Marrying Winterborne

BY LISA KLEYPAS

MARRYING WINTERBORNE

COLD-HEARTED RAKE

SCANDAL IN SPRING

DEVIL IN WINTER

IT HAPPENED ONE AUTUMN

SECRETS OF A SUMMER NIGHT

AGAIN THE MAGIC

WHERE'S MY HERO?
(with Kinley McGregor and Julia Quinn)

WORTH ANY PRICE

WHEN STRANGERS MARRY

LADY SOPHIA'S LOVER

SUDDENLY YOU

WHERE DREAMS BEGIN

SOMEONE TO WATCH OVER ME

STRANGER IN MY ARMS

BECAUSE YOU'RE MINE

SOMEWHERE I'LL FIND YOU

THREE WEDDINGS AND A KISS
(with Kathleen E. Woodiwiss,
Catherine Anderson, and Loretta Chase)

PRINCE OF DREAMS

MIDNIGHT ANGEL

DREAMING OF YOU

THEN CAME YOU

ONLY WITH YOUR LOVE

Marrying Winterborne

Lisa Kleypas

HARPER LUXE

An Imprint of HarperCollins*Publishers*

This is a work of fiction. Names, characters, places, and incidents are products of the author's imagination or are used fictitiously and are not to be construed as real. Any resemblance to actual events, locales, organizations, or persons, living or dead, is entirely coincidental.

MARRYING WINTERBORNE. Copyright © 2016 by Lisa Kleypas. All rights reserved. Printed in the United States of America. No part of this book may be used or reproduced in any manner whatsoever without written permission except in the case of brief quotations embodied in critical articles and reviews. For information address HarperCollins Publishers, 195 Broadway, New York, NY 10007.

HarperCollins books may be purchased for educational, business, or sales promotional use. For information please e-mail the Special Markets Department at SPsales@harpercollins.com.

FIRST HARPERLUXE EDITION

ISBN: 978-0-06-246738-6

HarperLuxe™ is a trademark of HarperCollins Publishers.

16 17 18 19 20 ID/RRD 10 9 8 7 6 5 4 3 2 1

To Greg—my husband and my hero.
Love always,
L.K.

Marrying Winterborne

Chapter 1

"Mr. Winterborne, a woman is here to see you."
Rhys looked up from the stack of letters on his desk with a scowl.

His personal secretary, Mrs. Fernsby, stood at the threshold of his private office, her eyes sharp behind round spectacles. She was a tidy hen of a woman, middle-aged and just a bit plump.

"You know I don't receive visitors at this hour." It was his morning ritual to spend the first half hour of the day reading mail in uninterrupted silence.

"Yes, sir, but the visitor is a lady, and she—"

"I don't care if she's the bloody Queen," he snapped. "Send her away."

Mrs. Fernsby's lips pinched into a disapproving

hyphen. She left promptly, the heels of her shoes hitting the floor like the staccato of gunfire.

Rhys returned his attention to the letter in front of him. Losing his temper was a luxury he rarely permitted himself, but for the past week he'd been invaded by a sullen gloom that weighted every thought and heartbeat, and made him want to lash out at anyone within reach.

All because of a woman he had known better than to want.

Lady Helen Ravenel . . . a woman who was cultured, innocent, shy, aristocratic. Everything he was not.

Their engagement had lasted a mere two weeks before Rhys had managed to ruin it. The last time he had seen Helen, he'd been impatient and aggressive, finally kissing her the way he'd wanted to for so long. She had gone stiff in his arms, rejecting him. Her disdain couldn't have been more obvious. The scene had ended in tears on her part, anger on his.

The next day, Kathleen, Lady Trenear, who had been married to Helen's late brother, had come to inform him that Helen was so distressed, she was bedridden with a migraine.

"She never wants to see you again," Kathleen had informed him bluntly.

Rhys couldn't blame Helen for ending the betrothal.

Obviously they were a mismatch. It was against the designs of God that he should take the daughter of a titled English family to wife. Despite his great fortune, Rhys didn't have the deportment or education of a gentleman. Nor did he have the appearance of one, with his swarthy complexion and black hair, and workingman's brawn.

By the age of thirty, he had built Winterborne's, his father's small shop on High Street, into the world's largest department store. He owned factories, warehouses, farmland, stables, laundries, and residential buildings. He was on the boards of shipping and railway companies. But no matter what he achieved, he would never overcome the limitations of having been born a Welsh grocer's son.

His thoughts were interrupted by another knock at the door. Incredulously he glanced up as Mrs. Fernsby walked back into his office.

"What do you want?" he demanded.

The secretary straightened her spectacles as she replied resolutely. "Unless you wish to have the lady removed by force, she insists on staying until you speak with her."

Rhys's annoyance faded into puzzlement. No woman of his acquaintance, respectable or otherwise, would dare to approach him so boldly. "Her name?"

"She won't say."

He shook his head in disbelief. How had the visitor made it past the outer offices? He paid a small army of people to prevent him from having to deal with this kind of interruption. An absurd idea occurred to him, and although he dismissed it immediately, his pulse quickened.

"What does she look like?" he brought himself to ask.

"She's dressed in mourning, with a veil over her face. Slender of build, and soft-spoken." After a brief hesitation, she added on a dry note, "The accent is pure 'drawing-room.'"

As realization dawned, Rhys felt his chest close around a deep stab of yearning. "*Yr Dduw*," he muttered. It didn't seem possible that Helen would have come to him. But somehow he knew she had, he knew it down to his marrow. Without another word, he stood and moved past Mrs. Fernsby with ground-eating strides.

"Mr. Winterborne," the secretary exclaimed, following him. "You're in your shirtsleeves. Your coat—"

Rhys scarcely heard her as he left his corner suite office and entered a foyer with leather-upholstered chairs.

He halted abruptly at the sight of the visitor, his breath catching sharp and quick.

Even though the mourning veil concealed Helen's face, he recognized her perfect posture, and the willowy slenderness of her form.

He forced himself to close the distance between them. Unable to say a word, he stood in front of her, nearly choking with resentment, and yet breathing in her sweet scent with helpless greed. He was instantly aroused by her presence, his flesh filling with heat, his heartbeat swift and violent.

From one of the rooms attached to the foyer, the *tappity-tap* of typewriting machines stuttered into silence.

It was madness for Helen to have come here unescorted. Her reputation would be destroyed. She had to be removed from the foyer and sent home before anyone realized whom she was.

But first Rhys had to find out what she wanted. Although she was sheltered and innocent, she wasn't a fool. She wouldn't have taken such an enormous risk without good reason.

He glanced at Mrs. Fernsby. "My guest will be leaving soon. In the meantime, make certain we're not disturbed."

"Yes, sir."

His gaze returned to Helen.

"Come," he said gruffly, and led the way to his office.

She accompanied him wordlessly, her skirts rustling as they brushed the sides of the hallway. Her garments were outdated and slightly shabby, the look of gentility fallen on hard times. Was that why she was here? Was the Ravenel family's need for money so desperate that she had changed her mind about lowering herself to become his wife?

By God, Rhys thought with grim anticipation, he would *love* for her to beg him to take her back. He wouldn't, of course, but he'd give her a taste of the torment he had endured for the past week. Anyone who had ever dared to cross him would have assured her that there would be no forgiveness or mercy afterward.

They entered his office, a spacious and quiet place with wide double-glazed windows and thick, soft carpeting. In the center of the room, a walnut pedestal desk had been piled with stacks of correspondence and files.

After closing the door, Rhys went to his desk, picked up an hourglass and upended it in a deliberate gesture. The sand would drain to the lower chamber in precisely fifteen minutes. He felt the need to make the point that they were in his world now, where time mattered, and he was in control.

He turned to Helen with a mocking lift of his brows. "I was told last week that you—"

But his voice died away as Helen pushed back her veil and stared at him with the patient, tender gravity that had devastated him from the first. Her eyes were the silver-blue of clouds drifting through moonlight. The fine, straight locks of her hair, the palest shade of blonde, had been pulled back neatly into a chignon, but a glinting wisp had slid free of the jet combs and dangled in front of her left ear.

Damn her, *damn* her for being so beautiful.

"Forgive me," Helen said, her gaze fastened to his. "This was the first opportunity I could find to come to you."

"You shouldn't be here."

"There are things I need to discuss with you." She cast a timid glance at a nearby chair. "Please, if you wouldn't mind . . ."

"Aye, be seated." But Rhys made no move to help her. Since Helen would never regard him as a gentleman, he'd be damned if he would act like one. He half-sat, half-leaned against his desk, folding his arms across his chest. "You don't have much time," he said stonily, giving a short nod toward the hourglass. "You'd better make use of it."

Helen sat in the chair, arranged her skirts, and removed her gloves with deft tugs at the fingertips.

Rhys's mouth went dry at the sight of her delicate fingers emerging from the black gloves. She had played the piano for him at Eversby Priory, her family's estate. He had been fascinated by the agility of her hands, darting and swooping over the keys like small white birds. For some reason she was still wearing the betrothal ring he'd given her, the flawless rose-cut diamond catching briefly on the glove.

After pushing back her veil so that it fell down her back in a dark mist of fabric, Helen dared to meet his gaze for a charged moment. Soft color infused her cheeks. "Mr. Winterborne, I didn't ask my sister-in-law to visit you last week. I wasn't feeling well at the time, but had I known what Kathleen intended—"

"She said you were ill."

"My head ached, that was all—"

"It seems I was the cause."

"Kathleen made far too much of it—"

"According to her, you said you never wanted to see me again."

Her blush deepened to brilliant rose. "I wish she hadn't repeated that," she exclaimed, looking vexed and ashamed. "I didn't mean it. My head was splitting, and I was trying to make sense of what had happened the day before. When you visited, and—" She tore her gaze from his and looked down at her lap, the light from the window sliding over her hair. The clasp of her hands was tight and slightly rounded, as if she held something fragile between her palms. "I need to talk to you about that," she said quietly. "I want very much to . . . reach an understanding with you."

Something inside him died. Rhys had been approached for money by too many people, not to recognize what was coming. Helen was no different from anyone else, trying to gain some advantage for herself. Although he couldn't blame her for that, he couldn't bear hearing whatever rationale she had come up with for how much he owed her, and why. He would rather pay her off immediately and be done with it.

God knew why he'd nourished some faint, foolish hope that she might have wanted anything from him other than money. This was how the world had always worked, and always would. Men sought beautiful women, and women traded their beauty for wealth. He had debased Helen by putting his inferior paws on her, and now she would demand restitution.

He walked around to the other side of his desk, pulled out a drawer, and withdrew a checkbook for a private account. Taking up a pen, he wrote an order for ten thousand pounds. After making a note on the left margin of the book for his own reference, he walked back around to Helen and gave it to her.

"There's no need for anyone to know where it came from," he said in a businesslike tone. "If you don't have a banking account, I'll see to it that one is opened for you." No bank would allow a woman to establish an account for herself. "I promise it will be handled discreetly."

Helen stared at him with bewilderment, and then glanced at the check. "Why would you—" She drew in a swift breath as she saw the amount. Her horrified gaze flew back to his. "*Why?*" she asked, her breath coming in agitated bursts.

Puzzled by her reaction, Rhys frowned. "You said you wanted to reach an understanding. That's what it means."

"*No*, I meant . . . I meant that I wanted for us to understand each other." She fumbled to tear the check into tiny pieces. "I don't need money. And even if I did, I would never ask you for it." Bits of paper flew through the air like snowflakes.

Stunned, he watched her make short work of the

small fortune he'd just given her. A mixture of frustration and embarrassment filled him as he realized that he'd misread her. What the hell did she want from him? Why was she there?

Helen took a long breath, and another, slowly reinflating her composure. She stood and approached him. "There's been something of a . . . windfall . . . at my family's estate. We now have means to provide dowries for me and my sisters."

Rhys stared at her, his face a hard mask, while his brain struggled to take in what she was saying. She had come too close. The light fragrance of her, vanilla and orchids, stole into his lungs with every breath. His body coursed with heat. He wanted her on her back, across his desk—

With an effort, he shoved the lurid image from his mind. Here in the businesslike surroundings of his office, dressed in civilized clothing and polished oxford shoes, he had never felt like more of a brute. Desperate to establish even a small measure of distance between them, he retreated and encountered the edge of the desk. He was forced to resume a half-sitting position while Helen continued to advance, until her skirts brushed gently against his knees.

She could have been a figure in a Welsh fairy tale, a nymph who had formed from the mist off a lake. There was something otherworldly about the delicacy of her porcelain skin, and the arresting contrast between her dark lashes and brows and her silver-blond hair. And those eyes, cool translucence contained in dark rims.

She'd said something about a windfall. What did that mean? An unexpected inheritance? A gift? Perhaps a lucrative investment—although that was unlikely, in light of the Ravenel family's notorious fiscal irresponsibility. Whatever manner of windfall it was, Helen seemed to believe that her family's financial troubles were over. If that were true, then any man in London would be hers for the choosing.

She had put her future at risk, coming to him. Her reputation was at stake. He could have ravished her right there in his office, and no one would have lifted a finger to help her. The only thing keeping her safe was the fact that Rhys had no wish to destroy something as lovely and fragile as this woman.

For her sake, he had to remove her from Winterborne's as quickly and discreetly as possible. With an effort, he looked over her head and focused on a distant point on the wood-paneled wall.

"I'll escort you from the building through a private exit," he muttered. "You'll return home with no one the wiser."

"I will not release you from our engagement," Helen said gently.

His gaze shot back to hers, while another of those deep stabs sank into his chest. Helen didn't even blink, only waited patiently for his response.

"My lady, we both know that I'm the last man you want to marry. From the beginning, I've seen your disgust of me."

"Disgust?"

Insulted by her feigned surprise, he continued savagely. "You shrink away from my touch. You won't speak to me at dinner. Most of the time you can't even bring yourself to look at me. And when I kissed you last week, you pulled away and burst into tears."

He would have expected Helen to be ashamed at being called out in a lie. Instead, she stared at him earnestly, her lips parted in dismay. "Please," she eventually said, "you must forgive me. I'm far too shy. I must work harder to overcome it. When I behave that way, it has nothing at all to do with disgust. The truth is, I'm nervous with you. Because . . ." A deep flush worked up from the high neck of her dress to the edge of her hairline. "Because you're very attractive," she continued awkwardly, "and worldly, and I don't wish for you to think me foolish. As for the other day, that . . .

that was my first kiss. I didn't know what to do, and I felt . . . quite overwhelmed."

Somewhere in the chaos of his mind, Rhys thought it was a good thing he was leaning against the desk. Otherwise, his legs would have buckled. Could it be that what he had read as disdain was actually shyness? That what he'd thought was contempt had been innocence? He felt a splintering sensation, as if his heart were cracking open. How easily Helen had undone him. A few words, and he was ready to fall to his knees before her.

Her first kiss, and he had taken it without asking.

There had never been a need for him to play the part of skilled seducer. Women had always been easily available to him, and they had seemed pleased with whatever he cared to do in bed. There had even been ladies now and then: the wife of a diplomat, and a countess whose husband had been away on a trip to the continent. They had praised him for his vigor, his stamina, and his big cock, and they hadn't asked for anything more.

In body and nature, he was as tough as the slate dug from the flanks of Elidir Fawr, the mountain in Llanberis, where he'd been born. He knew nothing of fine manner or good breeding. There were permanent callouses on his hands from years of building crates and loading merchandise onto delivery wagons. He was easily twice Helen's weight, and as muscular as a bull, and if he rutted on her the way he had with other women, he would rip her apart without even trying.

Holy hell. What had he been thinking in the first place? He should never have let himself even consider the idea of marrying her. But he had been too blinded by his own ambition—and by Helen's sweetness and fine-spun beauty—to fully consider the consequences for her.

Bitter with the awareness of his own limitations, he said in a low voice, "It's water under the bridge, it is. Soon you'll have your first season, and you'll meet the man you were meant for. The devil knows it's not me."

He began to stand, but Helen moved even closer, standing between his spread feet. The hesitant pressure of her hand on his chest sent desire roaring through him. Rhys sank back to the desk weakly, all his strength focused on maintaining his crumbling self-control. He was a terrifying hairsbreadth away from taking her down to the floor with him. Devouring her.

"Will you . . . will you kiss me again?" she asked.

He shut his eyes, panting, furious with her. What a joke Fate had played on him, throwing this fragile creature into his path to punish him for climbing higher than he'd been meant to. To remind him of what he could never become.

"I can't be a gentleman," he said hoarsely. "Not even for you."

"You don't have to be a gentleman. Only gentle."

No one had ever asked him for such a thing. To his despair, he realized it wasn't in him. His hands gripped the edges of the desk until the wood threatened to crack.

"*Cariad* . . . there's nothing gentle about how I want you." He was startled by the endearment that had slipped out, one he had never used with anyone.

He felt Helen touch his jaw, her fingertips delicate spots of cool fire on his skin.

All his muscles locked, his body turning to steel.

"Just try," he heard her whisper. "For me."

And her soft mouth pressed against his.

Chapter 2

Timidly Helen brushed her lips over Mr. Winterborne's, trying to coax a response from him. But there was no answering pressure. No hint of encouragement.

After a moment, she drew back uncertainly.

Breathing unevenly, he leveled a surly watchdog stare at her.

With a despairing sinking of her stomach, Helen wondered what to do next.

She knew little about men. Almost nothing. Since early childhood, she and her younger sisters, Pandora and Cassandra, had lived in seclusion at their family's country estate. The male servants at Eversby Priory had always been deferential, and the tenants and town tradesmen had kept a respectful distance from the earl's three daughters.

Overlooked by her parents, and ignored by her brother Theo, who had spent most of his short life at boarding schools or in London, Helen had turned to her inner world of books and imagination. Her suitors had been Romeo, Heathcliff, Mr. Darcy, Edward Rochester, Sir Lancelot, Sydney Carton, and an assortment of golden-haired fairy tale princes.

It had seemed as if she would never be courted by a real man, only imaginary ones. But two months ago, Devon, the cousin who had recently inherited Theo's title, had invited his friend Rhys Winterborne to spend Christmas with the family—and everything had changed.

The first time Helen had ever seen Mr. Winterborne was the day he had been brought to the estate with a broken leg. In a shocking turn of events, as Devon and Mr. Winterborne had traveled from London to Hampshire, their train had collided with some ballast wagons. Miraculously both men had survived the accident, but they had each sustained injuries.

As a result, Mr. Winterborne's brief holiday visit had been turned into nearly a month-long stay at Eversby Priory, until he had healed sufficiently to return to London. Even injured, he'd radiated a force of will that Helen had found as exciting as it was unsettling. Against every rule of propriety, she'd helped to take care of him. She had insisted on it, as a matter of fact. Although she had done it under the guise of simple compassion, that hadn't been the only reason. The truth was, she had never been so fascinated by anyone as she was by this big, dark-haired stranger with an accent like rough music.

As his condition had improved, Mr. Winterborne had demanded her companionship, insisting that she read and talk to him for hours. No one in Helen's life had ever taken such an interest in her.

Mr. Winterborne was strikingly handsome, not in the way of fairy tale princes, but with an uncompromising masculinity that made her nerves jump whenever he was near. The angles of his face were bold, the nose sturdy, the lips full and distinctly edged. His skin was not fashionably pale but a rich, glowing umber, and his hair was quite black. There was nothing of an aristocrat's ease about him, no hint of languid grace. He was sophisticated, keenly intelligent, but there was something not quite civilized about him. A hint of danger, a smolder beneath the surface.

After he had left Hampshire, the estate had been dull and quiet, the days monotonous. Helen had been haunted by thoughts of him . . . the suggestion of charm beneath his hard veneer . . . the infrequent but dazzling smile.

To her consternation, he didn't seem at all willing to take her back. His pride had been hurt by what must have appeared to be an insensitive rejection, and she longed to soothe it. If only she could turn the clock back to the day he had kissed her at Ravenel House, she would manage the situation far differently. It was only that she had been so profoundly intimidated by him. He had kissed her, put his hands on her, and she had reacted with startled dismay. After a few harsh words, he had left. That was the last time she had seen him until now.

Had there been a few flirtations in her girlhood—a stolen kiss or two from a young lad—perhaps the encounter with Mr. Winterborne wouldn't have been so alarming. But she'd had no experience at all. And Mr. Winterborne was no innocent boy, but an adult man in his prime.

The strange part—the secret she couldn't confess to anyone—was that in spite of her distress over what had happened, she had begun to dream every night about Mr. Winterborne pressing his mouth very hard against hers, over and over. In some of the dreams, he would begin to unfasten her dress, kissing her ever more compellingly and forcefully, all of it leading toward some mysterious conclusion. She would awaken breathless and agitated, and hot with shame.

A flicker of that same turmoil awakened low in her stomach as she looked up at him. "Show me how you want to be kissed," she said, her voice shaking only a little. "Teach me how to please you."

To her astonishment, one corner of his mouth curled with contemptuous amusement. "Hedging your bets, are you?"

She stared at him in confusion. "Hedging my . . ."

"You want to keep me on the hook," he clarified, "until you're sure about Trenear's windfall."

Helen was baffled and hurt by the scorn in his tone. "Why can't you believe that I want to marry you for reasons other than money?"

"The only reason you accepted me was because you had no dowry."

"That's not true—"

He continued as if he hadn't heard. "You need to marry one of your own kind, my lady. A man with pretty manners and a fine pedigree. He'll know how to treat you. He'll keep you in a country house, where you'll tend your orchids and read your books—"

"That's the *opposite* of what I need," Helen burst out. It wasn't at all like her to speak impetuously, but she was too desperate to care. Clearly he meant to send her away. How could she convince him that she genuinely wanted him?

"I've spent my entire life reading about the lives other people are having," she continued. "My world has been . . . very small. No one believes I would thrive if I weren't kept secluded and protected. Like a flower in a glasshouse. If I marry one of my kind, as you put it, no one will ever see me as I am. Only what I'm supposed to be."

"Why do you think I would be any different?"

"Because you are."

He gave her an arrested glance that reminded her of the gleam of light on a knife blade. After a peculiarly charged silence, he spoke brusquely. "You've known too few men. Go home, Helen. You'll find someone during the Season, and then you'll thank God, on your knees, that you didn't marry me."

Helen felt her eyes sting. How had everything been ruined so quickly? How could she have lost him so easily? Sickened with regret and grief, she said, "Kathleen shouldn't have spoken to you on my behalf. She thought she was protecting me, but—"

"She was."

"I didn't want to be protected from you." Fighting for composure was like trying to run through sand: She couldn't find traction amid the shifting angles of emotion. To her mortification, tears welled and a vehement sob escaped her. "I went to bed with a migraine for *one day*," she continued, "and when I woke up the next morning, our engagement was broken and I had *l-lost* you and I didn't even—"

"Helen, don't."

"I thought it was only a misunderstanding. I thought if I spoke to you directly, everything would be s-sorted out, and—" Another sob choked her. She was so consumed by emotion that she was only vaguely aware of Rhys hovering around her, reaching for her and snatching his hands back.

"No. Don't cry. For God's sake, Helen—"

"I didn't mean to push you away. I didn't know what to do. How can I make you want me again?"

She expected a jeering reply, or perhaps even a pitying one. The last thing she expected was his shaken murmur.

"I do want you, *cariad.* I want you too damned much."

She blinked at him through a bewildered blur, breathing in mortifying hiccups, like a child. In the next moment, he had hauled her firmly against him.

"Hush, now." His voice dropped to a deeper octave, a brush of dark velvet against her ears. "Hush, *bychan,* little one, my dove. Nothing is worth your tears."

"You are."

Mr. Winterborne went very still. After a minute, one of his hands came to her jaw, his thumb erasing the wake of a teardrop. The cuffs of his shirt had been rolled up to his elbows, in the manner of carpenters or farm workers. His forearms were heavily muscled and hairy, his wrists thick. There was something astonishingly comforting about being wrapped in his sturdy embrace. A dry, pleasant scent clung to him, a crisp mingling of starched linen and clean male skin, and shaving soap.

She felt him angle her face upward with great care. His breath fanned against her cheek, carrying the scent of peppermint. Realizing what he intended, she closed her eyes, her stomach lifting as if the floor had just disappeared from beneath her feet.

There was a brush of heat against her upper lip, so soft that she could scarcely feel it. Another touch at the sensitive corner of her mouth, and then at her lower lip, finishing with the hint of a tug.

His free hand slid beneath the fall of her veil to clasp the tender nape of her neck. His mouth came to hers in another brief, silky caress. The pad of his thumb drew over her lower lip, rubbing the kiss into the tender surface. The abrasion of a callus heightened the sensation, stimulating her nerve endings. She was suddenly lightheaded; her lungs wouldn't draw in enough air.

His lips returned to hers, and she strained upward, dying for him to kiss her harder, longer, the way he had in her dreams. Seeming to understand what she wanted, he coaxed her lips apart. Trembling, she opened to the glassy touch of his tongue, helplessly taking in the flavor of him, mint and heat and coolness, as he began to consume her with a slow hunger that unraveled runners of feeling all through her body. Her arms went around his neck, her hands sinking into his thick black hair, the locks curling slightly around her fingers. Yes, this was what she had needed, his mouth taking hers, while he held her as if he couldn't draw her close enough, tight enough.

She had never imagined that a man would kiss her as if he were trying to breathe her in, as if kisses were words meant for poems, or honey to be gathered with his tongue. Clasping her head in his hands, he tipped it back and dragged his parted lips along the side of her neck, nuzzling and tasting the soft skin. She gasped as he found a sensitive place, her knees slackening until they could barely support her weight. He gripped her closer, his mouth returning hungrily to hers. There was no thought, no will, nothing but a sensuous tangle of darkness and desire, while Mr. Winterborne kissed her with such blind, ravening intensity that she could almost feel his soul calling into her.

And then he stopped. With startling abruptness, he tore his mouth free and pried her arms from his neck. A protest slipped from Helen's throat as he set her aside with more force than was strictly necessary. Bewildered, she watched as Mr. Winterborne went to the window. Although he was recovering from the train accident with remarkable speed, he still walked with a faint limp. Keeping his back to her, he focused on the distant green oasis of Hyde Park. As he rested the side of his fist against the window frame, she saw that his hand was trembling.

Eventually he let out a ragged breath. "I shouldn't have done that."

"I wanted you to." Helen blushed at her own forwardness. "I . . . only wish the first time had been like that."

He was silent, tugging irritably at his stiff shirt collar.

Seeing that the hourglass was empty, Helen wandered to his desk and turned the timepiece over. "I should have been more open with you." She watched the stream of sand as it measured out second after yearning second. "But it's difficult for me to tell people what I think and feel. And I was worried about something Kathleen said, that you thought of me only as . . . well, as a prize to acquire. I was afraid she might have been right."

Mr. Winterborne turned and set his back against the wall, his arms folded across his chest. "She was right," he surprised her by saying. A corner of his mouth quirked wryly. "You're as pretty as a moonbeam, *cariad*, and I'm not a high-minded man. I'm a bruiser from North Wales, with a taste for fine things. Aye, you were a prize to me. You always would have been. But I did want you for more than just that."

The glow of pleasure Helen felt at the compliment had disappeared by the time he finished. "Why did you say that in the past tense?" she asked, blinking. "You . . . you still want me, don't you?"

"It doesn't matter what I want. Trenear will never consent to the match now."

"He was the one who suggested the match in the first place. As long as I make it clear that I'm *quite* willing to marry you, I'm sure he'll agree."

An unaccountably long pause ensued. "No one told you, then."

Helen gave him a questioning glance.

Shoving his hands in his pockets, Mr. Winterborne said, "I behaved badly, the day that Kathleen visited. After she told me that you no longer wanted to see me again, I—" He broke off, his mouth grim.

"You did what?" Helen prompted, her brow furrowing.

"It doesn't matter. Trenear interrupted when he came to fetch her. He and I nearly came to blows."

"Interrupted what? What did you do?"

He looked away then, his jaw flexing. "I insulted her. With a proposition."

Helen's eyes widened. "Did you mean it?"

"Of course I didn't mean it," came his brusque reply. "I didn't lay a blasted finger on her. I wanted *you*. I have no interest in the little shrew, I was only angry with her for interfering."

Helen sent him a reproachful glance. "You still owe her an apology."

"She owes me one," he retorted, "for costing me a wife."

Although Helen was tempted to point out the flaws in his reasoning, she held her tongue. Having been reared in a family notorious for its evil tempers and stubborn wills, she knew the value of choosing the right time to help someone see the error of his ways. At the moment, Mr. Winterborne was too much at the mercy of his passions to concede any wrongdoing.

But he had indeed behaved badly—and even if Kathleen forgave him, it was unlikely that Devon ever would.

Devon was madly in love with Kathleen, and along with that came all the jealousy and possessiveness that had plagued generations of Ravenels. While Devon was somewhat more reasonable than the past few earls, that wasn't saying much. Any man who frightened or offended Kathleen would earn his eternal wrath.

So this was why Devon had withdrawn his approval of the engagement so promptly. But the fact that neither he nor Kathleen had mentioned any of this to Helen was exasperating. Good heavens, how long would they insist on treating her like a child?

"We could elope," she said reluctantly, although the idea held little appeal for her.

Mr. Winterborne scowled. "I'll have a church wedding or none at all. If we eloped, no one would ever believe you went with me willingly. I'm damned if I'll let people say I had to kidnap my bride."

"There's no alternative."

A wordless interval followed, so full of portent that Helen felt her arms prickling beneath her sleeves, all the downy hairs lifting.

"There is."

His face had changed, his eyes predatory. Calculating. This, she understood in a flash of intuition, was the version of Mr. Winterborne that people regarded with fear and awe, a pirate disguised as a captain of industry.

"The alternative," he said, "is to let me bed you."

Chapter 3

Amid the chaos of Helen's thoughts, she retreated to one of the inset bookcases in the corner of the office.

"I don't understand," she said, even though she was terribly afraid that she did.

Mr. Winterborne prowled after her slowly. "Trenear won't stand in the way after he finds out you've been ruined."

"I would rather not be ruined." It was becoming more difficult to breathe by the minute. Her corset had clamped around her like a set of jaws.

"But you want to marry me." Reaching her, he rested a hand on the bookcase, cornering her. "Don't you?"

In moral terms, fornication was a mortal sin. In

practical terms, the risks of sleeping with him were enormous.

A horrid thought drained the color from her face. What if Mr. Winterborne slept with her and then refused to marry her? What if he were capable of such vindictiveness that he might dishonor and abandon her? No gentleman would ever offer for her. Any hope of gaining a home and family of her own would be lost. She would become a burden to her relations, condemned to a life of shame and dependence. If she conceived, she and her child would be social outcasts. And even if she didn't, her disgrace would still sabotage her younger sisters' marital prospects.

"How can I trust that you would do the right thing afterward?" she asked.

Mr. Winterborne's expression darkened. "Questions of my character aside, how long do you think Trenear would let me live if I tried something like that? Before nightfall, he'd have me hunted and felled like a carted deer."

"He might anyway," Helen said glumly.

He ignored that. "I would never abandon you. If I took you to my bed, you would be mine, as sure if we vowed it on an oathing stone."

"What is that?"

"A wedding ritual in my part of Wales. A man and

woman exchange vows with a stone held between their joined hands. After the ceremony, they go together to cast the stone into a lake, and the earth itself becomes part of their oath. From then on, they are bound to each other for as long as the world exists." His gaze locked with hers. "Give me what I ask, and you'll never want for anything."

He was overwhelming her again. Helen felt a light perspiration breaking out from her scalp to the soles of her feet. "I need time to consider it," she said.

Mr. Winterborne's determination seemed to feed from her distress. "I'll give you money and property of your own. A stable of thoroughbreds. A palace, and the market town around it, and scores of servants to wait on you hand and foot. No price is too high. All you have to do is come to my bed."

Helen reached up to rub her throbbing temples, hoping that another migraine wasn't coming on. "Couldn't we just say that I've been ruined? Devon would have to take my word for it."

Mr. Winterborne shook his head before she had even finished the question. "I'll need an earnest payment. That's how a deal is bound in business."

"This isn't a business negotiation," she protested.

He was adamant. "I want insurance in case you change your mind before the wedding."

"I wouldn't do that. Don't you trust me?"

"Aye. But I'll trust you more after we sleep together."

The man was *impossible*. Helen floundered for another solution, some means of countering him, but she could sense him becoming more intractable with every passing second.

"This is about your pride," she said indignantly. "You were hurt and angry because you thought I'd rejected you, and now you want to punish me even though it wasn't my fault."

"A punishment?" His black brows lifted mockingly. "Not five minutes ago you were enthusiastic about my kisses."

"Your proposition involves far more than kissing."

"It's not a proposition," he informed her in a matter-of-fact tone. "It's an ultimatum."

Helen stared at him in disbelief.

Her only choice was to refuse. Someday she would meet an eligible man her family would approve of. A member of the landed gentry, bland and reserved, with a very tall forehead. He would expect her to make his opinions and wishes her own. And her life would be planned out for her, every year the same as the last.

Marrying Winterborne, on the other hand . . .

There was still so much she didn't understand about him. What would be expected of a woman whose husband owned the largest department store in the world? What people would she become acquainted with, and what activities would fill her days? And Winterborne himself, who so often wore the look of someone who'd had more than a few quarrels with the world and had forgiven nothing . . . what would it be like, to live as his wife? His life was so large that she could easily imagine becoming lost in it.

Realizing that he was watching her closely, alert to every nuance of her expression, she turned her back to him. Rows of books confronted her, catalogues, manuals, ledgers. But lower down, amid a row of utilitarian volumes, she saw a collection of what appeared to be botanical titles. She blinked and looked at them more closely: *Bromeliads; Being a Concise Treatise on the Management of the Hothouse; Orchidaceae Genera and Species: An Enumeration of Known Orchids; and Orchid Cultivation.*

These books on orchids weren't in his office by happenstance.

Cultivating orchids had been a keen interest and hobby of Helen's ever since her mother had passed away five years ago, leaving a collection of approximately two hundred potted orchids. Since no one else in the family had been inclined to care for them, Helen had taken it upon herself. Orchids were demanding, troublesome plants, each with its own temperament. At first Helen had found no enjoyment in her self-appointed responsibility, but over time, she had become devoted to the orchids.

As she had once told Kathleen, sometimes one had to love something before it became lovable.

She touched the gilded book bindings with a hesitant fingertip, tracing the edge of a hand-painted flower. "When did you acquire these?" she asked.

Mr. Winterborne's voice came from close behind her. "After you gave me the potted orchid. I needed to know how to take care of it."

A few weeks earlier, he had come for dinner at Ravenel House, and Helen had impulsively given one of her orchids to him. A rare Blue Vanda, her most prized and temperamental plant. Although he hadn't seemed especially enthused about the gift, he had thanked her and taken it dutifully. But the moment their engagement had been broken, he had sent it back.

To Helen's amazement, she had discovered that the sensitive plant had thrived in his care.

"You looked after it yourself, then," she said. "I wondered about that."

"Of course I did. I had no intention of failing your test."

"It wasn't a test, it was a gift."

"If you say so."

Exasperated, Helen turned to face him. "I fully expected you to kill it, and I intended to marry you regardless."

His lips twitched. "But I didn't."

Helen was silent, trying to balance all her thoughts and feelings before making the most difficult decision of her life. But was it really that complicated? Marriage was always a risk.

One never knew what kind of husband a man might turn into.

For one last time, Helen allowed herself to consider the option of leaving. She imagined walking out of his office, entering the family carriage, and riding back to Ravenel House on South Audley. And it would be well and truly over. Her future would be identical to that of any young woman in her position. She would have a London Season and scores of dances and dinners with civilized suitors, all of it leading to marriage with a man who would never understand her nearly as well as she understood him. She would do her utmost never to look back on this moment and wonder what would have happened, or what she might have become, if she'd said yes.

She thought of the conversation she'd had with the housekeeper, Mrs. Abbott, before leaving this morning. The housekeeper a plump and neat silver-haired woman who had served in the Ravenel's employ for four decades, had objected strongly upon hearing that Helen intended to go out in the daytime with no companion. "The Master will sack the lot of us," she had exclaimed.

"I'll tell Lord Trenear that I slipped away without anyone's knowledge," Helen had told her. "And I'll say that I gave the driver no choice but to take me to Winterborne's or I threatened to go on foot."

"My lady, nothing can be worth such a risk!"

However, when Helen had explained that she intended to visit Rhys Winterborne in the hopes of renewing their engagement, it seemed to have given the housekeeper cause for second thought.

"I can't fault you," Mrs. Abbot had admitted. "A man such as that . . ."

Helen had stared at her curiously, noticing the way her face had softened with dreamy pensiveness. "You hold Mr. Winterborne in esteem, then?"

"I do, my lady. Oh, I know he's called an upstart by his social betters. But to the real London—the hundreds of thousands who work every blessed day and scrape by as best we can—Winterborne is a legend. He's done what most people don't dare dream of. A shop boy, he was, and now everyone from the queen down to any common beggar knows his name. It gives people reason to hope they might rise above their circumstances." Smiling slightly, the housekeeper had added, "And none can deny he's a handsome, well-made chap, for all that he's as brown as a gypsy. Any woman, highborn or low, would be tempted."

Helen couldn't deny that Mr. Winterborne's personal attractions were high on her list of considerations. A man in his prime, radiating that remarkable energy, a kind of animal vitality that she found both frightening and irresistible.

But there was something else about him . . . a lure more potent than any other. It happened during his rare moments of tenderness with her, when it seemed as if the deep, tightly locked cache of sadness in her heart was about to break open. He was the only person who had ever approached that trapped place, who might someday be able to shatter the loneliness that had always held fast inside her.

If she married Mr. Winterborne, she might come to regret it. But not nearly as much as she would regret it if she didn't take the chance.

Almost miraculously, everything sorted itself out in her brain. A feeling of calmness settled over her as her path became clear.

Taking a deep breath, she looked up at him. "Very well," she said. "I agree to your ultimatum."

Chapter 4

For several seconds, Rhys couldn't manage a response. Either Helen hadn't understood what she was saying, or he hadn't heard correctly.

"Here and now," he clarified. "You'll let me"—he tried to think of a decent word—"take you," he continued, "as a man takes a wife."

"Yes," Helen said calmly, shocking him all over again. Her face was very pale, with red banners of color emblazoned at the crests of her cheeks. But she didn't look at all uncertain. She meant it.

There had to be a drawback, some pitfall that would be discovered later, but he couldn't fathom what it might be. She had said yes. Within a matter of minutes, she would be in his bed. Naked. The thought set every internal rhythm off-kilter, his heart and lungs battling for room inside his constricted chest.

It occurred to him that his usual vigorous rutting wasn't going to work at all in this situation. Helen was vulnerable and innocent.

It would have to be lovemaking, not fucking.

He knew *nothing* about lovemaking.

Bloody buggering hell.

On the rare occasion when he'd enjoyed the favors of an upper-class lady, she had wanted to be taken roughly, as if he were a simple brute who was incapable of gentleness. Rhys had appreciated being spared any pretense of intimacy. He was no Byron, no poetry-spouting connoisseur of seduction. He was a Welshman with stamina. As for techniques and romance—well, obviously that was best left to the French.

But Helen was a virgin. There would be blood. Pain. Likely tears. What if he couldn't be gentle enough? What if she became overwrought? What if—

"I have two conditions," Helen ventured. "First, I should like to return home before dinnertime. And second . . ." She turned the color of a beetroot. "I wish to exchange this ring for a different one."

His gaze dropped to her left hand. The night he had proposed, he had given her a flawless rose-cut diamond the size of a quail egg. The priceless stone had been discovered in the Kimberley mines of South Africa, cut by a famed gemologist in Paris, and set in a platinum filigree mounting by Winterborne's master jeweler, Paul Sauveterre.

Seeing his confounded expression, Helen explained bashfully, "I don't like it."

"You told me you did when I gave it to you."

"To be precise, I didn't actually say that. It's only that I didn't say I *dis*liked it. But I have resolved to be outspoken with you from now on, to avoid future misunderstandings."

Rhys was chagrined to realize that Helen had never liked the ring he'd chosen for her. But he understood that she was trying to be straightforward with him now, even though she found the effort excruciating.

In the past, Helen's opinions had been ignored or trampled by her family. And perhaps, he reflected, by him as well. He might have asked her what kind of stones and settings she preferred, instead of deciding what he'd wanted her to have.

Reaching for her hand, he lifted it for a closer look at the glittering ring. "I'll buy you a diamond the size of a Christmas pudding."

"My goodness, no," Helen said hastily, surprising him yet again. "Just the opposite. This one sits very tall on my finger, you see? It slips from side to side, and makes it difficult to play the piano or write a letter. I would prefer a much smaller stone." She paused. "Something other than a diamond."

"Why not a diamond?"

"I'm not fond of them, actually. I suppose I don't mind the small ones that look like raindrops or little stars. But the large ones are so cold and hard."

"Aye, because they're diamonds." Rhys sent her a sardonic glance. "I'll have a tray of rings brought up at once."

A smile illuminated her face. "Thank you."

"What else would you like?" he asked. "A carriage and team of four? A necklace? Furs?"

She shook her head.

"There must be something." He wanted to inundate her with lavish gifts, make her understand what he was prepared to do for her.

"I can't think of anything."

"A piano?" As he felt the involuntary tightening of her fingers, he continued, "A Brinsmead grand concert piano, with patented check repeater action and a Chippendale mahogany case."

She gave a breathless laugh. "What a mind for detail you have. Yes. I would love to have a piano. After we're married, I'll play for you whenever you like."

The idea seized him. He would relax in the evenings

and watch her at the piano. Afterward he would take her to his room and undress her slowly, and kiss every inch of her. It didn't seem possible that this creature of moonlight and music would really be his. He felt himself at the edge of panic, needing to ensure that she wouldn't be stolen from him.

Carefully he worked the diamond ring from her finger and drew his thumb over the faint indentation left by the gold band. It felt too good to touch her, the awareness of her softness, her sweetness, coursing through him. He made himself let go before he ended up ravishing her there in the office. He had to think. Arrangements had to be made.

"Where is your driver waiting?" he asked.

"At the mews behind the store."

"An unmarked carriage?"

"No, the family carriage," came her innocent reply.

So much for discretion, Rhys thought ruefully, and gestured for her to precede him to his desk. "Write a note and I'll have it taken to him."

Helen allowed him to seat her. "When shall I have him return?"

"Tell him he won't be needed for the rest of the day. I'll see to it that you're delivered home safely."

"May I also send a message to my sisters, to keep them from worrying?"

"Aye. Do they know where you've gone?"

"Yes, and they were quite pleased. They're both fond of you."

"Or at least of my store," he said.

Helen struggled with a smile as she drew a sheet of writing paper from a silver tray.

At his invitation, the Ravenel family had visited Winterborne's one evening, after hours. Since they were still in mourning for the late earl, their activities in public were restricted. For the space of two hours, the twins, Cassandra and Pandora, had managed to cover an impressive amount of territory. They had been beside themselves with excitement over the displays of the newest, most fashionable merchandise, the glass cases and counters filled with accessories, cosmetics, and trimmings.

He noticed that Helen was staring in perplexity at the fountain pen on his desk.

"There's an ink reservoir inside the pen casing," he said, walking around the desk to her. "Apply light pressure to the tip as you write."

Picking up the pen cautiously, she made a mark with it, and paused in surprise as the pen created a smooth line across the paper.

"Haven't you seen one of those before?" he asked.

Helen shook her head. "Lord Trenear prefers an

ordinary pen and inkwell. He says this kind is prone to leak."

"They often do," he said. "But this is a new design, with a needle to regulate the flow."

He watched as she experimented with the pen, writing her name in careful script. When she finished, she studied it for a moment, and crossed out the surname. Rhys leaned over her from behind, his hands braced on either side of her as she wrote again. Together they stared down at the paper.

Lady Helen Winterborne

"It's a lovely name," he heard Helen murmur.

"Not quite so exalted as Ravenel."

Helen twisted in the chair to look up at him. "I'll be honored to take it as mine."

Rhys was accustomed to being flattered all the time, by a multitude of people who wanted things from him. Usually he could read their motives as easily as if they'd been written in the air above their heads. But Helen's eyes were clear and guileless, as if she meant it. She knew nothing of the world, or what kind of man she should marry, and she would only realize her mistake when it was too late to rectify it. If he had any decency, he would send her away this very moment.

But his gaze fell to the name she had written . . . *Lady Helen Winterborne* . . . and that sealed her fate.

"We'll have a grand wedding," he said. "So that all of London will know."

Helen didn't seem especially taken with the idea, but she offered no objection.

Still staring at the name, he absently stroked her cheek with a gentle fingertip. "Think of our children, *cariad*. Sturdy Welsh stock with a Ravenel strain. They'll conquer the world."

"I rather think you'll conquer it before they have a chance," Helen said, reaching for a fresh sheet of paper.

After she had written and sealed two notes, Rhys took them to the threshold of the office and called for Mrs. Fernsby.

The secretary answered the summons with unusual haste. Although her manner was professional as usual, the hazel eyes behind her round spectacles were bright with curiosity. Her gaze flickered to the room behind him, but his shoulders blocked her view.

"Yes, Mr. Winterborne?"

He gave her the notes. "Have these taken to the mews and delivered to the driver of the Ravenel carriage. I want them placed directly into his hands."

The name earned a quick double-blink. "So it *is* Lady Helen."

His eyes narrowed. "Not a word to anyone."

"Certainly not, sir. Will there be anything else?"

"Take this to the jeweler." He dropped the diamond ring into her extended hand.

Mrs. Fernsby gasped at the rich glittering weight in her palm. "Sweet heaven above. I assume you mean the master jeweler, Mr. Sauveterre?"

"Aye, tell him to bring up a tray of rings, in this size, that are suitable for betrothal. I'll expect him within the half hour."

"If he isn't immediately available, shall I ask one of the other—"

"I want Sauveterre," he repeated, "in my office, within the half hour."

Mrs. Fernsby responded with a distracted nod, and he could almost see the gears of her sensible brain spinning as she tried to piece together what was happening.

"Also," Rhys continued, "clear my schedule for the rest of the day."

The secretary stared at him fixedly. He had never made such a request before, for any reason. "The *entire* day? How shall I explain it?"

Rhys shrugged impatiently. "Invent something. And tell the household servants that I intend to spend a quiet afternoon at home with a guest. I don't want a soul in sight unless I ring." He paused, giving her a hard glance. "Make it clear to the office staff that if I hear so much as a whisper about this, from any quarter, I'll fire the lot of them without asking a single question."

"I would dismiss them myself," she assured him. Having personally supervised the interviewing and hiring of most of the office staff, Mrs. Fernsby took pride in their excellence. "However, their discretion is beyond question." Closing her fingers over the ring, she regarded him speculatively. "Might I suggest a tea tray? Lady Helen appears rather delicate. Refreshments might be just the thing while she awaits the jeweler."

Rhys's brows drew together. "I should have thought of that."

She couldn't quite repress a self-satisfied smile. "Not at all, Mr. Winterborne. That is what you employ me for."

As he watched her depart, Rhys reflected that Mrs. Fernsby could easily be forgiven for a touch of smugness: She was easily the best private secretary in London, performing her job with an efficiency that surpassed any of her male peers.

More than one person had suggested at the time that a male secretary would have been far more suitable for a man of Rhys's position. But he trusted his instincts in such matters. He could detect the same qualities in others: appetite, determination, vigor, which had driven him on the long, laborious climb from shop-boy to business magnate. It mattered not a whit to him about an employee's origins, beliefs, culture, or gender. All he cared about was excellence.

Mrs. Fernsby returned soon with a tea tray that had been sent up from the in-store restaurant. Although the secretary tried to remain inconspicuous as she set it on a small round table, Helen spoke to her gently.

"Thank you, Mrs. Fernsby."

The secretary turned to her with surprised pleasure. "You are quite welcome, my lady. Is there anything else you require?"

Helen smiled. "No, this is lovely."

The secretary lingered in the office, insisting on arranging a plate for Helen as if she were waiting on the Queen. Using a pair of silver tongs, she reached into a small basket adorned with white ribbon, and transferred tiny sandwiches and cakes to the plate.

"Enough fawning, Fernsby," Rhys said. "You have work to attend to."

"Of course, Mr. Winterborne." The secretary sent him a discreet but incinerating glance as she set aside the silver tongs.

Rhys accompanied Mrs. Fernsby to the door, and paused with her just beyond the threshold. They kept their voices low, mindful of being overheard.

"Fair smitten, you are," Rhys mocked.

The secretary's expression was utterly devoid of amusement. "Spending a few hours alone with you will destroy her honor. I will have your word, sir, that you intend to redeem it afterward."

Although Rhys didn't react outwardly, he was amazed that she would dare make such a demand. Mrs. Fernsby, the most loyal of all his employees, had always turned a blind eye and deaf ear to his past debaucheries. "You've never said a bloody word about the women I've brought to my house," he remarked coolly. "Why this sudden fit of scruples?"

"She's a lady. An innocent. I won't be party to ruining her."

Rhys gave her a warning glance. "I've asked for a tray of betrothal rings," he said curtly. "But I can't redeem her honor unless I ruin it first. Go see to your work."

Mrs. Fernsby straightened her neck and spine like a belligerent hen, continuing to view him with patent suspicion. "Yes, sir."

After closing the door, Rhys returned to Helen, who was pouring tea. She was poised on the edge of the chair, her back as straight as a lightning rod.

"Will you take some?" she asked.

He shook his head, watching her intently. Mrs. Fernsby had been right: Helen appeared delicate, more so than he had remembered. Her cameo-pale wrist was so slender, it scarcely seemed able to bear the weight of the teapot. Perhaps she didn't want to be treated like a hothouse flower, but she hardly seemed to have more substance than one.

Christ, how would she handle the demands he would make of her?

But then her steady gaze met his, and the impression of fragility faded. Whatever Helen might feel for him, it wasn't fear. She had come to him, sought him out, in an act of will and unexpected boldness.

He knew the ultimatum he'd given her was indecent, a contradiction of everything he aspired to, but he didn't give a damn. It was the only way he could be sure of her. Otherwise, she might back out of the engagement. He didn't want to think about what losing her again would turn him into.

Helen stirred a lump of sugar into her tea. "How long has Mrs. Fernsby been in your employ?"

"Five years, since she was widowed. Her husband succumbed to a wasting disease."

Sorrow and concern shadowed her sensitive face. "Poor woman. How did she come to work for you?"

Although Rhys was usually disinclined to talk about

his employees' personal lives, Helen's interest encouraged him to continue. "She had helped to manage and run her husband's hosiery and glove shop, which gave her a solid understanding of the retail business. After her husband passed away, she applied for a position at Winterborne's. She applied as a secretary to the manager of the advertising department, but the manager refused to interview her, as he felt only a man could handle such responsibility."

Helen's expression showed not a hint of surprise or disagreement. Like most women, she had been raised to accept the notion of male superiority in the world of business.

"However," Rhys said, "Fernsby outraged the hiring supervisor by asking to speak to me directly. She was turned away immediately. When I was told of it the next day, I sent for Fernsby, and interviewed her personally. I liked her pluck and ambition, and hired her on the spot as my private secretary." He grinned as he added, "She's lorded over the advertising department ever since."

Helen appeared to mull over the story as she proceeded to consume a tea sandwich, a sliver of Sally Lunn bun, and a tart so small it could encompass only one glazed cherry. "I'm not accustomed to the idea of a woman holding a position among men at a place of business," she admitted. "My father always said that the female brain was insufficient to the demands of professional work."

"You disapprove of Fernsby's actions, then?"

"I approve wholeheartedly," she said without hesitation. "A woman should have choices other than to marry or live with her family."

Although she probably hadn't meant that to sting, it did. Rhys gave her a dark glance. "Perhaps instead of proposing, I should have offered you a position alongside the secretaries in the front office."

Pausing with the teacup near her lips, Helen said, "I would rather marry you. It will be an adventure."

Somewhat mollified, Rhys picked up a light chair with one hand and moved it close to her. "I wouldn't count on much adventuring if I were you. I'm going to look after you and keep you safe. "

She glanced at him over the rim of the cup, her eyes smiling. "What I meant was, *you* are the adventure."

Rhys felt his heartbeats tumbling like a row of tin soldiers. He had always enjoyed women casually, sampling their favors with relaxed ease. Not one of them had ever caused this aching craving that Helen seemed to have unlocked from the center of his soul. God help him, he could never let her find out the power she had over him, or he would be at her mercy.

In a few minutes, Mr. Sauveterre, the jeweler, entered the office with a large black leather case held in one hand, and a small folding table in the other. He was a small, slim man with a prematurely receding hairline and a keen, incisive gaze. Although Sauveterre had been born in France, he spoke English with no accent, having lived in London since the age of two. His father, a successful glassmaker, had encouraged his son's artistic ability and eventually secured an apprenticeship for him with a goldsmith. Eventually Sauveterre had attended a Paris art school, and after graduation had worked as a designer in Paris for Cartier and Boucheron.

As a young man with a desire to distinguish himself, Sauveterre had leapt at the chance to become Winterborne's master jeweler. He possessed abundant skill and confidence in his own considerable talent, but just as important, he knew when to keep his mouth shut. A good jeweler protected the secrets of his clients, and Sauveterre knew an abundance of them.

Sauveterre bowed deftly. "My lady." He set the leather case on the floor. He proceeded to unfold the little campaign table in front of Helen, and pulled a tray from the case. "I understand you wish to view betrothal rings? The diamond was not to your taste?"

"I would prefer something smaller," Helen told him. "A ring that won't be a nuisance during needlework or piano practice."

The jeweler didn't bat an eye at hearing the priceless diamond described as a nuisance. "But of course, my lady, we will find something to suit you. Or failing that, I can create anything you desire. Do you have a particular gemstone in mind?"

She shook her head, her awestruck gaze moving over the sparkling rings arrayed along channels of black velvet.

"Perhaps there's a color you fancy?" Sauveterre prompted.

"Blue." She glanced at Rhys cautiously as she replied, and he gave her a slight nod to confirm that she could choose anything she liked.

Bending to rummage through the case, the jeweler began to nimbly arrange rings on a fresh tray. "Sapphires . . . aquamarines . . . opals . . . alexandrites . . . ah, and here is a blue topaz, quite rare, unearthed from the Ural Mountains in Russia . . ."

For at least a half-hour, Sauveterre sat beside Helen to show her various rings and discuss the merits of the stones and settings. As she became comfortable in the jeweler's presence, Helen began to speak more freely with him. In fact, she became positively chatty, discussing art and music, and asking about his work in Paris.

It was, arguably, a more relaxed exchange than she'd ever had with Rhys.

As jealousy stabbed him like a driven nail, Rhys strode to his desk and reached into a glass jar of peppermint creams. The jar, replenished once a week, occupied a permanent corner of his desk. Popping a soft white wafer into his mouth, he went to glare out the window. The confection, made of egg whites, icing sugar, and flavored essence, instantly dissolved in a melting flood of mint.

"What is this?" he heard Helen ask the jeweler.

"A moonstone surrounded by diamonds."

"How beautiful. What makes the stone glow that way?"

"The effect is called adularescence, my lady. The moonstone's natural layers refract the light and make it appear to shine from within."

Perceiving that the ring had caught Helen's fancy, Rhys went to have a look at it. She handed the ring to him, and he inspected it closely. The semiprecious stone was a smooth oval cabochon of an indeterminate color. As he turned it from side to side, ambient light struck hot and cool blue flashes from the pale depths.

It was a lovely ring, but even with the surround of diamonds, the central gem was infinitely humbler than the one he had first given her. It wasn't fit for the wife of a Winterborne. Silently he damned Sauveterre for having brought up such an unassuming piece of jewelry in the first place.

"Helen," he said shortly, "let him show you something else. This is the least valuable ring from the entire tray."

"To me it's the most valuable," Helen said cheerfully. "I never judge the worth of something by how much it actually costs."

"A pretty sentiment," Rhys commented. As the owner of a department store, it gave him chest pains. "But this isn't good enough for you."

Diplomatically the jeweler offered, "If you like, I could surround it with larger diamonds, and widen the shank—"

"I love it exactly as it is," Helen insisted.

"It's a semiprecious stone," Rhys said in outrage. Any of his past lovers would have scorned the thing.

Sauveterre broke the tense silence. "A stone of this quality, Mr. Winterborne, is perhaps more valuable than you may assume. For example, it's worth more than a middling sapphire or a ruby of the second water—"

"I want my wife to have a ring that's worthy of her," Rhys snapped.

Helen stared at him without blinking. "But this ring is what I want." Her voice was gentle, her expression mild. It would be easy to override her opinion—especially since it was clear that she didn't understand what she was asking for.

Rhys was about to argue, but something about her gaze caught his attention. She was trying not to be cowed by him, he realized.

Lucifer's flaming ballocks. There was no way in hell he could refuse her.

Enclosing the ring in his clenched fist, he gave the jeweler a glance of pure murder. "We'll take it," he said curtly.

While Sauveterre slid the glittering trays back into the case, Rhys muttered Welsh curses under his breath. Prudently, neither the jeweler nor Helen asked him to translate.

After Sauveterre closed the leather case, he took Helen's proffered hand and bent over it in a gallant gesture. "My lady, please accept my felicitations on your betrothal. I hope—"

"It's time for you to leave," Rhys said shortly, ushering him out.

"But the camp table—" Sauveterre protested.

"You can retrieve it later."

The jeweler strained to glance over his shoulder at Helen. "If I may be of service in any other—"

"You've helped enough." Rhys pushed him across the threshold and closed the door with a decisive shove.

"Thank you," Helen said in the silence. "I know it's not what you would have chosen, but it's made me happy."

She was smiling at him in a way she never had before, the corners of her eyes crinkling winsomely.

Rhys couldn't fathom why she was so pleased to have exchanged a diamond for a moonstone. All he understood was that she needed to be protected from her own naiveté. "Helen," he said gruffly, "when you have the upper hand, you must not give it away so easily."

She gave him a questioning glance.

"You just exchanged a costly ring for one that is only a fraction of its value," he explained. "It's a bad bargain, it is. You should demand something to make up the difference. A necklace, or a tiara."

"I don't need a tiara."

"You need to ask for a concession," he persisted, "to bring the ledger back into balance."

"There's no ledger in a marriage."

"There's always a ledger," he told her.

He saw from Helen's expression that she didn't agree. But rather than argue, she wandered to the jar of peppermint creams and lifted the lid, sniffing at the cool, bracing fragrance.

"So this is where it comes from," she said. "I've noticed the scent on your breath before."

"I've been fond of them ever since I was a boy," Rhys admitted, "carrying deliveries to the corner sweet shop. The confectioner used to let me have the broken ones." He hesitated before asking with a touch of uncertainty, "Do you dislike it?"

The line of her cheek curved as she looked down at the jar. "Not at all. It's . . . very pleasant. May I try one?"

"Of course."

Self-consciously she reached into the jar for a small white sphere, and placed it cautiously in her mouth. The quick dissolve and powerful rush of mint caught her off guard. "Oh. It's"—she coughed and laughed, her winter-blue eyes watering slightly—"strong."

"Do you need a glass of water?" he asked, amused. "No? Here, then—let me give this to you." Taking her left hand, he began to slide the moonstone onto her finger, and hesitated. "How did I propose the first time?" He had been nervous, steeling himself for a possible refusal; he could hardly remember a word he'd said.

Amusement tugged at her lips. "You laid out the advantages on both sides, and explained the ways in which our future goals were compatible."

Rhys absorbed that with chagrin. "No one has ever accused me of being a romantic," he said ruefully.

"If you were, how would you propose?"

He thought for a moment. "I would begin by teaching you a Welsh word. *Hiraeth.* There's no equivalent in English."

"*Hiraeth,*" she repeated, trying to pronounce it with a tapped R, as he had.

"Aye. It's a longing for something that was lost, or never existed. You feel it for a person or a place, or a time in your life . . . it's a sadness of the soul. *Hiraeth* calls to a Welshman even when he's closest to happiness, reminding him that he's incomplete."

Her brow knit with concern. "Do you feel that way?"

"Since the day I was born." He looked down into her small, lovely face. "But not when I'm with you. That's why I want to marry you."

Helen smiled. She reached up to curl her hand around the back of his neck, her caress as light as silk gauze being pulled across his skin. Standing on her toes, she drew his head down and kissed him. Her lips were smoother than petals, all clinging silk and tender dampness. He had the curious sensation of surrendering, some terrible soft sweetness invading him and rearranging his insides.

Breaking the kiss, Helen lowered back to her heels. "Your proposals are improving," she told him, and extended her hand as he fumbled to slide the ring onto her finger.

Chapter 5

Rhys kept Helen's hand in his as he led her along an enclosed passageway, a kind of gallery with windows that went from a door in his office to one of the upper floors of his house.

Not for the first time that day, a feeling of unreality crept through her. She was more than a little amazed by what she was doing. Step by step, she was departing her old life with no possibility of return. This was nothing like the madcap exploits of the twins, it was a serious decision with unalterable consequences.

Rhys's shoulders seemed to take up the entire breadth of the passageway as he led her to an enclosed stairwell. They proceeded to a small landing with a handsome door painted glossy black. After he unlocked the door, they entered a vast, quiet house, five floors arranged around a central hall and principal staircase. There wasn't a servant in sight. The house was very clean and smelled of newness—fresh paint, varnish, wood polish—but it was bare and sparsely furnished. A place of hard surfaces.

Helen couldn't help contrasting it with Eversby Priory's comfortable shabbiness, the profusion of fresh flowers and artwork, the floors covered with worn patterned carpeting. At home the tables were piled with books, the sideboards were heavy with crystal and porcelain and silver, and a pair of black spaniels named Napoleon and Josephine roamed freely in rooms lit by lamps with fringed shades. There was always afternoon teatime, with hot breads and pots of jam and honey. In the evenings, there was music and games, and sweets and mulled wine, and long conversations in deep cozy chairs. She had never lived any place other than Hampshire, a landscape of sun and rivers and meadows.

It would be very different living in the center of London. Glancing at her sterile, silent surroundings, Helen tried to imagine the house as a blank canvas waiting to be filled with color. Her gaze followed a row of tall sparkling windows up to the high ceiling.

"It's lovely," she said.

"It needs softening," Rhys replied frankly. "But I spend most of my time at the store."

He led her along a long hallway until they reached a suite of rooms. They passed through an unfurnished antechamber into a large, square bedroom with lofty ceilings and cream-painted walls. Helen's pulse raced until she began to feel slightly dizzy.

Here at least was a room that seemed lived-in, the air spiced faintly with candle wax and cedar and firewood ash. One wall was occupied by a long, low dressing-bureau topped with a carved wooden box and a tray containing various objects: a pocket watch, a flat brush and a comb. The floor was covered with a Turkish rug woven in shades of yellow and red. A massive mahogany bed with carved posts had been centered against the far wall.

Helen wandered to the fireplace, investigating the objects on the mantel: a clock, a pair of candlesticks, and a green glass vase of wood spills, used to light candles from the fire. The hearth had been lit. Had Rhys sent advance notice to his servants? Certainly the household was aware of his presence, there in the middle of the day. And his secretary, Mrs. Fernsby, knew exactly what was happening.

The recklessness of what she was about to do was nearly enough to make Helen's legs buckle.

But she had made her choice; she wouldn't turn back now, nor did she want to. And if one viewed the situation pragmatically—which she was trying very hard to do—she would have to submit to this sooner or later, as every bride did.

Rhys drew the curtains over the windows, casting the room into shadow.

Staring at the crackling, dancing flames, Helen spoke, trying to sound composed. "I must rely on you to tell me what . . . what I must do." Reaching up with trembling hands, she extracted the long pin, tugged the hat from her head, and wound the veil loosely about the small brim.

She was aware of Rhys coming up behind her. His hands came to her shoulders and slid to her elbows. Up and down again, in calming strokes. Tentatively Helen leaned back against his chest.

"We've shared a bed before," she heard him murmur. "Remember?"

Helen was momentarily confused. "You must mean when you were ill, at Eversby Priory?" Blushing, she said, "But that wasn't *sharing* a bed."

"I remember that I was burning with fever. And there was a killing pain from my leg. Then I heard your voice, and felt your cool hand on my head. And you gave me something sweet to drink."

"Orchid tea." She had learned a great deal about the

medicinal properties of the plants by poring over an extensive set of journals her mother had kept.

"And then you let me rest my head here." His free hand slid around her front, high on her chest.

Helen took an uneasy breath. "I didn't think you would remember. You were so very ill."

"I'll remember it to my last hour of life." His palm coasted gently over the curve of her breast, lingering until the tip tightened. The hat dropped from Helen's nerveless fingers. Shocked, she stayed motionless while he whispered, "I've never fought sleep as fiercely as I did at that moment, trying to stay awake in your arms. No dream could have given me more pleasure." His head bent, and he kissed the side of her neck. "Why did no one stop you?"

She quivered at the feel of his mouth on her skin, the erotic graze of warmth. "From taking care of you?" she asked dazedly.

"Aye, a rough-mannered stranger, common-born, and half-clothed in the bargain. I could have harmed you before anyone realized what was happening."

"You weren't a stranger, you were a family friend. And you were in no condition to harm anyone."

"You should have kept your distance from me," he insisted.

"Someone had to help you," Helen said pragmatically. "And you had already frightened the rest of the household."

"So you dared to walk into the lion's den."

She smiled up into his intent dark eyes. "As it turned out, there was no danger."

"No?" His voice held a gently mocking note. "Look where it's led. You're in my bedroom with your dress undone."

"My dress isn't—" Helen broke off as she felt her entire bodice come loose, the fabric sagging downward from the weight of her overskirts. "*Oh.*" Anxiety whipped through her as she realized that he had unbuttoned her gown while they had been talking. She clutched at the garment to halt its descent, all her nerves simultaneously burning and chilled.

"First we'll talk about what's going to happen." His mouth caressed her cheek. "But it's better if we're both comfortable."

"I'm already comfortable," she said, her insides as tight as an overwound watch mechanism.

Rhys pulled her against him, one of his palms sliding over her corseted back. "In this contraption?" he asked, tracing the ribbed channels of whalebone. "Or this?" His hand settled briefly on the small horsehair pad of her bustle. "I doubt any woman could feel at ease in so much rigging." He proceeded to untie the cords. "Besides, fashionable ladies no longer wear bustles."

"H-How do you know that?" Helen asked, flinching as the contraption thudded on the floor.

Lowering his mouth to her ear, he whispered as if imparting a great secret. "Undergarments and hosiery, second floor, department twenty-three. According to the manager's latest report, we're no longer stocking them."

Helen couldn't decide if she was more shocked by the fact that they were discussing undergarments, or by the fact that his hands were roaming freely beneath her dress. Soon her petticoats and corset cover landed on the floor with the bustle.

"I've never bought clothing from a department store," she managed to say. "It seems odd to wear something made by strangers."

"The sewing is done by women who support themselves and their families." He tugged the dress sleeves from her arms, and the gown sank to the floor in a shadowy heap.

Helen rubbed the gooseflesh on her bare arms. "Do the seamstresses work at your store?"

"No, at a factory I'm negotiating to purchase."

"Why—" She stopped, shrinking away as he unhooked the lowest fastening on the front of her corset. "Oh please don't."

Rhys paused, his gaze searching her tense face. "You're aware this is done without clothing?" he asked gently.

"May I keep my chemise on at least?"

"Aye, if that would make it easier."

As he proceeded to unfasten the corset with efficient tugs, Helen waited tensely, trying to focus on something other than what was happening. Finding that impossible, she brought herself to look up at him. "You're very accomplished at this," she said. "Do you undress women often? That is . . . I suppose you've had many mistresses."

He smiled slightly. "Never more than one at a time. How do you know about mistresses?"

"My brother Theo had one. My sisters eavesdropped on an argument between him and our father, and they told me about it afterward. Apparently my father said Theo's mistress was too expensive."

"Mistresses generally are."

"More expensive than wives?"

Rhys glanced at her left hand, which had come to rest tentatively on his shirtfront. The moonstone seemed to glow with its own inner light. "More than mine, it seems," he said wryly. Reaching up to her chignon, he eased the jet combs from her hair, letting the fine locks tumble over her shoulders and back. Feeling her shiver, he drew a calming hand along her spine. "I'll be gentle with you, *cariad*. I promise to cause you as little pain as possible."

"Pain?" Helen pulled back from him. "What pain?"

"Virgin's pain." He gave her an alert glance. "You don't know about that?"

She shook her head tensely.

Rhys looked perturbed. "It's said to be trifling. It's . . . Damn it, don't women talk about these things? No? What about when you began your monthly bleeding? How was that explained to you?"

"My mother never mentioned anything. I didn't expect it at all. It was . . . disconcerting."

"Disconcerting?" he repeated dryly. "It probably frightened the wits out of you." To her astonishment, he pulled her toward him slowly, until she was cuddled against his hard chest, her head on his shoulder. Unused to being handled so familiarly, she remained tense in his embrace. "What did you do when it happened?" she heard him ask.

"Oh—I can't discuss that with you."

"Why not?"

"It wouldn't be decent."

"Helen," he said after a moment, "I'm well acquainted with the realities of life, including the basic workings of a woman's body. No doubt a gentleman wouldn't ask. But we both know that's not an issue where I'm concerned." He tucked a kiss into the soft space just beneath her ear. "Tell me what happened."

Realizing that he wasn't going to relent, she forced herself to answer. "I awakened one morning with . . . with stains on my nightgown and the sheets. My tummy hurt dreadfully. When I realized the bleeding wasn't going to stop, I was very frightened. I thought I was going to die. I went to hide in a corner of the reading room. Theo found me. Usually he was away at boarding school, but he had come home on holiday. He asked why I was crying, and I told him." Helen paused, remembering her late brother with a mixture of fondness and grief. "Most of the time Theo was distant with me. But he was very kind that day. He gave me a folded handkerchief to . . . to put where I needed. He found a lap blanket to wrap around my waist, and helped me back to my room. After that, he sent a housemaid to explain what was happening, and how to use—" She broke off in embarrassment.

"Sanitary towels?" he prompted.

Her humiliated voice was muffled against the shoulder of his waistcoat. "How do you know about those?"

She felt a smile nudge against her ear. "They're sold in the store's apothecary department. What else did the housemaid tell you?"

Despite her nerves, Helen felt herself relaxing into his embrace. It was impossible not to. He was very large and warm, and there was such a nice smell about him, a mixture of peppermint and shaving soap and a pleasant resinous dryness like freshly cut wood. A thoroughly masculine fragrance that was somehow exciting and comforting at the same time.

"She said that one day, after I was married and shared a bed with my husband, the bleeding would stop for a time, and a baby would grow."

"But she mentioned nothing about how babies are made in the first place?"

Helen shook her head. "Only that they're not found underneath a gooseberry bush, as the nanny always said."

Rhys looked down at her with a mixture of concern and exasperation. "Are all young women of high rank kept so ignorant about such matters?"

"Most," she admitted. "It's for the husband to decide what his bride should know, and instruct her on the wedding night."

"My God. I can't decide which of them to pity more."

"The bride," she said without hesitation.

For some reason that made him chuckle. Feeling her stiffen, he hugged her more tightly. "No, my treasure, I'm not laughing at you. It's only that I've never explained the sexual act to anyone before . . . and I'm damned if I can think of a way to make it sound appealing."

"Oh dear," Helen whispered.

"It won't be terrible. I promise. You might even like some of it." He pressed his cheek to the top of her head, and spoke with cajoling softness. "It might be best if I explain as we go along, aye?" He waited patiently until he felt her incremental nod. "Come to bed, then."

Willing but reluctant, Helen accompanied him to the bed, discovering that her legs had turned to jelly. She tried to climb beneath the covers quickly.

"Wait." Rhys caught one of her ankles and tugged her back toward him deftly, while he remained standing at the side of the bed.

Helen turned a fearful shade of red. All that kept her from complete nakedness was a pair of stockings, a cambric chemise, and drawers with an open crotch seam.

Holding her stocking-clad ankle, Rhys ran one hand slowly over her shin. A frown notched between his brows as he saw that the knit cotton had been darned in several places. "A rough, poor stocking it is," he murmured, "for such a pretty leg." His hand traveled up to the garter cinched around her thigh. Since the stockinet bands had lost their elasticity, it was necessary to buckle the garter so tightly around her leg that it usually left a red ridge by the end of the day.

After unfastening the buckle, Rhys found a ring of chafed skin around her thigh. His frown deepened, and he let out a disapproving breath. "*Wfft.*"

Helen had heard him make the Welsh sound on previous occasions, when something had displeased him. After unrolling the stocking and casting it aside with distaste, he began on the other leg.

"I'll need those stockings later," Helen said, disconcerted to see her belongings handled so cavalierly.

"I'll replace them with new ones. And decent garters to go with them."

"My own stockings and garters are perfectly serviceable."

"They've left marks on your legs." After deftly knotting the second stocking into a ball, he turned and cast it toward the open grate. It landed perfectly into the fire and flared into a bright yellow blaze.

"Why did you burn it?" Helen asked in dawning outrage.

"It wasn't good enough for you."

"It was mine!"

To her vexation, Rhys seemed not all repentant. "Before you leave, I'll give you a dozen pair. Will that satisfy you?"

"No." She looked away with a frown.

"It was a worthless cotton stocking," he said derisively, "mended in a dozen places. I'll wager the scullery maid in my kitchen wears better."

Having learned forbearance over the years, from her role as the peacemaker in the Ravenel family, Helen held her tongue and counted to ten—twice—before she trusted herself to reply. "I have very few stockings," she told him. "Instead of buying new ones, I chose to mend them and use my pin money for books. Perhaps that scrap of cloth had no value to you, but it did to me."

Rhys was silent, his brows drawing together. Helen assumed that he was preparing for further argument. She was more than a little surprised when he said quietly, "I'm sorry, Helen. I didn't stop to think. I had no right to destroy something that belonged to you."

Knowing that he was not a man often given to apologizing, or humbling himself, Helen felt her annoyance fade. "You're forgiven."

"From now on I'll treat your possessions with respect."

She smiled wryly. "I won't come to you with many possessions, other than two hundred potted orchids."

His hands came to her shoulders, toying with the straps of her chemise. "Will you want all of them brought from Hampshire?"

"I don't think there's room for all of them."

"I'll find a way for you to keep them here."

Her eyes widened. "Would you?"

"Of course." His fingertips traced the curves of her shoulders with beguiling lightness. "I intend for you to have everything you need to be happy. Orchids . . . books . . . a silk mill dedicated to looming stockings only for you."

A laugh caught in her throat, her pulse quickening at his leisurely caresses. "Please don't buy a silk mill for me."

"I already own one, actually. In Whitchurch." He bent to kiss the pale curve of her shoulder, the brush of his mouth as warm and weightless as sunlight. "I'll take you there someday, if you like. A grand sight, it is: a row of huge machines throwing raw silk into threads even finer than strands of your hair."

"I would like to see that," she exclaimed, and he smiled at her interest.

"Then you shall." His fingers sifted through the loose blonde locks. "I'll keep you well supplied in ribbons and stockings, *cariad*." Easing her down to the bed, he began to reach beneath the chemise for the waist of her drawers.

Helen tensed, her hands catching at his. "I'm very shy," she whispered.

His lips wandered gently up to her ear. "How do shy women prefer their drawers to be removed? Fast, or slow?"

"Fast . . . I think."

Between one breath and the next, her drawers were tugged down and efficiently whisked away. Gooseflesh rose on her naked thighs.

Rhys stood and began to unknot his tie. Comprehending that he intended to undress right in front of her, she slid beneath the sheets and the eiderdown quilt, and yanked them up to her collarbone. The bed was soft and clean, scented with the dry tang of washing soda, a comforting smell because it reminded her of Eversby Priory. She stared fixedly at the fireplace, aware of Rhys's movements at the periphery of her vision. He worked on his collar and cuffs, and soon discarded his waistcoat and shirt.

"Have a look if you like," she heard him say casually. "Unlike you, I'm not shy."

Clutching the sheets higher against her neck, Helen risked a timid glance at him . . . and then she couldn't look away.

Rhys was a magnificent sight, dressed only in trousers with braces hanging loosely along his lean hips.

The flesh of his torso looked remarkably solid, as if it had been stitched to his bones with steel thread. Seeming comfortable in his half-naked state, he sat on the edge of the bed and began to remove his shoes. His back was layered with muscle upon muscle, the contours so defined that his sun-colored skin gleamed as if polished. As he stood and turned to face her, Helen blinked with surprise at the discovery that there was no hair at all on the broad expanse of his chest.

Often when her brother Theo had nonchalantly walked about Eversby Priory in his dressing-robe, a scruff of coarse curls had been visible on the upper portion of his chest. And when Devon's younger brother West had been put to bed after suffering an extreme chill, Helen had noticed that he was hairy as well. She had assumed all men were made that way.

"You're . . . smooth," she said, her face heating.

He smiled slightly. "A Winterborne trait. My father and uncles were the same." He began to unfasten his trousers, and Helen looked away hastily. "It was a curse in my teen years," he continued ruefully, "having a chest as bare as a young lad's, while the others my age were all growing a fair carpet. My friends baited and teased me near to death, of course. For a while they took to calling me 'badger.'"

"Badger?" Helen echoed, puzzled.

"Ever hear the expression 'bald as a badger's arse'? No? The long bristles on a shaving brush come from the area around the badger's tail. There's a joke that most of the badgers in England have had their backsides plucked bare."

"That was very unkind of them," Helen said indignantly.

Rhys chuckled. "It's the way of boys. Believe me, I behaved no better. After I grew big enough to thrash the lot of them, they didn't dare say a word."

The mattress sank beneath his weight as he climbed into bed with her. Oh, God. It was happening now. Helen wrapped her arms tightly around her midriff. Her toes curled like lambs' wool. She had never been so at the mercy of another human being.

"Easy," came his soothing voice. "Don't be afraid. Here, let me hold you." The tense bundle of her body was turned and gathered close against a wealth of muscle and hot skin. Her icy feet brushed against the wiry hair on his legs. His hand came to her back, nestling her closer, while firelight danced over them both. Steeping in the warmth of his body, she began to relax by degrees.

She felt his hand settle over the chemise, cupping her breast until the tip rose into the heat of his palm. His breathing changed, roughening, and he took her

mouth in a gently biting kiss, playing with her, rubbing and nudging with his lips. She responded uncertainly, trying to catch the half-open kisses with her
own mouth, the tender strokes and tugs exciting her.
He reached for the drawstring that tied the gathered
neck of her chemise, pulling decisively, and the garment fell loose and open.

"Oh," Helen said in dismay. She reached for the
drooping fabric, and he trapped her hand in his firm,
warm grip. "Oh please . . ."

But he wouldn't let go, only nuzzled across the
freshly revealed skin, the white curve, the shell-pink
aureole. A ragged sigh escaped him. He let the tip of
his tongue trail across the roseate peak, painting it with
heat before taking it into his mouth and flicking until
it ached and tensed even more, and then he moved to
her other breast. Dazed by the wicked pleasure, lost in
him and what he was doing, Helen inched closer, needing more closeness, more . . . *something* . . . but then
through the thin layer of her chemise, she felt an unexpected protrusion, a kind of swollen ridge. Startled, she
wrenched backward.

Rhys lifted his head. Embered light from the hearth
played across the damp surface of his lower lip. "No,
don't pull away," he said huskily. His hand slid over
her bottom and gently eased her back to him. "This

is"—he took an uneven breath as her hips settled tentatively against his—"what happens to me when I want you. There, where it's hard . . . that's the part that goes inside you." As if to demonstrate, he nudged against the cradle of her pelvis. "Understand?"

Helen froze.

Dear Lord.

No wonder the sexual act was such a secret. If women knew, they would never consent to it.

Although she tried not to look as aghast as she felt, some of it must have shown in her expression, because he gave her a glance of mingled chagrin and amusement.

"It's better than it sounds," he offered apologetically.

Although Helen dreaded the answer, she worked up the courage to ask timidly, "Inside where?"

For answer, he moved over her, spreading her beneath him. His hand coasted over her shrinking body, caressing the insides of her thighs and stroking them apart. She could scarcely breathe as he reached beneath the hem of the chemise. There was a light touch between her legs, his fingertips delving into the patch of intimate curls.

She went rigid at the peculiar feeling, the circling pressure that found a hollow place and began to push inward. And then, unbelievably, her body gave way to the silky-wet wriggle and glide of his finger as he . . . No, it was impossible.

"Inside here," he said quietly, watching her from beneath a sweep of ink-black lashes.

Moaning in confusion, she twisted to escape the invasion, but he held her firmly.

"When I enter you"—his finger sank to the last joint, retreated an inch, slipped in again—"you'll feel pain at first." He was stroking places she had never known existed, his touch clever and gentle. "But it won't hurt after the first time, ever again."

Helen closed her eyes, distracted by the curious sensation that had awakened inside her. Ephemeral, elusive, like a hint of perfume lingering in a quiet room.

"I'll move like this"—the subtle caresses acquired a rhythm, his finger nudging in, and in, her inner flesh becoming silkier and more slippery with each sinuous penetration—"until I spend inside you."

"Spend?" she asked through dry lips.

"A release . . . a moment when your heart begins to pound, and you struggle in every limb for something you can't quite reach. It's torture, but you'd rather die than stop." His mouth lowered to her scarlet ear, while he continued to tease her relentlessly. "You follow the rhythm and hold on tight," he whispered, "because you know the world is about to end. And then it does."

"That doesn't sound very comfortable," she managed to say, brimming with a strange, squirmy, guilty heat.

A dark tendril of laughter curled inside her ear. "Comfortable, no. But an unholy pleasure, it is."

His finger withdrew, and she felt him stroke along the delicately closed seam of her sex. Parting the soft crevice, he began to toy with the pink folds and frills, grazing a place so exquisitely tender that her entire body jerked.

"Does this hurt, *cariad*?"

"No, but . . ." There seemed no way to make him understand an upbringing in which certain areas of the body were too shameful to be acknowledged, let alone touched, except for purposes of washing. One of many rules instilled by a stout nanny who had been fond of smacking naughty children's palms with a ruler until they were red and sore. Such lessons could never be entirely unlearned. "That's . . . a shameful place," she finally said breathlessly.

His reply was immediate. "No, it isn't."

"It is." When he shook his head, she insisted, "I was taught that it most definitely *is*."

Rhys looked sardonic. "By the same person who told you that babies are found under gooseberry bushes?"

Forced to concede the point, Helen fell into a dignified silence. Or at least as dignified as she could manage in the circumstances.

"Many people are ashamed of their own desires," he said. "I'm not one of them. Nor do I want you to be." Lightly resting his palm on the center of her chest, he drew it slowly down her body. "You were made for pleasure, *cariad*. No part of you is shameful." He seemed not to notice the way she stiffened as his hand drifted down between her thighs. "Especially not this sweet place . . . ah, you're so pretty here. Like one of your orchids."

"*What?*" she asked faintly, wondering if he were mocking her. "No."

"You're shaped like petals." One of his fingertips traced her outer folds. Resisting her desperate tugs at his wrist, he spread her open. Gently he took a rosy inner flange between his thumb and forefinger and rubbed with the softest possible pressure. "And these. Sepals . . . aye?"

It was then that Helen understood what he meant, the accuracy of the comparison. She went crimson all over. If it were possible to faint from embarrassment, she would have.

A smile flickered across his lips. "How can you not have noticed?"

"I've never looked down there before!"

Absorbed in every minute variation of her expression, he swirled his fingertip up to the crest of her sex. Gently his thumb pressed the hood back, while he tickled around the little bud. "Tell me the word for this. The tip inside the blossom."

Writhing in his hold, she gasped, "Anther." Something was happening to her. Fire was creeping up the backs of her legs and gathering in her stomach, every sensation feeding into a pool of heat.

His finger slipped inside her again, where it had become deep and liquid. What was it? What—her body closed on the invasion, pulling at him in a way she couldn't control. He brushed silken kisses over her mouth, catching at her lips as if he were sipping from a fragile cup. The tip of his thumb found the sensitive peak. Electric tension spread through her in widening ripples, an alarming wave of feeling approaching . . . too strong . . . almost like pain. Sliding out from beneath him with a low cry, she rolled to her stomach, suffocating on her own heartbeat.

Instantly she felt Rhys at her back, his soothing hands running over her trembling limbs.

His voice was at her ear, velvety with amused chiding. "*Cariad*, you're not supposed to pull away. It won't hurt. I promise. Turn over."

Helen didn't move, stunned by the anguished rush

of pleasure that had begun to overwhelm her. It had nearly stopped her heart.

Pushing aside the tangled disorder of her hair, Rhys kissed the nape of her neck. "Is this the kind of wife you'll be? It's too soon for you to begin disobeying me."

Her lips felt swollen as she managed to reply. "We're not married yet."

"No, and we won't be until I manage to compromise you properly." His hand went to her bare bottom, kneading gently. "Turn over, Helen."

An approving sound, very nearly a purr, left his throat as she obeyed. He looked down at her with eyes as bright as the reflection of stars in a midnight ocean. So brutally handsome, like one of the volatile gods of mythology, wreaking havoc on hapless mortal maidens at a whim.

And he was hers.

"I want to know what you feel like," she surprised herself by whispering.

His breath caught, his lashes lowering as she reached down the sleek muscled terrain of his body. Her trembling hand curved around the thick, erect length of him. The skin beneath her fingers was thin and astonishingly satiny, slipping easily over the hard shaft. She gripped him lightly, discovering fever-hot flesh, dense in texture, full of mysterious pulses. Daring to caress him lower down, she trundled the loose, cool weights in the cup of her palm, and he responded with an inarticulate sound. He wasn't breathing well. For once he seemed as overwhelmed by her as she had always been by him.

In the next moment, she found herself dominated by a large expanse of amorous naked male. He covered her chest and shoulders with voracious kisses, his hands cupping her breasts high while he fastened his mouth over the tips. With a quiet grunt, he grasped a handful of her chemise and tugged until the hem was around her waist. He settled over her, and she felt the stunning texture of naked flesh, hardness pressing against soft, furry, shivery heat.

He kissed her, ravishing her mouth, moving to her breasts, then lower. The tangled chemise was in his way, and he gripped it in both hands, rending it in half as if it were made of paper lace. With a savage flick of his arm, the ruined chemise sailed through the air in a ghostlike arc. He slid downward and she felt him lick across her navel. The slithery tickle drew a protracted groan from her. Indecent kisses wandered to the edge of damp curls and into the hollows of her inner thighs.

His arms slid beneath her legs, pushing upward until her knees hooked over his shoulders. The tip of his tongue separated the furled petals and traced an erotic pattern around the tender bud, and she whimpered in confusion. Turning ruthless, he sucked the full center of her into his mouth and licked at every throb and pulse, teasing and teasing until she felt a low, hot pressure inside. A loss of control was approaching, something powerful and frightening. The more she tried to contain it, hold it back, the stronger it grew, until finally she was wracked with violent spasms of pleasure. She stiffened, every muscle tightening and releasing, quivers running out to her fingers and toes. Eventually the sensations quieted until she was limp with exhaustion. Her sex had become so sensitive that even the gentlest stroke was painful.

With an incoherent protest, Helen pushed at his head, his shoulders, but he was rock-solid, impossible to budge. His tongue trailed lower, searching wetly until it pushed into the trembling entrance of her body. Opening her eyes, she stared at the dark shape of his head silhouetted against dancing firelight.

"Please," she faltered, although she wasn't quite certain what she was asking for.

Both of his hands went to her sex, spreading it softly, his thumbs caressing over the little bud with alternating flicks. To her shame and astonishment, her body squeezed intimately at every inward surge of his tongue, as if to capture and hold it there.

Before she had even realized it, another tide of release rolled up to her. She dug her heels into the mattress, her hips lifting high and tight as wave after wave of heat went through her. He drew out the feeling, shaping it with delicate whisks and cat licks, feeding on her pleasure.

Panting and disoriented, Helen collapsed back onto the bed. She made no move to resist as Rhys rose over her. Something smooth and stiff nudged into the wetness between her thighs. He reached down, circling the head of his sex against her, pushing harder. It began to burn, and she recoiled instinctively, but the pressure was steady and insistent. A weak moan escaped her as her flesh stretched and pulsed around him in jabs of fire. More of him, impossibly more, until finally his hips met hers, and she was utterly filled. There was too much of him inside her, and no way to escape the piercing ache.

Taking her head in his hands, Rhys stared down at her, his gaze not quite focused. "I'm sorry to cause you pain, little dove." His voice was uneven. "Try to open to me."

She lay still, willing herself to relax. As Rhys continued to hold her, his lips pressing to her shoulder, then drifting to her throat, she felt the stabbing discomfort ease a little.

"Aye," he whispered. "That's the way."

A flash of embarrassment assailed her as she realized he had felt the slight loosening of those small, private muscles. She lifted her arms, her hands coming to rest on the powerful surface of his back. To her surprise, his muscles turned to steel. Intrigued by his reaction to the light touch, she trailed her fingers gently from his shoulders down to his waist, letting the oval tips of her nails scratch delicately at the small of his back.

He groaned and lost control, quaking violently just as she had, and she realized that he was experiencing his own release. Feeling curiously protective of him, she tightened her arms across his back. After a long moment, Rhys withdrew with a groan and eased to his side to keep from crushing her.

As the invasion slid away, there was a hot, disconcerting trickle between her thighs. Her flesh was sore and smarting, closing oddly on emptiness. But she felt sated, her body agreeably tumbled and lazy, and it was exquisite to feel the roughness and strength and smoothness of him all around her. With the last of her strength, she turned to her side and nestled into the crook of his shoulder.

Her thoughts were dissolving before she could fully grasp them. It was daytime, even though it felt like deepest night. Soon she would have to dress herself, and go out into the bright, cold light, when all she wanted was to stay in this safe warm darkness and sleep, and sleep.

Rhys sought to arrange the covers, pausing to tug at something caught half-beneath her. A remnant of her chemise. Helen knew she ought to feel concerned—how could she return home without a chemise?—but in her exhaustion, it didn't seem to matter nearly as much as it should have.

"I meant to respect your possessions," he said rue-fully.

"You were distracted," she managed to whisper.

Rhys made a faint sound of amusement. "'Un-hinged' would be the word." After using the torn gar-ment to blot the wetness between her thighs, he tossed it aside and shaped his hand over her skull in a brief, comforting gesture. "Sleep, *cariad*. I'll wake you now in a minute."

Now in a minute . . . a Welsh phrase she'd heard him say before. *Later*, it seemed to mean, with no particular urgency.

Her body quivered with relief as she let herself suc-cumb, sinking into the inviting darkness. And she fell asleep in a man's arms for the first time in her life.

For more than an hour, Rhys did nothing but hold her. He felt drugged with satisfaction, drunk on it.

No matter how long he stared at Helen, he couldn't have his fill. Every detail of her struck fresh notes of pleasure in him: the supple lines of her body, the pretty curves of her breasts. The white-blonde hair that spilled and streamed over his forearm, catching light as if it were liquid. And most of all her face, innocent in sleep, bereft of its usual composed mask. The wistful softness of her mouth went straight to his heart. How was it that he could hold her so close and still want more of her?

Helen was not a placid sleeper. At times her lashes trembled and her lips parted with an anxious breath, and her fingers and toes twitched involuntarily. Whenever she became restless, he caressed and cradled her more closely. Without even trying, she pulled something from him, a tenderness he'd never shown to anyone. He had pleasured women, taken them in every conceivable way. But he'd never made love to anyone the way he just had, as if his fingers were drinking sensation from her skin.

Beneath the covers, her slender thigh hitched higher on his leg as she turned more fully on her side. His cock answered vigorously. He wanted her again, now, even before she had healed from the first time, before he'd washed the virgin's blood and his seed from her. Somehow in yielding to him so completely, she had gained a mysterious advantage, something he couldn't yet identify.

He had to steel himself from rolling over her and thrusting into her defenseless body. Instead he savored the feel of her tucked against his side.

A log snapped in the hearth, the implosion of flame sending ruddy light through the room. He relished the way it gilded Helen's skin, a sheen of gold over ivory. Very softly he touched the perfect curve of her shoulder. How strange it was to lie here so utterly contented, when he usually couldn't abide inactivity. He could lie here for hours, even now at the middle of the day, just holding her.

He couldn't remember the last time he'd been abed at this hour, save for those three weeks at Eversby Priory while he'd recovered from the train accident.

Before that experience, he'd never been sick in his life. And the thing he had always feared most was to be at someone else's mercy. But somewhere in the miasma of heat and pain, he had become aware of a young woman's cool hands and lulling voice. She had wiped his face and neck with iced cloths, and given him sips of sweetened tea. Everything about her had soothed him: the delicacy of her, the vanilla sweetness of her scent, the gentle way she had spoken to him.

For the most blissful few minutes of Rhys's life, she

had cradled his feverish head and told him stories about mythology and orchids. Until his last day on earth, that memory was the one he would return to most often. It was the first time he hadn't envied a single man on earth, because for once he had felt something close to happiness. And it hadn't been something he'd had to hunt down and devour in dog-hungry gulps . . . it had been gently, patiently spooned to him. Kindness that had asked for nothing in return. He had craved it . . . craved *her* . . . ever since.

A delicate blond tendril dangled over Helen's nose, fluttering with each soft exhalation. Rhys stroked back the glinting strands and let his thumb trace over a slender dark brow.

He still didn't understand why Helen had come to him. He had believed that his wealth was the attraction, but that didn't seem to be the case. Obviously she wasn't drawn to his scholarly turn of mind or his distinguished lineage, since he possessed neither of those things.

She'd said she wanted adventure. But adventures had a way of becoming tiresome, and then it was time to return to everything that was safe and familiar. What would happen when she wanted to go back and realized her life could never be what it was?

Troubled, he disentangled himself from Helen and

arranged the covers snugly around her. Leaving the bed, he dressed in the bracing air of the bedroom. His mind fell back into its customary brisk pace, setting out lists and plans like marbles on a solitaire board.

Hell and damnation, what had he been thinking earlier? A grand wedding to show off his blue-blooded bride . . . why had he thought that mattered? *Idiot,* he told himself in disgust, feeling as if he were finally thinking clearly after spending days in a fog.

Now that Helen belonged to him, he couldn't give her back. Not even for a brief interval until the wedding. He needed to keep her close at hand, and he damned well couldn't risk having her back under Devon's control. Although Rhys was convinced that Helen genuinely wanted to marry him, she was still too unworldly. Too malleable. Her family might try to send her far from his reach.

Thank God it wasn't too late to rectify his mistake. Striding from the bedroom suite, he went to his private study and rang for a footman.

By the time the footman had reached the study, Rhys had made a list, sealed it, and addressed it to his private secretary.

"You sent for me, Mr. Winterborne?" The young footman, an enterprising fellow named George, had been well trained and highly recommended by an aristocratic London household. Unfortunately for the upper-class family—but quite fortunately for Rhys—they had recently been forced to economize and reduce the number of servants in their employ. Since many peerage families found themselves in straitened circumstances nowadays, Rhys had the luxury of hiring servants they could no longer afford. He had his pick of any number of competent people in service, usually the young or the very old.

Rhys motioned the footman to approach the desk. "George, take this list to my office and give it to Fernsby. Wait there while she collects the items I've requested, and bring it all here within the half-hour."

"By your leave, sir." The footman was gone in a flash.

Rhys grinned briefly at the young man's speed. It was no secret, both in his household and at his store, that he liked his orders to be carried out quickly and with enthusiasm.

By the time the requested items had been brought, all packed in cream-colored boxes, Rhys had drawn a bath for Helen and gathered up her scattered clothes and hair combs.

He sat on the edge of the mattress and reached down to caress Helen's cheek.

As he watched her struggle into consciousness, Rhys

was caught off guard by a pang of tenderness, almost painful in its intensity. Helen opened her eyes, wondering for a bewildered instant where she was, and why he was there. Remembering, she looked up at him uncertainly. To his delight, one of her shy smiles emerged.

He pulled her up against him, his lips finding hers. As he caressed the naked length of her spine, he felt gooseflesh rise on her skin.

"Would you like a bath?" he whispered.

"Could I?"

"It's ready for you." He reached for the dressing-robe he'd laid over the foot of the bed, a kimono style that wrapped across the front. Helen slipped out of bed and allowed him to help her into it, trying to conceal herself in the process. Charmed by her modesty, Rhys tied the belt at her waist and proceeded to roll the sleeves back. His robe was twice her size, the hem pooling on the floor. "You shouldn't be shy," he told her. "I'd give my soul for a glimpse of you without your clothes."

"Don't joke about that."

"About seeing you naked? I wasn't joking."

"Your soul," Helen said earnestly. "It's too important."

Rhys smiled and stole another kiss from her.

Taking her hand, he led her to the bathroom, which was paved with white onyx tile, the upper half of the walls lined with mahogany paneling. The French double-ended tub was tapered at the base, the sides flared to allow the bather to lean back comfortably. Nearby, an inset cabinet with glass doors featured stacks of white toweling.

Gesturing to the small mahogany stand beside the tub, Rhys said, "I had a few things sent over from the store."

Helen went to investigate the objects on the stand: a rack of hairpins, a set of black combs, an enamel-backed hairbrush, a collection of soaps wrapped in hand-painted paper, and a selection of perfumed oils.

"You usually have a maid to attend you," Rhys remarked, watching as she twisted up her hair and anchored it in place.

"I can manage." A touch of pink infused her cheeks as she glanced at the high rib of the tub. "But I may need help to step in and out of the bath."

"I'm at your service," Rhys said readily.

Still blushing, she turned away from him and let the robe slip from her shoulders. He pulled it from her, nearly dropping the garment as he saw the slim length of her back and the perfect heart shape of her bottom. His fingers literally trembled with the urge to touch her. Draping the robe over one arm, he extended his free hand. Helen took it as she stepped into the tub, every movement graceful and careful, like a cat finding her way across uneven ground. She settled into the water, wincing as the heat of the bath soothed the intimate aches and stings from their earlier encounter.

"You're sore," he said in concern, remembering how delicate she was, how tight.

"Only a little." Her lashes lifted. "May I have the soap?"

After unwrapping a cake of honey soap, he handed it to her along with a sponge, mesmerized by the pink shimmer of her body beneath the surface of the water. She rubbed the soap over the sponge and began to wash her shoulders and throat.

"I feel relieved," she commented, "now that our course has been set."

Rhys went to occupy the mahogany chair next to the inset cabinet. "That leads to something I need to discuss," he said casually. "While you were sleeping, I reflected on the situation, and I've reconsidered our agreement. You see—" He broke off as he saw her face turn bleach-white, her eyes huge and dark. Realizing that she had misunderstood, he went to her in two strides, lowering to his knees beside the tub. "No— no, it's not that—" He reached for her hastily, heedless of the water soaking his sleeves and waistcoat. "You belong to me, *cariad*. And I'm yours. I would never—

Jesus, don't look like that." Pulling her to the side of the tub, he spread kisses over her sweet, wet skin. "I was trying to say that I can't wait for you. We have to elope. I should have said so at the beginning, but I wasn't thinking clearly." He captured her tense mouth with his, kissing her until he felt her relax.

Drawing back, Helen looked at him in amazement, her cheeks dappled with water, her lashes spiked. "Today?"

"Aye. I'll take care of the arrangements. There's nothing you need worry about. I'll have Fernsby pack a valise for you. We'll travel to Glasgow by private train carriage. It has a sleeping compartment with a large bed—"

"Rhys." Her fingers, scented of soap, came to rest on his lips. She took an extra breath to steady herself. "There's no need to alter our plans. Nothing has changed."

"Everything's changed," he said, a shade too aggressively. Swallowing hard, he moderated his tone. "We'll leave this afternoon. It's far more practical this way. It solves more than one potential problem."

Helen shook her head. "I can't leave my sisters alone in London."

"They're in a household full of servants. And Trenear will return soon."

"Yes, tomorrow, but even so, the twins can't be left to their own devices until then. You know how they are!"

Pandora and Cassandra were a pair of little devils, there was no denying it. They were both full of mischief and imagination. After having been brought up on a quiet estate in Hampshire all their lives, they thought of London as a giant playground. Neither of them had any idea of the perils that might befall them in the city.

"We'll take them with us," Rhys said reluctantly.

Her brows lifted. "And have Devon and Kathleen return from Hampshire to discover that you've kidnapped all three Ravenel sisters?"

"Believe me, I intend to give the twins back at the first opportunity."

"I don't understand the need for elopement. No one would deny us a wedding now."

Steam rose from the water and clung to her fair skin in a glistening veil. Rhys was distracted by a cluster of soap bubbles that slid down the upper slope of her breast in a lazy path, finally coming to rest on the soft shell-pink tip. Unable to resist, he reached out to cup her breast, his thumb brushing away the bit of foam. He circled the nipple gently, watching it tighten into a perfect bud.

"There might be a baby," he said.

Helen slipped from his grasp, as elusive as a mermaid. "Will there?" she asked, clutching the sponge until water streamed between her fingers.

"We'll know if you miss your monthly bleeding."

She applied more soap to the sponge and continued to bathe. "If that happens, it may become necessary to elope. But until then—"

"We'll do it now," Rhys said impatiently, "to avoid any hint of scandal if the child is born early." The soaked waistcoat and shirt had turned clammy and cold. He stood and began to unfasten them. "I don't want to provide gossip fodder for wagging tongues. Not where my offspring is concerned."

"An elopement would cause just as much of a scandal as a baby coming early. And it would give my family more cause to disapprove of you."

Rhys gave her a speaking glance.

"I would rather not antagonize them," Helen said.

He dropped the waistcoat to the floor, where it landed with a wet smack. "Their feelings don't matter to me."

"But mine do . . . don't they?"

"Aye," he muttered, working on his wet cuffs.

"I would like to have a wedding. It would give everyone, including me, time to adjust to the situation."

"I've already adjusted."

There was a suspicious tension at her lips, as if she were trying to hold back a sudden smile. "Most of us don't live at the same pace as you. Even the Ravenels. Couldn't you try to be patient?"

"I would if there was a need. But there isn't."

"I think there is. I think a large wedding is still something you desire, although you're not willing to admit it at the moment."

"I wish I'd bloody well never said it," Rhys said, exasperated. "I don't care if we're married in a church, the office of the Registrar General, or by a shaman wearing antlers in the wilds of North Wales. I want you to be mine as soon as possible."

Helen's eyes widened with curiosity. She seemed on the verge of asking more about shamans and antlers, but instead she kept to the subject at hand. "I would prefer to be married at a church."

Rhys was silent as he opened his collar and began on the front placket of his shirt. The situation was of his own making, he thought, damning himself. He couldn't believe he'd allowed his pride and ambition to stand in the way of marrying Helen as soon as possible. Now he would have to wait for her, when he could have had her in his bed every night.

Helen watched him solemnly. After a long moment,

she said, "It's important that you keep your promises to me."

Defeated and fuming, he stripped off his wet shirt. Apparently Helen wasn't quite as malleable as he'd assumed. "We'll be married in six weeks. Not a day more."

"That's not nearly enough time," she protested. "Even if I had unlimited resources, it would take much longer than that to make plans and place orders, and have things delivered—"

"I have unlimited resources. Anything you want will be delivered here faster than a rat up a drainpipe."

"It's not just that. My brother Theo hasn't been gone a year. My family and I will be in mourning until the beginning of June. Out of respect for him, I would like to wait until then."

Rhys stared at her. His brain staggered around the words.

Wait until then. Wait until . . . *June?*

"That's five months," he said blankly.

Helen looked back at him, seeming to believe she had said something rational.

"*No*," he said in outrage.

"Why not?"

It had been many years, and tens of millions of

pounds ago, since anyone had asked Rhys to justify why he wanted something. The mere fact that he wanted it was always enough.

"It's what we originally planned," Helen pointed out, "the first time we became engaged."

Rhys didn't know why he'd agreed to that, or how it had even seemed tenable. Probably because he'd been so elated about marrying her that he hadn't been inclined to quibble over the wedding date. Now, however, it was painfully clear that five days was too long to wait for her. Five weeks would be torment.

Five months didn't even merit a discussion.

"Your brother won't know or care if you marry before the mourning period is over," Rhys said. "He probably would have been glad that you'd found a husband."

"Theo was my only brother. I would like to honor him with the traditional year of mourning if at all possible."

"It's not possible. Not for me."

She gave him a questioning glance.

Rhys leaned over her, gripping the sides of the tub. "Helen, there are times when a man has to—if his needs aren't satisfied—" The heat from the water wafted up to his darkening face. "I can't go without you that long. A man's natural urges—" He broke off uncomfortably.

"*Damn it!* If he can't find relief with a woman, he's driven to self-abuse. Do you understand?"

She shook her head, mystified.

"Helen," he said with growing impatience, "I haven't been chaste since the age of twelve. If I tried now, I would probably end up killing someone before the week was out."

Perplexity wove across her forehead. "When we were engaged before . . . how were you planning to manage? I suppose . . . you were going to lie with other women until we were married?"

"I hadn't considered it." At that point, it might not have been entirely out of the question. But now . . . he was appalled to realize that the thought of trying to substitute someone else for Helen was repellent. Bloody hell, what was happening to him? "It has to be you. We're bound to each other now."

Helen's gaze slid bashfully over his bare torso, and by the time her eyes returned to his face, she looked flushed and a little shaken. With a hot stab in the pit of his stomach, he realized she was aroused by him.

"You'll need it too," he said huskily. "You'll remember the pleasure I gave you, and want more."

Helen looked away from him as she replied. "I'm sorry. But I would rather not marry while I'm still in mourning."

Gentle as her tone was, Rhys heard the underlying intractability in it. After a lifetime of bartering and bargaining, he had learned to recognize when the other party had reached the point at which they would not yield.

"I intend to marry you in six weeks," he said, making his voice hard to mask his desperation, "whatever the cost. Tell me what you want. Tell me, and you'll have it."

"I'm afraid there's nothing you can bribe me with." Looking sincerely apologetic, Helen added, "You already promised me the piano."

Chapter 6

The elegant unmarked carriage came to a halt at the porticoed side entrance of Ravenel House. An afternoon rain had descended from the January sky, swept along by brisk icy breezes that whistled through the streets of London. As Helen had peeked through the carriage's window blinds during the ride from Cork Street to South Audley, she had seen pedestrians clutching wool coats and capes more closely around their bodies, heading to covered shop doorways to stand in tight clusters. The shower of raindrops, heralding worse to come, had imparted a dark shimmer to the pavement.

But warm yellow light poured through the glass-paned doors that opened onto Ravenel House's spacious double library, filled with mahogany shelves and acres of books, and heavy well-cushioned furniture. A shiver of anticipation went through Helen at the thought of returning to her cozy house.

Rhys slid a hand over both her gloved ones, giving them a slight squeeze. "I'll call on Trenear tomorrow evening to tell him about the engagement."

"He may not take the news well," Helen said.

"He won't," Rhys replied flatly. "But I can handle him."

Helen was still concerned about Devon's reaction. "Perhaps you should wait to call until the day after tomorrow," she suggested. "He and Kathleen will be weary from traveling. I think they'll receive the news more easily if they've had a sound night's rest. And I could—" She paused as a footman began to open the carriage door.

Rhys glanced at the footman and said brusquely, "A few minutes."

"Yes, sir." The door closed at once.

Turning in his seat, Rhys leaned over Helen, toying with the folds of her veil. "Go on."

"I could explain things to Devon before you arrive," she continued, "and try to pave the way."

He shook his head. "If he loses his temper, I won't have you bear the brunt of it. Let me be the one to tell him."

"But my cousin would never harm me in any way—"

"I know that. All the same, he'll be picking for a fight. It's for me to deal with him, not you." Carefully he adjusted an edge of her collar that had folded over. "I want this settled by tomorrow night, for both our sakes. I can't bear to wait longer than that. Will you agree to say nothing until then? And let me take care of it?" His tone was not dictatorial, but rather concerned. Protective. He paused before saying with gruff unwillingness, as if the word threatened to choke him, "Please."

Helen stared into his coffee-black eyes. This was new, this feeling of being looked after and wanted. It seemed to spread inside her like delicate tendrils.

Realizing that he was waiting for an answer, she replied with a touch of impishness, "Aye."

After a blink of surprise, Rhys hauled her up into his lap. His eyes glinted with amusement. "Mocking my accent, are you?"

"No." A breathless giggle escaped her. "I like it. Very much."

"Do you, then?" His tone had deepened. "I'll have to send you inside, now soon. Give me a kiss, *cariad*. One to make up for all the kisses I would have had from you tonight."

She pressed her mouth to his, and his lips parted, letting her explore him with little flirting tastes. Realizing that he was letting her take the lead, she nudged him more fully open, enjoying the firm silken texture of his mouth. Tentatively she changed the angle of the kiss, and the fit was so lush and delicious that she locked her mouth onto his. She wanted to stay like this forever, caught in his lap with the mass of her skirts bunched all around them, her bottom sinking into the space between his muscular thighs. Gripping his shoulders, she hugged herself closer to the hard contours of his body.

His chest moved in a forceful breath or two, like pumps from fireplace bellows, and he broke the kiss with a groan. A shaken laugh escaped him as her mouth continued to seek his. "No—Helen—ah, how you please me—we have to stop." He leaned his forehead against hers. "Before I take you here in this carriage."

Befuddled, Helen asked, "It can be done in a carriage?"

His color heightened, and he closed his eyes briefly, as if he'd been pushed to the limit of his endurance. "Aye."

"But how—"

"Don't ask me to explain, or I might end up showing you." Clumsily he set her back on the seat beside him, and leaned forward to rap on the carriage door.

The footman came to help Helen descend, first placing a movable step on the flagstone tiled ground, then extending his gloved hand for her to take. Before Helen reached the French doors, she could already see the twins through the paned glass, their slim forms practically vibrating with eagerness.

"Milady, shall I carry this inside?"

Helen glanced at the cream-colored box he held, approximately the size of a dinner plate, tied with a narrow matching satin ribbon. She realized it was the box containing a selection of stockings from the store. "I'll take it now," she said. "Thank you"—she tried to remember what Rhys had called him—"George, isn't it?"

He smiled at her as he opened the door. "Yes, milady."

Immediately upon entering the house Helen was beset by the twins, who danced around her in excitement.

She cast one last glance through the glass panes, watching the carriage depart.

"You're back!" Pandora shouted. "*Finally!* Whatever took you so long? You've been gone for most of the day!"

"It's almost teatime," Cassandra chimed in.

Helen smiled, nonplussed by their wildness.

The twins were nineteen, soon to be twenty, but one could be excused for thinking they were younger than their actual age. Raised in an atmosphere largely devoid of authority, they had run free on a country estate with few diversions other than those they created for themselves. Their parents had spent much of their time in London society, leaving their daughters in the care of servants, governesses, and tutors. None of them had been able or willing to take a firm hand with them.

To be certain, Pandora and Cassandra were high-spirited but also affectionate, intelligent, and endearing. And they were as beautiful as a pair of pagan goddesses, both of them long-limbed and glowing with health. Pandora was perpetually disheveled and full of energy, her dark hair falling from its pins as if she'd just been running through the woods. Cassandra, the golden-haired twin, was more compliant and romantic in nature, more willing to abide by rules.

"What happened?" Cassandra demanded. "What did Mr. Winterborne say?"

Helen set aside the cream-colored box. After tugging off a black glove, she held out her left hand.

The twins crowded close, wide-eyed with wonder.

The moonstone seemed illuminated, glowing with shimmers of green, blue, and silver.

"A new ring," Pandora said.

"A new engagement," Helen told her.

"But the same fiancé," Cassandra said with a questioning lilt.

Helen laughed. "One can't simply go shopping for one of those. Yes, it's the same fiancé."

That set off a fresh burst of enthusiasm, both girls whooping and jumping without restraint.

Perceiving there was no use in trying to curb them, Helen stood back. Noticing movement at the doorway, she turned to find the housekeeper waiting at the threshold.

Mrs. Abbott tilted her head and regarded her expectantly, asking a silent question.

Helen beamed and nodded.

The housekeeper sighed with what appeared to be an equal measure of relief and worry. "May I take your things, Lady Helen?"

After giving her hat and gloves, Helen said quietly, "You and the other servants must not worry, even for a moment, about the consequences of my outing. I will take full responsibility. All I ask is that the staff refrain from saying anything to Lord or Lady Trenear when they arrive tomorrow."

"They will hold their tongues and go about their work as usual."

"Thank you." Impulsively Helen touched the older

woman's shoulder, patting it softly. "I've never been so happy."

"There's no one who deserves happiness more," Mrs. Abbott said gently. "I hope Mr. Winterborne will be half so deserving of you."

The housekeeper departed through the main library room, while Helen went back to her sisters. They had settled onto a leather-upholstered settee, staring at her eagerly.

"Tell us everything," Cassandra urged. "Was Mr. Winterborne upset when you approached him? Angry?"

"Was he confuming?" Pandora, who liked to invent words, asked.

Helen laughed. "As a matter of fact, he was terribly confuming. But after I convinced him that I sincerely wished to be his wife, he seemed much happier."

"Did he kiss you?" Cassandra asked eagerly. "On the lips?"

Helen hesitated before replying, and both twins squealed, one from excitement and the other from aversion.

"Oh lucky, lucky Helen," Cassandra exclaimed.

"I don't think she's lucky at all," Pandora said frankly. "Fancy putting your mouth on someone else's—what if his breath is nasty or there's a wad of dipping snuff in his cheek? What if there are crumbs in his beard?"

"Mr. Winterborne has no beard," Cassandra said. "And he doesn't dip snuff."

"Still, mouth kisses are revolting."

Cassandra looked at Helen with great concern. "Was it revolting, Helen?"

"No," she said, turning scarlet. "Not at all."

"What was it like?"

"He held my cheeks in his hands," Helen said, remembering the touch of Rhys's strong, gentle fingers, and the way he'd murmured *You belong to me, cariad* . . . "His mouth was warm and soft," she continued dreamily, "and his breath was cool with peppermint. It was a lovely feeling. Kissing is the best thing lips do other than smiling."

Cassandra drew up her knees and hugged them. "I want to be kissed someday," she exclaimed.

"I don't," Pandora said. "I can think of a hundred things better than kissing. Decorating for Christmas, petting the dogs, extra butter on the crumpets, having someone scratch the itch on your back that you can't quite reach—"

"You haven't tried kissing," Cassandra told her. "You might like it. Helen does."

"Helen likes Brussels sprouts. How can anyone trust

her opinion?" Curling up in the corner of the settee, Pandora gave Helen a shrewd glance. "You needn't worry that we'll let anything slip to Devon or Kathleen. We're good at secrets. But all the servants know you went somewhere."

"Mrs. Abbott promises they will hold their silence."

Pandora grinned crookedly. "Why is everyone willing to keep Helen's secrets," she asked Cassandra, "but not ours?"

"Because Helen's never naughty."

"I rather was today," Helen said before she thought better of it.

Pandora glanced at her with keen interest. "What do you mean?"

Deciding that a distraction was in order, Helen retrieved the ivory box and handed it to them. "Open this." She sat in a nearby chair, smiling as the twins untied the ribbon and lifted the lid.

Inside, three rows of folded silk stockings had been arranged like bonbons . . . pink, yellow, white, lavender, cream, all of them with stretchy lace welts.

"There are twelve pair," Helen said, enjoying her sisters' awestruck expressions. "The three of us will divide them evenly."

"Oh they're so beautiful!!" Cassandra reached out with a single finger to touch the tiny embroidered forget-me-nots bordering a lace top. "May we wear them now, Helen?"

"Only take care that no one sees them."

"I suppose these might be worth a kiss on the mouth," Pandora conceded. After counting the stockings, she glanced quizzically at Helen. "There are only eleven."

Unable to think of an evasive answer, Helen was compelled to admit, "I'm already wearing one pair."

Pandora regarded her speculatively, and grinned. "I think you *have* been naughty."

Chapter 7

When Rhys awakened the next morning, the first thing he saw was a dark object on the white sheets beside him, a little wisp of shadow.

Helen's black cotton stocking, the one he hadn't destroyed. He had deliberately left it next to his pillow, to forestall any fears that it might have all been a dream.

His hand reached out to close over it, while his mind swam with images of Helen in his bed, his bath. Before taking her home, he had dressed her before the warm hearth. Choosing a brand new pair of stockings from a box that had been sent from the store, he had knelt before her and slid them up her slender legs, one by one. After pulling the knitted silk to the middle of her thighs, he had fastened the lace welts with elastic satin garters embroidered in tiny pink roses. With Helen's naked body so close to his face, he hadn't been able to resist nudging his mouth and nose against the juncture of her thighs, where the fine blond fleece was still damp and scented of flowery bath soap.

Helen had gasped as he had cupped her naked bottom in his hands and let his tongue play among the tender curls. "Please," she had begged. "No, *please*, I'll fall. You mustn't kneel like that . . . your leg is stiff . . ."

Rhys had been tempted to demonstrate a far more critical stiffness than the one in his leg. However, he had relented and released her. He had continued to dress her, helping her into a pair of drawers sewn of silk so fine that they could have been pulled through the band of a wedding ring, and a matching chemise trimmed with handmade lace as delicate as cobwebs. There had been a new long-line corset as well, but Helen had declined it, explaining that she had to wear the old-fashioned shaped corset and bustle, or her dress wouldn't fit properly.

Garment by garment, Rhys had reluctantly covered her back up in heavy black mourning layers. But it had filled him with satisfaction to know that she was wearing something from him against her skin.

Stretching and rolling to his back, Rhys toyed absently with the purloined cotton stocking, rubbing the little mended places against the pad of his thumb. He inserted a finger into the top of the stocking, and then another, stretching the soft fabric.

He frowned as he recalled Helen's insistence about having the wedding in five months. He was tempted to kidnap her, and ravish her all the way up to Scotland in a private train carriage.

But that probably wasn't the best way to begin a marriage.

Tucking all four fingers inside the stocking, he brought it to his nose and mouth, hunting for any scent of Helen.

Tonight he would go to Ravenel House and ask for Devon's consent to the marriage. It was certain that Devon would refuse, and Rhys would have no choice but to reveal that he had dishonored Helen.

And then Devon would attack him like a feral wolverine. Rhys had no doubt in his ability to defend himself. Still, brawling with a Ravenel in a rage was something any rational man would try to avoid if at all possible.

His thoughts strayed to the subject of Devon's recent good fortune, which, according to Helen, had something to do with mineral rights on his twenty-thousand-acre estate. The portion of land in question had just been leased to a mutual friend, Tom Severin, a railway magnate who intended to build tracks across it.

After his morning rounds today, Rhys decided, he would visit Severin to learn more about the situation.

Keeping the stocking against his lips, he blew a soft breath through the fabric. His eyes half-closed as he thought of Helen's lips parting for his kisses, the light-spun locks of her hair wound around his fists. The feel of her intimate flesh, tightening as if it were greedy for every inch of him.

Kidnapping, he decided in a haze of lust, was still a possibility.

After Rhys met with Severin at his office, the two men walked to a local fried fish shop for lunch, a place they both visited often. Neither of them was fond of having a long, leisurely meal during the middle of a workday, preferring the light refreshment shops that were to be found in every quarter of London. Well-heeled gentlemen and common working-men alike frequented such establishments, where one could buy a plate of ham or beef, dressed crabs or lobster salad, and be done with the meal in a half-hour. Food stalls along the street offered fare such as boiled eggs, a ham sandwich, a batter pudding or a cup of hot green peas, but that was a dodgy proposition, since one could never be certain how the food had been adulterated.

After sitting at a corner table and ordering plates of fried fish and mugs of ale, Rhys considered how to broach the subject of Devon Ravenel's land.

"Hematite ore," Severin said, before Rhys had uttered a syllable. He smiled easily at Rhys's questioning glance. "I assume you were going to ask, since everyone else in London is trying to find out."

The phrase "too smart for his own good" was far too often applied to people who weren't in the least deserving of it. In Rhys's opinion, Tom Severin was the only person he'd ever met who actually was too smart for his own good. Severin often appeared relaxed and inattentive during a conversation or meeting, but later could recall every detail with almost perfect accuracy. He was bright, articulate, confident in his razor-edged intellect, and frequently self-mocking.

Rhys, who had been raised by stern and joyless parents, had always liked people with Severin's quality of irreverence. They were of the same generation, with the same humble beginnings, the same appetite for success. The main difference between them was that Severin was highly educated. However, Rhys had never envied him for that. In business, instinct was equally as valuable as intelligence, sometimes even more so. Whereas Severin could sometimes talk himself into the wrong side of an issue, Rhys trusted the promptings of his own nature.

"Trenear found hematite ore on his land?" Rhys asked. "What's the significance? It's a common mineral, isn't it?"

Severin loved nothing better than explaining things. "This grade of hematite ore is of unusually high quality—rich in iron, low in silica. It doesn't even need to be smelted. There's no deposit like it south of Cumbria." An ironic grin twisted his lips. "Even more conveniently for Trenear, I've already planned to run rail tracks through the area. All he has to do is quarry the stuff, load it onto a hopper, and transport it to a rolling mill. With the demand for steel so high, he has a fortune on his hands. Or more accurately, beneath his feet. According to the surveyors I sent, rock-boring machines were pulling up samples of high-grade ore across at least twenty acres. Trenear could garner a half-million pounds or more."

Rhys was glad for Devon, who deserved a stroke of good luck. During the past few months, the former carefree rake had learned to shoulder a burden of responsibilities that he'd never wanted nor expected.

"Naturally," Severin continued, "I did my damnedest to get the mineral rights before Trenear realized what he had. But he's a stubborn bastard. I finally had to concede near the end of the lease negotiations."

Rhys glanced at him alertly. "You knew about the hematite deposit and didn't tell him?"

"I needed it. There's a shortage."

"Trenear needed it more. He's inherited an estate near bankruptcy. You should have told him!"

Severin shrugged. "If he wasn't smart enough to discover it before I did, he didn't deserve to have it."

"*Iesu Mawr.*" Rhys lifted his ale mug and downed half of its contents in a few swallows. "A fine pair of fellows, we are. You tried to swindle him, and I propositioned the woman he loves." He felt distinctly uncomfortable. Devon was no saint, but he had always been a solid friend, and he merited better treatment than this.

Severin seemed fascinated and entertained by the information. He was dark haired and fair skinned, with lean, sharp-cut features, and the kind of gaze that tended to make people feel targeted. His eyes were unusual, blue with uneven swaths of green around the pupils. The green was so much more pronounced on the right side that in certain light it appeared as if he had two entirely different-colored eyes.

"What woman?" Severin asked. "And why did you make a play for her?"

"It doesn't matter who she is," Rhys muttered. "I did it because I was in the devil's own mood." Kathleen, Lady Trenear, had told him—without malice—that he would never be able to make Helen happy, that he wasn't worthy of her. It had touched that raw nerve in himself that he had never fully understood, and his reaction had been mean. Ugly.

Thereby proving her right.

Bloody hell, he wouldn't blame Devon for thrashing him to a fare-thee-well.

"Was this around the time Trenear's little cousin ended her betrothal with you?" Severin asked.

"We're still betrothed," Rhys replied curtly.

"Is that so?" Severin looked even more interested. "What happened?"

"Damned if I'll tell you—the devil knows when you might use it against me."

Severin laughed. "As if you hadn't fleeced more than a few unlucky souls in your business dealings."

"Not friends."

"Ah. So you would sacrifice your own interests for those of a friend—is that what you're saying?"

Rhys took another deep drink of ale, trying to drown a sudden grin. "I haven't yet," he admitted. "But it's possible."

Severin snorted. "I'm sure it is," he said, in a tone

that conveyed exactly the opposite, and gestured for a barmaid to bring more ale.

The conversation soon turned to business matters, especially the recent flurry of speculative building to address the housing needs of the middle class and working poor. It seemed that Severin was interested in helping an acquaintance who had fallen into debt after investing too heavily with a low rate of return. Some of his property had been given to a firm of auctioneers, and Severin had offered to take over the rest of his mortgaged properties, to keep him from becoming sold up altogether.

"Out of the goodness of your heart?" Rhys asked.

"Naturally," came Severin's arid response. "That, and the fact that he and three other large property owners in the Hammersmith district are part of a provisional committee for a proposed suburban railway scheme I want to take over. If I pull my friend out of the mess he's made for himself, he'll convince the others to support my plans." His tone turned offhand as he added, "You might be interested in one of the properties he's selling. It's a block of tenements that are being torn down as we speak, to be replaced with model dwellings for three hundred middle-class families."

Rhys gave him a sardonic glance. "How would I make a profit from that?"

"Rack-renting."

He shook his head with scorn. "As a boy living on High Street, I saw too many workingmen and their families crushed when their rents doubled with no warning."

"All the more reason to buy the property," Severin said without pause. "You can save three hundred families from rack-renting, whereas some other greedy bastard—me, for example—wouldn't."

It occurred to Rhys that if the residential buildings were of good quality, well plumbed and ventilated, the project actually might be worth buying. He employed approximately a thousand people. Although they were well paid, most had difficulty finding good quality housing in town. He could think of several advantages to acquiring the property as a residence for his employees.

Settling back in his chair, Rhys asked with deceptive indolence, "Who's the builder?"

"Holland and Hannen. A reputable firm. We could walk to the construction site after lunch, if you'd care to see it for yourself."

Rhys shrugged casually. "It won't hurt to take a look."

After the meal concluded, they walked north toward King's Cross, their breaths ghosting in the raw air. Handsome building facades, with their ornamental brickwork and terracotta panels, gave way to soot-colored tenements separated by narrow alleys and gutters filled with muck. Windows were covered with paper instead of glass, and cluttered with laundry hung out on broken oars and poles. Some of the lodgings were doorless, imparting a sense that the buildings were gaping at their own decaying condition.

"Let's cross to the main thoroughfare," Severin suggested, wrinkling his nose at the sulfurous taint of the air. "It's not worth a shortcut to breathe in this stench."

"The poor sods who live here have to breathe it all the time," Rhys said. "You and I can endure ten minutes of it."

Severin slanted a mocking glance at him. "You're not becoming a reformer, are you?"

Rhys shrugged. "A walk through these streets is enough to make me sympathize with reformist views. A sin, it is, for a decent workingman to be forced to live in squalor."

They continued along the constricted street past blackened facades that had turned soft with rot. There was a dismal-looking cook-shop, a gin shop, and a small hut with a painted sign advertising a supply of gamecocks for sale.

It was a relief when they turned a corner onto a wide,

well-drained roadway and approached the construction site, where a row of buildings was in the process
of being torn down. The scene was one of controlled
turmoil as a wrecking crew systematically dismem-
bered the three-story structures. It was dangerous and
difficult work: More skill was required to take down a
large structure than to build it. A pair of mobile steam
cranes mounted on wheels polluted the air with thun-
derous rattling, whistling, and clacking. Heavy steam
boilers counterbalanced the jibs, making the machines
remarkably stable.

Rhys and Severin walked behind a row of wagons
being loaded with waste lumber to be hauled off and
split for kindling wood. The grounds swarmed with
men carrying pick-axes and shovels, or pushing wheel-
barrows, while masons sorted through bricks to save
the ones that could be reused.

A frown crossed Rhys's face as he saw tenants being
evicted from the building that was next in line to be de-
molished. Some of them were defiant, others wailing,
as they carried their belongings outside and set them in
heaps on the pavement. It was a pity for the poor devils
to be turned out into the street in the dead of winter.

Following his gaze to the distraught residents, Severin looked momentarily grim. "They were all given
a period of notice to vacate," he said. "The building

would have been condemned in any case. But some people stayed on. It always happens."

"Where would they go?" Rhys asked rhetorically.

"God only knows. But it's no good, allowing people to live among open cesspools."

Rhys's gaze rested briefly on a young boy, perhaps nine or ten years of age, sitting alone amid a small heap of belongings, including a chair, a frying pan, and a heap of soiled bedding. The lad appeared to be guarding the pile of possessions while waiting for someone to return. Most likely his mother or father was out looking for accommodations.

"I've had a glimpse of the plans," Severin said. "The new buildings will be five stories tall, with running water and a water-closet on each floor. As I understand it, the basements will house communal kitchens, washhouses, and drying rooms. At the front, they'll install iron railings to form a protected play area for children. Are you interested in seeing copies of the architectural schemes?"

"Aye. Along with deeds, bills of sale, building agreements, mortgages, and a list of all contractors and subcontractors."

"I knew you would," Severin said with satisfaction.

"With the condition," Rhys continued, "that some of your Hammersmith railway shares are on the table as well."

Severin's smug expression faded. "Look here, you sticky-fingered bastard, I'm not going to sweeten the deal with bloody railway shares. That's not even my building. I'm just showing it to you!"

Rhys grinned. "But you do want someone to buy it. And you won't find many prospective buyers with all the cheap undeveloped land available in the boroughs."

"If you think—"

The rest of Severin's words were drowned out by an ominous cracking sound, a deafening rumble, and shouts of alarm. Both men turned to look as the upper portion of one of the condemned buildings began to collapse. Rotting beams and timbers had given way to gravity, slate tiles sliding downward and tumbling over the eaves.

The abandoned boy, perched on his pile of belongings, was directly below the deadly cascade.

Without thinking, Rhys raced toward the child, forgetting the stiffness of his leg in his haste to reach him. He threw himself over the boy, making a shelter of his body, just before he felt a tremendous blow on his shoulder and back. His entire skeleton quivered. Through the burst of white sparks in his head, some distant part of his brain calculated that he'd been struck heavily—there would be considerable damage—and then everything went dark.

Chapter 8

"Winterborne. *Winterborne.* Come now, open your—yes, there's a good fellow. Look at me."

Rhys blinked, awakening slowly to the bewildered awareness that he was on the ground, in the perishing cold. There was a crowd around him, exclaiming, questioning, shouting advice, and Severin was leaning over him.

Pain. He was submerged in it. Not the worst pain he'd ever experienced, but considerable nonetheless. It was difficult to move. He could tell that something was drastically wrong with his left arm, which had gone numb and motionless.

"The boy—" he said, recalling the roof collapse, the tumble of wood and slate.

"Unharmed. He was trying to pick your pocket before I shooed him away." Giving him a mocking glance, Severin continued, "if you're going to risk your life for someone, do it for a useful member of society, not a street urchin." He extended a hand, intending to help Rhys up.

"My arm won't move."

"Which one? The left? You've probably broken it. I shouldn't have to tell you this, but when a building is falling down, you run *away* from it, not toward it."

A commanding female voice pierced the cacophony of voices and steam engines. "Let me through! Move to the side, please. Out of my way."

A woman dressed in black with a jaunty green necktie at her throat, pushed her way through the crowd with brisk determination, deftly employing a curved-handle walking stick to prod slow-moving bystanders. She looked at Rhys with an assessing gaze and knelt beside him, heedless of the muddy ground.

"Miss," Severin began with a touch of annoyance, "no doubt you're trying to be of use, but—"

"I'm a physician," she said curtly.

"You mean a nurse?" Severin asked.

Ignoring him, she asked Rhys, "Where is the worst pain?"

"Shoulder."

"Move your fingers, please." She watched as he complied. "Does the arm feel numb? Tingly?"

"Numb." Clenching his teeth, Rhys looked up at her. A young woman, still in her twenties. Pretty, with brown hair and large green eyes. Despite her slim form and fine features, she conveyed an impression of sturdiness. Very gently, she took hold of his arm and elbow and tested the range of motion. Rhys grunted as a spear of agony went through his shoulder. Carefully the woman settled the arm back against his midriff. "Pardon," she murmured, reaching beneath his coat to feel his shoulder. An explosion of icy heat sent sparks across his vision.

"Agghh!"

"I don't believe it's fractured." She withdrew her hand from his coat.

"That's enough," Severin said in exasperation. "You're going to make his injuries worse. He needs a doctor, not some—"

"I have a medical degree. And your friend has a dislocated shoulder." She untied the green bow at her throat and pulled the scarf free. "Give me your necktie. We have to secure his arm before we move him."

"Move him where?" Severin asked.

"My practice is two streets away. Your necktie, please."

"But—"

"Give it to her," Rhys snapped, his collapsed shoulder on fire.

Grumbling, Severin complied.

Deftly the woman improvised a sling with the green scarf, knotted it at the level of Rhys's collarbone, and adjusted the edge around his elbow. With Severin's help, she slid the necktie around Rhys's midriff and over the numb arm, securing it close to his body.

"We'll help you to your feet," she told Rhys. "You won't have to walk far. I have the proper facilities and supplies to treat your shoulder."

Severin scowled. "Miss, I have to object—"

"Dr. Gibson," she said crisply.

"Dr. Gibson," he said, with an emphasis on the "Dr." that sounded distinctly insulting. "This is Mr. Winterborne. The one with the department store. He needs to be treated by a real physician with experience and proper training, not to mention—"

"A penis?" she suggested acidly. "I'm afraid I don't have one of those. Nor is it a requirement for a medical degree. I am a real physician, and the sooner I treat Mr. Winterborne's shoulder, the better it will go for him." At Severin's continued hesitation, she said, "The limited external rotation of the shoulder, impaired elevation of the arm, and the prominence of the coracoid process all indicate posterior dislocation. Therefore, the joint must be relocated without delay if we are to prevent further damage to the neurovascular status of the upper extremity."

Had Rhys not been in such acute discomfort, he would have relished Severin's stunned expression.

"I'll help you move him," Severin muttered.

During the short but torturous walk, Severin persisted in questioning the woman, who answered with admirable patience. Her name was Garrett Gibson, and she had been born in East London. After enrolling at a local hospital as a nursing student, she had begun to take classes intended for doctors. Three years ago, she had earned a medical degree at the University of Sorbonne in Paris, and subsequently returned to London. As was common, she had established her practice out of a private home, which in this case happened to be her widowed father's residence.

They reached the three-story house, tucked in a row of comfortably middle-class Georgian-style terraces built with crimson cutting bricks. Such buildings were invariably designed with one room in the front and one in the back on each story, with a passageway and a staircase on one side.

A maid opened the door and welcomed them inside. Dr. Gibson ushered them into the back room, a scrupulously clean surgery that had been furnished with an examination table, a bench, a desk, and a wall of mahogany cabinets. She directed Rhys to sit on the examination table, constructed with a padded leather top over a cabinet base. The top was divided into hinged sections that could be adjusted to raise the head, upper torso, or feet.

After quickly shrugging out of her coat and pulling off her hat, Dr. Gibson handed them to the maid. She approached Rhys and gently removed the makeshift sling. "Before you lie down, Mr. Winterborne," she said, "we'll need to remove your coat."

He nodded, cold sweat trickling down his face.

"How can I help?" Severin asked.

"Begin with the sleeve on the uninjured side. I'll take the other. Pray do not jostle the arm any more than necessary."

Despite their extreme care during the process, Rhys winced and groaned as he was divested of the coat. Closing his eyes, he felt himself sway in his seated position.

Severin immediately steadied him with a hand on his good shoulder. "I think we should cut off the shirt and waistcoat," he suggested.

"I agree," Dr. Gibson said. "Keep him steady while I attend to it."

Rhys blinked his eyes open as he felt his upper garments being removed with a few strokes of a wickedly sharp blade. One thing was certain—the woman knew how to wield a knife. Glancing at her small, dispassionate face, he wondered about what it must have taken for her to earn a place for herself in a man's profession.

"Holy hell," Severin murmured, as the bruised flesh of Rhys's back and shoulder became visible. "I hope saving that ragamuffin was worth it, Winterborne."

"Of course it was," Dr. Gibson said, having turned to rummage through a cabinet. "He saved the boy's life. One never knows what a child might become someday."

"In this case, definitely a criminal," Severin said.

"Possibly," the woman said, returning with a small glass filled with amber liquid. "But not definitely." She handed the glass to Rhys. "Here you are, Mr. Winterborne."

"What is it?" he asked warily, taking it in his good hand.

"Something to help you relax."

Rhys took an experimental taste. "Whisky," he said, surprised and grateful. A decent vintage at that. He downed it in a couple of swallows, and extended the glass for more. "It takes more than one to relax me," he told her. At her skeptical glance, he explained, "Welsh."

Dr. Gibson smiled reluctantly, her green eyes sparkling, and she went to pour another.

"I need to relax as well," Severin told her.

She looked amused. "I'm afraid you'll have to remain sober," she replied, "as I shall require your assistance." After retrieving the glass from Rhys and setting it aside, she slid a strong arm behind his back. "Mr. Winterborne, we'll help you to lie down. Slowly, now. Mr. Severin, if you will lift his feet . . ."

Rhys eased to the leather surface, letting out a few curses in Welsh as his back settled on the table. Agony radiated through him in continuous spikes.

Dr. Gibson used her foot to depress a pedal several times in succession, raising the level of the table. She moved to his injured side. "Mr. Severin, please take a position on his other side. I will need you to reach an arm across him, and place your hand on the side of the ribcage to stabilize him. Yes, there."

Severin grinned down at Rhys as he followed the doctor's directions. "How do you feel about those Hammersmith shares now that you're at my mercy?" he asked.

"Still want them," Rhys managed to say.

"I doubt you'll need this, Mr. Winterborne," Dr. Gibson said, bringing a section of leather strap to his mouth, "but I'd advise it as a precaution." Seeing Rhys's hesitation, she said, "It's clean. I never re-use supplies."

Rhys took it between his teeth.

"Are you physically strong enough for this?" Severin asked Gibson doubtfully.

"Would you like to arm-wrestle?" she offered with such cool aplomb that Rhys let out a huff of amusement.

"No," Severin said at once. "I can't take the chance that you might win."

The doctor smiled at him. "I doubt I would win, Mr. Severin. But I would at least make it difficult for you." She took Rhys's wrist in her right hand. With her other hand, she gripped beneath his upper arm. "Keep him steady," she warned Severin. Slowly, smoothly, she exerted traction while pushing the arm upward and rotating it until the joint popped back into place.

Rhys made a sound of relief as the stabbing misery eased. Turning his head, he spat out the leather and drew in a shaking breath. "Thank you."

"Right as rain," the woman said in satisfaction, feeling the shoulder to make certain everything was in place.

"Well done," Severin said. "You're very clever, Dr. Gibson."

"I prefer the word 'competent,'" she said. "But thank you all the same." Using the table's foot pedal mechanism, she lowered the level of the table. "I apologize for the loss of your shirt and waistcoat," she commented, reaching into a lower cabinet for a length of white cloth.

Rhys shook his head to indicate that it was of no importance.

"The shoulder will become increasingly sore and swollen over the next few days," she continued, "but you must try to use your arm naturally in spite of the discomfort. Otherwise the muscles will weaken from disuse. For the rest of today, keep it supported in a sling and refrain from exertion." After she helped him to sit upright, she expertly tied a sling around his neck and arm. "You may have difficulty sleeping for the next few nights: I'll prescribe a tonic that will help. Take one spoonful at bedtime, no more." She retrieved his coat and carefully draped it over his shoulders.

"I'll step outside and wave down a hackney," Severin said. "We can't have Winterborne walking outside in all his bare-chested glory or the pavement will be cluttered with swooning females."

As Severin left the room, Rhys awkwardly reached

for his wallet, tucked in an inside pocket of his coat. "What is your fee?" he asked.

"A florin will be sufficient."

The sum was half of the four shillings that Dr. Havelock, the staff physician at Winterborne's, would have charged. Rhys fished out the coin and gave it to her. "You're very competent, Dr. Gibson," he said gravely.

She smiled, neither blushing nor denying the praise. He liked her, this proficient and unusual woman. Despite the obvious odds against her, he hoped she would succeed in her profession.

"I won't hesitate to recommend your services," Rhys continued.

"That is very kind, Mr. Winterborne. However, I'm afraid my practice will close by the end of the month." Her tone was matter-of-fact, but her eyes became shadowed.

"May I ask why?"

"Patients are few and far between. People fear that a woman has neither the physical stamina nor mental acuity to practice medicine." A mirthless smile curled her lips. "I have even been told that women are unable to hold their tongues, and therefore a lady doctor would constantly violate her patients' privacy."

"I understand all about prejudice," Rhys said quietly. "The only way to fight it is to prove them wrong."

"Yes." But her gaze became absent, and she went to busy herself with rearranging a tray of supplies.

"How good are you?" Rhys asked.

She stiffened and glanced at him over her shoulder. "Pardon?"

"Recommend yourself to me," he said simply.

Gibson turned to face him with a thoughtful frown. "While I worked as a surgery nurse at St. Thomas's, I undertook private tuition to obtain certificates in anatomy, physiology, and chemistry. At the Sorbonne, I took honors in anatomy for two years, and the top prize in midwifery for three. I also studied for a brief time with Sir Joseph Lister, who instructed me in his techniques of antiseptic surgery. In short, I'm very good. And I could have helped a great many people, given the . . ." Her voice faded as she saw Rhys withdraw a card from his wallet.

He extended it to her. "Bring this to Winterborne's on Monday morning at nine o'clock sharp. Ask for Mrs. Fernsby."

"May I ask for what purpose?" The doctor's eyes had widened.

"I keep a staff physician on retainer to look after the health of a thousand employees. He's an old codger, but a good man. He'll have to agree to hiring you, but I don't expect he'll object. Among other things, he needs someone to help with midwifery—it takes hours at a time, and he said the process is hard on his rheumatism. If you're willing—"

"Yes. I would be. Thank you. Yes." Dr. Gibson held the card with whitening fingertips. "I'll be there Monday morning." A wondering grin crossed her face. "Although it hasn't turned out to be a fortunate day for you, Mr. Winterborne, it seems to have turned out well for me."

Chapter 9

"**M**r. *Winterborne*," Fernsby exclaimed in horror as she entered the office and saw that Rhys was filthy, battered, and bare-chested save for his coat. "Dear heaven, what happened? Were you set upon by thugs? Thieves?"

"By a building, actually."

"What—"

"I'll explain later, Fernsby. At the moment, I need a shirt." Uncomfortably he fished the prescription from his coat pocket and gave it to her. "Give this to the apothecary and have him mix a tonic—my shoulder was dislocated, and it aches like the devil. Also, tell my solicitor to be in my office within the half hour."

"Shirt, medicine, solicitor," she said, committing

them to memory. "Are you going to sue the owners of the building?"

Wincing in discomfort, Rhys lowered into the chair at his desk. "No," he murmured. "But I need to revise my will immediately."

"Are you certain you wouldn't like to go to your house to wash first?" she asked. "You're rather . . . begrimed."

"No, this can't wait. Tell Quincy to bring hot water and a towel. I'll scrub off what I can here. And bring some tea—no, coffee."

"Shall I send for Dr. Havelock, sir?"

"No, I've already been treated by Dr. Gibson. She's coming for an interview on Monday at nine, by the way. I'm going to hire her to assist Havelock."

Mrs. Fernsby's brows arched high over the rims of her spectacles. "She? Her?"

"Haven't you heard of female doctors?" Rhys asked dryly.

"I suppose so, but I've never seen one."

"You will Monday."

"Yes, sir," Mrs. Fernsby muttered, and rushed from the office.

With effort, Rhys reached for the jar of peppermint creams, took one and popped it into his mouth, and resettled his coat around his shoulders.

As the peppermint disintegrated on his tongue, he forced himself to confront the thought that had horrified him during the ride back to Winterborne's.

What would have become of Helen if he had died?

He had always lived fearlessly, taking calculated risks, doing whatever he pleased. Long ago he had accepted that his business would someday go on without him: He had planned to leave the company to his board of directors, the group of trusted advisors and friends whom he'd collected over the years. His mother would be handsomely taken care of, but she neither wanted nor merited any controlling interest in the company. There were also generous bequests to certain employees, such as Mrs. Fernsby, and sums to be distributed to distant relatives.

But so far Helen hadn't been mentioned in his will. As things stood, if the building accident had been fatal, she would have been left with nothing—after he had taken her virginity and possibly left her with his child.

It terrified him to realize how vulnerable Helen's position was. Because of him.

His head throbbed viciously. Bracing his good arm on the desk, he lowered his forehead to the crook of his elbow, and trammeled his frantic thoughts into coherence.

He would have to move quickly to safeguard Helen's

future. The question of how to protect her in the long term, however, was a more complicated question.

As usual, his staff was fast and efficient. Quincy, the elderly valet he had hired away from Devon Ravenel only a few months ago, brought a fresh shirt, waistcoat, a can of hot water, and a tray of grooming supplies. Upon witnessing Rhys's condition, the concerned valet clucked and murmured in dismay as he washed, brushed, combed, dabbed, and smoothed until Rhys was presentable. The worst part was donning the fresh shirt and waistcoat; as Dr. Gibson had predicted, the injured shoulder was becoming more painful.

After Mrs. Fernsby had brought a dose of tonic from the apothecary, and a tray with both coffee and brandy, Rhys was ready for the solicitor.

"Winterborne," Charles Burgess said as he entered the office, glancing over him with a mixture of amusement and concern. "You remind me of a rough and tumble lad I once knew on High Street."

Rhys smiled at the stocky, gray-haired solicitor, who had once worked for his father on small legal matters. Eventually he had become one of Rhys's advisors as the grocer's shop expanded into a vast mercantile business. Now Burgess was on the private company's board of directors. Meticulous, insightful, and creative, he was able to pick his way through legal obstacles like a North Wales sheep through upland heath.

"Mrs. Fernsby says that you were caught in a construction mishap," Burgess commented, sitting on the other side of the desk. He extracted a notebook and pencil from the inside of his coat.

"Aye. Which brought to my attention the need to revise my will without delay." He proceeded to explain about his engagement to Helen, giving Burgess a carefully expurgated version of recent events.

After listening closely and writing a few notes, Burgess said, "You wish to secure Lady Helen's future contingent upon a legal and consummated marriage, I assume."

"No, starting now. If something should happen to me before the wedding, I want her to be taken care of."

"You have no obligation to make any provision for Lady Helen until she becomes your wife."

"I want to put five million pounds in trust for her without delay." At the solicitor's stunned expression, Rhys said bluntly, "There may be a child."

"I see." Burgess's pencil moved rapidly across the page. "If a child is born within nine months after your demise, would you wish to make a provision for him?"

"Aye. He—or she—will inherit the company. If there is no child, everything goes to Lady Helen."

The pencil stopped moving. "It's not my place to say anything," Burgess said. "But you've only known this woman for a matter of months."

"It's what I want," Rhys said flatly.

Helen had risked everything for him. She had given herself to him without conditions. He would do no less for her.

He certainly didn't plan on meeting his maker any time soon—he was a healthy man with the greater part of his life still ahead of him. However, the accident today—not to mention the train collision a month ago—had demonstrated that no one was exempt from the vagaries of fate. If something did happen to him, he wanted Helen to have everything that was his. *Everything*, including Winterborne's.

Kathleen and Devon arrived at Ravenel House just in time for afternoon tea, which had been set out on a long, low table in front of the settee.

Striding into the room, Kathleen went to Helen first, embracing her as heartily as if they'd been apart for two months instead of two days. Helen returned the hug with equal strength. Kathleen had become like an older sister to her, at times even a bit maternal. They had confided in each other and grieved together over Theo. In Kathleen, Helen had found a generous and understanding friend.

When Theo had married Kathleen, everyone had hoped it would help to settle him down. Generations of Ravenels had been cursed with the volatile temperament that had distinguished them in battle as they fought alongside the Norman conquerors in 1066. Unfortunately it had been repeatedly proven in the following centuries that the Ravenels' warlike nature wasn't suited for any place other than the battlefield.

By the time Theo had inherited the earldom, the estate of Eversby Priory had nearly fallen to ruins. The manor house was decaying, the tenants starving, and the land had gone without improvements or decent drainage for decades. No one would ever know what Theo might have accomplished as the earl of Trenear. Only three days after his wedding, he had lost his temper and gone out to ride an unbroken horse. He had been thrown, and died of a snapped neck.

Kathleen, Helen, and the twins had expected that they would have to leave the estate as soon as Devon, a distant Ravenel cousin, took possession. To their surprise, he had allowed all of them to stay, and he had devoted himself to saving Eversby Priory. Along with his younger brother West, Devon was making the estate viable again, learning everything he could about farming, land improvement, agricultural machinery, and estate management.

Kathleen turned from Helen to embrace the twins. In the gray winter light from the windows, Kathleen's auburn hair was a lively shock of color. She was a little slip of a thing with distinctive feline beauty, her brown eyes tip-tilted and her cheekbones prominent.

"My dears," she exclaimed, "I've missed you—everything is glorious—I have so much to tell you!"

"So do I," Helen said with an uneasy smile.

"To begin with," Kathleen said, "we brought some company from Eversby Priory."

"Has Cousin West come to visit?" Helen asked.

At that exact moment, the sound of high-pitched barking echoed from the entrance hall.

"Napoleon and Josephine!" Pandora exclaimed.

"The dogs were pining for you," Kathleen said. "Let's hope they don't cause trouble, or back to Hampshire they go."

A pair of black cocker spaniels burst in the room, yapping excitedly and jumping on the twins, who both dropped to the floor to play with them. Pandora was on all fours, pretending to pounce on Napoleon, who flopped onto his back in joyful surrender. Kathleen opened her mouth to protest, but shook her head in resignation, recognizing that any attempt to calm the boisterous girls would be useless.

Devon, Lord Trenear, entered the room and grinned at the mayhem. "How soothing," he remarked to the room at large. "Like a Degas painting: 'Young Ladies at Afternoon Tea.'"

The earl was a handsome man, dark-haired and blue-eyed, with a seasoned air that suggested a past full of misadventure. His gaze went to Kathleen and turned absorbed and hot, the look of a man in love for the first time in his life. He went to stand just behind her, one hand sliding over her narrow shoulder, while his chin rested gently on the ruddy curls pinned atop her head. Helen had never seen him touch Kathleen in such an openly familiar manner.

"Have you all behaved in our absence?" he asked.

"Two of us have," Cassandra said from the floor.

Kathleen glanced at the other twin. "Pandora, what did you do?"

"Why do you assume it was me?" Pandora protested with faux indignation, making everyone laugh. She grinned and stood, holding the dog as he wriggled to lick her face. "While we're asking questions— Kathleen, why is there a ring on your finger?"

All gazes shot to Kathleen's left hand. Looking bashfully pleased, she extended it for them to see. Cassandra abandoned Josephine and leapt to her feet, joining Pandora and Helen as they crowded close for a look. The ring, featuring a ruby of the rare shade known as "pigeon's blood," was set in yellow gold filigree.

"Just before we took the train to Hampshire," Kathleen confided, "Devon and I were wed at the registrar's office."

All three Ravenel sisters burst out with joyful exclamations. The news wasn't altogether surprising: In the past few months, the household had become aware of the growing attraction between Devon and Kathleen.

"How wonderful," Helen said, beaming. "Everyone knows you belong together."

"I hope you won't think too badly of me for marrying while I'm still in mourning," Kathleen said in a muffled voice. Drawing back, she continued earnestly, "I wouldn't wish for any of you to feel that I'd forgotten Theo, or that I didn't respect his memory. But as you know, I have developed a very deep respect and fondness for Devon, and we decided—"

"*Fondness?*" Devon interrupted, his brows lifting. But there was a spark of mischief in his blue eyes. Kathleen had been raised in a strict household where declarations of emotion had always been discouraged, and Devon delighted in teasing her out of her reserve.

Self-consciously Kathleen muttered, "Love."

He pretended not to hear, cocking his head. "Hmm?"

Blushing, Kathleen said, "I'm in love with you. I adore you. May I continue now?"

"You may," Devon said, gathering her more closely against him.

"As I was saying," Kathleen went on, "we decided that it was best to marry sooner rather than later."

"I couldn't be happier," Cassandra said. "But why couldn't you wait to have a proper wedding?"

"I'll explain later. For now, let's have tea."

"You could explain during tea," Pandora persisted.

"It's not appropriate for teatime," Kathleen replied evasively.

Then Helen understood, with insight gained from very recent experience, that Kathleen was expecting a child. It was the most logical explanation for a hasty marriage and an inability to explain why to a nineteen-year-old girl.

A faint blush rose in Helen's cheeks as she reflected that Devon and Kathleen must have shared a bed, in the way of a husband and wife. It was a bit shocking.

But not nearly as shocking as it would have been if Helen hadn't done the same thing with Rhys Winterborne only yesterday.

"But why—" Pandora persisted.

"Oh dear," Helen interceded, "the dogs are sniffing around the tea table. Come, let's all sit while I pour. Kathleen, how is Cousin West?"

Kathleen settled into a wingback chair, sending Helen a grateful glance.

The subject of West instantly diverted the twins, as Helen had known it would. Devon's brother, a handsome young rake who pretended to be far more cynical than he actually was, had become the twins' favorite person in the world. He treated both of them with casual affection and benevolent interest, acting as the older brother they'd never really had. Theo had always lived away at boarding school, and then London.

Talk soon turned to the subject of Eversby Priory. Devon described the massive hematite ore deposit that had been discovered, and how they were developing plans to quarry and sell it.

"Are we rich now?" Pandora asked.

"It's not polite to ask," Kathleen said, lifting her teacup. But just before she took a sip, she winked over the rim and murmured, "But yes."

The twins chortled.

"As rich as Mr. Winterborne?" Cassandra inquired.

"Silly," Pandora said, "no one's as rich as Mr. Winterborne." Noticing the scowl dawning on Devon's face, she said apologetically, "Oh. We're not supposed to mention him."

Devon steered the conversation back to Eversby Priory, and the girls listened avidly as he described proposed plans for a station in the village. They all agreed that it would be marvelously convenient to have access to the railway so close to home, rather than go to the station at Alton.

Teatime was a lavish affair, an indulgence the Ravenels had always maintained no matter what else might have to be sacrificed. A flowered porcelain tea service had been brought out on a heavy silver tray, along with three-tiered stands filled with crisp golden scones, mincemeat puffs, slices of sweet Damson cheese on toast, and tiny sandwiches filled with butter and cress, or egg salad. Every few minutes, a servant came to refresh the hot water or replenish the pitchers of milk and cream.

As the family laughed and chatted, Helen did her best to participate, but her gaze strayed frequently to the mantel clock. Half past five: only ninety minutes until acceptable calling hours would end. She broke off a portion of scone and carefully pressed a morsel of comb honey onto it, waiting until the comb was warm and melting before popping it into her mouth. It was delicious, but in her anxiety, she could hardly swallow. Sipping her tea, she nodded and smiled, only half-listening to the conversation.

"This was lovely," Kathleen finally pronounced, setting her napkin beside the plate. "I'll believe I'll rest now—it has been a tiring day. I will see you all at dinner."

Devon stood automatically and went to help her from the chair.

"But it's not yet seven," Helen said, trying to conceal her dismay. "Someone may call. It is a visiting day, after all."

Kathleen gave her a quizzical smile. "I doubt anyone will call. Devon has been away, and we've extended no invitations." She paused, focusing more closely on Helen's face. "Unless . . . we're expecting someone?"

The mantel clock was absurdly loud in the absence of conversation.

Tick. Tick. Tick.

"Yes," Helen said impulsively, "I'm expecting company."

Simultaneously, Kathleen and Devon asked, "*Who?*"

"My lord." The first footman had come to the doorway. "Mr. Winterborne is here on a personal matter."

Tick. Tick. Tick.

Helen's nerves were rioting, her blood coursing as

Devon glanced at her sharply. His expression drove Helen's heartbeat up into her throat.

He returned his attention to the footman. "Did you show him in?"

"Yes, my lord. He's waiting in the library."

"Please don't turn Mr. Winterborne away," Helen said with forced composure.

"There's no chance of that," Devon replied. The words were hardly reassuring; on the contrary, they were uttered with soft menace.

Kathleen touched her husband's arm lightly and murmured to him.

Devon looked down at her, and some of the violence left his eyes. But still, an unsettling suggestion of ferocity practically radiated from him. "Stay up here," he muttered, and strode from the room.

Chapter 10

Kathleen looked remarkably collected as she sat in her upholstered chair. "Helen, will you have another cup of tea?"

"Yes." Helen sent a quick, beseeching glance to Pandora and Cassandra. "Perhaps you should take the dogs out to the garden?"

The twins hurried to comply, snapping for the spaniels, who bounded after them as they departed.

As soon as they were alone, Kathleen asked urgently, "Helen, why on earth is Mr. Winterborne here, and how did you know he was coming?"

Slowly Helen reached to the high neck of her dress and hooked her forefinger around a thin silk ribbon tied around her neck. The comforting weight of the moonstone ring dangled beneath her bodice, hidden in the space between her breasts. She pulled it out, tugged the ring free of its tether, and slid it onto her finger.

"I went to him," she said simply, laying her hand lightly over Kathleen's to display the moonstone. "Yesterday."

Kathleen stared down at the ring in bewilderment. "You went to see Mr. Winterborne alone?"

"Yes."

"Did he arrange it? Did he send someone for you? How—"

"He knew nothing about it. It was my idea."

"And he gave this ring to you?"

"I asked for it." Helen smiled wryly. "Demanded, rather." Withdrawing her hand, she sat back in her chair. "As you know, I never liked the diamond."

"But why—" Kathleen fell silent, staring at her in confusion.

"I want to marry Mr. Winterborne," Helen said gently. "I know that you and Cousin Devon have my best interests at heart, and I trust your judgment. But since the engagement was broken, I haven't had a moment's peace. I realized that I had formed an attachment to him, and—"

"Helen, there are things you don't know—"

"I do. Yesterday Mr. Winterborne told me that he behaved in a coarse and insulting manner to you. He regrets it very much, and he's come here to apologize. It was a mistake born of impulse—you must believe that he didn't mean it."

Kathleen rubbed her eyes wearily. "I knew the moment he said it that he didn't mean it. The problem is that Devon walked into the room and overheard enough to send him into a rage. He still hasn't had sufficient time to view the situation in its proper perspective."

"But you do?" Helen asked anxiously.

"I can certainly understand and forgive a few rash words. My objection to Mr. Winterborne has nothing to do with what happened that day, it's the same as always: You and he have nothing in common. Soon you'll be out in society, and you'll meet a score of very nice gentlemen, cultured and educated and—"

"None of whom would have been willing to spend a minute in my company if I had no dowry. And I don't need them for comparison: Mr. Winterborne is the man I would choose above all others."

Kathleen was obviously struggling to understand. "Only a week ago you were in tears, telling me how he'd frightened you when he kissed you."

"He did. But you gave me the perfect advice, as usual. You said that someday, with the right man, kissing would be wonderful. And it is."

"He . . . you let him . . ." Kathleen's eyes widened.

"I have no illusions about Mr. Winterborne," Helen continued. "Or at least, not many. He's ruthless, ambitious, and too accustomed to having his way. Perhaps he's not always a gentleman in the formal sense of the word, but he has his own code of honor. And"—Helen felt a wondering smile tug at her lips—"he has a soft spot for me. I think I've become a weakness of his, and he's a man who desperately needs a few weaknesses."

"How much time did you spend with him yesterday?" Kathleen asked distractedly. "Were you at the store, or his house? Who saw you together?" She was already calculating how to minimize the damage to Helen's reputation. Undoubtedly Devon's reaction would be the same.

It was becoming clear to Helen that Rhys's insistence on sleeping with her, although manipulative, had made perfect sense. It was the perfect weapon to cut through any number of arguments.

There was no choice now but to use it.

"Kathleen," she said gently, "I've been compromised."

"Not necessarily. There may be rumors, but—"

"I have to marry him." Seeing her sister-in-law's perplexed expression, Helen repeated the words with quiet emphasis. "I *have* to marry him."

"*Oh,*" Kathleen faltered, understanding. "You and he . . ."

"Yes."

Kathleen was silent, trying to take in the revelation. Her golden-brown eyes glimmered with concern. "My poor Helen," she finally said. "You didn't know what to expect. You must have been frightened. Please tell me, darling, did he coerce you, or—"

"No, it wasn't like that," Helen said urgently. "You must believe that I was completely willing. I had every opportunity to refuse. Mr. Winterborne explained what would happen. It was not at all unpleasant. It was—" She dropped her gaze. "I found pleasure in it," she finished in a small voice. "I'm sure that's wicked of me."

In a moment, Kathleen patted her hand reassuringly. "It's not wicked," she said. "Some claim that women shouldn't enjoy the act, but in my opinion, it certainly makes the process far more appealing."

Helen had always loved Kathleen's pragmatic nature, but never so much as at that moment. "I thought you would disapprove of me for having slept with him," she said with relief.

Kathleen smiled. "I wouldn't go so far as to say I'm *happy* about it. But I can hardly fault you for doing exactly as I have done. As long as we're speaking frankly . . . I'm expecting Devon's child."

"Are you?" Helen asked with delight. "I thought that might be the reason why you and he married so quickly."

"It is. That, and I love him madly." Kathleen reached for the bowl of sugar, picked out a medium-sized lump, and began to nibble on it. Tentatively she said, "I have no idea how much you know about these matters. You understand the possible consequences of sleeping with a man?"

Helen nodded. "There might be a baby."

"Yes, unless he . . . took preventive measures?" At Helen's blank look, Kathleen continued, "Dear, may I ask something quite personal?"

Helen nodded cautiously.

"Did he . . . finish . . . inside you? At the last moment?"

Bewildered, Helen said, "I'm not sure."

Kathleen smiled ruefully as she saw Helen's confusion. "We'll have a talk later. It appears that Mr. Winterborne didn't quite explain everything." Absently she picked up the little gold timepiece that hung on a long chain around her neck, and tapped the smooth metal casing against her lips. "What are we to do?" she asked, more to herself than Helen.

"I was hoping that you and Devon would withdraw your objections to the match."

"I've withdrawn them already," Kathleen said. "In practical terms, no one is in a position to object to it now. And I owe you my support after the way I meddled in your relationship. I'm sorry, Helen. I truly was trying to help."

"Of course you were," Helen said in relief. "Don't give it another thought. Everything has turned out beautifully."

"Has it?" Kathleen regarded her with a wondering smile. "How happy you seem. Can Mr. Winterborne really be the reason?"

"He is." Helen put her hands up to her flushed cheeks, and laughed breathlessly. "I'm all pangs and palpitations, just knowing that he's downstairs. I feel hot and cold, and I can scarcely breathe." She hesitated. "Is that what love feels like?"

"That's infatuation," Kathleen said. "It's love when you can breathe." Occupied with her thoughts, she repeatedly folded and unfolded a table napkin on her knee. "The situation must be handled with care. Devon must *not* find out that you and Mr. Winterborne slept together—he won't be nearly as reasonable as I am about it. He'll take it as an affront to the family honor, and—oh I don't want to contemplate it. But I'll talk him into accepting the match. It may take a few days, but—"

"Mr. Winterborne is going to tell him tonight."

Kathleen looked at her alertly, setting aside the napkin. "What? I thought you said he'd come to apologize."

"Yes, but after that, he's going to ask for Devon's approval of our engagement. If Devon refuses, he'll tell him that he has no choice but to consent since I'm no longer a virgin."

"Good God," Kathleen exclaimed, leaping to her feet. "We have to stop him."

"Mr. Winterborne may have told him already," Helen said in dismay.

"He hasn't yet," Kathleen said, striding from the room while Helen dashed after her. "If he had, we would hear bellowing and things breaking, and—"

At that moment, an unholy clamor erupted downstairs: swearing, shattering, cracking, rattling, a heavy thud, a violent tumble. The walls of the house vibrated.

"Hang it," Kathleen muttered, "he's told him."

Together the two women rushed downstairs, crossed the entrance hall, and ran full bore to the library. By the time they reached it, the room was already in a shambles, with a small table overturned, books strewn across the floor, and a porcelain vase shattered. Belligerent grunts and muffled curses thickened the air as the two men grappled viciously. Managing to gain traction, Devon shoved Rhys with enough force to slam his back against the wall.

With a hoarse sound, Rhys dropped to all fours.

Crying out in alarm, Helen ran to him as he collapsed slowly to his side.

"*Devon*," Kathleen shouted, running into her husband's path.

"Get out of my way," Devon snarled, his face dark with bloodlust. He was in a fury, the kind that grew exponentially the more one tried to calm it. His kinswoman had been defiled, and nothing less than murder would suffice. There were only two people on earth who could handle him in this state: his brother West, and Kathleen.

"Leave him be," Kathleen said, positioning herself between her husband and Rhys. "You've hurt him."

"Not enough." He moved as if to push by her.

"Devon, *no*." Kathleen stubbornly stood her ground. Without realizing it, she slid a hand over her abdomen. Later she would confide to Helen that it had made no sense, the impulse to shield her stomach long before the baby had even begun to show, before she'd even accustomed herself to the idea of it.

However, that small, unconscious action was all it took to disarm Devon completely. His gaze shot to her stomach, and he halted, breathing heavily.

Comprehending her advantage, Kathleen told him promptly, "I shouldn't be distressed in my condition."

Devon gave her a glance of mingled rage and protest. "Are you going to use that against me for the next nine months?"

"No, darling, only for the next seven and a half months. After that, I'll have to find something else to use against you." Kathleen went to him, hugging herself against his rigid form. As his arms went around her, she slipped a soothing hand over the nape of his neck, coaxing him to relax. "You know I can't let you murder people before dinner," she murmured. "It throws the entire household off schedule."

Rhys was in too much pain to pay attention to the exchange. He remained on his side, half-curled, his healthy bronze complexion bleached of color.

Sitting on the floor beside him, Helen eased his black head into her lap. "Where are you hurt?" she asked anxiously. "Is it your back?"

"Shoulder. Dislocated . . . this morning."

"Have you seen a doctor?"

"Aye." Letting go of her skirt fabric, Rhys flexed his fingers experimentally. "It's all right," he muttered. Moving stiffly, he began to sit up, and paused with a groan of agony.

Helen moved to help him, wedging herself beneath

his good arm. She felt him jolt as she accidentally pressed against a sore place on his side. "It's more than your shoulder," she said in worry.

Rhys let out a scraping laugh. "*Cariad*, I haven't a single moving part that doesn't ache." He struggled to a sitting position and propped his back against the edge of a nearby settee. Closing his eyes, he let out an unsteady breath and tried to accommodate the multitude of pains that assailed him.

"What do you need?" Helen asked urgently. "What can I do?" A few locks of heavy dark hair had tumbled over his forehead, and she stroked them back with tender fingertips.

His lashes lifted, and she found herself staring into hot, black-brown eyes. "You can marry me."

Smiling in spite of her worry, Helen laid her palm against his lean cheek. "I've already said I would."

Devon, who had come to stand behind her, asked irritably, "What the devil is the matter with you, Winterborne?"

"You slammed him against the wall," Kathleen pointed out.

"I've done worse in the past, and it's never sent him to the floor." The two men routinely boxed and trained at a club that taught both pugilism and *Savate*, a form of combat that had originated on the streets of Paris.

Helen twisted to glance at them as she explained. "Mr. Winterborne's shoulder was dislocated this morning."

Devon looked surprised and then furious. "Damn it, why didn't you say anything?"

Rhys's eyes narrowed. "Would it have made a difference?"

"Not after the rubbish you were spouting!"

"What rubbish?" Kathleen asked in an excessively calm tone, stroking her husband's arm.

"He said that Helen went to visit him yesterday. *Alone*. And they—" Devon broke off, unwilling to repeat the offensive claim.

"It's true," Helen said.

It was rare to see Devon, who'd become accustomed to frequent surprises over the past year—caught so entirely off guard. But his jaw sagged like the lid of an unlatched valise as he stared at her.

"I've been ruined," Helen added, perhaps a bit too cheerfully. But after twenty-one years of being shy and predictable and sitting quietly in corners, she had discovered an untoward enjoyment in shocking people.

In the stunned silence that followed, she turned back to Rhys and began to unknot his silk necktie.

Rhys reached up to stop her, but flinched in agony. "*Cariad*," he said gruffly, "what are you doing?"

She pushed back the lapels of his coat. "Having a look at your shoulder."

"Not here. I'll have a doctor see to it later."

Helen understood his desire for privacy. But there was no way that she could allow him to leave Ravenel House while he was injured and in pain. "We must find out whether it has been dislocated again."

"It's sound." But he grunted in pain as she pulled the coat carefully off his shoulder.

Immediately Kathleen came to help, kneeling by his other side. "Don't move," she cautioned. "Let us do the work."

They began to divest him of the garment. Rhys steeled himself, but as they tugged at the coat, he shoved them back. "*Argghh!*"

Helen paused and looked at Kathleen in worry. "We'll have to cut it off."

Rhys was trembling, his eyes closed.

"The devil you will," he muttered. "I've already had a shirt cut off me this morning. Let it be."

Kathleen cast an imploring glance at her husband.

With an explosive sigh, Devon went to pick up something from the library table, and returned to the group on the floor. As he approached, he flicked open a silver folding knife with a long gleaming blade.

The sound, quiet as it was, caused Rhys to flinch

reflexively, his eyes flying open. He moved to confront the threat, and cursed with pain, sitting down hard on his rump.

"Easy, arsewit," Devon said acidly, sinking to his haunches beside him. "I'm not going to kill you. Your valet will do that for me when he realizes you've ruined two bespoke shirts and a coat in one day."

"I don't—"

"Winterborne," Devon warned softly, "you've insulted my wife, debauched my cousin, and now you're delaying my dinner. This would be an excellent time to keep your mouth shut."

Rhys scowled and held still while Devon employed the blade with meticulous skill. The knife slid along the seams of the garments until they began to peel from his body like bark from a silver birch. "My lady," he said to Kathleen, and paused, his breath hissing between his clenched teeth. "I apologize. For how I behaved that day. For what I said. I"—a groan escaped him as Kathleen gently pulled the sleeve from his aching arm—"have no excuse."

"I'm equally to blame," Kathleen said, folding the coat and setting it aside. Meeting Rhys's surprised gaze, she continued resolutely. "I acted on impulse, and created a difficult situation for everyone. I knew better than to go to a gentleman's house alone, but in my worry over Helen, I made a mistake. I accept your apology, Mr. Winterborne, if you'll accept mine."

"It was my fault," he insisted. "I shouldn't have insulted you. I didn't mean a word of it."

"I know," Kathleen assured him.

"I've never been attracted to you. I couldn't desire a woman less."

Kathleen's lips quivered with a repressed laugh. "The repulsion is quite mutual, Mr. Winterborne. Shall we cry pax and start over?"

"What about what he's done to Helen?" Devon asked in outrage.

Rhys watched warily as the knife sliced through his shirt.

"That was my fault," Helen said hastily. "I went uninvited to the store yesterday and demanded to see Mr. Winterborne. I told him that I still wanted to marry him, and I made him exchange my ring for a new one, and then I—I had my way with him." She paused, realizing how that sounded. "Not *in* the store, of course."

Straight-faced, Kathleen said, "Dear me, I hope he didn't put up a struggle."

Devon gave his wife a sardonic glance. "Kathleen, if you would be so kind, have Sutton fetch one of my shirts. One of the looser-fitting ones."

"Yes, my lord." Kathleen rose to her feet. "Perhaps he should also bring—" She broke off as the shirt fell away, revealing the broad expanse of Rhys's bare chest, and the violently discolored shoulder. It looked intensely painful, the muscles visibly knotted beneath the flesh.

Helen was silent with anguish at the sight. She let her fingers curl gently over the knob of his wrist, and felt the subtle inclination of his body toward her, as if he were trying to absorb her touch.

"What caused this?" Devon asked curtly, nudging Rhys to lean forward so he could glance at his back, where several more black bruises marked the smooth amber skin.

"I went with Severin to look at a block of property near King's Cross," Rhys muttered. "Some debris fell from a condemned building."

Devon's scowl deepened. "When did you become so damned accident-prone?"

"Since I began spending more time with my friends," Rhys said acidly.

"I suppose it's too much to hope that debris fell on Severin as well?" Devon asked.

"Not a scratch on him."

Sighing, Devon turned to Kathleen. "We'll need brandy and ice bags as well as the shirt. And a camphor poultice—the kind we used on my cracked ribs."

Kathleen smiled at him. "I remember." She strode to the door and flung it open, and halted abruptly as she discovered a crowd eavesdropping at the threshold. Her gaze moved over three housemaids, a footman, Mrs. Abbott, and Devon's valet.

The housekeeper was the first to react. "As I was telling all of you," she said loudly, "it's time to go about your work, and mind your p's and q's."

Kathleen cleared her throat as if trying to choke back a laugh. "Sutton," she said to the valet, "I shall need you to bring a few items for our guest. Did you overhear Lord Trenear quite clearly, or should I repeat the list?"

"Brandy, ice, a poultice, and a shirt," the valet replied with great dignity. "I will also obtain a length of fabric to fashion a sling for the gentleman's arm."

As Sutton left, Kathleen turned to address the housekeeper. "Mrs. Abbott, I'm afraid a porcelain vase has been accidentally overturned."

Before the woman could reply, all three housemaids excitedly volunteered to sweep up. One couldn't help but question whether their enthusiasm was for their work, or the desire to be in the same room with the half-naked Winterborne. Judging from the way they were craning their necks to glance at him, definitely the latter.

"I'll do it myself, my lady," the housekeeper declared, shooing the housemaids away. "I'll return momentarily with the broom."

Kathleen turned to the twins, who had remained at the threshold. "Is there something you would like to ask, girls?"

Pandora looked at her hopefully. "May we say hello to Mr. Winterborne?"

"Later, darling. He's in no condition for that right now."

"Please tell him we're so very sorry that a building fell on him," Cassandra said earnestly.

A smile wove through Kathleen's voice as she replied. "I'll convey your kind wishes. Now, off you go."

Reluctantly the twins trudged from the library.

After closing the door, Kathleen headed back to the group near the settee. Along the way, she retrieved a lap blanket that had been draped over the arm of a chair.

Devon was examining Rhys's shoulder, palpating it carefully to discern whether or not the bone had come loose from the socket. "You should be at home in bed," he said brusquely, "not traipsing across London proposing to young women you've ruined."

Rhys scowled. "First, I don't traipse, and second, Helen's—*devil take you*, that hurts!" Exhausted, he dropped his head to his chest.

Helen regarded him sympathetically, knowing how he hated not being in control. Rhys was always well dressed and in command of himself. His very name connoted success, luxury, and elegance. None of that was consistent with finding himself on the floor, battered, bruised, and forcibly divested of his clothing.

"And second?" she prompted gently, bringing him back to his unfinished thought.

"You're not ruined," he said gruffly, his head still down. "You're perfect."

Helen's heart twisted with painful sweetness. She wanted badly to comfort and cradle him. Instead she had to settle for stroking his black hair very lightly. He pushed his head against the caress, like an affectionate wolf. Her palm moved along the side of his face to his jaw and down to the firm, perfect line of his good shoulder.

"It seems stable," Devon said, sitting back on his heels. "I don't think it's been reinjured. Helen, if you continue to fondle the bastard right in front of me, I'll have to dislocate his other shoulder."

Helen withdrew her hand sheepishly.

Lifting his head, Rhys gave Devon a baleful glance. "She's leaving with me tonight."

Devon's face hardened. "If you think—"

"But we would rather have a June wedding," Helen interrupted hastily. "And above all, we would like to have your blessing, Cousin Devon."

"Here you are, Mr. Winterborne," Kathleen said brightly, coming forward to drape the lap blanket over his tawny exposed torso. "Let's help him up onto the settee—the floor is too drafty."

"I don't need help," Rhys grumbled. With effort, he managed to hoist himself onto the leather upholstery. "Helen, go pack your belongings."

Helen was filled with consternation. She couldn't bring herself to oppose Rhys, especially when he was injured and vulnerable. But she didn't want to leave Ravenel House on these terms. Devon had been extraordinarily kind, letting her and the twins stay at Eversby Priory, when anyone else in his position would have cast them out without a second thought. Helen had no desire to divide the family by eloping and excluding them all from her wedding.

She glanced at Kathleen, silently pleading for help.

Understanding at once, Kathleen spoke to Rhys in a placating tone. "Surely there's no need for that, Mr. Winterborne. You both deserve a proper ceremony, with family and friends around you. Not some hasty slap-and-dash affair."

"Slap-and-dash was good enough for you and Trenear," Rhys retorted. "If he didn't have to wait for a wedding, why do I?"

Kathleen hesitated before replying with amused chagrin. "We had no choice."

It took approximately two seconds for Rhys's agile brain to process the implications. "You're expecting," he said flatly. "Congratulations."

"You didn't have to tell him," Devon muttered.

Kathleen smiled at him as she seated herself. "But my lord, Mr. Winterborne will be part of the family soon."

Devon rubbed the upper half of his face with one hand, as if the statement had caused an instant migraine.

"The same circumstances may soon apply to Helen," Rhys said, deliberately provoking him further. "She could also be with child."

"We don't know that yet," Helen said, reaching out to arrange the blanket over his chest. "If it turns out to be the case, the plan must change, of course. But I would rather wait until we find out for certain."

Rhys stared at her, making no effort to conceal the desire smoldering beneath his stillness. "I can't wait for you," he said.

"But you will," Devon said coolly. "That's the condition of my consent. You've treated Helen like a pawn in a chess game and manipulated the situation to your advantage. Now you'll bloody well have to wait until June, because that's how long it will take before I'll be able to look at you without wanting to throttle you. In the meantime, I've had enough of Ravenels running amok in London. Now that our affairs are in order, I'm taking the family back to Hampshire." He glanced at Kathleen with an arched brow, and she nodded in agreement.

At the same time, a distant wail came from the farthest threshold of the double library. *"Noooo!"*

Kathleen glanced quizzically toward the sound. "Pandora," she called out, "do not eavesdrop, if you please."

"It's not Pandora," came the disgruntled reply, "it's Cassandra."

"It is *not*," another young voice said indignantly. "I'm Cassandra, and Pandora is trying to land me in trouble!"

"You're both in trouble," Devon called back. "Go upstairs."

"We don't want to leave London," one of them said, while the other added, "The country is so drear-itating."

Devon glanced at Kathleen, and in the next moment they both struggled to hold back grins.

"When am I going to see Helen?" Rhys demanded.

Devon seemed to relish his former friend's suppressed wrath. "If I have my way, not until the day of the wedding."

Rhys returned his attention to Helen. "*Cariad*, I want you to—"

"Please don't ask that of me," Helen begged. "A June wedding is what we had planned before. You've lost nothing. We're betrothed again, and this way, we'll have my family on our side."

She saw the struggle on his face: fury, pride, need.

"*Please*," she asked gently. "Say you'll wait for me."

Chapter 11

After they had sent Mr. Winterborne home in his carriage, with his arm secured in a sling and rubber ice bags packed around his shoulder, the Ravenels had dinner and retired early for the evening. Kathleen had been pleased and not at all surprised that Devon, despite his lingering resentment, had made certain that his friend was well taken care of before he departed. Although Mr. Winterborne had angered and disappointed him, there was no doubt that Devon would forgive him.

Kathleen watched appreciatively as he shed his dressing-robe to join her in bed. Her husband, who loved riding, pugilism, and sports of all kinds, was an athletic and superbly fit man.

Settling on his back, Devon stretched with a pleasured sigh.

Kathleen propped herself up on an elbow and drew her fingertips idly through the dark hair on his chest. "Do you think it might be a bit severe," she asked, "not to let them see each other for the next five months?"

"There's no chance in hell that Winterborne will stay away from her that long."

Kathleen smiled, tracing the sturdy edge of his collarbone. "Why did you forbid him, then?"

"The bastard tramples through life like a conquering army—if I didn't force him to retreat now and then, he'd have nothing but contempt for me. Besides, I'd still like to kill him for what he did to Helen." Devon sighed shortly. "I knew we shouldn't have left the girls alone, even for a day. To think I was worried about the twins, when Helen was the one who went out seeking a scandal."

"She wasn't seeking scandal," Kathleen countered reasonably. "She went to . . . well, to reclaim her fiancé. And one must view the situation in balance; it's not fair to blame him entirely."

His brows lifted. "Why are you taking Winterborne's side, when you've been against the match from the beginning?"

"Because of Helen," she admitted. "I knew she

would do anything for the good of the family, even marry a man she didn't love. I also knew that Mr. Winterborne intimidated her. But that's changed. I believe she truly wants him now. She's no longer afraid of him. The way she stood her ground with him this evening altered my opinion of the match entirely. If this is what she wants, I will support her."

"I can't overlook Winterborne's actions," Devon grumbled. "Out of regard for me, if for no other reason, he shouldn't have taken the innocence of a young woman under my protection. It's a matter of respect."

Kathleen hoisted herself more fully over him, staring down into his blue eyes. "*This*," she mocked gently, "from a man who seduced me in nearly every room, stairwell and hay-nook of Eversby Priory. Where was your regard for innocence then?"

His frown disappeared. "That was different."

"Why, may I ask?"

Devon flipped her over, reversing their positions neatly and surprising a giggle from her. "Because," he said huskily, "I wanted you *so much* . . ."

She writhed and laughed as he unfastened her nightgown.

". . . and as lord of the manor," he continued, proceeding to strip her naked, "I thought it was time to exercise my *droit de seigneur.*"

"As if I were some medieval peasant girl?" she asked, shoving him onto his back and climbing over him.

Grabbing his marauding hands, she tried to pin him down with her entire weight.

A deep laugh escaped him. "Love, that won't work. You're no heavier than a butterfly." Clearly enjoying their play, he lay unresisting as she gripped his thick wrists more tightly. "A determined butterfly," he conceded. As he stared up at her, his smile faded, and his eyes darkened to intense blue. "I was a selfish bastard," he said softly. "I shouldn't have seduced you."

"I was willing," Kathleen pointed out, inwardly surprised by his remorse. He was changing, she thought, rapidly gaining maturity as he shouldered the responsibilities that had been forced on him so unexpectedly.

"I would do it differently now. Forgive me." He paused, frowning in self-reproach. "I wasn't raised to be honorable. It's damned difficult to learn."

Kathleen slid her hands over his until their fingers interlaced. "There's nothing to forgive, or regret."

Devon shook his head, not allowing her to absolve him. "Tell me how to atone."

She bent to brush her lips against his. "Love me," she whispered.

With great care, Devon rolled until she was caught beneath him. "Always," he said huskily, and possessed her mouth while his hands slid over her body. He made love to her slowly, with exquisite skill. Long after he'd made her ready for him, he finally nudged her thighs apart and eased inside. She wriggled in frustration as he refused to press deeper, no matter how she tried to urge him.

"Devon . . ." Her breath came in little flurries. "I need more."

"More of what?" His mouth drifted to the base of her throat.

She scowled and squirmed. "Oh I hate it when you tease me!"

He smiled. "Almost as much as you love it." Relenting, he slid an inch forward.

"Deeper," she gasped. "Please, Devon—"

"Like this?" he asked gently.

Kathleen arched beneath him, her lips parted in a silent cry as he took her with fierce, tender urgency, loving her body and soul.

"Fernsby," Rhys called out, frowning as he sorted through the sheaf of papers on his desk with a frown.

The private secretary appeared promptly at the threshold of his open door. "Yes, Mr. Winterborne?"

"Come in." He straightened the paper into a neat stack, replaced it in a cardboard file envelope, and tied the attached string around it. "I've just looked through the documents sent by Mr. Severin's office." He handed her the envelope.

"The ones pertaining to the block of residential buildings near King's Cross?"

"Aye. Deeds, mortgages, contractor's agreements, and so forth." He gave her a dark glance. "But there's not one piece of paper in that entire file that bears the owner's name. Severin knows better than to expect me to buy property without knowing who's selling it."

"I would have thought it was legally required for the owner's name to be listed."

"There are ways around it." Rhys nodded toward the file in Fernsby's hands. "The mortgage wasn't financed by a bank, but through a loan from a cooperative building society. According to the deed, the property is owned by a private investment company. I'd bet a hundred pounds that it's being held in trust for an unnamed party."

"Why would someone go to such trouble instead of buying it in his own name?"

"In the past, I've bought property anonymously to keep the asking price from going through the roof when they hear my name. And I have business adversaries who would enjoy putting me in my place now and then, by denying me something I want. Likely this man's reasons are similar. But I want his name."

"Would Mr. Severin be willing to tell you, if you asked him directly?"

Rhys shook his head. "He would have told me already. I suspect he knows it would ruin the deal if I found out."

"Shall I give this information to the same man we hired to research the canning factory purchase?"

"Aye, he'll do."

"I'll take care of it right away. Also, Doctor Havelock is waiting to have a word with you."

Rhys rolled his eyes impatiently. "Tell him my shoulder is as good as—"

"I don't give a tinker's damn about your shoulder," came a gravelly voice from the threshold. "I've come about a more important matter."

The speaker was Dr. William Havelock, formerly the private physician to a handful of privileged London families. He had also been a medical journalist with progressive views, writing about poor-law medicine and public health issues. Eventually his wealthy patients had been irked by the political debates he had stirred up, and had turned to other, less controversial practitioners.

Rhys had hired Havelock ten years ago, ever since the store had first broken ground on Cork Street. It had made sense to hire a permanent staff doctor to take care of his employees, keeping them healthy and productive.

The middle-aged widower was a fit, sturdy man with a lionesque head, a shock of snow-white hair, and eyes that had seen humanity at its highest and lowest. His craggy face was routinely set in truculent lines, but when he was with his patients, his features softened with a grandfatherly kindness that immediately earned their trust.

"Dr. Havelock," Mrs. Fernsby said with a touch of annoyance, "I asked you to wait in the visitors' foyer."

"Winterborne doesn't mind interfering with my schedule," he said testily, "so I've decided to interfere with his."

They exchanged narrow-eyed glances.

More than a few employees had speculated that beneath the habitual antagonism between Havelock and Mrs. Fernsby, the two were secretly attracted to each other. Seeing the pair at this moment, Rhys was inclined to believe the rumor.

"Good morning, Havelock," Rhys said. "How have I interfered with your schedule?"

"By foisting an unexpected visitor on me during a day when I have at least a dozen patients to attend to."

Rhys sent Mrs. Fernsby a questioning glance.

"He's referring to Dr. Gibson," she told him. "I interviewed her as you asked. Having found her both qualified and agreeable, I sent her to Dr. Havelock."

Havelock asked brusquely, "How can you judge her qualifications, Fernsby?"

"She has a medical degree with honors and top prizes," Mrs. Fernsby retorted.

"From *France*," Havelock said with a slight sneer.

"Considering how English doctors failed to save my poor husband," Mrs. Fernsby snapped, "I would take a French doctor any day."

Before the argument could develop into a full-fledged brawl, Rhys interceded quickly. "Come in, Havelock, and we'll discuss Dr. Gibson."

The physician entered the office, saying pointedly as he passed the secretary, "I would like some tea, Fernsby."

"That's *Mrs.* Fernsby to you. And you may find all the tea you want at the staff canteen."

Pausing, Havelock turned to give her an offended glance. "Why can he call you Fernsby?"

"Because he is Mr. Winterborne, and you are not." Mrs. Fernsby focused her attention on Rhys. "Sir, would you care for some tea? If so, I suppose I could place an extra cup on the tray for Dr. Havelock."

Rhys struggled to conceal his amusement before replying blandly, "I believe I would. Thank you, Fernsby."

After the secretary had left the office, Rhys said to Havelock, "I made it clear to Dr. Gibson that her hiring was subject to your approval."

A scowl divided the older man's forehead into a ladder of ridges. "She informed me it was *a fait accompli*, the presumptuous chit."

"You did say last month that you needed an assistant, aye?"

"One of my choosing, since I'm the one who will be called upon to train and guide him."

"Do you doubt her proficiency?" Rhys asked.

Havelock could have destroyed Garrett Gibson's incipient career with a simple "yes." However, he was too honest to take that route. "Had any man come to me with her qualifications, I would have hired him on the spot. But a woman? There's too much prejudice to overcome. Even the female patients will prefer a male doctor."

"At first. Until they become accustomed to the idea." Seeing the objection on the older man's face, Rhys continued with a hint of amused chiding, "Havelock, I employ hundreds of hardworking women who demonstrate their skill every day. Recently I promoted a salesgirl to manager of her department, and her performance has been equal to that of any man at her level. And obviously Fernsby's abilities are beyond question. I'm not a radical, Havelock; these are facts. Therefore, as men of reason, let's give Dr. Gibson a chance to prove herself."

Havelock reached up to tug fractiously at a lock of white hair as he considered the situation. "I've fought enough battles for one lifetime. I have no desire to take part in women's struggles against injustice."

Rhys smiled, his gaze unrelenting.

The doctor let out a sighing groan, acknowledging that he was being given no choice in the matter. "Damn you, Winterborne."

The day was bitterly cold, the air laced with frost that stung the nose and chilled the teeth. Helen shivered and gathered her wool half-cape more tightly about her neck, and pressed her numb lips together in a futile effort to warm them.

According to the rules of mourning, enough time had passed since Theo's death that the Ravenel sisters could now respectably leave their faces uncovered in public, so long as they wore veils draped down the backs of their hats or bonnets. Helen was grateful that she no longer had to squint through a layer of black crepe.

The Ravenel family and a handful of servants were about to depart London on a train bound for Hampshire. It seemed to Helen that Waterloo Station, a ten-acre system of sheds filled with a complex web of platforms and additions, could not have been more perfectly designed to cause the maximum amount of confusion for travelers. The volume of travelers practically doubled each year, forcing the station to expand in an ad hoc fashion. To make matters worse, the railway employees often gave contradictory information about where a train would arrive or depart. Porters carried luggage to the wrong trains and guided people to the wrong hackney carriage ranks and booking offices. Passengers seethed and shouted in frustration as they milled inside the open-sided sheds.

Helen jumped at the sound of a nearby brass orchestra that began to play a regimental march with strident enthusiasm. The first battalion of the Coldstream regiment had been brought down from Chichester, and a crowd had gathered to cheer their arrival.

Annoyed by the uproar, Devon said to Kathleen, "I'm going to find out where our blasted train is. Don't move an inch until I return. I've already told the footman that any man who approaches you or the girls is to be beaten to a pulp."

Looking up at him, Kathleen placed her feet firmly on the planks as if rooting herself.

Devon shook his head with a reluctant grin. "You don't look obedient in the least," he informed her, stroking her cheek with a gloved finger.

"Am I supposed to?" Kathleen called out as he left.

"It would be interesting to see at least once," he retorted over his shoulder without breaking stride.

Laughing, Kathleen went to stand beside Helen.

While the wide-eyed twins viewed the procession of Coldstreams, dressed in brilliant scarlet tunics trimmed with gold buttons, Kathleen sobered and glanced at Helen's subdued expression with concern. "I'm sorry we have to leave London."

"There's nothing to be sorry for," Helen said. "I'm perfectly content."

It wasn't true, of course. She was worried about being separated from Rhys for so long. Especially in light of how infuriated he'd been at her refusal to elope. He wasn't accustomed to waiting or being denied something he wanted.

Ever since Rhys had left Ravenel House, Helen had written to him daily. In the first letter, she had asked about his health. In the second she had told him about the family's travel plans, and in the third, she had dared to ask, in a moment of uneasiness and self-doubt, if he regretted their engagement.

After each of the first two letters, a succinct response, written in a remarkably precise copperplate hand, had arrived within hours. In the first, Rhys had assured her that his shoulder was mending quickly, and in the second, he had thanked her for the information about the Ravenels' imminent departure.

But there had been no reply to Helen's third letter.

Perhaps he did regret the engagement. Perhaps she had been a disappointment to him. Already.

To keep from troubling the rest of the family, Helen did her best to conceal her low spirits, but Kathleen was sensitive to her mood.

"The time will pass quickly," Kathleen murmured. "You'll see."

Helen managed a strained smile. "Yes."

"We would have had to return to the estate even if it weren't for the situation with Mr. Winterborne. There's much to be done now that the ground is being prepared for the railway and the quarry, and it can't all fall to West."

"I understand. But . . . I do hope that Cousin Devon will not continue to be severe upon Mr. Winterborne."

"He'll relent soon," Kathleen assured her. "He's not trying to be severe, it's only that you and the twins are under his protection, and he cares very much for you." After glancing around them, Kathleen lowered her voice. "As I told Devon," she continued, "it's hardly a crime for a man to make love to a woman he intends to marry. And he couldn't argue. But he didn't like the way Mr. Winterborne manipulated the situation."

"Will they become friends again?" Helen dared to ask.

"They're still friends, dear. After we've settled in and let a few weeks pass, I'll persuade Devon to invite Mr. Winterborne to Hampshire."

Helen clenched her gloved hands together, striving to contain her excitement before she made a spectacle of herself in public. "I would appreciate that."

Kathleen's eyes twinkled. "In the meantime, there will be more than enough to keep you occupied. You must go through the house to choose the things you'll want to take to London. You'll want your personal possessions, of course, but also any furniture and ornaments that will help to make your new home feel snug."

"That's very generous—but I wouldn't wish to take anything that you might want later."

"There are two hundred rooms in Eversby Priory. Scores of them are filled with furniture that no one ever uses and paintings no one ever views. Take whatever you like, it's your birthright."

Helen's smile faded at that last word.

Their conversation was drowned out by the roar and blast of a train arriving on the other side of the platform. Smells of metal, coal dust, and steam poured out into the shed, while the wood planks beneath their feet seemed to shake with impatience. Helen shrank back instinctively, even though the locomotive posed no threat. The band continued to play, soldiers marched, and people cheered. Passengers emerged from the railway carriages to be met by porters with barrows, and there was so much calling and shouting that Helen covered her ears with her gloved hands. Kathleen went to gather in the twins as the crowd pressed forward. Bodies moved and collided all around them, while the footman, Peter, did his best to keep the women from being jostled.

A sharp gust came from the open side of the railway shed, whipping the front of Helen's half-cape apart. The button of a frog fastening had slipped free of a braided silk loop. Gripping the edges of the cape, Helen turned her back to the wind and fumbled with the loop. Her fingers were so cold they wouldn't work properly.

A pair of young women, clutching valises and hatboxes, brushed by her in their haste to leave the platform, and Helen was bumped sideways. Taking an extra step or two to maintain her balance, she collided with a huge, solid form.

A shocked breath escaped her as she felt a pair of hands steady her.

"I beg your pardon, sir," she gasped, "I—"

Helen found herself looking up into a pair of midnight eyes. A deep flutter went through her stomach, and her knees weakened.

"Rhys," she whispered.

Wordlessly he reached for the fastening of her cape and hooked the silk loop around the button. He was smartly dressed in a beautiful black wool overcoat and a pearl gray hat. But his civilized attire did nothing to soften the hard-edged tension of a dangerous mood.

"Why did you come?" she managed to ask, her pulse in her throat.

"Do you think I'd let you leave London without saying good-bye?"

"I didn't expect—but I wanted—that is, I'm glad—" Flustered, she fell silent.

Sliding a hand to the center of her back, Rhys murmured, "Come with me." He guided her toward a tall wooden barrier that had been set up partially across the platform. The wall was plastered with advertisements and notices about alterations to train services.

"My lady!" Helen heard from behind her, and she stopped to glance over her shoulder.

The family footman, Peter, stared at her distractedly as he tried to buffer the rest of the family from the onslaught of departing passengers. "My lady, the earl bade me to keep you all together."

"I'll look after her," Rhys told him curtly.

"But sir—"

Kathleen, who had just noticed Rhys's presence, interrupted the footman. "Allow them five minutes, Peter." She sent Helen an imploring glance and held up five fingers to make certain she understood. Helen responded with a hasty nod.

Rhys pulled her to a sheltered corner created by the wooden barrier and a cast-iron support column. He turned his back to the crowd, concealing her from view.

"I had a devil of a time finding you." His low voice undercut the din around them. "You're at the wrong platform."

"Cousin Devon has gone to find out where we should wait."

An icy breeze teased a few white-blond wisps of hair loose from her coiffure and seemed to slip beneath the collar of her dress. She shivered violently, trying to huddle deeper into her cape.

"I can hear your teeth chattering," Rhys said. "Come closer."

With mingled dismay and longing, she saw that he was unfastening the front of his double-breasted coat. "I don't think—there's no need—"

Ignoring her protests, he pulled her against his body and wrapped the sides of the coat around her.

Helen closed her eyes as warmth and private darkness surrounded her, the thick wool muffling the busy clamor of their surroundings. She felt like a small woodland creature nestling in its burrow, hidden from dangers that lurked outside. He was large and strong and warm, and she couldn't help relaxing into his embrace, her body recognizing his as a source of comfort.

"Better?" His voice was soft against her ear.

Helen nodded, her head on his chest. "Why didn't you reply to my last letter?" she asked in a muffled voice.

The fine leather of his black-gloved fingers slid beneath her chin, nudging it upward. The mocking glint in his eyes was unmistakable. "Perhaps I didn't like your question."

"I was afraid—that is, I thought—"

"That I might have changed my mind? That I might not want you any longer?" His voice was edged with something that sent a prickle down the back of her neck. "Would you like proof of how I feel, *cariad*?"

Before she could reply, his mouth crushed over hers in a demonstration that was nothing less than scandalous. He didn't care. He wanted her, and he intended for her to know it, feel it, taste it. Her hands inched up his shoulders and around his neck, clinging for balance as her knees gave way. The kiss went on in timeless suspension, his lips restless and searing, while his hand cradled her cheek in cool black leather. It wasn't anger that drove him, she realized dazedly. He had come because he wanted reassurance. He was no more certain of her than she was of him.

With a rough vibration in his throat, he ended the kiss and lifted his head. His breath came in bursts of steam that scalded the wintry air. He loosened the coat from around her and stepped back, leaving her to stand on her own again.

Helen's body quivered at the onslaught of fresh cold air.

Rhys reached into his coat, rummaging through an inner pocket. Taking Helen's gloved hand, he pressed a small sealed envelope against her palm. Before she could ask what it was, he said, "Tell your family to go to platform eight, by way of the footbridge."

"But when—"

"Hwyl fawr am nawr." He took a last look at her, a lonely-demon flicker in his eyes. "'Good-bye for now,' that means." After turning her in the direction of her family, he nudged her forward. Helen paused and turned to look back, his name on her lips. But he was already walking away, cutting through the crowd with purposeful strides.

Helen tucked the letter in her close-fitting sleeve and didn't read it until much later, after Devon had bustled the family to the correct train at platform eight, and they were all seated in a first-class carriage. When the train had pulled away from Waterloo Station, beginning the two-hour journey to Hampshire, she carefully inched out the envelope.

Seeing that the twins were staring outside the window, and Kathleen was engaged in conversation with Devon, Helen broke the dark red wax seal and unfolded the letter.

> *Helen,*
>
> *You ask if I regret our engagement.*
>
> *No. I regret every minute that you're out of my sight. I regret every step that doesn't bring me closer to you.*
>
> *My last thought each night is that you should*

be in my arms. There is no peace or pleasure in my empty bed, where I sleep with you only in dreams and wake to curse the dawn.

If I had the right, I would forbid you to go anywhere without me. Not out of selfishness, but because being apart from you is like trying to live without breathing.

Think on that. You've stolen my very breath, cariad. And now I'm left to count the days until I take it back from you, kiss by kiss.

Winterborne

Chapter 12

Kneeling in front of a bookcase in an upstairs reading nook, Helen sorted through rows of books and set aside the ones she wanted to pack. In the three weeks since she had returned to Eversby Priory, she had accumulated a room full of possessions to take to her new home. Each item held personal meaning, such as a rosewood sewing box that had belonged to her mother, a porcelain dresser tray painted with a parade of cherubs, a children's bath rug embroidered with Noah's ark and its animal passengers, and a mahogany parlor chair with a triangular seat that her maternal grandmother had always occupied during visits.

Staying busy was the only way Helen could find to distract herself from the melancholy longing that had invaded her heart. *Hiraeth*, she thought gloomily. The familiar comforts of home had lost their appeal, and her ordinary habits had turned into drudgery. Even caring for her orchids and practicing the piano had become tedious.

How could anything seem interesting in comparison with Rhys Winterborne?

She'd had so little time alone with him, but in those few hours she had been possessed and pleasured with such intensity that now her days were dull by comparison.

Reaching the row of her mother's orchid journals, Helen pulled them out and placed them one by one in a canvas overland trunk. The set comprised twelve inexpensive notebooks covered in plain blue cloth, with pages that had been glued to the spine rather than stitched. Their value to Helen, however, was inestimable.

Jane, Lady Trenear, had filled each one with information about orchids, including sketches of different varieties and notations about their individual temperaments and properties. Sometimes she had used the journals as a diary, weaving personal thoughts and observations throughout.

Reading the journals had helped Helen to understand her elusive mother far more than she ever had in life. Jane had stayed in London for weeks or months at a time, and left the rearing of her children to governesses and servants. Even when Jane had been at Eversby Priory, she had seemed more like a glamorous guest than a parent. Helen couldn't remember ever having seen her mother less than perfectly attired and perfumed, with jewels at her ears, throat, and wrists, and a fresh orchid in her hair.

No one would have thought that Jane, generally admired for her beauty and wit, had a care in the world. However, in the privacy of her journals, Jane had revealed herself as an anxious, lonely woman, frustrated by her inability to produce more than one son.

I've been split open like a sausage, Jane had written after the twins were born, *by a pair of daughters. Before I even arose from my childbed, the earl thanked me for producing "two more parasites." Why couldn't at least one of them have been a boy?*

And in another notebook . . . *Little Helen is proving to be a help with the twins. I own, I like her better than I once did, although I fear she'll always be a pale, rabbit-faced creature.*

Despite the stinging words, Helen felt sympathy for Jane, who had been increasingly unhappy in her marriage to Edmund, Lord Trenear. He'd been a disenchanted and difficult husband. His temper had veered from scorching to freezing, rarely lingering in-between.

It wasn't until after her mother's death that Helen had finally understood why her parents had always seemed reluctant to acknowledge her existence.

She had learned the truth while nursing her father through his last illness, brought on by a day of hunting out in the cold and damp. Edmund had gone into a rapid decline despite the doctor's efforts to heal him. As the earl sank into a half-delirium, Helen had taken turns with Quincy, his trusted valet, to sit at his bedside. They had administered tonic and sage tea to soothe his sore throat, and applied poultices to his chest.

"The doctor will return soon," Helen had murmured to her father, gently wiping traces of saliva from his chin after he'd suffered a coughing fit. "He was called away to see a patient in the village, but he said it wouldn't take long."

Opening his rheumy eyes, the earl had said in a dry, scoured voice, "I want one of my children . . . with me . . . at the end. Not you."

Thinking that he hadn't recognized her, she had replied gently, "It's Helen, Papa. I'm your daughter."

"You're not mine . . . never were. Your mother . . . took a lover . . ." The exertion of talking had provoked more coughing. When the throat spasms had calmed, he had rested silently with his eyes closed, refusing to look at her.

"There's no truth to it," Quincy had told Helen later. "The poor master is raving mad from fever. And your mother, God bless her, was admired by so many men that it poisoned his lordship with jealousy. You're every spit a Ravenel, my lady. Never doubt it."

Helen had pretended to believe Quincy. But she had known that the earl had told her the truth. It explained why she had neither the temperament nor the looks of the Ravenels. No wonder her parents had despised her—she was a child born of sin.

During the earl's last lucid moments, Helen had brought the twins to his bedside to say good-bye. Although she had sent for Theo, he hadn't been able to arrive from London in time. After their father had fallen insensate, Helen hadn't been able to find it in her heart to make the twins attend his deathwatch.

"Do we have to stay?" Cassandra had whispered, swabbing her red eyes with a handkerchief as she sat with Pandora on a little bench by the window. They had no affectionate memories of him to share, no advice or stories they could reminisce over. All they could do was sit silently and listen to his faint rattling breaths, and wait miserably for him to pass.

"He wouldn't want us here anyway," Pandora had said in a monotone. "He's never cared beans for either of us."

Taking pity on her young sisters, Helen had gone to embrace and kiss them both. "I'll stay with him," she had promised. "Go say a prayer for him, and find something quiet to do."

They had left gratefully. Cassandra had paused at the threshold to steal one last glance at her father, while Pandora had walked out in a brisk stride without looking back.

Going to the bedside, Helen had looked down at the earl, a tall, lean man who appeared shrunken in the vast bed. His complexion was gray-tinged and waxen, his swollen neck obscuring the shape of his jaw. All his great will had burned down to the frailest flicker of life. Helen had reflected that the earl seemed to have faded slowly in the two years after Jane had died. Perhaps he had been grieving for her. Theirs had been a complex relationship, two people who had been bound by disappointments and resentments the way others were bound by love.

Helen had dared to take the earl's lax hand, a collection of veins and bones contained in a loose envelope of skin. "I'm sorry Theo isn't here," she had said humbly. "I know I'm not the one wanted with you at the end. I'm sorry for that, too. But I can't let you face this alone."

As she had finished, Quincy had entered the room,

his deep-set black eyes gleaming with tears that slipped down to his white-whiskered jowls. Without a word, he had gone to occupy the bench at the window, determined to wait with her.

For an hour, they had watched over the earl as each strained breath grew softer than the last. Until finally Edmund, Lord Trenear, had passed away in the company of a servant and a daughter who possessed not a drop of his blood.

After the earl's passing, Helen had never dared to talk to Theo about her parentage. She felt certain that he must have known. It was why he had never wanted to bring her out in society, and why his attitude toward her had held echoes of his father's contempt. Neither had Helen been able to bring herself to confide in Kathleen or the twins. Even though she hadn't done anything wrong, she felt the shame of her illegitimate birth acutely. No matter how she tried to ignore it, the secret had lurked inside like a dose of venom waiting to be released.

It bothered Helen a great deal that she hadn't yet told Rhys. She knew how he loved the idea of marrying a daughter of the peerage. It would be incredibly difficult to confess that she wasn't a Ravenel. Rhys would be disappointed. He would think less of her.

Still . . . he had a right to know.

Sighing heavily, Helen packed the rest of the journals into the trunk. As she cast a cursory glance at the empty bookshelf, she noticed a little pale bundle wedged in the dusty corner. Frowning, she lowered to her elbows and reached into the bookcase to pry it loose.

A wad of writing paper.

Sitting up, she opened the crumpled mass carefully and discovered a few lines of her mother's handwriting. The words were more widely spaced than usual, sloping downward within their sentences.

My dearest Albion,

It is foolish, I know, to appeal to your heart when I have come to doubt its existence. Why has there been no word from you? What of the promises you made? If you abandon me, you ensure that Helen will never be loved by her own mother. I watch her sob in the cradle and cannot bring myself to touch her. She must cry alone, uncomforted, just as I must now that you have forsaken me.

I won't observe the decencies. My passion cannot be commanded by reason. Come back to me, and I swear I will send the baby away. I will tell everyone that she is sickly and must be raised by a nurse in a warm, dry climate. Edmund won't object—he'll be only too glad to have her removed from the household.

Nothing has to change for us, Albion, as long as we are discreet.

There was nothing more. Helen turned over the unfinished letter, but the other side was blank.

Helen found herself laying the wrinkled rectangle of paper on the floor and pressing it flat with her palm. She felt hollow, distanced from a host of feelings that she had no desire to acknowledge or examine.

Albion.

She had never wanted to know her father's name. But she couldn't help wondering what kind of man he had been. Was he still alive? And why had Jane never completed the letter?

"Helen!"

The unexpected cry caused her to start. Blindly she lifted her head as Cassandra raced into the room.

"The mails have been delivered," Cassandra exclaimed, "and there's a crate from Winterborne's! The footman is carrying it into the receiving room downstairs. You must come directly, we want to—" She paused with a frown. "Your face is all red. What's the matter?"

"Book dust," Helen managed to say. "I've been packing away Mama's journals, and it made me sneeze dreadfully."

"Won't you finish that later, *please*, dear Helen? We want to open your presents right away. Some of the boxes are marked 'perishable' and we think there may be sweets inside."

"I'll come down in a few minutes," Helen said distractedly, sliding the letter beneath a fold of her skirts.

"Shall I help you with the books?"

"Thank you, dear, but I would rather take care of it myself."

Cassandra heaved a sigh and said wistfully, "It's so difficult to wait."

Helen's gaze remained on her sister, as she noticed that Cassandra had recently lost the gangly, coltish look of childhood. She bore an astonishing resemblance to Jane, with the immaculate prettiness of her bone structure and bow-shaped lips, the sunlight-colored curls, and heavily lashed blue eyes.

Fortunately Cassandra was a softer, infinitely kinder version of their mother. And Pandora, for all her prankish high spirits, was the most sweet-natured girl imaginable. Thank God for the twins—they had always been the constant in her life, a source of love that had never faltered.

"Why don't you start opening the boxes without me?" Helen suggested. "I'll be down there quite soon. If anyone objects, tell them I've designated you as my official representative."

Cassandra grinned with satisfaction. "If there are sweets, I'll set some aside for you before Pandora eats them all." She bolted from the room with unladylike vigor, screaming out as she hurried down the grand staircase, "Helen says to start without her!"

Helen smiled absently and sat for a moment, pondering the canvas trunk with its invisible weight of secrets and painful memories. Both Jane and Edmund had gone to their eternal rest, and yet it seemed they still had the power to hurt their children from the grave.

But she wouldn't let them.

Decisively she closed the lid of the canvas trunk, silencing the whispers of the past. She picked up her mother's unfinished letter, carried it to the hearth, and laid it over a cluster of glowing coals. The dusty paper contracted and writhed on the heat before erupting into white flame.

She watched until every last word had disintegrated into ash.

And she dusted her hands together briskly as she left the room.

Chapter 13

Helen's spirits lightened as she entered the cheerful bustle of the front receiving room. West and the twins sat on the carpeted floor, unpacking hampers and boxes, while Kathleen opened correspondence at the writing desk in the corner.

"I always thought I didn't like courtship," West said, sorting through a hamper from Winterborne's. "But it turns out that I was merely on the wrong side of it. Courtship is one of those activities in which it's better to receive than give."

Weston Ravenel bore a close resemblance to his older brother, handsome and blue-eyed, with the same strapping build and air of disreputable charm. In the past few months, he had thrown himself into learning as much as possible about agriculture and dairying. The former rake was never happier than when he had spent a day in the company of tenants, working the land and coming home with muddy boots and breeches.

"Have you ever courted anyone, Cousin West?" Pandora asked.

"Only if I was certain the lady was too intelligent ever to accept me." West stood in an easy movement as he saw Helen come into the room.

"You don't wish to marry, then?" Helen asked lightly, taking a place on the unoccupied settee.

Smiling, West placed a flat blue satin box in her lap. "How could I ever be satisfied with only one sweet from the entire box?"

Helen lifted the lid, her eyes widening as she discovered a treasure trove of caramels, jelly creams, candied fruit, toffees and marshmallow drops, all wrapped in twists of waxed paper. Her wondering gaze traveled to the nearby mountain of accumulating delicacies . . . a smoked Wiltshire ham and collar bacon, a box of dry-cured salmon, pots of imported Danish butter, tinned sweetbreads, and a sack of fat glossed dates. There was a basket of hothouse fruits, wheels of Brie in papery white rinds, cunning little cheeses wrapped in netting, jars of rich fig paste, pickled quail eggs, bottles of jewel-colored fruit liqueur meant to be sipped from tiny glasses, and a gold-colored tin of cocoa essence.

"What can Mr. Winterborne be thinking?" she asked with a flustered laugh. "He's sent enough food for an army."

"Obviously he's courting the entire family," West told her. "I can't speak for everyone else, but I for one feel thoroughly wooed."

Kathleen's wistful voice came from the corner. "I could eat that entire ham by myself." In the past few days, she had begun to experience insatiable cravings one moment and incipient nausea the next.

West grinned. Rising to his feet, he brought a pressed-glass jar of almonds to her. "Will these do?"

Kathleen pried the lid open and ate one of the almonds. As she crunched it between her teeth, the sound could be heard across the room. Evidently finding them to her liking, she devoured several in rapid succession.

West looked both amused and mildly perturbed. "Not so fast, darling, you'll choke." He went to the sideboard to pour some water for her.

"I'm starving," Kathleen protested. "And these almonds are exactly what I've been craving, I just didn't know it until now. Did Mr. Winterborne send only one jar?"

"I'm sure he'll send more if I ask," Helen volunteered.

"Would he? Because—" Kathleen fell abruptly silent, her attention fixed on the letter in her hand.

Helen felt a creeping sensation along her spine, warning that something terrible had happened. She saw Kathleen's narrow shoulders hunch forward, as if she were trying to protect herself from something. Blindly Kathleen fumbled to set the jar on the desk, but placed it too close to the edge. The container crashed to the floor. Fortunately it landed on a bit of carpet, preventing the glass from shattering. Kathleen didn't even seem to notice, her attention fixed on the letter.

Helen hurried to her, reaching her just before West did. "What's wrong, dear?"

Kathleen's complexion had turned chalky, her breath shallow and fitful. "My father," she whispered. "I could only read the first part. I can't think." Helplessly she handed the letter to Helen.

The news couldn't be good. Approximately a month earlier, Kathleen's father, Lord Carbery had suffered an accident at his riding arena in Glengarriff, when his horse had reared and caused his head to hit the edge of a support beam. Although Carbery had survived the blow, his health had been poor ever since.

West gave the water glass to Kathleen, pressing both her small hands around it as if she were a child. "Drink this, sweetheart," he said quietly. His concerned gaze met Helen's. "I'll fetch Devon. He should be close by. He's meeting with the timberman about felling the oak on the east side."

"There's no need to interrupt him," Kathleen said, her voice strained but calm. "This can wait until he's finished. I'm perfectly fine." Unsteadily she lifted the glass to her lips and drained at least half of it in painful gulps.

Looking over her head at West, Helen told him soundlessly "*Go*," and he left with a short nod.

Helen returned her attention to the letter. "He passed away two days ago," she murmured, scanning the written lines. "The farm manager writes that Lord Carbery was troubled by headaches and seizures since the accident. He went to bed early one night and died in his sleep." She settled a gentle hand on Kathleen's shoulder, feeling the fine tremors of tightly leashed emotion. "I'm so sorry, dear."

"He was a stranger," Kathleen said quietly. "He sent me away to be raised by someone else. I don't know what I should feel for him."

"I understand."

Kathleen's cold fingers came to cover hers. "I know you do," she said with a faint, bleak smile.

They stayed like that for a quiet moment. Pandora and Cassandra approached hesitantly.

"Is there something we can do, Kathleen?" Pandora asked, kneeling by her chair.

Glancing into the girl's earnest face, Kathleen shook her head and reached out to draw her close. Cassandra knelt on the other side and embraced them both.

"There's no need to worry," Kathleen said. "I'll be all right. How could I not be, when I have the dearest sisters in the world?" Closing her eyes, she leaned her head against Pandora's. "We've been through a great deal together in a short time, haven't we?"

"Does this mean another year of mourning?" Pandora asked.

"Not for you," Kathleen reassured her, "only for me." She sighed. "Huge with child, and lumbering about dressed in black—I'll look like one of those hopper-barges loaded with refuse and sent out to sea."

"You're too small to be a barge," Cassandra said.

"You'll be a tugboat," Pandora added.

Kathleen let out a dry chuckle and kissed them both. Some of the color had returned to her cheeks. She stood from the chair and straightened her skirts with a few deft tugs. "There's much to do," she said. "The funeral will be in Ireland." She gave Helen a stricken glance. "I haven't been there since I was a child."

"You don't have to make decisions right now," Helen said. "Perhaps you should go upstairs and lie down."

"I can't, there are things I must—" Kathleen stopped as Devon entered the room.

His intent gaze swept over her, coming to rest on her bleached white face. "What is it, love?" he asked gently.

"My father's gone." She tried very hard to sound prosaic. "It's not a surprise, of course. We knew that he was in ill health."

"Yes." Devon came forward and took her rigid form against his, wrapping her in his arms.

"I'm perfectly calm," she said against his shoulder.

"Yes." Devon kissed her temple. His face was taut with concern, the blue eyes hazed with tenderness.

"I'm not going to cry." Her tone was matter-of-fact. "He certainly wouldn't have wanted my tears."

Devon smoothed her hair, his hand covering half her small head. "Give them to me, then," he said softly.

Kathleen hid her face in his shirtfront, her slight form seeming to wilt. In a few seconds, a low, broken keening sound began to emerge without stopping. Her husband laid his cheek on her head and cradled her closer against the solid reassurance of his body.

Realizing that they were all *de trop* in what had become a deeply private moment, Helen gestured for the twins to leave the room with her.

After closing the door, Helen suggested, "Let's go to the library and send for tea."

"I wish we'd brought the sweets with us," Pandora fretted.

"Helen, what's going to happen?" Cassandra asked as they walked through the entrance hall. "Will Kathleen really go to Ireland for the funeral?"

"I think she should, if possible," Helen said reflectively. "It's important to say good-bye."

"But her father won't know," Pandora pointed out.

"Not for his sake," Helen murmured, linking an arm with her younger sister's and patting her hand affectionately. "For hers."

Chapter 14

POST OFFICE TELEGRAM
MR. RHYS WINTERBORNE
CORK STREET LONDON

HAVE JUST LEARNED THAT MY WIFE'S FATHER LORD CARBERY IS DECEASED. ALTHOUGH CIRCUMSTANCES LESS THAN IDEAL YOUR PRESENCE WOULD BE GREATLY WELCOME IN HAMPSHIRE.

OBLIGED IF YOU WOULD SEND SALTED ALMONDS FOR LADY TRENEAR.

—TRENEAR

"Fernsby," Rhys said curtly, looking up from the telegram, "clear my schedule for the week and arrange for two tickets on the next train from London to Hampshire. Have someone run to Quincy and tell him to pack for me and himself. And tell a clerk at the food hall to pack all the salted almonds we have, in a bag to be hand-carried."

"All?"

"Every last jar."

As the secretary rushed out of the office with lunatic speed, Rhys lowered his forehead to the surface of his desk. "*Diolch i Dduw*," he muttered. *Thank God.*

If an invitation hadn't come soon, he would have had no choice but to storm Eversby Priory like an invading army. He was sorry for the death of Kathleen's father, but more than anything he was desperate to see Helen again. It had seemed impossible that Helen was beyond his reach when he wanted her so badly. All he'd been able to do was wait, which was the thing in life he had always been worst at.

Helen had sent three or four letters a week, telling him the latest news about the family and recent events in the village, the restoration work being done on the house, and the progress of the hematite ore quarry. She had sprinkled in descriptions of things like candle making, or harvesting the forced rhubarb they had grown in one of the glasshouses. Prim, cheerful, chatty letters.

He was mad with longing, sick with it.

His work, his store, had always absorbed his unlimited energy, but now it wasn't enough. He burned with desire, a constant fever beneath his skin. He wasn't sure if Helen was the illness or the cure.

As it turned out, the next train departed in three hours. Since there wasn't nearly enough time to have his private train car made ready, nor was there an immediately available locomotive to couple it with, Rhys was more than happy to go by regular train. By some miracle, the unflappable Quincy managed to pack their bags with such efficiency that they were able to reach the station in time. Had there been any lingering question in Rhys's mind about the merit of having a valet, it was forever silenced.

During the two-hour journey from London to Alton Station, Rhys found himself leaning forward in his seat as if to urge the toiling engine to a greater speed. At last the train stopped at Alton Station, and Rhys found a hired carriage to convey him and his valet to Eversby Priory.

The massive Jacobean manor house was in the process of being restored, and had been ever since Devon had inherited it. Richly ornamented with parapets, and arcade arches, and bristling with rows of elaborate chimneystacks, the Jacobean house surveyed its surroundings like a dignified dowager at a ball. The discovery of a hematite deposit on the estate had come none too soon—without a heavy infusion of capital, the manor would have fallen to ruins before the next generation could inherit.

Rhys and Quincy were greeted by the butler, Sims, who said something to the effect that they hadn't been expected quite so soon. Quincy agreed that their arrival had indeed been precipitate, and the two servants exchanged a quick glance of mutual commiseration over the difficulties posed by rash and demanding employers.

As Rhys prowled restlessly around the front receiving room, waiting for someone to appear, it occurred to him that his surroundings were deeply comfortable in a way that his modern house was not. He'd always preferred newness, associating old things with decay and dowdiness. But the faded charms of Eversby Priory were soothing and welcoming. It had something to do with the way the furniture was arranged in cozy groups on the flowered rug. Books and periodicals were stacked on small tables, and there were cushions and lap blankets everywhere. A pair of friendly black spaniels wandered in to sniff at his hand, and left at the sound of some distant noise in the house. Baked sweet smells wafted into the room, heralding the approach of afternoon tea.

He hadn't known what to make of the fact that he had been invited to Eversby Priory at a time of mourning. From what he knew of mourning rituals—which wasn't much, save for the merchandise he sold at his store—a recently bereaved family did not invite or accept visitors. Calls of condolence weren't encouraged until after the funeral.

However, Quincy, who was versed in such matters and had known the Ravenels for decades, had explained the significance of the invitation. "It would appear, sir, that Lord and Lady Trenear have decided to treat you as one of the family, even though you have not yet married Lady Helen." Turning away, he had added with a hint of disapproval, "This new generation of Ravenels is not always traditional."

Rhys's thoughts snapped back to the present as Devon entered the room.

"Good God, Winterborne." Devon looked bemused and a bit weary. "I only sent the telegram this morning." But he smiled in the old comfortable way, and reached out to shake Rhys's hand firmly. It seemed that their differences had been set aside.

"How is Lady Trenear?"

Devon hesitated, as if debating how much to admit. "Fragile," he finally said. "She's grieving not for the father she lost so much as the father she never had.

I've sent for Lady Berwick, who will arrive tomorrow from Leominster. Kathleen will find comfort in her presence—the Berwicks took her in after her own parents sent her away from Ireland."

"The funeral will be there?"

Devon nodded a slight frown. "Glengarriff. I'll have to take her. Needless to say, the timing is bloody inconvenient."

"Couldn't you find a suitable traveling companion for her?"

"Not in her condition. I need to be with her. She's having morning sickness, and is more at the mercy of her emotions than usual."

Rhys considered the logistics of the trip. "The fastest way is to go from Bristol to Waterford by steamer, and stay the night at the Granville—it's a fine hotel with a railway station close by. You could take a train to Glengarriff the next day. If you wish, I'll wire my office to make travel arrangements. They know the schedules of every ship and steam packet route going to and from England, as well as every railway station and halt in existence."

"I would be much obliged," Devon said.

Wordlessly Rhys picked the black leather Gladstone bag he'd carried inside, and gave it to him.

Lifting his brows, Devon unlatched the end catches,

pulled the top apart, and looked inside the bag. A slow grin crossed his face as he beheld two dozen glass jars of salted almonds packed among layers of tissue paper.

"I gather Lady Trenear has a fondness for them?" Rhys asked.

"Cravings," Devon said, his smile lingering. "Many thanks, Winterborne." Closing and latching the bag, he said affably, "Come to the library, we'll have a brandy."

Rhys hesitated. "Where is everyone?"

"West is at the quarry site and will return soon. The twins are out walking, and my wife is resting upstairs. Helen is most likely still out at the glasshouse with her orchids."

Knowing that Helen was nearby—alone, in the glasshouse—caused Rhys's heart to pound out a few extra beats. After a discreet, desperate glance at the mantel clock, he said, "Four o'clock is a bit early for brandy, aye?"

Devon gave him an incredulous look, followed by a low laugh. "My God. What kind of Welshman are you?" Before Rhys could reply, he continued, "Very well. I'm going to deliver this"—he hefted the bag in his hand—"to my wife. As repayment for your generosity, I'll deny all knowledge of your whereabouts for as long as possible. But if you and Helen are late for tea, it's on your head." He paused. "She's at the first glass-house past the walled garden."

Rhys gave him a short nod. He could feel himself bracing inwardly, a knot tightening at the pit of his stomach as he wondered how Helen would react to seeing him.

Devon's lips twitched. "No need to brood, Heathcliff. She'll be glad to see you."

Although the reference escaped Rhys—he was not one for novels—he was annoyed to realize that his rampaging nerves were obvious. Damning himself silently, he couldn't keep from asking, "Has she mentioned me?"

Devon's brows flew upward. "*Mentioned* you? You're all Helen talks about. She's been reading Welsh history books and plaguing the family with accounts of *Owain Glyndŵr* and something called the *Eistedfodd*." His eyes sparkled with friendly mockery. "Helen was hacking and spitting so much the other day that we thought she was coming down with a cold, until we realized she was practicing the Welsh alphabet."

Ordinarily Rhys would have made some sarcastic retort, but he'd barely noticed the gibe. His chest had gone tight with pleasure.

"She doesn't have to do that," he muttered.

"Helen wants to please you," Devon said. "It's her nature. Which leads to something I want to make clear: Helen is like a younger sister to me. And although I'm obviously the last man alive who should lecture anyone about propriety, I expect you to behave like an altar boy with her for the next few days."

Rhys gave him a surly glance. "I *was* an altar boy, and I can tell you that reports of their virtue are highly exaggerated."

With a reluctant grin, Devon turned and headed back toward the main hall.

Rhys went to find Helen. Since it wouldn't do to alarm her by running and leaping on her like a madman, he forced himself to walk at a measured pace. Exiting the back of the house through the conservatory, he crossed a section of neatly mown lawn.

A sinuous graveled path led past sweeps of winter-flowering shrubs, and ancient stone walls covered with climbing vines that twisted together like lace. The estate gardens were clean and spare, the frosted ground biding its time until spring came to soften it. A breeze scented of peat smoke and sedge reminded him of the vale where he had lived in early childhood until his family had moved to London. Not that Llanberris, with its stony ground and abundant tarns, was anything like these manicured surroundings. But there was a particular smell of a place with lakes and rain, and Hampshire had it.

As he approached the row of four glasshouses, he saw movement in the first one, a slim black-clad shape gliding past frosted panes. His heart jolted, and a flush heated his face despite the biting February air. He didn't know what he expected, or why he was as nervous as a lad with his first sweetheart. Not long ago, he would have scoffed at the suggestion that an unworldly young woman, a girl, could reduce him to this state.

He used one knuckle to rap gently on a glass pane. Carefully he ascended a stone step, let himself into the building, and closed the door.

Rhys had never been inside the glasshouse before. Helen had described it to him in detail while he had stayed at Eversby Priory, but he'd been encumbered by crutches and a leg cast. He had regretted not being able to walk out to see it, having understood how important it was to her.

The indoor climate was moist, warm, loamy. It seemed a world away from England, a glass palace filled with brilliant color and exotic shapes. He was greeted with the pungency of potting soil and dense greenery, and thin sharp orchid perfumes, and a pervasive smell of vanilla. His wondering gaze traveled over row upon row of tall plants, tables of orchids in pots and jars, orchid vines growing over the walls and curling upward toward a glittering glass firmament.

A slender figure emerged from behind an inflorescence of snow-white blooms. Helen's crystalline eyes caught the light, and her pretty lips rounded like a tea rose as she said his name in soundless bewilderment. She moved toward him, stumbling a little as she came around the table too fast. The hint of clumsiness, her obvious haste, electrified him. She had missed him. She had wanted him, too.

Reaching her in three swift strides, Rhys caught her up against him so tightly that her toes left the floor. Momentum turned them in a half-circle. Letting her back down, he dove his face into the warm fragrant skin of her neck and breathed her, absorbed her.

"*Cariad*," he said huskily, "that was the first time I've ever seen you move with less than swanlike grace."

She gave an unsteady laugh. "You surprised me." Her warm, delicate hands came to the cold sides of his face. "You're here," she said, as if trying to make herself believe it.

Breathing unevenly, Rhys nuzzled her, amazed by the silkiness of her skin and hair, the tenderness of her flesh. Something like elation, only stronger, was pouring into his veins, intoxicating him. "I could eat you," he muttered, pushing past her caressing hands to find her lips, feeling her mouth with his. Helen responded eagerly, her fingers sliding into his hair and shaping against his skull.

He murmured rough-soft endearments between kisses, while Helen clung to him. Her sweet little tongue stroked against his in the way he'd taught her, and the sensation shot down to his groin. Staggering slightly, he had to reach down to the edge of the table to steady himself. *Holy hell.* He had to stop now, or he wouldn't be able to stop at all. Taking his mouth from hers, he let out a shuddering sigh, and another, laboring to bring his desire under control. The muscles of his arms trembled as he forced them to loosen.

It didn't help that Helen was stringing flowerlike kisses along the taut line of his jaw, infusing fresh sensation into his blood. "I thought you might come tomorrow or the next day—"

"I couldn't wait," he said, and felt her cheek curve against his.

"This must be a dream."

Too full of heat to restrain himself, Rhys reached down and gripped her hips snugly against his. "Is this real enough for you, *cariad*?" A coarse gesture that no gentleman would have made. But Helen knew what to expect of him by now.

Her eyes widened as she felt the taut pressure of him

even through the layers of her skirts. But she didn't pull back. "You feel very . . . healthy," she said. "How is your shoulder?"

"Why don't you cut off my shirt and take a look?"

That drew a quick, throaty chuckle from her. "Not in the glasshouse." Lowering to her heels, she twisted to reach for one of the plants on the table beside them. After breaking off a small, perfect green orchid, she inserted it into the buttonhole of his left lapel.

"*Dendrobium*?" Rhys guessed, looking down at the flower.

"Yes, how did you know?" She felt for the tiny silk boutonniere latch underneath the lapel and tucked the end of the stem into it. "Have you been reading about orchids?"

"A bit." He ran a teasing fingertip down the length of her nose. It was impossible to stop touching her, playing with her. "Trenear said you've been studying Welsh history."

"I have. It's fascinating. Did you know that King Arthur was Welsh?"

Amused, Rhys stroked her hair, finding the intricate mass of pinned-up braids at the back. "If he existed, he would have been."

"He did exist," Helen said earnestly. "There's a

stone that bears his horse's footprint near a lake named *Llyn Barfog*. I want to see it someday."

His smile widened. "You pronounce that well, *cariad*. But the double L sounds more like *thl*. Let a breath of air slip around the sides of your tongue."

Helen repeated the sound a few times, not quite able to match his pronunciation. She was so adorable with the tip of her tongue fitted behind her front teeth that he couldn't help stealing another kiss, sucking briefly at the warm satin of her lips.

"You don't have to learn Welsh," he told her.

"I want to."

"A difficult language, it is. And in these times, there's no advantage to knowing it." Ruefully he added, "My mother always said, 'Avoid speaking in Welsh as you would sin.'"

"Why?"

"It was bad for business." Rhys let his hands coast slowly over her arms and back. "You know of the prejudice against my kind. People who believe the Welsh are morally backward, lazy . . . even unclean."

"Yes, but it's nonsense. Civilized people would never say such things."

"Not in public. But some say that, and worse, in the privacy of their own parlors." He frowned as he continued. "Some will think less of you for marrying me. They won't admit it to your face, but you'll see it in their eyes. Even when they smile."

It wasn't something they had discussed during their previous engagement—Rhys had been touchy about his social inferiority, and Helen hadn't been willing to risk offending him. He was relieved to finally be frank with her. But at the same time, the admission that it would lower her to marry him left a bitter taste in his mouth.

"I'll be a Winterborne," Helen said calmly. "They should worry about what I'll think of them."

That drew a grin from him. "So they shall. You'll be a woman of influence, with the means to accomplish whatever you like."

She touched his face, her fingers shaping to his cheek with gentle, thrilling pressure. "My first concern will be to keep my husband happy."

Rhys leaned over her, gripping the table on either side of her to make a living cage of his body. "You'll have your work cut out for you, wife," he warned softly.

Her silvery eyes searched his. Gently the tip of her thumb traced the edge of his lower lip. "Is it difficult for you to be happy, then?"

"Aye. It happens only when you're near." He seized her mouth ardently, sending his tongue deep, feeding pleasure into her until she was too dazed to refuse anything he wanted. His hand closed on her skirts, and for a fraction of a second, he was tempted to take what his tortured body clamored for, just have her right there. It would be easy to hoist her up to the table, lift her skirts, spread her legs—

Ending the kiss with a groan, he rested his forehead against hers. "I've been too long without you, *cariad*." He filled his lungs with air and exhaled slowly. "Say something to distract me."

Helen's face was very pink, her lips slightly puffy. "You mentioned your mother," she said. "When will I meet her?"

A dry chuckle escaped him—she couldn't have chosen a more effective way to dampen his ardor. "After I've put it off for as long as possible."

His mother, Bronwen Winterborne, was a stern, severe woman, lean and straight as a broomstick. Her wiry arms had delivered a wealth of punishments throughout his childhood, but Rhys couldn't remember a single time when they had encircled him with tenderness. Still, she had been a good mother, keeping him fed and clothed, teaching him the values of discipline and hard work. It had always been easy to admire her, but not nearly as easy to love her.

"Will she disapprove of me?" Helen asked.

Rhys tried to imagine what his mother would make

of this subtle, incandescent creature with a mind full of books and music in her fingers.

"She'll think you're too pretty. And too soft. She doesn't understand your kind of strength."

Helen looked pleased. "You think I'm strong?"

"I do," he said without hesitation. "You have a will like a steel blade." With a dark glance, he added, "Otherwise you couldn't manage me half so well."

"Manage you?" With adroit grace, Helen ducked beneath one of his arms and wandered to another table. "Is that what I was doing by giving in to your ultimatum and sleeping with you?"

The flirtatious reprimand caused his pulse to leap. Captivated and inflamed, he followed at her heels as she walked between rows of orchids. "Aye, and then leaving London after setting me to longing for you. Now you have me like a dog on a leash, begging for more."

Amusement curled through her voice. "I see no dog on a leash. Only a very large wolf."

Catching her from behind, Rhys lowered his mouth to the side of her neck. "Your wolf," he said gruffly, and grazed her skin with the edge of his teeth.

Helen arched a little, leaning back against him. He could feel the yearning in her, the way she shivered at his touch. "Shall I come to you tonight?" she whispered. "When it's dark and everyone's abed?"

The question turned his blood to fire. *God, yes. Please.* He was starved for sensation and release, for the feel of her beautiful soft flesh yielding to his. But most of all, his heart ached for the peaceful minutes afterward, when she would lie in his arms and belong only to him.

Closing his eyes, he pressed his jaw gently against her small ear. A half-minute passed before he could find his voice. "You've read the fairy tales. You know what happens to little girls who visit wolves."

Helen turned in his arms. "I do indeed," she whispered, and lifted her smiling lips to his.

Chapter 15

"Cousin Devon, won't you play?" Pandora entreated. "We need more people or the game won't last long enough." She was seated at the game table with Cassandra in the upstairs parlor, where everyone relaxed after dinner.

The twins had pulled out the only board game they possessed, called "The Mansion of Happiness." The old-fashioned game, a board printed with a spiral track of spaces representing virtues and vices, had been designed to teach values to children.

Devon shook his head with a lazy smile, pulling Kathleen into the crook of his shoulder as he sat with her on the settee. "I played the last time," he replied. "It's West's turn now."

Helen watched with amusement as West sent Devon

a deadly glance. Both Ravenel brothers detested the preachy and high-minded game, which the twins frequently coerced them into playing.

"It's a foregone conclusion that I'll lose," West protested. "I always end up in the House of Correction."

"All the more reason to play," Helen told him. "It will teach you moral behavior."

West rolled his eyes. "No one ever thinks their own behavior is immoral, only other people's." Bringing his snifter of cognac along with him, he went to take a seat at the table.

"We need a fourth," Pandora said. "Helen, if you would set aside the mending—"

"No, don't ask her," Cassandra protested, "she always wins."

"I'll join you," Rhys volunteered, tossing back the last swallow of his cognac and going to take the last chair at the game table. He grinned at West, in the way of fellow sufferers.

Helen was delighted by Rhys's newfound ease with her family. When he had visited the Ravenels in London, his manner had been controlled and cautious. Now, however, he was relaxed and charming, participating freely in the conversation.

"You've just become a drunkard," Pandora informed Rhys sternly when his playing piece landed on one of the vices. "Off to the whipping post you go, and stay there for the next two turns."

Helen smiled as Rhys tried to look suitably chastened.

Cassandra spun the little wooden teetotum and triumphantly advanced her piece to a space marked Sincerity.

Next came West's turn. His piece advanced to a space bearing the ominous label "Sabbath Breaker."

"It's three turns in the stocks for you," Cassandra told him.

"Clapped in the stocks, merely for breaking the Sabbath?" West asked indignantly.

"It's a severe game," Cassandra said. "It was invented at the turn of the century, and back then you could be put in the stocks or hanged even for stealing a piece of bacon."

"How do you know that?" Rhys asked.

"We have a book about it in the library," Pandora said. "*Crimes of Fallen Humanity.* It's all about terrible criminals and horrid gruesome punishments."

"We've read it at least three times," Cassandra added.

West regarded the twins with a frown before turning toward the settee and asking, "Should they be reading a book like that?"

"No, they should not," Kathleen said flatly. "I would have removed it, had I known it was there."

Pandora leaned toward Rhys and said conspiratorially, "She's too short to see the books above the sixth shelf. That's where we keep all the naughty ones."

West coughed in the effort to disguise a laugh, while Rhys stared down at the game board with sudden undue interest.

"Helen knows about it too," Pandora added.

Cassandra frowned at her. "Now you've done it. They'll take away all the interesting books."

Pandora shrugged. "We've read all of them anyway."

Rhys deftly changed the subject. "There's a newer version of this game," he commented, looking at the board. "An American company bought the rights, and they've revised it to make the punishments less harsh. My store carries it."

"By all means, let's purchase the less bloodthirsty version," West said. "Or better yet, let's teach poker to the twins."

"West," Devon warned, his eyes narrowing.

"Poker is positively wholesome compared to a game with more whippings than a novel by de Sade."

"*West*," Devon and Kathleen said at the same time.

"Mr. Winterborne," Pandora asked, her blue eyes

lively with interest, "where do these board games come from? Who invents them?"

"Anyone who designs one could contract a printer to make some copies."

"What if Cassandra and I make one?" she asked. "Could we sell it at your store?"

"I don't want to make a game," Cassandra protested. "I only want to play them."

Pandora ignored her, focusing intently on Rhys.

"Come up with a prototype," he told her, "and I'll take a look at it. If I think I can sell it, I'll be your backer and pay for the first printing. In return for a percentage of your profits, of course."

"What is the usual percentage?" Pandora asked. "Whatever it is, I'll give you half."

Raising one brow, Rhys asked, "Why only half?"

"Don't I deserve an in-law discount?" Pandora asked ingenuously.

Rhys laughed, looking so boyish that Helen felt her heart quicken. "Aye, you do."

"How will I know what games have already been done?" Pandora was becoming more enthusiastic by the minute. "I want mine to be different from everyone else's."

"I'll send you one of every board game we sell, so you can examine all of them."

"Thank you, that would be most helpful. In the meantime . . ." Pandora's fingers drummed the table in a pale blur. "I can't play any more tonight," she announced, standing up quickly, obliging West and Rhys to rise to their feet as well. "There's work to be done. Come with me, Cassandra."

"But I was winning," Cassandra grumbled, looking down at the game board. "Isn't it too late at night to begin something like this?"

"Not when one has a dire case of imagine-somnia." Pandora tugged her sister from the chair.

After the twins had left, Rhys glanced at Helen with a slight smile. "Has she always made up words?"

"For as long as I can remember," she replied. "She likes to try to express things like 'the sadness of a rainy afternoon' or 'the annoyance of finding a new hole in one's stocking.' But now she's trying to break herself of the habit, fearing that it might expose her to ridicule during the Season."

"It would," Kathleen said regretfully. "Vicious tongues are always wagging, and high-spirited girls like Pandora and Cassandra rarely have an easy time of it during the Season. Lady Berwick was forever scolding me for laughing too loudly in public."

Devon regarded his wife with a caressing gaze. "I would have found that charming."

She grinned at him. "Yes, but you never took part in the Season. You and West were elsewhere in London, doing whatever rakes do."

Rhys went to the sideboard to pour a cognac for himself. Glancing at Devon, he asked, "Will Lady Helen and the twins stay at the estate while you and Lady Trenear are in Ireland?"

"That would be for the best," Devon said. "We've asked Lady Berwick to chaperone them during our absence."

"It would raise eyebrows otherwise," Kathleen explained. "Even though we all know West is like a brother to Helen and the twins, he's still a bachelor with a wicked reputation."

"Which I worked hard to acquire, by God." West went to lounge in a chair by the hearth. "In fact, I insist on a chaperone: I can't have my bad name tarnished by the suggestion that I could be trusted around three innocent girls."

"Lady Berwick will be a good influence on the twins," Kathleen said. "She taught me and her two daughters, Dolly and Bettina, how to conduct ourselves in society, and that was no easy task."

"We'll depart for Ireland the day after tomorrow," Devon said with a slight frown. "God willing, we'll return soon."

West stretched his legs before the fire and laced his fingers across his midriff. "I suppose I'll have to postpone Tom Severin's visit. I invited him to come to Hampshire in two days' time, to view the progress on the groundwork for the quarry and railway tracks."

Rhys spoke in a flat tone that chilled Helen's nerves. "It would be best to keep Severin far away from me."

They all looked at him alertly. Rhys stood at the sideboard, his long-fingered hand cupped around the bowl of the cognac glass to warm the amber liquid. Swirling the cognac gently, he stared into its depths with eyes that had turned colder than Helen had ever seen them.

Devon was the first to speak. "What has Severin done now?"

"He's been trying to convince me to buy a block of property near King's Cross. But the owner's name wasn't listed on any of the documents. Not even the mortgages."

"How is that possible?" Devon asked.

"A private investment company holds it all in trust. I hired an investigator to find out what's behind all the elaborate legal papering. He uncovered a transfer agreement, already signed and notarized, that will take effect upon completion of the purchase. The entire price of the property will go to the last man on earth

I would ever willingly do business with. And Severin knows it."

Devon withdrew his arm from around Kathleen and leaned forward, his gaze lit with interest. "Mr. Vance?" he guessed.

Rhys responded with a single nod.

"Damn," Devon said quietly.

Perplexed, Helen looked from one man to the other.

"You know how Severin is," West said in the tense silence. "There's no malice in him. He probably decided that if you found out about it later, it would be water under the bridge."

Rhys's eyes flashed dangerously. "If the deal had gone through before I found out that the money would go to Vance, I'd have made certain that Severin's lifeless body was under the bridge. The friendship is over for good."

"Who is Mr. Vance?" Helen asked.

No one replied.

Warily Kathleen broke the silence. "He's Lord Berwick's nephew, actually. Since the Berwicks never had a son, Mr. Vance is the heir presumptive to the estate. When Lord Berwick passes away, everything will go to Mr. Vance, and Lady Berwick and her daughters will be dependent on his goodwill. So, they've always tried to be hospitable to him. I've met Mr. Vance on a few occasions."

"What is your opinion of him?" Devon asked.

Kathleen made a face. "A loathsome man. Petty, cruel, and self-important. Always in debt, but he believes himself to be a financial wizard of the age. In the past he tried more than once to borrow against his future inheritance. Lord Berwick was livid."

Helen glanced at Rhys, troubled by the bleakness of his expression. His friend's actions seemed to have cut deeply. "Are you certain," she asked hesitantly, "that Mr. Severin understood the extent of your dislike for Mr. Vance?"

"He understood," Rhys said shortly, and took a swallow of cognac.

"Then why did he do it?"

Rhys shook his head, remaining silent.

In a moment, Devon answered pensively. "Severin can be callous in pursuit of a goal. He has an extraordinary mind, it's no exaggeration to call him a genius. However, such ability often comes at the expense of—" He hesitated, searching for the right word.

"Decency?" West suggested dryly.

Looking rueful, Devon nodded. "When dealing with Severin, one must never forget that above all, he's an opportunist. His brain is so busy trying to engineer a certain outcome that he doesn't bother to consider anyone's feelings, including his own. That being said, there have been times when I've seen Severin go to great lengths to help other people. He's not all bad." He shrugged. "It seems a pity to give up the friendship entirely."

"I'd give up anyone or anything," Rhys retorted, "to make certain I never have any connection to Albion Vance."

Chapter 16

Helen lowered her head as if to concentrate on the mending in her lap. A sickening, strange, stomach-dropping feeling came over her. Somehow her hands continued the familiar task of sewing, jerkily stabbing the needle through the torn seam of a shirt. Panicked thoughts became ensnarled in her head, and she worked to pull them apart and make sense of them.

Albion was an uncommon name, but not entirely out of the ordinary. It could be a coincidence.

Please, God, please let it be a coincidence.

Oh that look on Rhys's face. The kind of hatred a man would take to his grave.

Anxiety seethed inside her, making it the effort to remain outwardly calm excruciating. She had to leave the room. She had to go somewhere private, and take a few deep breaths . . . and she had to find Quincy.

He had come to the estate with Rhys. Quincy knew more of her family's secrets than anyone. She would insist that he tell her the truth.

While the conversation continued, Helen tied off the thread of her mending and slowly reached into the sewing box near her foot. She felt for the pair of tiny sewing scissors in the top compartment, and nudged the wickedly sharp blades apart. Deliberately she ran the side of her forefinger against the blade until she felt a pinching sensation and a hot sting. Drawing her hand back quickly, she glanced with feigned dismay at the drop of bright red blood welling from the cut.

Rhys noticed immediately. He made a Welsh sound of disgruntlement, a flick of breath pushed between the edge of teeth and lower lip. "*Wfft.*" Tugging a handkerchief from inside his coat, he came to her in a few strides. Wordlessly he sank to his haunches in front of her and clamped the folded cloth around her finger.

"I should have looked before reaching for the scissors," Helen said sheepishly.

His eyes had lost that chilling hardness and were now filled with concern. Carefully, he lifted the handkerchief to look at the cut on her finger. "It's not deep. But you need a plaster."

Kathleen spoke from the settee. "Shall I ring for Mrs. Church, dear?"

"I'd rather go to her room," Helen said lightly. "It will be easier there, with all her supplies at hand."

Rhys rose to his feet, pulling Helen up with him. "I'll go with you."

"No, do stay," Helen said quickly, holding the handkerchief around her finger. "You haven't finished your cognac." She stepped back from him. Avoiding his searching gaze, she sent a quick smile to the room in general. "The hour is late," she said. "It's time for me to retire. Good night, everyone."

After the family responded in kind, Helen left the parlor with measured steps, fighting the urge to break into a run. She continued down the grand staircase, crossed through the main hall, and descended the servants' stairs. In contrast to the quiet emptiness of the first floor, belowstairs bustled with activity. The servants had finished their dinner and were clearing away dishes and flatware, while the cook supervised advance preparations for the next day's meals.

A burst of laughter came from the servants' hall. Inching closer to the doorway, Helen saw Quincy sitting at the long table with a group of footmen and maids. He appeared to be regaling them with stories of his new life in London. Quincy had always been a well-liked member of the staff, and he had surely been missed since he had been hired away by Rhys.

As Helen wondered how she might attract his attention without causing a scene, she heard the housekeeper's voice behind her.

"Lady Helen?"

She turned to face Mrs. Church, whose plump face was trestled with concern.

"What brings you belowstairs, my lady? You have only to ring, and I'll send someone up to you."

With a rueful smile, Helen held up her injured finger. "A slight mishap with the sewing scissors," she explained. "I thought it best to come to you directly."

Mrs. Church clucked over the little wound, and led her to the housekeeper's room, just two doors away. It served as both a sitting room and a place where Mrs. Church conducted the business of household management. From the earliest time Helen could remember, Mrs. Church had kept a large medicine chest there. Whenever Theo, Helen, or the twins had injured themselves or had felt ill, they had gone to the housekeeper's room to be bandaged, dosed, and comforted.

Sitting at the small table, Helen remarked, "Everyone seems merry tonight."

Mrs. Church opened the medicine chest. "Yes, they're fair tickled to have Quincy back for a visit.

They've asked a thousand questions, mostly about the department store. Quincy brought a catalog for everyone to marvel over. None of us can imagine so many goods to be found under one roof."

"Winterborne's is very grand," Helen said. "Like a palace."

"So Quincy says." After dabbing tincture of benzoin onto the cut, Mrs. Church cut a small strip from a piece of white sarcenet imbued with isinglass, and moistened it with lavender water solution. Deftly she wrapped the plaster around Helen's finger. "Quincy seems to have been invigorated by working for your Mr. Winterborne. I haven't seen him so spry in years."

"I'm glad to hear it. As a matter of fact . . ." Helen tried to make her tone casual. ". . . I would like to speak privately with Quincy, if you would bring him here."

"Now?"

Helen replied with a single nod.

"Of course, my lady." An unaccountable pause followed. "Is something wrong?"

"Yes," Helen said quietly. "I think so."

Mrs. Church stood, frowning. "Shall I bring some tea?"

Helen shook her head.

"I'll fetch Quincy straightaway."

In less than two minutes, there was a tap at the

door, and Quincy's short, stocky figure entered the housekeeper's room. "Lady Helen," he said, his blackcurrant eyes smiling beneath the heavy white swags of his eyebrows.

It was a relief to see him. In the absence of any affection or interest from her father or Theo, Quincy had been the only kind male presence in Helen's life. As a child, she had gone to him whenever she was in trouble. He had always helped her without hesitation, such as the time she had accidentally torn an entry in the *Encyclopædia Britannica* and he had removed the entire page with a razor blade, assuring her that the family would be no worse off for being deprived of the history of Croatian astronomy. Or the time she had knocked over a porcelain figurine, and Quincy had glued the head back on so precisely that no one had ever detected it.

Helen gave him her hand. "I'm sorry to have interrupted your evening."

"Not an interruption," Quincy said, pressing her palm warmly, "but a pleasure, as always."

Gesturing to the other chair at the table, Helen said, "Please join me."

The valet remained standing, his eyes crinkling at the corners. "You know that would not be fitting."

Helen nodded slightly, her smile turning strained.

"Yes, but this isn't an ordinary conversation. I'm afraid—" She paused, the words jamming inside, refusing to emerge. As she tried again, all she could seem to do was repeat numbly, "I'm afraid."

Quincy stood before her, his expression patient and encouraging.

"I have something important to ask," Helen finally managed to say. "I need you to tell me the truth." To her annoyance, raw salt tears collected in the corners of her eyes. "I think I already know the answer," she said. "But it would help if you would tell me—" She stopped as she saw the way his face had changed.

Quincy's shoulders were sinking as if from the weight of a terrible burden. "Perhaps," he ventured, "you shouldn't ask."

"I have to. Oh, Quincy . . ." Helen's temples throbbed as she fixed her gaze on him. "Is Albion Vance my father?"

Slowly the valet reached for the empty chair, repositioned it, and sat heavily. Folding his hands into a compact bale of fingers, he rested them on the table. He focused on the lone casement window on the outside wall. "Where did you hear such a thing?"

"I found an unfinished letter that my mother had written to him."

Quincy was silent. His gaze was distant, as if he were

staring all the way to the farthest edge of the world. "I wish you had not."

"So do I. Please tell me, Quincy . . . is he my father?"

His attention returned to Helen. "Yes."

She flinched. "Do I look like him?" she whispered.

"You look like neither of them," he said gently. "You resemble only yourself. A unique and lovely creation."

"Rabbit-faced," Helen said, and could have bitten her tongue at the self-pitying remark. With chagrin, she explained, "She wrote that too."

"Your mother was a complicated woman. Competitive with every female in the world, including her own daughters."

"Did she ever love my father?"

"Until her last day of life," he surprised her by saying.

Helen gave him a skeptical glance. "But she and Mr. Vance . . ."

"He was not her only indiscretion. Nor was the earl always faithful to her. But your parents cared for each other in their own fashion. After your mother's liaison with Mr. Vance had ended, and you were born, your parents resumed their relationship." After removing his spectacles, he fished in his coat for a handkerchief and cleaned the lenses meticulously. "You were the sacrifice. You were kept upstairs in the nursery, out of sight and out of mind."

"What about Mr. Vance? Did he love my mother?"

"No man can see inside another's heart. But I don't believe he is capable of that particular emotion." He replaced his spectacles. "It would be best to pretend that you never learned about this."

"I can't," Helen said, digging her elbows into the table and pressing the sockets of her eyes into her palms. "Mr. Winterborne hates him."

Quincy's tone was uncharacteristically dry. "There isn't a Welshman who doesn't."

Helen lowered her hands and looked at him. "What has he done?"

"Mr. Vance's loathing of the Welsh is well-known. He wrote a pamphlet that is widely quoted by those who seek to eradicate the use of Welsh language in schools. He believes their children should be forced to speak only English." He paused. "But in addition to that, Mr. Winterborne has a personal grudge against him. I don't know what it is, only that it is so vile, he won't speak of it. The subject is dangerous and best left alone."

Helen gave him a bewildered glance. "You're suggesting that I keep this from Mr. Winterborne?"

"You must never say a word to him, or to anyone."

"But he'll find out someday."

"If he does, you can deny knowledge of it."

Helen shook her head in dazed misery. "I couldn't lie to him."

"There are rare times in life when a lie serves the greater good. This is one of them."

"But Mr. Vance may approach Mr. Winterborne someday and tell him. Or he may even approach me." Distraught, she rubbed the corners of her eyes. "Oh God."

"If he does," the valet replied, "you will pretend to be astonished. No one will know that you were the wiser."

"*I'll* know. Quincy, I must tell Mr. Winterborne."

"Don't. For his sake. He needs you, my lady. In the short time I have known him, he has changed for the better because of you. If you care for him, don't force him to make a choice that will hurt him beyond healing."

Her eyes widened. "A choice? Then you believe he would end the engagement if he knew?"

"It would be unlikely. But not impossible."

Helen shook her head slightly. She couldn't fathom it. Not after the things Rhys had said and done, the way he'd held and kissed her that very afternoon. "He wouldn't."

Quincy's eyes glimmered with some strong emotion. "Lady Helen, forgive me for speaking freely. But
I've known you since you were an infant in the cradle.
I always thought it a great injustice, and a pity, that an
innocent child was so scorned and neglected. You were
blamed by both of your parents, God rest their souls,
for sins that were theirs, not yours. Why should you
continue to pay the price? Why shouldn't you allow
yourself to be cherished as you have always deserved?"

"I want to. But first I must tell Mr. Winterborne the
truth about who I am."

Quincy paused, looking troubled. "Mr. Winterborne is a good master. Demanding, but fair and generous. He looks after his people, and treats them with
respect, down to the lowest scullery maid. But there
are limits. Last week, Mr. Winterborne saw one of
his footmen, Peter, cuff a beggar boy that had run up
to him on the street. He blistered Peter's ears with a
shaming lecture, and dismissed him on the spot. The
poor footman apologized and begged for forgiveness,
but Mr. Winterborne wouldn't relent. Some of the
other servants and I tried to approach him on Peter's
behalf, and he threatened to dismiss us if we dared to
say another word. He said there were some mistakes he
could not forgive." He was silent for a moment. "With
Mr. Winterborne, there is a line never to be crossed. If

someone does, he cuts them out completely, and never looks back."

"He wouldn't do that to his wife," Helen protested.

"I agree." Quincy looked away before adding with difficulty, "But, you're not his wife yet."

Stunned, Helen wondered if he was right, if it was truly that dangerous to tell Rhys about her father.

"Mr. Winterborne is not an ordinary man, my lady. He fears nothing, and answers to no one. He's above scandal, and in some ways he's even above the law. I daresay he conducts himself better than most would, in his position. But he can be unpredictable. If you want to marry Mr. Winterborne, my lady, you must keep your silence."

Chapter 17

The distant chimes of a clock drifted through the house as Helen slipped from her room and navigated the shadows of the upstairs hallway. Rhys had been lodged in a guest room in the east wing, for which she was thankful. They would need privacy for the conversation they were about to have.

She was as afraid as she had ever been about anything. Her heart pounded so hard that it felt as if something were striking her chest from the outside. She didn't know Rhys well enough to be certain how he would react when she told him. Whatever he might feel for her, it was founded on some ideal of perfection, of an aristocratic wife on a pedestal. The news she was about to tell him wasn't a step down from the pedestal—it was a leap off a cliff.

The problem was not with something she had done. The problem was with *who she was,* and there was no solution for that. Would Rhys ever be able to look at her without seeing shades of Albion Vance? She had spent most of her life with people who were supposed to love her, and hadn't. She couldn't endure spending the rest of it with a husband who would do the same.

By the time Helen reached the east wing, she was desperately cold despite the wool lining of her dressing gown and the thickness of her embroidered slippers. Shivering, she approached Rhys's door and knocked tentatively.

Her stomach lurched as she was confronted with Rhys's huge dark form, silhouetted against the glow of the hearth and a small bedside lamp. He was dressed only in a robe, his chest and feet bare. Reaching an arm around her waist, he drew her past the threshold, closed the door, and locked it decisively.

As Rhys pulled her against him, Helen pressed her cheek against the exposed part of his chest.

Feeling the way she trembled, he cuddled her closer. "You're nervous, *cariad.*"

She nodded against his chest.

One of his hands gently cupped the side of her face. "Are you afraid that I'll hurt you?"

She understood that he was referring to the physical joining that had left her sore after their first time. What she feared, of course, was a far different kind of pain. Licking her dry lips, she forced herself to reply. "Yes. But not in the way you—"

"No, no," he soothed, "it will be different this time." He bent his head and hugged her as if he were trying to surround her with himself. "Your pleasure means more to me than anything in life." One of his hands slid low on her hips to the beginning curve of her bottom. His hand traveled to her front, gently pressing her stomach before sliding to the place between her thighs.

The teasing stroke sent a thrill of sensation through her, and her legs quaked until she could hardly stand. She took a breath to speak, but it stuck in her throat as a half-sob. Swallowing it back, she said unsteadily, "It's not that, it's . . . I'm afraid because I think . . . I might lose you."

"Lose me?" Rhys looked down at her keenly, and her gaze fell from his. After a moment, she heard him ask, "Why would you worry about that?"

Now was the time to tell him. She tried to blurt it out—*Albion Vance is my father*—but she couldn't make herself do it. Her mouth refused to shape the words. All she could do was stand there and shiver like a treble wire of a piano, fine vibrations of cowardice singing through her.

"I don't know," she finally said.

As she kept her face averted, continuing to tremble, Rhys bent to nudge a kiss against her cheek. "Ah you've made yourself upset," he exclaimed quietly, and scooped her up with an ease that stole her breath away.

He was so strong, the heavy muscles of his chest and arms capable of crushing her. But he was gentle, careful, carrying her to an upholstered chair near the hearth and sitting with her sideways in his lap. Removing one of her slippers, he grasped her ice-cold foot in his big, warm hand and began to knead it slowly. His thumb rubbed into her arch, easing soreness she hadn't even been aware of. She bit back a quiet moan as he proceeded to massage every vulnerable place on her sole. Gently he squeezed each of her toes between his thumb and forefinger, and made small, firm circles on the ball of her foot. In a while he reached for her other foot, rubbing and pressing patiently until she had relaxed in his lap, her head resting against his heartbeat. Her breathing slowed as a kind of trance came over her, a drowsing-awake feeling.

Outside the windows, the winter wind raced over the close-grazed downs, causing tree limbs and branches to sway like unbolted gates. Creaks and settling noises came from the house's bones as the night deepened.

Rhys cradled her comfortably while they listened

to the crackling of the seasoned oak on the hearth and watched sparks dance and rise. No one had ever held Helen so close, for so long.

"Why do old houses creak so much?" he asked idly, playing with her braid and drawing the silky end across his cheek.

"When all the warmth fades at night, it makes the old boards contract and slip against each other."

"A bloody massive house, it is. And you were left to your own devices in this place for too long. I didn't understand before, how alone you were."

"I had the twins for company. I watched over them."

"But there was no one to watch over you."

A sense of uneasiness came over her, as it always did whenever she reflected on her childhood. It had seemed as if her very survival had depended on never complaining or drawing attention to herself. "Oh I—I didn't need that."

"All little girls need to feel safe and wanted." He stroked back the fine loose locks around her face, his fingertips gently following the changing patterns of firelight against her hair. "When you grow up without something, the lack of it is always with you. Even when you finally have it."

Helen looked up at him in wonder. "Do you ever feel that way?"

His smile turned self-mocking. "My fortune is so large, *cariad*, that the numbers would frighten any reasonable man. But something inside me always insists that every last shilling could disappear tomorrow." His hand charted the shape of her hip and followed the line of her thigh. Clasping her knee, he stared into her wide eyes. "When we were in London, you told me that your world was very small. Well, my world is very large. And you're the most important person in it. You're safe and wanted now, Helen. In time, you'll become used to that, and you won't worry." As she turned her face against his chest, he lowered his mouth to her ear. "We're bound to each other," he whispered, "for as long as the world exists. Remember?"

Helen rubbed her cheek against his velvet robe. "We haven't made our vows yet."

"We did that afternoon, when you came to my bed. That's what it meant." His fingers slid beneath her chin, coaxing her to look at him. Amusement deepened the faint whisks at the outer corners of his eyes. "I'm sorry, sweetheart, but there's no getting rid of me."

Desperately she stared at the face above hers, all strong, stark angles and shadows, a striking framework for those compelling sable eyes. Rhys hid nothing, letting her see the tenderness that was reserved for her alone. She felt the overwhelming pull between them, like the force of gravity between twin stars.

Rhys adjusted her higher on his chest, his powerful body flexing beneath her. Her breasts felt hot and full, and she turned to press them against him. Dizzy with guilt and longing, she linked her arms around his neck. She wanted more of him, his skin, his taste, his body inside hers.

Tell him, her tortured conscience screamed. *Tell him!*

Instead, she heard herself whisper, "I want to go to bed now."

Beneath her weight, where she rested on him intimately, she felt a thickening pressure.

His brows lifted in subtle teasing. "Alone?"

"With you."

Chapter 18

Rhys didn't understand why Helen seemed especially vulnerable tonight, at the mercy of some private anxiety she wouldn't explain. She always held something in reserve, an edge or two of her soul turned inward. The mystery of her, the hint of elusiveness, fascinated him. God help him, he had never wanted to be inside another human being the way he did her.

He carried her to the bed and deposited her on the mattress.

With a decisiveness that caught him off guard, Helen reached for the belt of his robe and untied it. The garment listed open, revealing his aroused body . . . and then her cool fingers settled on him. His mouth went dry, and his flesh throbbed viciously as she explored the shape and texture of his aroused flesh.

Shrugging out of his robe, he stood with his hands suspended in midair, not quite sure where to put them. Never in his wildest dreams would he have imagined that Helen would do such a thing of her own accord. It inflamed him further to see how ladylike she was about it, her pretty hands touching him with the same lightness she used on her piano keys or to hold a porcelain teacup.

Noticing the way he jumped and caught his breath as she reached the head of his erection, Helen asked in an abashed voice, "It's more sensitive here?"

Unable to muster a coherent word, Rhys nodded with a gruff sound.

Slowly she caressed the shaft with the flat of her palm. He saw the luminous blue glow of the moonstone ring, the symbol of his claim on her, as her fingers glided to the swaying weight of him below. She cupped him so gently, as if she were handling something dangerously volatile. Which she was. His body was nothing but a container brimming with lust, ready to explode. The primitive part of his brain took obscene satisfaction in the lurid sight of her, a fair-haired nymph, sweetly caressing his cock. The contrast of grace and crudeness appealed to him on the most primitive level.

Taking hold of him at the base, she made a delicate cuff of her fingers and slid them upward. Her thumb touched the exposed tip and made a mild circling stroke, and for a few seconds he couldn't see past the shower of sparks over his vision. A heavy pulse began deep in his pelvis, warning that he was only seconds from climax. With a groan, he tried to push her hands away. "No more . . . no . . . sweetheart . . ."

But she only leaned closer, her breath flowing gently against him. She kissed him, her lips lingering on the moist tip. A shock of response nearly unmanned him. Panting, he pulled away and lowered to the bed on his stomach, feverishly willing the sensation to die down. His chest heaved as he pulled in huge draughts of air.

"Helen," he muttered, gripping savage handfuls of the bedclothes. "My God, Helen."

There were movements beside him, her slight weight depressing the mattress. "Did you like that?" she asked cautiously.

His sound of vigorous assent was buried in the sheets.

"Oh good." She sounded relieved. In a moment, he felt her climbing over him. She had removed her nightgown, and was draping her naked body all along his, catlike. He tensed, smoldering at the enticing weight of her. Silky female skin . . . the curves of her breasts . . . the little fluff of curls teasing his backside . . .

"I talked with Kathleen," she said, her breath causing the hair at his nape to prickle and lift. "She explained a few things about the marital relationship that she thought I should know." As he flexed and shivered beneath her, she wriggled to conform more closely to the masculine terrain of his body.

"Helen. Hold still."

She stopped moving at once. "Is it uncomfortable when I lie on you like this?"

"No, it's just that I'm trying not to spend."

"Oh." Helen pressed her cheek against his nape. "Some men can more than once," she said helpfully.

In spite of his raging arousal, Rhys found himself burying a grin against the mattress. "You're so well-informed, *cariad*."

"I want to learn everything a mistress would know, so that I can satisfy you."

Carefully he rolled to his side, letting her slide off his back before he moved over her. His hands clasped her head, her silvery-gold hair spilling between his fingers.

"My own," he said, "don't ever worry about that. Everything about you is a delight to me."

Her gaze turned wary. "I'm sure you'll discover things you won't like."

"I hope so. If you had no flaws, mine would throw us off-balance."

"I'll balance yours," she assured him with a touch of irony he'd never heard from her before.

"If by that you mean your shyness," Rhys said, "you'll learn to overcome it." He nudged his hips against hers. "Just look at the progress you've made with me."

Helen laughed, turning pink up to her hairline. One of her hands drew along his flank and slipped cautiously between their bodies. "What's the word for this?" she asked, taking hold of him again. "What do you call it?"

"Your sister-in-law didn't include that in her lecture?"

"She told me some of the English words," Helen admitted, "but I want to know what it's called in Welsh."

"Is this how you mean to begin learning Welsh?" he asked in mock disapproval. "With profanity?"

"Yes."

Rhys smiled and kissed her. "Mind you, most Welsh love-talk sounds like a farming manual. The word for a man's part is *goesyn*. Stalk."

She repeated the syllables, her fingers gripping and stroking him with maddening gentleness.

"When the man thrusts inside the woman," he said, breathing with increasing difficulty, "the word is *dyrnu*. To thresh." He began to kiss his way down her body, savoring her warm skin with its faint dusting of talcum. After blowing lightly against the protective curls of her sex, he murmured, "This is a *ffwrch*. A furrow to be plowed." He leaned close enough for her to feel the tip of his tongue as he drew it along the innocently closed seam. Her thighs trembled on either side of him. "And the word for this"—he paused to search deeper, finding the shy bud still hidden beneath its hood—"is *chrib*, a bit of honeycomb." He delved again, tickling the little peak to wakefulness until it was hot and distinct against the tip of his tongue.

Slowly he continued to lick and tease her, while she squirmed beneath him. He was lost in her, aware of nothing outside this room, this bed. How finely made she was, her skin pearly, the palms of her hands and the soles of her feet as soft as a kitten's paws. She was sensitive everywhere, her toes spreading reflexively as he kissed the arch of her foot, her leg jerking when his tongue slipped behind her knee.

Rising back over her, he braced his weight carefully, settling his shaft against that exquisite channel and letting her feel what he was about to give her. She looked disoriented, flushed, a pulse visible in her neck.

"Do you want me, Helen?"

"Yes. Yes."

Afraid of hurting her by thrusting too hard, he pinned her writhing hips and whispered that she had to keep still, he needed to enter her slowly. Her flesh was wet but tight, refusing to yield easily. She locked her arms around his neck, gasping, making soft noises as he pushed up inside her, working in short thrusts, sliding deeper each time. He kissed her lips, her throat. His brain flooded with thoughts of the other time they'd been together and how he'd caused her pain, and how much he wanted it to be good for her now.

After he had slid forward the last inch, he paused to stare down at her in wonder. Her skin was misted and gleaming, her eyes shimmering. She was like something wrought of myth and make-believe, some lovely lost angel who had fallen into his arms. He sank deeper into the tender cradle of her hips and thighs, luxuriating in the feel of her trembling body beneath his, the air settling like cool silk against his sweating back. His mouth skimmed over the slope of her breast, his ears thrilling to her low-throated moan. Playing with her breasts, he shaped the firm curves with his hands, lifting them as he teased and nibbled at the peaks.

"When I push against you, *cariad,*" he said huskily, sliding a hand beneath her bottom, "lift your hips like this." He pulled her up into his slow thrust. Taking his time, he drew back and drove forward again, and she hitched against him in a bashful movement that sent a rush of white fire through him. He fought to find his breath. "Aye, just like that—my good girl, my—Ah, God, you'll kill me—"

He felt Helen bracing her feet for leverage, rolling her hips upward as he sank into her. It seemed as if they were doing something other than fucking, this was so new, so unbelievably raw and sweet. He'd never been so hard, so wild with need. He could feel pleasure leaking from him as he rode her steadily, the crisis racing forward with irresistible momentum.

But he didn't want it to end yet. Gritting his teeth, he managed to stop. She whimpered, writhing beneath him.

"Wait," Rhys said.

"I can't—"

"I want you to."

"Oh please—"

"Now in a minute." He weighted her so that she couldn't move.

"That means never," she protested, and he laughed unsteadily.

When his desire was back under control, he began again, building the rhythm gradually, while the voltage of lightning gathered in his spine. He stopped every few minutes, holding himself deep inside her, letting his desire subside until he could continue thrusting. Her moans became louder, her movements more demanding. He saw the moment when she lost control, her eyes closing, her face deeply flushed.

Hooking his arms beneath her knees, he pushed her legs back, her hips up until her feet dangled and swayed, and he entered her more deeply. She was fully open to him now, her body working him, clamping sweetly. Sharp cries pushed between her clenched teeth, and he bent to seal his mouth over hers, forcing it open, licking at the sounds she made. She shuddered as her climax began, and that was all he could endure, the lightning releasing and shooting to the top of his skull. He pumped into her, yielding every drop of his essence as she pulled it from him in endless shocks.

Dazed by the force of his release, he let down her legs and hung over her, panting. Her arms tightened around his midriff, compelling him to lower over her until they were flattened together like the pages of a book. He wanted to stay that way, fused and clasped and caressed inside her, for the rest of his days. Instead, using the last flicker of his strength, he collapsed to his side and slid free of her.

After a while, Helen left the bed wordlessly, returning with a cloth she had dampened at the washstand in the corner. As she began to wipe it gently over his groin, he rolled to his back and linked his hands behind his head, enjoying the sight of her performing the intimate service for him.

"No one has ever given me such pleasure, *cariad*."

She paused to send him a sideways smile. After finishing her ministrations, she set aside the cloth, turned down the lamp, and climbed back into bed. He pulled the covers over them both and settled her in the crook of his shoulder.

Helen snuggled against him. "Have you been with many women?" she dared to ask.

Rhys slid his hand over the supple line of her back, considering his answer. How much was a man supposed to tell his wife—future wife—about the women he'd known before her?

"Does it matter?" he countered.

"No. But I'm curious about how many mistresses you've had."

"The store has always been my most demanding mistress."

She pressed her lips against his shoulder. "You must hate being away from it."

"Not half as much as I hate being away from you."

Her kiss spread into a smile. "You still haven't answered my question."

"If you mean the traditional arrangement—setting a

woman up in her own house, paying her bills—I've had only one mistress. It lasted a year." After a pause, he said frankly, "It's an odd bargain to make, it is. Paying for a woman's company out of bed as well as in it."

"Why did you do it?"

He shrugged uncomfortably. "Other men of my position kept mistresses. A business associate introduced her to me after her previous arrangement had ended. She needed a new protector, and I found her attractive."

"Did you come to care for her?"

Rhys wasn't accustomed to reflecting on his past, or discussing his feelings about it. He couldn't fathom what good could come of airing his weaknesses to her. But faced with her questioning silence, he continued reluctantly. "I never knew if her affection was real, or if it was included on the bill of sale. I don't think she knew, either."

"Did you want her to feel affection for you?"

He shook his head at once. Her hand smoothed over his chest and stomach, and the moment was so peaceful that he found himself telling her more than he'd intended. "I've had lovers, from time to time. Women who didn't want to be kept, and sometimes liked a bit o' rough."

"A bit of rough?" Helen repeated quizzically.

"A lower-class sort," he explained. "A rowdy in bed."

Her hand paused on his chest. "But you're gentle."

Rhys was torn between amusement and shame as his mind recollected some of the more lurid episodes of his past. "I'm glad you think so, *cariad*."

"And you're not lower-class." She began to trace invisible patterns on his torso again.

"The devil knows I'm not from the upper," he said wryly. "'Codfish aristocracy' is what they call us. Men who've made a fortune in business, but are common-born."

"Why codfish?"

"It used to refer to the rich merchants who settled the American colonies and made their money in the cod trade. Now it means any successful businessman."

"*Nouveau riche* is another term," Helen said. "It's never used as a compliment, of course. But it should be. Being self-made is something to be admired." As she felt his soundless chuckle, she insisted, "It is."

Rhys turned his head to kiss her. "You've no need to flatter my vanity."

"I'm not flattering you. I think you're remarkable."

Whether she really felt that way, or was merely playing the role of loyal spouse, her words smoothed over the rough-hewn, ragged places of his soul like some healing balm. God, he needed this, had always needed it. Her sleek young body pressed against his as she drew her hands over him tentatively. He lay still and let her explore him, satisfying her curiosity.

"Was there ever a woman you thought of marrying?" she asked.

Rhys hesitated, unwilling to have his past probed and exposed. But she was underneath his armor now. "There was a girl I fancied," he admitted.

"What was her name?"

"Peggy Gilmore. Her father was a furniture-maker who supplied my store." His mind sifted through unwanted memories, pulling out ghostly images, words, shades of feeling. "A pretty girl with green eyes. I didn't court her—it never went that far."

"Why not?"

"I knew that a good friend of mine, Ioan, was in love with her."

Helen draped herself along his side, a slender leg hitching over one of his. "That's a Welsh name, isn't it?"

"Aye. Ioan's family, the Crewes, lived on High Street, not far from my father's shop. They made and sold fishing tackle. There was a giant stuffed salmon in the window." He smiled slightly, remembering his fascination with the shop's displays of taxidermied fish and reptiles. "Mr. Crewe talked my parents into letting me take penmanship lessons with Ioan two afternoons a week. He convinced them that it would help their business to have someone who could write a good legible hand. Years later, when I began to expand my store, I hired Ioan as the merchandise controller. A fine, honest man, he was, good as gold. I couldn't blame Peggy for preferring him to me—I'd never have loved her the way he did."

"Did they marry? Does he still work at the store?"

A dark feeling came over Rhys, as it always did when he thought about Ioan. He regretted having mentioned him, or Peggy—he didn't want to let the past intrude on his time with Helen. "Let's talk no more of it, *cariad*—it's not a pretty story, and the telling of it brings out the worst in me."

But Helen was intent on prying the information from him. "Did you have a falling-out?"

Rhys was irritably silent, responding with a single shake of his head. He thought Helen would retreat then. But he felt her lips press against his cheek, while one of her hands slid into his hair and lay lightly against his skull. The silent consolation, so unexpected, undermined him completely.

Baffled by his inability to withhold anything from her, he let out a sigh. "Ioan's been dead these four years past."

Helen was still and quiet as she absorbed the information. After a moment she kissed him again, this time on his chest. Over his heart. *Damn it,* he thought, realizing that he was going to tell her everything. He couldn't put any distance between them when she did something like that.

"He and Peggy married," he said. "They were happy for a while. They were well matched, and Ioan had made a fortune with his private shares in the store. Anything Peggy wanted, he provided." Rhys paused before admitting ruefully, "Except his time. Ioan worked the same hours he always had, staying late at the store each night. He left her alone for too long. I should have put a stop to that. I should have told him to go home and pay attention to his wife."

"Surely that wasn't your place."

"As his friend, I could have said it." He felt Helen's head settle on his chest. "It won't be an issue in our marriage," he muttered. "I won't keep bachelor's hours."

"Our house is next to the store. If you work too late, I'll simply come and fetch you."

Helen's pragmatic reply nearly made him smile.

"You'll have no trouble tempting me from my work," he said, playing with her hair as it streamed over his chest in pale ribbons.

Gently Helen prompted, "Peggy became discontent?"

"Aye, she needed more companionship than Ioan provided. She went to social events without him, and eventually fell prey to the attentions of a man who charmed and seduced her." Rhys hesitated, conscious of the same choking tightness that had invaded his throat the other spare handful of times he'd related the story. He forced himself to go on, laying out the events as if setting up a game of solitaire. "She came to Ioan, shamed and weeping, and told him that she was with child, and it wasn't his. He forgave her, and said he'd stand by her. The fault was his, he said, because he'd made her lonely. He promised to claim the babe as his own, and love it as a true father."

"How honorable of him," Helen said softly.

"Ioan was a better man than I could ever be. He devoted himself to Peggy. He was with her every possible moment during her confinement, from the quickening until the labor began. But it went wrong. The labor lasted two days, and the pains became so bad that they gave Peggy chloroform. She reacted badly—they'd given it to her too fast—she was dead in five minutes. When he was told, Ioan collapsed from shock and grief. I had to carry him to his room."

Rhys shook his head, hating the memory of his own helplessness, his overwhelming need to fix everything and make it all right, the way he'd slammed repeatedly into the fact that he couldn't. "He went mad with despair," he continued. "For the next few days he saw visions, talked to people who weren't there. He asked when Peggy's labor would be finished, as if the clock had stopped in that moment and couldn't be started again." His lips curved with a humorless smile. "Ioan was the friend I always talked to when there was a problem I couldn't solve, when I needed to mull something over. I began to wonder if I'd gone a bit mad myself: More than once I caught myself thinking, 'By God, I need to talk to Ioan about this, so we can figure out what to do.' Except that he was the problem. He was a broken man. I brought doctors to him. A priest. Friends and relations, anyone who might reach through to him." He paused and swallowed. "A week after Peggy's death, Ioan hanged himself."

"Oh my dear . . ." he heard Helen whisper.

They were both silent for a long time.

"Ioan was like a brother," Rhys eventually said. "I've waited for the memory to fade. For time to make it better. But so far it hasn't. All I can do is shut it away, and not think of it."

"I understand," Helen said, as if she truly did. Her palm moved in a gentle circle on his chest. "Did the baby die?"

"No, it survived. A girl. Peggy's family didn't want

it, in light of its origins, so they sent it to the natural father."

"You don't know what became of her?"

"I don't give a damn," he said bitterly. "She's Albion Vance's daughter."

A strange, numb feeling invaded Helen, as if her soul had just been jarred loose from her body. She lay still against him, her thoughts whirling like moths in the darkness. Why hadn't it occurred to her before that her mother probably wasn't the only woman that Vance had seduced and abandoned?

Poor unwanted infant—she was four now—what had Vance done with her? Had he taken her in?

Somehow Helen didn't think so.

No wonder Rhys hated him.

"I'm sorry," she said quietly.

"For what? You've nothing to do with it."

"I'm just . . . sorry."

She felt him take a tight-banded breath, and her numbness was swept away in a wave of compassion and tenderness. She wanted badly to comfort him, for the pain of the past and the hurt yet to be inflicted.

The fire had sunk down to red coals in their beds of ash, throwing off a thin buttered glow. Most of the heat in the room came from the big masculine form beside her. She moved along his body, feeling her way with lips and hands. He was still, clearly curious about what she intended. The drum-tight surface of his stomach contracted as she drew her mouth across it. Reaching his groin, she breathed in the intimate scent of him, musk and a hint of sharpness that reminded her of whittled birch, and sweetness, like a hot summer meadow. She heard his low exclamation as she touched the hard length of him, gripping until it swelled thickly against her fingers.

Rhys gasped out a few words, beseeching and urgent. Helen didn't think he realized that he was speaking in his native language, which of course she hadn't a hope of understanding. But he sounded so violently appreciative that she bent to kiss him as she'd done before. His hips jerked reflexively, and he grunted as if he were in pain. Helen hesitated. His shaking hand came to her head and smoothed over her hair in what seemed to be a mixture of pleading and benediction. She dared to wrap her lips around him, tasting salt as she pulled back slowly. He tensed like a man strung on a torture rack, groaning as she repeated the caress.

In the next moment, he had rolled Helen onto her side, fitting their bodies together like a pair of spoons. One of his muscled arms hooked beneath her top knee, lifting it high, and Helen tensed in surprise as she felt him entering her. He kissed the side of her neck and murmured in Welsh, words like audible caresses. His mouth found the vulnerable spot low behind her ear, where he knew she was especially sensitive. She relaxed helplessly against him as he centered himself and rocked firmly upward, the angle teasing a new place inside her. After adjusting her top leg to rest on his, he slid a hand between her thighs.

Moaning, she abandoned herself to the rhythm he set, his strength all around her, the vital force of him sinking deep. His hips lunged with increasing power, driving the sensations to a higher pitch, until pleasure seemed to come from every direction. A scalding flush came over her, followed by a stronger one. She turned her mouth against the hard arm beneath her neck, biting into the dense muscle, trying to muffle her cries. His scorching breath struck her neck in rapid gusts, and she felt the graze of his teeth and the scrape of his bristle on the tender skin. Twisting, convulsing, she forced her hips down on his, taking his full length, and he poured into her with a ragged groan, holding deep and fast.

They were both still, relaxing slowly. When Helen could finally move, she eased her top leg down. She was limp and heavy, replete with satisfaction. Deep within her belly, where Rhys still pressed, she felt an insistent pulse, and she couldn't tell whether it came from him or her.

His hand coasted gently over her body, caressing her hip and waist. Helen quivered as he bit gently at her earlobe. He had drawn his legs up behind hers, the hair on his limbs pleasantly coarse against her skin.

"You forgot to speak in English," she said after a moment, her voice languid. "During."

His lips toyed with the rim of her ear. "I was so wild for you, I couldn't have told you my own name."

"You don't think anyone heard us, do you?"

"I think it was no accident that I was given a room far away from the family."

"Perhaps they were afraid you would snore," she said lightly, and paused. "*Do* you snore?"

"I don't think so. You'll have to tell me."

Helen snuggled deeper into his embrace. Sighing, she said, "I can't be found here in the morning when the maid comes to light the grate. I should go back to my room."

"No, stay." His arms tightened. "I'll wake you early. I never sleep past dawn."

"Never? Why not?"

Rhys smiled lazily against her neck. "It's what comes of being raised a grocer's son. My day started at first light, delivering baskets of orders to families around the neighborhood. If I was fast enough, I could stop for a five-minute game of marbles with friends before going back to the shop." He chuckled. "Whenever my mam heard marbles clicking in my pocket, she took them and gave me a clout to the side of the head. There was no time for play, she would say, with so much work to be done. So I took to wrapping them in a handkerchief to keep them quiet."

Helen pictured him as a gangly boy, hurrying through his morning chores with a cache of forbidden marbles in his pocket. A bloom of emotion expanded in her chest, an electrifying happiness that almost bordered on pain.

She loved him. She loved the boy he had been, and the man he was now. She loved the look and smell and feel of him, the brusque charm of his accent, the touchy pride and determined will that had taken him so far in life, and the thousand other qualities that made him so extraordinary. Turning in his arms, she pressed herself as tightly to him as she could, and gradually surrendered to an uneasy sleep.

Chapter 19

"The carriage is coming down the drive," Cassandra said, kneeling on the settee and staring through the receiving room window. "They've almost reached the house."

It had fallen to West to collect Lady Berwick and her lady's maid at the Alton railway station, and bring them to Eversby Priory.

"Oh God," Kathleen muttered, putting a hand to her chest as if to calm a rampaging heartbeat.

She had been tense and distracted throughout the morning, walking from room to room to make certain that every detail was perfect. Flower arrangements had been scrutinized and divested of any drooping blossoms. Carpets had been ruthlessly beaten and brushed, silver and glass had been polished with soft linen, and all the candleholders had been loaded with new bees-wax tapers. Every sideboard was weighted with bowls of fresh fruit, and bottles of chilled champagne and soda water had been set in ice-filled urns.

"Why are you so worried about how the house looks?" Cassandra asked. "Lady Berwick has already seen it once before, when you married Theo."

"Yes, but I wasn't responsible for anything at the time. Now I've been living here for almost a year, and if anything is amiss, she'll know it's my fault."

Pacing in a continuous circle, Kathleen spoke distractedly. "Remember to curtsy when Lady Berwick arrives. And don't say 'How do you do'—she doesn't like that—just tell her 'Good afternoon.'" She stopped abruptly and cast a wild glance at their surroundings. "Where are the dogs?"

"In the upstairs parlor," Pandora said. "Do you want them down here?"

"*No*, dear God, no, Lady Berwick doesn't allow dogs in the receiving room." Kathleen stopped in her tracks as an uncomfortable thought occurred to her. "Also, don't say anything about the pet pig we had living in the house last year." The pacing resumed. "When she asks a question of you, try to answer simply, and don't be amusing. She doesn't like wit."

"We'll do our best," Pandora said. "But she already

doesn't like Cassandra and me. After we met her at the wedding, I heard her telling someone that we behaved like a pair of Bilberry goats."

Kathleen continued to pace. "I wrote to her that you'd both become accomplished and well-mannered young ladies."

"You lied?" Pandora asked, her eyes widening.

"We had just begun our etiquette lessons at the time," Kathleen said defensively. "I assumed our progress would go a bit faster."

Cassandra looked worried. "I wish I'd paid more attention."

"I don't care a pickle if Lady Berwick approves of me or not," Pandora said.

"But Kathleen does," Helen pointed out gently. "That's why we're going to try our best."

Pandora heaved a sigh. "I wish I could be perfect like you, Helen."

"Me?" Helen shook her head with an uncomfortable laugh. "Darling, I'm the least perfect person in the world."

"Oh, we know you've make mistakes," Cassandra said cheerfully. "What Pandora meant was that you always *appear* to be perfect, which is all that really matters."

"Actually," Kathleen said, "that's not what really matters."

"But there's no difference between *being* perfect and *seeming* perfect as long as no one can tell," Cassandra said. "The result is the same, isn't it?"

Looking perturbed, Kathleen rubbed her forehead. "I know there's a good answer for that. But I can't think of what it is right now."

In a minute or two, the butler, Sims, brought Lady Berwick to the receiving room.

Eleanor, Lady Berwick, was a woman built on a majestic scale, tall, broad-shouldered, and bosomy, with a way of moving that reminded Helen of the prow of a great sailing ship gliding through calm waters. The effect was enhanced by the complex draperies that formed the skirts of her dark blue dress, rippling in her wake as she proceeded into the room. With her narrow face, paper-thin lips, and large, heavy-lidded eyes, the countess was not a beautiful woman. However, she possessed an air of stunning assurance, a shrewd confidence that she knew the answers to any questions worth asking.

Helen saw the automatic pleasure on Lady Berwick's face as her gaze fell upon Kathleen, who had rushed forward. Clearly Kathleen's fondness for her was returned. However, as Kathleen threw her arms around her, Lady Berwick looked nonplussed by the demonstration of affection. "My dear," she exclaimed with a touch of reproof.

Kathleen didn't let go. "I was going be dignified." Her voice was muffled against the older woman's shoulder. "But as you walked in just now, I felt as if I were five years old again."

Lady Berwick's gaze turned distant, one of her long pale hands settling on Kathleen's back. "Yes," she eventually said. "It isn't easy to lose one's father. And you've had to do it twice, haven't you?" Her voice was like unsweetened tea, crisp with tannins. After a few fond pats, she said, "Let us don our armor of control."

Kathleen pulled back and cast a bemused glance at the empty doorway. "Where has Cousin West gone?"

"Mr. Ravenel was eager to escape my presence," Lady Berwick said dryly. "He did not seem to enjoy our conversation in the carriage." After a meaningful pause, she commented without a smile, "A merry fellow, isn't he?"

Helen was fairly certain the statement was not intended as a compliment.

"Cousin West may seem a trifle irreverent," Kathleen began, "but I can assure you—"

"There is no need to explain his character, which is indeed a trifle: nothing but sugar and air."

"You don't know him," one of the twins said beneath her breath.

Hearing the quietly rebellious murmur, Lady Berwick turned sharply to gaze at the three Ravenel sisters.

Kathleen hastened to introduce them, while they each curtsied in turn. "Lady Berwick, my sisters-in-law—Lady Helen, Lady Cassandra, and Lady Pandora."

The countess's dispassionate gaze fell on Cassandra first, and she motioned for the girl to approach. "The posture is merely adequate," she observed, "but that can be corrected. What are your accomplishments, child?"

Having been prepared for the question in advance, Cassandra replied hesitantly. "My lady, I am able to sew, draw, and watercolor. I play no instruments, but I am well-read."

"Have you studied languages?"

"A little French."

"Have you any hobbies?"

"No, ma'am."

"Excellent. Men are afraid of girls with hobbies." Glancing at Kathleen, Lady Berwick remarked in an aside, "She's a beauty. With a bit more polish, she'll be the belle of the season."

"I have a hobby," Pandora volunteered, speaking out of turn.

Lady Berwick turned to her with raised brows. "Indeed," she said frostily. "What is it, my bold miss?"

"I'm making a board game. If it turns out well, I will sell it in stores, and earn money."

Seeming astonished, Lady Berwick sent Kathleen a questioning glance. "Board game?"

"The kind meant for parlor amusements," Kathleen explained.

Lady Berwick turned back to Pandora with narrowed eyes. Unfortunately Pandora forgot to keep her gaze lowered, and stared back at her audaciously.

"An excess of vitality," Lady Berwick said. "The eyes are a pleasing shade of blue, but the gaze is that of a wild stag."

Helen risked a quick glance at Kathleen, who looked defensive on Pandora's behalf.

"Ma'am," Kathleen began, "Pandora is merely—"

But Lady Berwick gestured for her to be silent. "Does it not concern you," she asked Pandora, "that this hobby, along with the distasteful desire to earn money, will alienate prospective suitors?"

"No, ma'am."

"It should. Don't you wish to marry?" At Pandora's lack of response, she pressed impatiently, "Well?"

Pandora glanced at Kathleen for guidance. "Should I say the conventional thing or the honest thing?"

Lady Berwick replied before Kathleen was able. "Answer honestly, child."

"In that case," Pandora said, "No, I don't wish to marry, ever. I like men quite well—at least the ones I've been acquainted with—but I shouldn't like to have to obey a husband and serve his needs. It wouldn't make me at all happy to have a dozen children, and stay at home knitting while he goes out romping with his friends. I would rather be independent."

The room was silent. Lady Berwick's expression did not change, nor did she blink even once as she stared at Pandora. It seemed as if a wordless battle were being waged between the authoritative older woman and the rebellious girl.

Finally Lady Berwick said, "You must have read Tolstoy."

Pandora blinked, clearly caught off guard by the unexpected statement. "I have," she admitted, looking mystified. "How did you know?"

"No young woman wants to marry after reading Tolstoy. That is why I never allowed either of my daughters to read Russian novels."

"How are Dolly and Bettina?" Kathleen burst in, trying to change the subject by asking after the countess's daughters.

Neither Lady Berwick nor Pandora would be side-tracked.

"Tolstoy isn't the only reason I don't wish to marry," Pandora said.

"Whatever your reasons, they are unsound. I will explain to you later why you *do* wish to marry. Furthermore, you are an unconventional girl, and you must learn to conceal it. There is no happiness for any individual, man or woman, who does not dwell within the broad zone of average."

Pandora regarded her with baffled interest. "Yes, ma'am."

Privately Helen suspected that the two women were looking forward to a ripping argument.

Lady Berwick gestured to Helen. "Come hither."

Helen obeyed, and stood patiently as the countess surveyed her.

"Graceful deportment," Lady Berwick said, "with a modest downcast eye. Quite lovely. Do not be too shy, however, as that will cause people to accuse you of pride. You must cultivate a proper air of confidence."

"I will try, ma'am. Thank you."

The countess surveyed her with an appraising

glance. "You are affianced to the mysterious Mr. Winterborne."

Helen smiled faintly. "Is he mysterious, ma'am?"

"He is to me, as I have not personally encountered him."

"Mr. Winterborne is a gentleman of business," Helen replied carefully, "with many obligations that keep him too busy to attend many social events."

"Nor is he invited to the exclusive ones, as he is of the merchant class. You must be distressed by the prospect of an unequal marriage. He is beneath you, after all."

Although the words stung, Helen schooled her features into impassiveness, aware that she was being tested. "Mr. Winterborne is in no way beneath me, ma'am. Character is a far more important measure of a man than birth."

"Well said. Fortunately for Mr. Winterborne, marriage to a Ravenel will elevate him sufficiently that he will be allowed to mix in good society. One hopes he will prove worthy of the privilege."

"I hope aristocratic society will be worthy of *him*," Helen said pointedly.

The gray eyes sharpened. "Is he high-minded? Refined in his tastes? Exquisite in his comportment?"

"He is well-mannered, intelligent, honest, and generous."

"But not refined?" Lady Berwick pressed.

"Whatever refinements Mr. Winterborne does not possess, he will certainly acquire them if he wishes. But I wouldn't ask him to change anything about himself, as there is already far too much to admire, and I would be in danger of excessive pride on his behalf."

Lady Berwick gazed at her steadily, her gray eyes warming. "What an extraordinary girl. 'Cool as callar air,' as my Scottish grandfather used to say. You'll be wasted on a Welshman—I vow, we could have married you to a duke. Still, this sort of union—the alliance of wealth with breeding—is necessary for even the best families nowadays. We must reconcile ourselves to it with grace and forbearance." She glanced at Kathleen. "Does Mr. Winterborne appreciate his good fortune in acquiring such a wife?"

Kathleen smiled. "You will be able to decide for yourself when you meet him."

"When will this occur?"

"I expect Mr. Winterborne and Lord Trenear to arrive momentarily. They rode out to the eastern perimeter of the estate, to view the site being prepared for railway tracks and a platform halt. They promised to return and change in time for afternoon tea."

Before Kathleen had even finished the sentence, Devon had come to the doorway. He smiled at his wife.

"And so we have." A swift conversation took place in their shared gaze—an unvoiced question, concern, reassurance—before he strode in to meet Lady Berwick.

He was followed by Rhys, who was similarly dressed in riding clothes: cord-breeches and boots, and a coat of heavy woolen broadcloth.

Rhys paused beside Helen, smiling down at her. He smelled like the outdoors: cold morning air, wet leaves, and horses. As usual, there was the snap of peppermint on his breath. "Good afternoon," he said, in the same soft way he'd murmured, "Good morning" upon waking her much earlier that day. Remembering their night together, Helen felt a dreadful blush coming on, the kind only he could inspire, a blaze of color that kept building on itself until it seemed she'd been thrown into a bonfire.

She'd had a restless sleep, tossing and turning, her mind plagued with worries. More than once she'd become aware of Rhys soothing and stroking her back to sleep. When he had finally awakened her at dawn, she had given him an apologetic glance and mumbled, "You'll never want to share a bed with me again."

Rhys had laughed quietly, pulling her up against his chest and caressing her naked back. "Then you'll be surprised when I insist on it again tonight." After that, he made love to her one last time, disregarding her feeble protests that she had to leave.

Now, trying to control her blush, Helen tore her gaze from his. "Did you have a pleasant ride?" she asked softly, watching as Kathleen introduced Devon to Lady Berwick.

"Which ride are you referring to?" His tone was so bland that at first she didn't perceive his implication.

Helen shot him a shocked glance. "Don't be wicked," she whispered.

Rhys grinned and took her hand, lifting it to his lips. The gentle pressure of his mouth on the backs of her fingers did little to calm the rioting color in her face.

Lady Berwick's brittle voice came from several feet away. "Not so cool and composed now, I see. Lady Helen, introduce me to the gentleman who seems to have set you all aflutter."

Helen went to her with Rhys at her side. "Lady Berwick," she murmured, "this is Mr. Winterborne."

A curious change came over the countess's face as she stared at the big, black-haired Welshman before her. Her steely eyes turned as soft as mist, and a hint of girlish color rose in her cheeks. Instead of giving him a nod, she extended her hand.

Without hesitation, Rhys enclosed the older woman's jewel-laden fingers in a gentle grip, and bowed over her hand with easy grace. He straightened and smiled at her. "A pleasure."

Lady Berwick studied him, her gaze wide and almost wondering, although her voice remained coolly assessing. "A young man. I confess, I expected someone of more advanced years, in light of your accomplishments."

"I was set to learn my father's trade at an early age, my lady."

"You have been described to me as a 'business magnate.' It is my understanding that the term is used for a man who has amassed wealth so great that it cannot be measured on any ordinary scale."

"I've had a stroke of luck now and then."

"False modesty is evidence of secret pride, Mr. Winterborne."

"The subject makes me uncomfortable," he admitted frankly.

"As well it should—any discussion of money is vulgar. However, at my age, I will ask whatever I like, and let anyone reproach me if they dare."

Rhys laughed suddenly in that free, attractive way he had, his teeth white against his amber complexion. "Lady Berwick, I would never reproach nor refuse you anything."

"Well then, I have a question for you. Lady Helen

insists that in taking you for a husband, she is not marrying down. Do you agree?"

Rhys glanced at Helen, his eyes warm. "No," he said. "Every man marries above himself."

"Do you believe, then, that she should wed a man of noble pedigree?"

Returning his attention to the countess, Rhys hitched his shoulders in a nonchalant shrug. "Lady Helen is so far above all men that none of us deserve her. Therefore, it might as well be me."

Lady Berwick let out a reluctant cackle, staring at him as if spell-struck. "Charmingly arrogant," she said. "I almost find myself in agreement with you."

"Ma'am," Kathleen said, "Perhaps we should send the gentlemen to refresh themselves and change into more appropriate attire for tea. The housekeeper will have a conniption at the sight of these muddy boots clomping across the carpets."

Devon grinned. "Whatever a conniption is, I feel certain I don't want to be the cause of one." He leaned down and kissed his wife's forehead, in spite of all her previous warnings about Lady Berwick's dislike of physical demonstrations.

After making polite bows, the men left the receiving room.

Lady Berwick's mouth twisted wryly. "There is no

lack of manly vigor in this household, is there?" Her gaze turned absent as she stared at the empty doorway. As she continued, she seemed almost to be speaking to herself. "When I was a girl, there was a footman-in-waiting at my father's estate. A handsome rascal from North Wales, with hair black as night, and a knowing gaze . . ."

A distant memory had stirred her, something withheld but tender radiating through the temporary softening of her expression. "A rascal," she repeated gently, "but gallant." Recovering herself, she cast a stern glance at the young women around her. "Mark my words, girls. There is no greater enemy of virtue than a charming Welshman."

Feeling Pandora's elbow poking discreetly against her side, Helen reflected with chagrin that she could vouch for that.

Chapter 20

"Do not cross your legs, Pandora. Occupy your chair entirely. Cassandra, try not to fling the drapery of your skirts all about while sitting down." Lady Berwick dispensed these and many other instructions to the twins during afternoon tea, with the expertise of a woman who had trained many young ladies in the arts of deportment.

Pandora and Cassandra did their best to follow the countess's commands, although there would be private bemoaning later about how the older woman could turn the pleasant ritual of teatime into a trial of endurance.

Kathleen and Devon managed to focus most of the conversation on one of Lady Berwick's favorite subjects: horses. Both Lord and Lady Berwick were keen horse enthusiasts, occupying themselves with the training of thoroughbreds at their Leominster estate. In fact, that was how they had originally become acquainted with Kathleen's parents, Lord and Lady Carbery, who had owned an Arabian stud farm in Ireland.

Lady Berwick displayed a lively interest upon learning that Kathleen would inherit at least two dozen horses of purebred Arabian stock, and a parcel of land comprising a riding school, stables, paddocks, and an arena. Even though Lord Carbery's title and estate lands would be passed on to the nearest male issue, a great-nephew from his father's side, the stud farm had been built by Kathleen's parents and had never been entailed.

"We'll arrange for three or four of the horses to be brought here," Devon said, "but the rest of the stock will have to be sold."

"The difficulty will be in finding buyers who understand the nature of Arabians," Kathleen said with a frown. "They have to be managed differently than other breeds. Placing an Arabian with the wrong kind of owner could lead to many problems."

"What will you do with the farm?" Rhys asked.

"I'd like to sell it to the next Lord Carbery and have done with it," Devon said. "Unfortunately, according to the farm manager, Carbery has no interest in horses."

"No interest in horses?" Lady Berwick echoed, seeming aghast.

Kathleen nodded ruefully. "When Lord Trenear and I reach Glengarriff, we'll be able to take account of all that must be done. I'm afraid we may have to stay a fortnight to resolve everything. Perhaps even a month."

The countess knit her brows. "I'm afraid it won't do for me to remain at Eversby Priory so long."

West, who had seated himself as far away from Lady Berwick as possible, said insincerely, "Oh that's too bad."

"My daughter Bettina is in her first confinement," Lady Berwick continued. "The birth is expected to occur soon, and I must be with her in London when the labor begins."

"Why don't you stay at Ravenel House with Helen and the twins?" Devon suggested to the countess. "You could manage them just as easily in London as here."

Pandora clapped her hands together in enthusiasm. "I would *love* that, there is *so much more* to do in town—"

"Oh *do* say yes, my lady!" Cassandra exclaimed, bouncing in her chair.

The countess gave them both a stern glance. "This display is unseemly." When the girls had fallen completely silent, she said to Devon, "My lord, that would seem an ideal solution. Yes, we will do that."

Helen was quiet and still, but her heart quickened at the thought of returning to London, where she would be closer to Rhys. She didn't dare look in his direction, even when she heard him speak calmly to Lady Berwick.

"I'll escort you and the girls on the train to London, if that would be agreeable."

"It would, Mr. Winterborne," came the decisive reply.

"I'm at your service," Rhys continued. "It would be a privilege to assist with anything you require while you're in town."

"Thank you," the countess said with great dignity. "Coming from a man of your extensive connections, I realize that is no small offer. We will prevail on you if necessary." She paused to stir another lump of sugar into her tea. "Perhaps you might call on us at Ravenel House from time to time."

Rhys smiled. "It would be my pleasure. In return, I would like to invite you to Winterborne's as my personal guest."

"A department store?" Lady Berwick sounded disconcerted. "I only frequent small shops, where the tradesmen are acquainted with my preferences."

"My sales clerks would show you the greatest variety of luxury goods you've ever seen in one place. Gloves, for example—how many pairs do they bring out for you at a little shop? A dozen? Two dozen? At the glove counter at Winterborne's, you'll view ten times that many, made of glacéed kid, calf suede, doeskin, elk, peccary, antelope, even kangaroo." Seeing her interest, Rhys continued casually, "No fewer than three countries have a part in making our best gloves. Lambskin dressed in Spain, cut in France, and hand-stitched in England. Each glove is so delicate, it can be enclosed in the shell of a walnut."

"You offer those at your store?" the countess asked, clearly weakening.

"Aye. And we have eighty other departments featuring items from all over the world."

"I am intrigued," the older woman admitted. "But hobnobbing with the common herd . . . the crowds . . ."

"You could bring the girls after-hours, when the daytime customers have gone," Rhys said. "I'll have some of the sales clerks stay to assist you. If you like, my assistant will make a private appointment for Lady Helen to consult with the store's dressmaker. It's time to begin designing her trousseau, aye?"

"It's beyond time," Kathleen said, sending her husband an inquiring glance.

"Knowing little of these matters," Devon replied, "I'll leave it to your judgment."

"Then if Lady Berwick consents," Kathleen said, "and Helen wishes it, the dressmaker at Winterborne's could begin on the trousseau while Lord Trenear and I are away."

Helen nodded. "That would be lovely." She looked at Rhys for just an instant, seeing past his relaxed veneer. Judging from the gleam in his eyes, he was coming up with all manner of plans.

"I will give the matter due consideration," Lady Berwick remarked, frowning as Pandora tapped the fingers of both hands on the table in a burst of excitement. "Child, do not make a tambourine of the tea table."

Helen found it both a pleasure and torture to go through an ordinary day with Rhys there at Eversby Priory. He was within her sight, her reach, but they were always in the company of others. It was exhausting to have to conceal how much she felt, how her heart raced whenever he entered the room. She had never expected how powerful the combination of physical desire and love would be. At some moments she was filled with melancholy, reflecting that her time with him was slipping through her fingers like fine white sand. She had to tell him about her father . . . she just couldn't make herself do it yet.

The hours before midnight dragged by slowly, while Helen paced and fidgeted and waited in her room until the household had finally settled. She hurried barefoot through the hallways to the east wing in her white nightgown and robe, impatience pumping through her veins.

She arrived at Rhys's door, and it opened before she even touched it, a strong arm reaching out to pull her inside. The key turned firmly in the lock, and Rhys caught her close with a soft laugh. Helen was electrified by the feel of him all along her, the aggressive pressure of him against her belly. His mouth blotted out every thought as he searched her hungrily, unlocking a flood of desire that she was too inexperienced to control. She responded blindly, desperate for him, her hands sliding into his thick hair to pull his head down harder over hers.

After undressing her where she stood, Rhys carried her to the bed. Stretching her out beneath him, he began to feast on her with deliberate slowness, biting and licking on the pulses in her throat, breasts, wrists. She felt the touch of his hand between her thighs, teasing lightly. He splayed the soft flesh open, his fingers cool and gentle as they stroked on either side of the hot bud. She couldn't stop twisting, straining, twining her limbs around his at every possible opportunity. He resisted, wanting to play, wanting to indulge in lavish variety when all she wanted was to have him inside her *now.*

His whisper curled into her ear like smoke. "You're not wet enough for me, *cariad.*"

"I am," she managed to say between labored gasps.

"Show me."

After the briefest of hesitations, she reached down to clasp his erection. A shallow gasp escaped her as she felt the heavy pulse of his flesh, the shaft thickening until she was unable to close her fingers around it. Guiding him between her thighs, she rubbed the head of his sex over soft feminine layers and pleats, circling the most sensitive part of him against her until it was glossed with moisture and they were both shaking.

Rhys pushed against the swollen opening, stretching her, coaxing her flesh to yield. She arched, helpless and overtaken, aware of nothing but the pleasure of him filling her. He grasped her hips, pushing and pulling her slowly on his hard shaft, and she made sounds she'd never made in her life, moaning and purring at the intense delight of his possession.

When the last shudders had left her, and Helen had regained her breath, Rhys rolled and maneuvered her easily. She found herself straddling his lap as he sat on the edge of the bed. The position felt strange and awkward, and she linked her arms around his neck, fearing she might fall backwards.

Rhys slid a reassuring hand low on her spine. His mouth tugged at hers, his teeth lightly grazing her lower lip. He seemed to be waiting for something. She glanced down in confusion at the rampant erection pressed between them, wondering what he expected of her.

He laughed quietly, the lamplight striking sparks in his midnight eyes. "You look like a dove caught in a snare."

"I don't know what to do," she protested, hot and mortified.

Cupping her bottom with his free hand, Rhys guided her upward and gently brought her closer to his body. "Lower yourself onto me, *cariad*."

Her eyes widened as she understood what he intended.

She gripped his shoulders and obeyed, easing downward inch by cautious inch. Unable to take all of him, she stopped in discomfort. His supportive hand lifted her at once, lessening the inner pressure.

The black crescents of his lashes lowered, the space between his brows contracting. A sheen of perspiration had given his face and chest the look of cast bronze. He bit his lip and muttered something in Welsh.

"I can't understand what you're saying," Helen whispered.

After taking a raw breath, he let out a rasp of amusement. "Just as well. I paid you a compliment—but a crude one. Hold onto me." He eased back and supported himself on his elbows, letting her rest partially on his torso. "Is this better?"

Helen nodded with a little gasp of relief. In this position, she was able to control his depth. What an amazing feeling it was to have all that sinewy power beneath her, his robust body braced between her thighs.

There was a flicker of challenge in his eyes, and his hips nudged upward in playful invitation.

Helen moved carefully, rising and lowering, catching her breath at the hot slide of him within her. He was patient, letting her experiment, while his heart beat like a trip-hammer beneath her flattened palms. She found a gliding back-and-forth motion that sent spasms of heat through her. Judging from his ardent groan, he seemed to enjoy it as well. His mouth caught at the tips of her breasts whenever she moved high enough, and she began to delight in teasing him, sometimes letting him have what he wanted, sometimes withholding. The ribbon had come loose from her hair, the curtain of silvery locks tickling his face and chest.

"You like to torment me," Rhys said, his eyes heavy-lidded with pleasure.

"Yes." In fact, it was fun, enormously exciting fun of a kind she'd never imagined.

The hint of a grin crossed his lips and vanished quickly as she plunged harder, filling herself with him. He began to answer her rhythm in earnest, fisting his hands in the bedclothes. She loved the sight of him lost to passion, his head tilted back and his strong throat exposed, the muscles of his chest sharply delineated. A storm of sensation swept through her, and her shuddering body locked on him. He continued to thrust, the movements becoming jerky and forceful, finishing in a powerful shove that arched his hips and most of his back completely off the bed.

As soon as he was able, he sank back down and pushed Helen's hair back with an unsteady hand to look at her face. "Was I too rough with you, *cariad*?"

"No." Helen stretched luxuriously over him. "Was I too rough with you?"

He chuckled and relaxed. "Aye, did you not hear me begging for mercy?"

"Is that what you were doing?" She bent to let her mouth hover teasingly above his. "I thought you were urging me on."

A slow smile crossed his face. "I was doing a bit of both," he conceded, and drew her down to him.

They talked lazily for a while, while the night drowsed around them and shadows subsided in the corners.

"You charmed Lady Berwick despite herself," Helen told him, leaning back against his chest as he sat with his shoulders propped on the headboard. "I think she invited you to call on us at Ravenel House before she even realized what she was doing."

His warm hand coasted along the slender length of her arm. "I'll visit as often as she'll allow."

"I'm certain she'll want to see Winterborne's now, after all your talk of gloves. How did you know that would tempt her?"

"Most women her age go first to the glove counter when they enter the store."

"What counter do women my age first go to?"

"Perfumes and powder."

Helen was amused. "You know all about women, don't you?"

"I wouldn't say that, *cariad*. But I know what they like to spend their money on."

Turning sideways, Helen laid her head on his shoulder. "I'll persuade Lady Berwick to invite you for dinner as soon as we're settled in London." She sighed. "It will be difficult to see you and behave in a formal manner."

"Aye, you'll have to keep your hands to yourself."

She smiled and kissed his chest. "I'll try."

Rhys fell silent for a minute before saying abruptly, "I don't like the connection between Lady Berwick and Vance. I'll tell Trenear to make it clear to her that I don't want Vance to come within a mile of you or the twins."

Helen fought to remain relaxed, although the remark had chilled her. To meet her real father—the prospect was horrifying—and yet she was curious about him. Was it wrong to be curious? "No, I wouldn't want that either." Her heart had begun to beat unpleasantly fast. "Does Mr. Vance have any family?"

"His wife died of pneumonia last year. They had no surviving children—all were stillborn. The rest of his relations live far north and don't usually come to town."

"How ironic that he should have an illegitimate daughter by your friend's wife, but no legitimate children of his own." A shadow of sadness fell over her. "I wonder if the poor little thing has survived."

"Better if she hasn't," Rhys said flatly. "Any child of his is demon spawn, and would come to no good."

Helen stiffened, even though she understood why he said it.

Theirs was a culture in which blood meant everything. Society itself was founded on the principle that a person's bloodline determined his entire life—his morals, temperament, intelligence, status, everything he would ever accomplish. People couldn't go against the blood of their ancestors—their futures had already been decided by the past. It was why so many blue bloods thought of marrying commoners as a degradation. It was why a successful self-made man with five hundred years of low ancestry would never be respected as much as a peer. It was why people believed that criminals, lunatics, and fools would only beget more of themselves.

Blood will tell.

Feeling the change in her body, Rhys lowered her to the bed and leaned over her, with her head resting in the crook of his elbow. "What's the matter?"

She was slow to answer. "Nothing, only . . . you sounded rather callous just now."

Rhys was quiet for a moment. "I don't like the side of me that Vance brings out, but there's no help for it. We won't speak of him again."

As he settled beside her, Helen closed her eyes and swallowed back the pressure of tears. Miserably she wished she could talk to someone about the situation. Someone besides Quincy, who had made his opinion clear. Helen wished she could confide in Kathleen. But Kathleen already had more than enough worries heaped on her plate, and in her condition, she didn't need another.

Her thoughts were interrupted as Rhys gathered her against his warm body. "Rest now, sweetheart," he whispered. "When you wake in the morning, I promise your ill-tempered beast will have turned back into a man again."

Chapter 21

The next day was consumed with a fury of packing as the servants frantically filled trunks, portmanteaus, dressing-cases, valises, and hatboxes for every member of the family except West. As it happened, Kathleen, Devon, Sutton, the valet, and Clara, the lady's maid, would have to depart for Bristol by train that very evening. They would spend the night at a port hotel, and catch a steamer to Waterford the next morning. At Rhys's request, the transport office at Winterborne's had planned their trip with meticulous attention to detail.

A few minutes before departing for Alton Station, Kathleen found Helen in her bedroom, packing a small valise to be carried by hand.

"Darling, why are you doing that?" Kathleen asked breathlessly. "Clara should have taken care of it."

"I offered to help," Helen replied. "Clara needs a few more minutes to pack her own belongings."

"Thank you. Goodness, it's been a madhouse. Have you and the twins finished packing your things for London?"

"Yes, we leave in the morning with Mr. Winterborne and Lady Berwick." Helen opened the valise, which sat on the bed, and displayed its contents. "Come have a look—I hope I've thought of everything."

She had packed Kathleen's favorite shawl of colorful ombré-shaded wool, a jar of salted almonds, a notebook and pencil, a sewing kit with tiny scissors and pincers, a hairbrush, and a rack of pins. She had also included extra handkerchiefs and gloves, a jar of cold cream, a bottle of rosewater, a drinking cup, a tin of lozenges, an extra pair of linen drawers, a little purse jingling with coins, and a three-volume novel.

"The twins tried to persuade me to include a pair of pistols, in case your steamer should be overtaken by pirates," Helen said. "It fell to me to point out that pirates haven't sailed the Irish Sea for two and a half centuries."

"How disappointing. I'm sure I would have made short work of them. Oh, well—in lieu of adventure, at least I'll have a novel to read." Picking up one of the volumes, Kathleen read the title and began to laugh. "*War and Peace?*"

"It's long and very good," Helen explained, "and I knew you hadn't read it yet, since we've been keeping it above the sixth shelf in the library. And even if Tolstoy does tend to sour one on marriage, as Lady Berwick claims, you're already married and it's too late."

Still chuckling, Kathleen placed the book back into the valise. "Nothing could sour me on marriage, after the way Devon has been with me. Steady as the polar star, and so very tender. I've discovered that I need him even more than I thought."

"He needs you also."

Kathleen closed the valise and gave her an affectionate glance. "I'll miss you so much, Helen. But it will make my heart lighter to know that you and the twins will be enjoying yourselves in London. I expect Mr. Winterborne will be at Ravenel house often, and he'll do anything short of performing backward somersaults if it would make you happy." She paused before adding quietly, "He loves you, you know. It's obvious."

Helen didn't know how to reply. She longed to pour out her heart, and confide that no matter how much Rhys loved her, it wouldn't be enough to overcome the terrible fact of who she was. It would devastate him when he found out.

Forcing a smile, she averted her face, affecting shyness.

In a moment, Kathleen's arms went around her. "This will be a happy time for you, darling. You'll have no trouble with Lady Berwick. She's the most honorable woman I've ever known, and the wisest. You and the twins must trust and rely on her while we're gone."

"I will." Helen hugged her tightly. "Don't worry about anything. We'll have a relaxing and pleasant time while we wait for you to return."

Anyone who had witnessed the Ravenel family's drawn-out good-byes would have been forgiven for assuming the group was about to be separated for a period of years instead of weeks. Fortunately, Lady Berwick, who would have deplored the display of emotion, was in her room at the time. Rhys, for his part, had tactfully elected to withdraw to the library to allow the family privacy.

Both Pandora and Cassandra tried to be light and amusing, but when it came time to say farewell, they both became tearful and hugged Kathleen simultaneously, until one could hardly see her small form sandwiched between them. For the better part of a year,

Kathleen had treated the twins with a mixture of interest and affection that was undeniably maternal in nature. The twins would miss her sorely.

"I wish we were going with you," Pandora said unsteadily.

Cassandra gave a little sob.

"There, there," came Kathleen's voice from amid the girls' enveloping embrace. "We'll be together soon, dear ones. In the meantime, you'll have a lovely time in London. And I'll be coming back with a beautiful horse for each of you—just think of that!"

"What if my horse isn't a good sailor?" Cassandra asked.

Kathleen tried to reply, but since she was still engulfed by the twins, it was difficult to make herself heard.

Amused, Devon stepped forward and pried his wife out of the enthusiastic tangle of arms. "The horses will have padded stalls onboard the ship," he explained. "There'll also be wide canvas belts underneath them, like hammocks, to keep them from foundering or falling. I'll stay belowdecks with the horses to keep them calm."

"So will I," Kathleen added.

Devon gave her a warning glance. "As we discussed earlier, my job during the return voyage will be to take care of the horses, while your job is to take care of my future son or daughter."

"I'm not an invalid," Kathleen protested.

"No," he said, "but you're the most important thing in the world to me, and I won't risk your safety."

Crossing her arms, Kathleen tried to look indignant. "How am I supposed to argue with that?"

Devon smiled and kissed her soundly. "You can't." Turning to the twins, he took them both in his arms, and kissed the tops of their heads. "Good-bye, imps. Try not to cause too much trouble for Lady Berwick, and take care of Helen."

"It's time to leave," West said from the doorway. "Are you certain you don't need me to accompany you to the station?"

Devon grinned at his brother. "Thank you, but the carriage will be crowded enough as it is. Moreover, I don't want to take you away when you should be acting as host to Lady Berwick."

"Quite right," West replied blandly, but as he turned, he executed a discreet hand gesture meant only for Devon's gaze.

"Kathleen," Pandora said, "Cousin West did that thing with his finger again."

"It was a hand cramp," West said quickly, and shot a narrow-eyed glance at Pandora.

Kathleen grinned and went to put her arms around his neck. "West," she said fondly, "whatever are you going to do when all of us leave you in peace?"

Sighing, West kissed her forehead. "I'll miss you, damn it."

Before the rest of the family departed the next morning, West drew Helen aside for a private conversation. They walked slowly to the conservatory, a room of glass and stone that was lushly crowded with potted palms and ferns. The glazed windows revealed a nearby stand of Weeping Beech trees, their pendulous branches draping and sagging as if exhausted by the tribulations of winter. A flock of plump orange-and-gray bramblings descended from the ash-colored sky to feed on the carpet of beech mast around the gnarled trunks.

"It occurs to me," West said, ducking his head to keep from colliding with a hanging basket filled with mixed plants, "that this is the first time you and the twins will have stayed in London for more than a night with no family to look after you."

"There's Lady Berwick," Helen pointed out.

"She's not family."

"Kathleen thinks well of her."

"Only because Lady Berwick took her in after her parents tried to set her out on a street corner with a sign saying FREE CHILD hung around her neck. Oh, I know Kathleen regards her as the fount of all wisdom and benevolence, but you and I are both aware that this isn't going to be easy. The countess and Pandora will go at it beak-and-claw the entire time."

Helen smiled up at him, seeing the concern in his dark blue eyes. "It's only for a month. We'll learn how to get on with her. And Mr. Winterborne will be nearby."

West's frown deepened. "That doesn't make me feel any better."

Perplexed, Helen asked, "What are you concerned about?"

"That you'll be manipulated and taken advantage of until you feel like you've been flattened in a washing mangle."

"Mr. Winterborne won't take advantage of me."

West snorted. "You only say that because he already has." Taking Helen by the shoulders, he looked into her upturned face. "Little friend, I want you to be cautious, and remember that London is not a magical land of happiness and cake-shops, and every stranger is not a hero in disguise."

Helen gave him a reproachful glance. "I'm not *that* unworldly."

One of his brows arched. "Are we sure about that? Because the last time you were there, you decided to gallivant off to Winterborne's unaccompanied, and—oddly enough—returned home thoroughly deflowered."

Her color heightened. "He and I made a bargain."

"There was no need for a bargain. He would have married you anyway."

"You don't know that."

"Darling, everyone knew it, except apparently you. No, don't bother arguing, we haven't time. Just bear in mind that if you have any trouble at all, if anything goes wrong for you or the twins, I want you to send for me. Have a footman run a note to the nearest telegraph office, and I'll be there like a shot. Promise me you'll do that."

"I promise." Helen stood on her toes to kiss his cheek, and told him, "I think you're a hero in disguise."

"Do you?" West shook his head ruefully. "Then it's a good thing you don't know more about me." He offered her his arm. "Come, it's time to join the others in the entrance hall. Do you happen to have a pocket-mirror?"

"I'm afraid not. Why?"

"I've made you late, which means by now Lady Berwick has sprouted serpents from her head, and I can't look at her directly."

To no one's surprise, Lady Berwick insisted that Rhys occupy the seat next to hers on the journey up to London. He obliged her, of course, but every now and then he twisted to glance longingly at Helen, who sat in the row behind them with her embroidery hoop.

As Helen worked on an appliqué flower, attaching the edges of a leaf with a delicate featherstitch, she listened unobtrusively to their conversation. Rhys treated Lady Berwick with respectful interest but didn't seem awed by her in the least. He asked about her favorite subject, horses and their training, saying frankly that he knew little about it and was an adequate rider at best. The admission produced an enthusiastic response from the countess, who loved nothing better than to dispense information and advice.

Helen's attention was diverted by the twins, who were talking in the seats behind her.

". . . that word from *Othello* that we're not supposed to know," Pandora was saying.

"Fustilarian?" Cassandra guessed.

"No, silly. And that's not from *Othello*, that's from one of the Henrys. I'm referring to the thing that Othello calls Bianca when he thinks she loves another man." At her twin's perplexed expression, Pandora whispered the forbidden word.

"I don't know that one," Cassandra said.

"That's because you read the abridged version. But I read the original, and I looked up the word in the dictionary. It means 'a woman who lies with a man for money.'"

"Why would a man pay a woman to sleep with him?" Cassandra asked, sounding puzzled. "Unless it's very cold, and there aren't enough blankets. But it would be simpler to buy more blankets, wouldn't it?"

"I'd rather sleep with dogs. They're much warmer than people."

Perturbed, Helen reflected that it wasn't right to keep the twins so sheltered. Years ago, she had taken it upon herself to tell them in advance about their monthly courses, so that when it happened, neither of them would be shocked and terrified, as she had been. Why should they be kept in ignorance of the rest of it? After all, forewarned was forearmed. She decided to explain the basic facts to the twins at the first available opportunity, rather than let them come to the wrong conclusions on their own.

The train arrived at Waterloo Station, the sheds crowded and milling, the air thick with the usual cacophony of noise. As soon as the Ravenels and their retinue descended to the platform, they were met by four blue-uniformed employees from Winterborne's, who collected their luggage, placed it on wheeled carts, and cleared a path with magical efficiency. Helen was privately amused by Lady Berwick's struggle not to appear impressed as they were escorted out to a pair of private carriages—one for family, one for the servants—and a wagon for surplus luggage.

Rhys's carriage was a magnificent vehicle of modern design, finished in glossy black lacquer with the familiar ornate W monogrammed on the side. Standing at the door of the carriage, Rhys personally handed each occupant into the vehicle, beginning with Lady Berwick and then Helen. He paused as one of the twins tugged at his sleeve imploringly. Casting a brief glance at the seated women, he said ruefully, "I beg your indulgence for a moment."

The door closed, leaving Helen and Lady Berwick inside.

The countess frowned. "What is this about?"

Helen shook her head slightly, mystified.

The door opened with a smooth *click*, swung out a few inches, and closed again. *Click*. It opened and closed once more.

Helen bit back a grin as she realized that the twins

were playing with the newfangled outer handle, which opened by slightly pressing the handle down, instead of turning it partway around in the ordinary manner.

"Girls!" Lady Berwick exclaimed in annoyance, the next time the door opened. "Come inside at once."

Looking abashed, Pandora and Cassandra entered the carriage and sat beside Helen.

The countess stared at them icily. "We do not play with door handles."

"Mr. Winterborne said we could," Pandora mumbled.

"I daresay he knows little about the proper deportment of young ladies."

As Rhys settled into the seat next to the countess, he replied in a sober manner, but the outer corners of his eyes had creased slightly. "Forgive me, my lady. When I saw their interest, I thought to show them how the mechanism worked."

Mollified, the countess said in a quieter tone, "One must exert restraint on active young minds. Too much thinking will excite the sparks of vice."

Helen pressed her elbow against Pandora's side, warning her to stay silent.

"My parents were of the same opinion," Rhys said

easily. "An overactive mind, my father said, would make me insolent and unsatisfied. 'Know your place,' he told me, 'and keep to it.'"

"Did you heed him?" Lady Berwick asked.

He laughed softly. "If I had, my lady, I would be keeping shop on High Street at this moment—not sitting in a carriage with a countess."

Chapter 22

To Helen's disappointment, there was little opportunity to see Rhys during their first week in London. After the days he had been absent from his office, work had accumulated and there were many matters that required his attention. When he paid a call to Ravenel House one afternoon, his interaction with Helen was limited to small talk, with the countess and the twins seated nearby. Lady Berwick's rules about visiting were explicit and unyielding: Calls must be paid during specified hours, and the visitor should stay no longer than fifteen minutes. After a quarter of an hour had passed, the countess glanced meaningfully at the clock.

Rhys's gaze met Helen's in a moment of shared impatience and yearning, and the corners of his lips twitched as he stood. "I believe I've stayed long enough."

"We've quite enjoyed your visit, Mr. Winterborne," Lady Berwick said, rising to her feet also. "You are welcome to dine with us the evening after next, if your schedule can accommodate it."

"Friday?" Rhys frowned in regret. "I would love nothing better, my lady, but I've already committed to attending a private dinner with the prime minister."

"Mr. Disraeli?" Helen asked, her eyes widening. "Is he a friend of yours?"

"An acquaintance. He wants my support for a labor law reform bill, to allow workers the legal right to go on strike."

"I didn't realize it was illegal," Helen said.

Rhys smiled at her interest. "Only a handful of craft societies—carpenters, bricklayers, iron founders—are legally allowed. But many other union members do it nevertheless, and are jailed as a result."

"Do you want them to have the right to strike?" Helen asked. "Even though you're a business owner?"

"Aye, the working class should enjoy the same rights as everyone else in society."

"It is not for women to concern ourselves with such matters," Lady Berwick said, waving away the matter.

"I shall endeavor to find a mutually acceptable date for dinner, Mr. Winterborne."

"I will see him out, ma'am," Helen said, striving to tamp down her frustration at not having even a second alone with him.

Lady Berwick shook her head decisively. "My dear, it is improper to accompany a gentleman all the way to the door."

Helen sent her sisters a pleading glance.

Instantly Pandora nudged her chair with the back of her leg, toppling it over. "*Blast*," she exclaimed. "How did that happen?"

The countess turned to face her. "Pandora, that word!"

"What should I say when I knock something over?"

There was a brief silence as Lady Berwick considered the question. "You may say 'alas.'"

"'Alas?' Pandora echoed in distaste. "But that's such a flabby word."

"What does it even mean?" Cassandra asked.

While the twins kept Lady Berwick occupied, Helen slipped out into the hallway with Rhys.

Without a word, he slid a hand to the nape of her neck and brought her mouth to his, devouring her with heat and pure male hunger. She inhaled sharply as he pulled her hard against him, his breath striking her cheek in scorching rushes.

"Helen?" The countess's voice came from the front parlor.

Rhys let go of her instantly. He stared at her, his hands opening and closing as if they itched for the feel of her.

Dazed, Helen tried to steady her wobbly knees. "You should probably leave," she whispered. With an attempt at humor, she added lamely, "Alas."

Rhys gave her a sardonic glance before going to fetch his hat and gloves from a demilune table. "I can't call again during visiting hours, *cariad*. For the past fifteen minutes, I've suffered like a starving man outside a bakery window."

"When will I see you next?"

He settled the hat on his head and tugged on his gloves. "I'll make certain she brings you to the store on Monday evening."

"Will we have any privacy there?" Helen asked doubtfully, following him to the door.

Pausing to look down at her, Rhys stroked her cheek with his forefinger, and she shivered at the caress of smooth black leather. Gently he gripped her jaw and stared at her mouth. "The store is my territory," he said. "What do you think?"

The following day, the parlor was filled with no less than a dozen women whom Lady Berwick had invited for a special visit. These were the matrons who supervised the most important events of the season. It was their responsibility to shape the next generation of wives and mothers, and the fates of all marriageable young women depended on their good favor.

"Say as little as possible," Lady Berwick told the girls severely. "Remember that silence is golden." Glancing at Pandora, she added, "In your case, it's platinum."

The three sisters occupied a corner of the parlor, quiet and wide-eyed as the group of matrons chatted and drank tea to the health of the Queen. A genial discussion of the weather led to a consensus that it had been unusually cold, and spring would certainly be late that year.

Helen paid close attention as Lady Berwick sought the general opinion on the dressmaker at Winterborne's, and was reassured from all sides that the lady in question, Mrs. Allenby, produced fashions of exceptional quality. Now that Mrs. Allenby had become an official court dressmaker, one could not secure an appointment without first being placed on a waiting list.

"One assumes, however," a dowager remarked with a smile, "that Lady Helen will be able to obtain an appointment without having to wait."

Helen kept her gaze modestly down.

"Indeed she will," Lady Berwick answered for her. "Mr. Winterborne has been most accommodating."

"You've made his acquaintance?" one of the ladies asked.

A multitude of chairs creaked in unison as the group leaned forward, ears twitching to catch the countess's reply.

"He escorted us to London on the train."

As excited murmurs fluttered among the group, Lady Berwick cast Helen a meaningful glance.

Helen instantly took the cue. "If your ladyship has no objection," she said demurely, "my sisters and I will withdraw to study our history lessons."

"Very good, my dear, attend to your education."

Helen and the twins curtsied to the group, and left the room. As they crossed the threshold, a barrage of questions about Mr. Winterborne filled the parlor.

"Let's go upstairs," Helen told the twins uncomfortably as they paused to listen. "Eavesdroppers hear no good of themselves."

"Yes," Pandora conceded, "but they hear *fascinating* things about other people."

"Hush," Cassandra urged in a whisper, straining to listen.

". . . his features are pleasing, although not as delicate as one might wish," Lady Berwick was saying. She paused, her voice lowering marginally. "He has an abundant crop of hair—jet black—a virile development of beard, a strapping build, and a robust physique."

"And his temperament?" someone asked.

"As high-spirited as a Barbary stallion," Lady Berwick replied with relish. "Obviously he is well-adapted for the duties of paternity."

An excited volley of comments and questions followed.

"I wonder if they ever actually talk about charity events at their meetings," Cassandra whispered drolly, while Helen tugged her away.

Having managed to survive the ladies' gathering without committing social suicide, Pandora, Cassandra, and Helen were all excused from the obligation of receiving callers during visiting hours the next day. Pandora cajoled Cassandra into helping with the artwork for her board game, while Helen sat alone with a book in the upstairs parlor.

For several minutes, she stared at the words without reading them, while her mind spun in a weary carousel. Chilled despite the warmth of the room, she set the book aside and wrapped her arms around herself.

"My lady." The footman, Peter, had come to the threshold of the parlor. "Lady Berwick wishes for you to join her in the receiving room."

Straightening in her chair, Helen gave him a perplexed glance. "Did she explain why?"

"To help entertain a visitor."

Helen stood uneasily. "Did she send for the twins as well?"

"No, my lady, only you."

"Please tell her that I'll be down directly."

After smoothing her hair and straightening her skirts, Helen descended the stairs and went to the receiving room. She blinked, her steps slowing, as she saw that Lady Berwick was waiting for her at the threshold.

"Ma'am," she said with a questioning frown.

The countess kept her back turned to the visitor in the receiving room. Her posture was upright and elegant as always, but something about her reminded Helen of a starling she'd once seen perched on the hand of an itinerant bird seller. The bird's wings had been pinned to its sides with fetters and a length of packthread . . . but its eyes had been wild and bright with the longing for freedom.

"Unexpectedly," Lady Berwick said in a soft undertone, "my husband's heir has come to meet you. You need say very little to him. Straighten your spine."

With no more preparation than that, Helen found herself pulled into the receiving room.

"Lady Helen," the countess said evenly, "this is my nephew, Mr. Vance."

Chapter 23

Helen felt an all-over sting, as if she'd been dropped into a flash-fire. Then she couldn't feel anything at all except the brutal pounding of her heart, like a fist beating against a closed door. She curtsied without lifting her gaze.

"How do you do?" she heard him murmur. A pleasant voice, dry and smooth, not too deep.

Some outside force seemed to be guiding Helen's actions. She entered the room and went to a chair near the settee, arranging her skirts by force of habit. After Vance had occupied the settee, she brought herself to look at him.

Albion Vance was singularly handsome in a way that made her skin crawl. She had never seen anyone who looked like him, his complexion white and incongruously youthful, his eyes pale gray-blue, his cropped hair snow-colored and gleaming like the inside of an oyster shell. His honed features reminded her of the thin-nosed wax heads in barbershop windows, set out to display the latest hairdressing styles. He was an average-sized man, lean and compactly built, his legs crossed with feline grace.

With an unpleasant shock of recognition, Helen saw that his brows and lashes were dark, just as hers were. Oh, how peculiar this was—she was grateful for the unearthly calm that had settled over her, muffling every sensation.

Vance regarded her with a detached stare. There was something corrupt and magnetic about him, the sense of an icy flame animating a self-interested spirit.

"You remind me of your mother," he observed. "Although you are more delicate."

Perfectly aware that she had instantly been assessed and found lacking, Helen asked, "Were you acquainted with her, Mr. Vance? I don't recall having seen you at Eversby Priory."

"From time to time I saw her at social events, when she was at town." He smiled, revealing a perfect row of small white teeth. "A captivating beauty. Childlike in her impetuosity. She loved to dance and couldn't keep her feet still when music was playing. One time I told her that she reminded me of that charming tale, the one with the red shoes."

Helen had always hated that story, in which a little girl who had dared to wear red shoes to her confirmation had been doomed to dance in them until she died. "You're referring to the one by Hans Christian Andersen? It's a morality tale about the wages of sin, is it not?"

His smile faded, and his gaze returned to hers, now appraising rather than dismissive. "I confess, I don't recall the moral of the story."

"No doubt it's been a long time since you've read it." Helen made her face into the inscrutable mask that had always annoyed the twins and provoked them to call her a sphinx. "The red shoes become instruments of death, after a girl yields to temptation."

Vance regarded her suspiciously, clearly wondering if that had been a deliberate dig. "I was sorry to learn of your mother's passing, and more recently, of your father and brother. These have been tragic times for the Ravenels."

"We hope for better days ahead," Helen said in a neutral tone.

Vance turned to Lady Berwick with an unsettling, foxlike grin. "The Ravenels seem to be recovering nicely. Our clever Kathleen has certainly wasted no time in snapping up the next Earl of Trenear."

The countess couldn't entirely conceal her annoyance at the implication that Kathleen had married Devon out of calculation and opportunism. "It is a love match," she said shortly.

"So was her first marriage. How convenient for Kathleen that she loves so easily."

Helen loathed him. There was something polluted about him, something unappeasably cruel. She was appalled that his blood ran through her veins. She remembered what Rhys had said a few nights earlier: *Any child of his is demon spawn, and would come to no good.* Now having met Vance, she had to agree. How could her mother have fallen under the spell of a man like this? How could Peggy Crewe?

It must be that evil had its own attractions, just as goodness did.

Vance turned back to her. "Lady Helen, I have heard that you are engaged to marry Mr. Winterborne. A pity that you must take a husband outside your appropriate sphere. But still, my congratulations to you both."

The comment rankled far more than when Lady Berwick had said the same thing in Hampshire. Only the awareness that Vance was goading her deliberately kept Helen from losing her composure. But she was sorely tempted to reply that if he were so concerned about people staying within their "appropriate spheres," he should have refrained from having affairs with married women.

"I do hope someone has cautioned you," Vance continued, "that your children may turn out to be a coarse, rebellious lot, no matter how gently they're reared. It's in the blood. One might tame a wolf, but its offspring will always be born wild. The Welsh are volatile and dishonest by nature. They lie easily and often, even when the truth would serve just as well. They love nothing more than to spite their betters, and they will do or say anything to avoid honest work."

Helen thought of Rhys, who had worked ceaselessly for his entire life, and had done nothing to deserve the contempt of a man born to a life of privilege. Feeling her hands begin to ball into tight fists, she forced them to remain folded in her lap. "How have you come to be so informed on the subject?" she asked.

Lady Berwick tried to intercede. "Mr. Vance, I think—"

"Much of it is common knowledge," he told Helen. "But I also toured throughout Wales to gather information for a pamphlet I was writing. I felt it my obligation to establish the necessity of banishing the

Welsh language from their schools. It's a poor medium of instruction, and yet they stubbornly insist on clinging to it."

"Imagine," Helen said softly.

"Oh yes," Vance said, either missing the edge of sarcasm, or choosing to ignore it. "Something must be done to awaken their intelligence, and it begins with forcing English on them, whether they like it or not." As he continued, Helen saw that he was no longer posturing or trying to provoke her, but rather speaking with sincere conviction. "The Welsh must be saved from their own sloth and brutality. As things stand now, they don't even make fit servants."

Lady Berwick glanced quickly at Helen's stiff face, and sought to ease the tension. "You must have found it a relief to return to England from your tour," she said to Vance.

His reply was emphatic. "I would rather be thrown in the fiery pit of hell than return to Wales."

Unable to tolerate him for another second, Helen stood and said coolly, "I'm sure that can be arranged, Mr. Vance."

Caught off guard, Vance rose slowly to his feet. "Why, you—"

"Do excuse me," Helen said. "I have correspondence to attend to." And she left the room without another word, fighting every instinct to keep from breaking into a run.

Helen had no idea how many minutes passed as she lay curled on her bed, using one hand to press a folded handkerchief against her streaming eyes. She tried to breathe around the sharp repeated pains in her throat.

Having no father at all would have been infinitely better than this. Albion Vance was more hateful than she could ever have imagined, warped in all directions. And she had come from him. His blood ran in her veins like venom.

The sins of the fathers shall be visited on the children. Everyone knew that Biblical principle. Somewhere in her nature, something vile must have been passed down from him.

There came a brief tap at her door, and Lady Berwick entered, carrying two glasses of amber liquid. "You handled yourself very well," she remarked, pausing at the foot of the bed.

"By insulting your guest?" Helen asked in a waterlogged voice.

"He was not my guest," the countess said tersely. "He's a despicable parasite. A worm who would feast on the cankered sores of Job. I had no idea that Vance would appear today without a word of warning."

Peeling the damp handkerchief from her eyes, Helen blew her nose. "Mr. Winterborne will be angry," she said. "He made it clear that I wasn't to associate with Mr. Vance in any way."

"Then I shouldn't tell him, if I were you."

Helen's fingers closed around the handkerchief, compressing it into a ball. "You're advising me to keep a secret from him?"

"I believe you and I are both aware of why it is very much in your interest *not* to tell Mr. Winterborne."

Helen stared at her dumbly. Oh, God, she knew, *she knew.*

Coming around to the side of the bed, Lady Berwick gave her one of the glasses. "Brandy," she said.

Lifting the drink to her lips, Helen took a cautious sip, and another. It burned her lips, and the taste was very sharp. "I thought ladies weren't supposed to drink brandy," she said huskily.

"Not in public. However, one may take it in private when a stimulant is required."

As Helen sipped the brandy, the countess spoke to her without superiority, but rather unsparing honesty tempered with a surprising touch of kindness. "Last year, when I informed Vance that Kathleen was to marry into your family, he confided in me about his affair with your mother. He claimed you were his child.

The first time I saw you, I had no doubt of it. Your hair is the color his once was, and your brows and eyes are the same."

"Does Kathleen know?"

"No, she has no idea. I wasn't certain if you yourself knew, until I saw your face just before you entered the parlor. But you composed yourself quickly. Your self-possession was admirable, Helen."

"Did Mr. Vance intend to reveal the news to me today?"

"Yes. However, you foiled his plans for a dramatic scene." The countess paused to sip her brandy, and said darkly, "Before he left, he asked me to make it perfectly clear to you that he's your father."

"That word doesn't apply to him."

"I agree. A man is not entitled to be called a father merely because he once had a well-timed spasm of the loins."

Helen smiled faintly despite the fog of gloom. It sounded like something Kathleen might have said. Propping herself higher on the bed, she rubbed the sore corners of her eyes with a thumb and forefinger. "He'll want money," she said flatly.

"Obviously. You will soon become a conduit to one of the greatest fortunes in England. I have no doubt that in the future, he will also ask you to influence your husband's business decisions."

"I wouldn't do that to Mr. Winterborne. Besides . . . I couldn't live with Mr. Vance's threats hanging over my head."

"I have for decades, my girl. Since the day I married Lord Berwick, I knew that until I produced male issue, I would have to kowtow to Vance. Now you must as well. If you don't comply with his demands, he will ruin your marriage. Possibly before it even begins."

"He won't have the chance," Helen said dully. "I'm going to tell Mr. Winterborne myself."

Lady Berwick's eyes enlarged until the whites were fully visible. "You're not so foolish as to believe that he would still want you if he knew."

"No, he won't want me. But I owe him the truth."

After swallowing the rest of her brandy in an impatient gulp, the countess set the glass aside and spoke with irritated conviction. "Good heavens, child, I want you to mind every word I'm about to say." She waited until Helen's tormented gaze had met hers. "The world is unkind to women. Our futures are founded on sand. I am a *countess*, Helen, and yet in the winter of life I am likely to become a poor widow, a mere nullity. You must do whatever is necessary to marry Mr. Winterborne, because there is one thing a woman needs above all else: security. Even if you should lose your husband's affections, the smallest splinter of his fortune will guarantee that you will never suffer degradation or poverty. Better still if you should bear a son—*there* is the source of a woman's true power and influence."

"Mr. Winterborne won't want a child who is descended from Albion Vance."

"There's nothing he can do about it after it happens, is there?"

Helen's eyes widened. "I couldn't deceive him that way."

"My dear," Lady Berwick said crisply, "you are naïve. Do you think there aren't parts of his life, past and present, which he keeps secret from you? Husbands and wives are never completely honest with each other—no marriage could survive it."

Becoming aware of a throbbing at her temples, and a gathering nausea in her stomach, Helen wondered desperately if a migraine were coming on. "I feel ill," she whispered.

"Finish your brandy." The countess went to the window and pushed a fold of the curtain aside to take in the outside view. "Vance wants to meet with you tomorrow. If you refuse, he'll go to Mr. Winterborne before the day is out."

"I won't refuse," Helen said, thinking grimly that she would tell Rhys the truth at a time she chose, on her own terms.

"I'll send word for him to meet us on neutral territory. It won't do to have him call at Ravenel House again."

Helen thought for a moment. "The British Museum," she suggested. "The twins have been asking to see the Zoological Galleries. He and I could exchange a few words there without anyone noticing."

"Yes, I think that would do. What should I suggest as a meeting-place?"

Helen paused in the act of lifting the glass to her lips. "The poisonous serpents exhibit," she said, and took another sip.

Lady Berwick smiled slightly, and then looked grim. "I already know the way Vance will present the situation to you, as I am all too familiar with the way his mind works. He won't like the word blackmail; he'll frame it as something like an annual tax, in return for allowing you to find happiness with Mr. Winterborne."

"There's no such thing as a tax on happiness," Helen said, rubbing her forehead.

The countess regarded her with rueful sympathy. "My poor girl . . . it certainly can't be had for free."

Chapter 24

"Helen, are you certain there's nothing wrong?" Cassandra asked, after they had descended from the family carriage. "You've been so quiet, and your eyes are glazed."

"My head aches a little, that's all."

"Oh I'm sorry. Should we go to the museum another day?"

"No, I won't feel any better for being at home. Perhaps some walking will set me to rights."

They linked arms and proceeded together, while far ahead of them, Pandora hurried toward the imposing stone portico of the British Museum.

Lady Berwick puffed impatiently as she hastened after the girl. "Pandora, do not gallop like a chaise-horse!"

The British Museum, a Grecian-styled quadrangle with a two-acre courtyard, was so large that despite a half-dozen visits in the past, they still had seen only a third of its exhibits. Last night, when Lady Berwick had casually suggested a jaunt to the museum, the twins had been overjoyed. Helen, knowing the real reason for the visit, had been far more subdued.

After purchasing tickets and collecting printed maps in the Hall, the group proceeded toward the principal staircase that led to the upper floors. A trio of towering giraffes had been artfully arranged at the top of the staircase, at the entrance of the Zoological Galleries. The front legs of the largest animal were even taller than Lady Berwick. A little wooden railing had been erected in front of the giraffes to keep the public at bay.

The women paused to regard the taxidermied creatures with awe.

Predictably, Pandora went forward with her hand outstretched.

"Pandora," Lady Berwick snapped, "if you molest the exhibits, we will not be returning to the museum."

Turning, Pandora gave her a pleading glance. "A giraffe is *right there*—it once roamed the African savannah—don't you want to know how it feels?"

"Indeed not."

"There's no sign that says we can't."

"The railing implies it."

"But the giraffe is *so* close," Pandora said woefully. "If you would look the other way for five seconds, I could reach out and touch it so easily . . . and then I wouldn't have to wonder anymore."

Sighing and scowling, Lady Berwick glanced at their surroundings to make certain they were unobserved. "Be quick about it," she said tersely.

Pandora darted forward, reached over the railing to feel the creature's limb and furrowed knee, and scurried back to the group. "It's like a horse's coat," she reported with satisfaction. "The hairs are no longer than a half-inch. Cassandra, do you want to feel it?"

"No, thank you."

Pandora took her twin's hand. "Come on, then—shall we go to the hoofed beasts, or the ones with claws?"

"Claws."

Lady Berwick began to follow the girls, but she paused to take another glance at the giraffe. In a few hasty strides, she went to the exhibit, furtively touched its leg, and glanced guiltily at Helen.

Biting back a smile, Helen looked down at her map, pretending not to have seen.

After the countess joined the twins in the southern gallery, Helen headed to the northern one, consisting of five vast rooms filled with exhibits contained in enormous glass cases. Finding the second room, she walked past displays of reptiles. She paused at the sight of a lizard with a large frill around its neck, which reminded her of Queen Elizabeth's ruff. According to the placard beside it, the lizard could expand the frill to make itself look threatening.

Before Helen proceeded to the next case, containing a variety of serpents, a man came to stand beside her. Knowing that he was Mr. Vance, she closed her eyes briefly, her muscles tensing with instant antagonism.

He studied a pair of African chameleons. Eventually he murmured, "Your scent . . . it's the same one your mother wore. *Calanthe* orchids and vanilla . . . I've never forgotten it."

It caught her off guard, the notion that he had been so familiar with her mother's scent. No one had ever noticed that Helen wore the same fragrance. "I found the recipe in one of her journals."

"It suits you."

Helen looked up to find his evaluating gaze on her.

Albion Vance was riveting at this close distance, his high-cheeked face fashioned with sharply androgynous delicacy. His eyes were the color of a November sky.

"You're a pretty girl, though not as beautiful as she was," he commented. "You favor me. Did she resent you?"

"I would prefer not to discuss my mother with you."

"I want you to understand that she meant something to me."

Helen returned her attention to the case of lizards. Mr. Vance seemed to expect a reply, but she couldn't think of one.

Her lack of response seemed to annoy him.

"I, of course, am the heartless seducer," Mr. Vance said in an arid tone, "who abandoned his lover and newborn daughter. But Jane had no intention of leaving the earl, nor did I want her to. As for you . . . I was in no position to do anything for you, nor you for me."

"But now that I'm engaged to a wealthy man," Helen said coolly, "you've finally taken an interest. Let's not waste time, Mr. Vance. Do you have a shopping list of demands, or would you rather name a simple financial figure?"

His fine dark brows lifted. "I had hoped we could come to an arrangement without being crass."

Helen was silent, waiting with forced patience, staring at him in a way that seemed to make him uncomfortable.

"A little icicle, aren't you?" he asked. "There's something vestal about you. No spirit. That is why you lack your mother's beauty."

She refused to rise to the bait. "What do you want, Mr. Vance?"

"Among Lady Berwick's many philanthropic concerns," he finally said, "is a charity that administers pensions to blind paupers. I want you to persuade Winterborne to donate twenty thousand pounds to the charity's board of trustees. You will explain that his generous gift will be used to purchase freehold ground rents at West Hackney, which will produce annual dividends for the benefit of the blind pensioners."

"But instead," Helen said slowly, "you've worked out a way to benefit yourself."

"The donation must be made right away. I have immediate need of capital."

"You want me to ask this of Mr. Winterborne before he and I are even married?" Helen asked incredulously. "I don't think I could convince him to do it."

"Women have their ways. You'll manage."

Helen shook her head. "He won't hand over money without having the charity investigated. He'll find out."

"There will be no documents for him to uncover," Mr. Vance replied smugly. "I can't be attached either to the charity or the property at West Hackney, the arrangements are verbal."

"What will happen to the blind pensioners?"

"Some of the money will filter down to them, of course, to make everything appear aboveboard."

"Just so I understand the situation clearly," Helen said, "you're blackmailing your daughter to enable you to steal from blind paupers."

"No one is stealing from the paupers; the money isn't theirs to begin with. And this is not blackmail. A daughter has a natural obligation to help her father when he is in need of assistance."

"Why am I obligated to you?" Helen asked, bewildered. "What have you ever done for me?"

"I gave you the gift of life."

Seeing that he was perfectly serious, Helen gave him a disbelieving glance. An irrepressible, half-hysterical burst of giggles rose from her chest. She pressed her fingers to her lips, trying to hold the laughter back, but that only made it worse. It didn't help to see Mr. Vance's offended expression.

"You find that amusing?" he asked.

"P-pardon me," Helen sputtered, struggling to be quiet. "But it didn't take much effort on your part, did it? Other than a . . . a timely spasm of the loins."

Mr. Vance glared at her with frosty dignity. "Don't demean the relationship I had with your mother."

"Oh yes. She 'meant something' to you." The wild,

mirthless giggles faded, and Helen took an unsteady breath. "I suppose Peggy Crewe did as well."

His cold gaze fixed on hers. "So Winterborne told you about that. I thought he might."

Becoming aware of a woman and three children coming to view the lizard display, Helen was forestalled from replying. She affected interest in a glass case of turtles and tortoises, and wandered to it slowly, while Mr. Vance accompanied her.

"There's no reason for Winterborne to harbor everlasting hatred toward me," Vance said, "for doing something that most men have done. I'm not the first to sleep with a married woman, nor will I be the last."

"Because of you," Helen pointed out, "Mrs. Crewe died in her childbed, and her husband—a man whom Mr. Winterborne loved like a brother—ended up dead as well."

"Is it my fault that the husband was so weak-minded as to commit suicide? Is it my fault if a woman hasn't the constitution for childbirth? The entire situation could have been avoided had Peggy chosen not to spread her legs in the first place. I only took what was eagerly offered."

His callousness stole Helen's breath away. He seemed to have no more conscience than a shark. What had made him this way? She stared at him, searching for any hint of humanity, any flicker of guilt, regret, or sadness. There was nothing.

"What did you do with the baby?" she asked.

The question seemed to surprise him. "I found a woman to look after her."

"When was the last time you saw her?"

"I've never seen her. Nor do I intend to." Mr. Vance looked impatient. "That has nothing to do with the matter at hand."

"You have no interest in her welfare?"

"Why should I, when her mother's family doesn't? No one wants the misbegotten bastard."

No doubt he had thought the same thing about her. Helen felt a nagging, anxious, rapidly increasing concern for the little girl, her half-sister. Was the child being nurtured and educated? Neglected? Abused?

"What is the name of the woman who takes care of her?" she asked. "Where does she live?"

"It's none of your concern."

"Apparently it's none of *yours*," Helen shot back, "but I would like to know."

Mr. Vance smirked. "So you can use her against me in some way? Attempt to embarrass me?"

"Why would I try to embarrass you? It's in my interest to avoid scandal just as much as it is yours."

"Then I advise you to forget the child."

"Shame on you," Helen said quietly. "Not only have you rejected responsibility for your own child, you're also trying to prevent someone else from helping her."

"I've paid for her upkeep these past four years— what else would you have me do? Personally spoon-feed the brat?"

Helen tried to think above a rush of inchoate rage. She wouldn't be able to find out about her half sister's welfare unless she could pry the information from Mr. Vance. Racking her brains, she recalled what Rhys had once told her about business negotiations.

"You've demanded a large sum of money and will expect more in the future," she said, "but all you've offered in return is to let me keep something I already have. I won't agree to a bargain without a concession from you. A small one: It will cost you nothing to tell me who has your daughter."

A long silence passed before Mr. Vance replied. "Ada Tapley. She's a charwoman for my solicitor's relations in Welling."

"Where—"

"It's a village on the main road from London to Kent."

"What is the child's name?"

"I have no idea."

Of course you don't, Helen thought, writhing inwardly with fury.

"We agree on the bargain, then?" Mr. Vance asked. "You'll convince Winterborne to make the charity donation as soon as possible."

"If I intend to marry him," Helen said woodenly, "I have no choice."

Something in his face eased. In a moment, he grinned. "I find it delicious, that he thinks he's bought a Ravenel to breed, and instead he'll be furthering *my* lineage. Welsh Vances, God help us all."

For a few minutes after he left her, Helen stared into the case of artfully preserved and arranged creatures. Their sightless glass eyes were permanently wide with surprise, as if they couldn't fathom how they'd come to be there.

The full awareness of her own ruin sank in, and with it, a new feeling. Self-loathing.

She would never ask Rhys for the so-called charity donation. Nor could she marry him. Not now. She would never inflict Albion Vance—or herself—on him.

Telling Rhys the truth would be a nightmare, more hideous than she could imagine. She didn't know how she would find the courage to do it, but there was no choice.

A shadow of grief hovered around her, but she

couldn't give in to it yet. There would be time to grieve later.

Years, in fact.

Much later in the day, after they had returned from the museum, Helen sat alone at the upstairs parlor writing desk, and dipped a pen into a well of India ink.

Dear Mrs. Tapley,

Recently I learned about a female child who was given into your care as a newborn infant, some four years ago. I would like to inquire if she is still residing with you, and if so, I would appreciate any information you could give about her . . .

Chapter 25

"This all seems rather untoward," Lady Berwick said, frowning as the Ravenel carriage approached the mews behind the enormous department store building. "Shopping at six o'clock in the evening, and at such a place. But Mr. Winterborne was most insistent."

"It's *private* shopping," Pandora reminded her. "Which, when one thinks of it, is really much more discreet than shopping along a promenade at midday."

The countess didn't seem pacified by the idea. "The sales clerks won't know my preferences. They might be impertinent."

"I promise your ladyship," Helen said, "they will be very helpful." She would have continued, but the throbbing, pulsing pain in her was worsening. Her anxiety over seeing Rhys tonight had set off a migraine. She didn't know how she could behave as though nothing were wrong. How could she talk and smile and behave affectionately to him when she knew they were never going to marry? The ache spread behind her forehead and eyes like a stain.

"I only want to see the gloves," Lady Berwick said primly. "After that I will occupy a chair and wait during your appointment with the dressmaker."

"I don't expect it will last long," Helen murmured, keeping her eyes closed. "I may have to return home soon."

"Does your head hurt?" Cassandra asked in concern.

"I'm afraid so."

Cassandra touched her arm gently. "Poor you."

Pandora, however, was not quite as sympathetic. "Helen, *please* try to rise above it. Think of something soothing—imagine your head is a sky filled with peaceful white clouds."

"It feels like a drawer full of knives," Helen murmured ruefully, rubbing her temples. "I promise to hold out for as long as I'm able, dear. I know you want time to shop."

"We'll take you to the furniture department and you can lie on a chaise," Pandora said helpfully.

"Ladies do not recline in public," Lady Berwick said.

The footman assisted them from the vehicle and guided them to one of the back entrances, where a uniformed doorman awaited them.

Occupied with the stabbing pain in her head, Helen followed blindly as they were shown into the store. She heard Lady Berwick's murmurs of astonishment upon being led through opulent spaces with arched openings and lofty ceilings, with brilliant chandeliers showering light down to the polished wood floors. Tables and counters were heaped with treasure, and glass cases featured row upon row of luxurious merchandise. Instead of small, closed-in rooms, the departments were airy, open halls, encouraging customers to wander freely. The air smelled like wood polish and perfume and newness, an expensive smell.

As they reached the six-story central rotunda, with scrollwork balconies at every floor and a massive stained-glass dome ceiling, Lady Berwick couldn't conceal her amazement.

Following the countess's gaze upward, Pandora said reverently, "It's the church of shopping."

The countess was too bemused to reprimand her for the blasphemy.

Rhys approached them, relaxed and handsome in a

dark suit of clothes. Even Helen's oncoming migraine couldn't inhibit a glow of pleasure at the sight of him, so powerful and self-assured in this world he had created. His gaze connected with hers for a brief, hot instant, then switched to Lady Berwick. He bowed over the older woman's hand and smiled as he straightened.

"Welcome to Winterborne's, my lady."

"This is extraordinary." Lady Berwick sounded bewildered, almost plaintive. She looked on either side of her, at the halls that seemed to go on and on, as if a pair of mirrors had been set up to reflect each other infinitely. "There must be two acres of floor space."

"Five acres, including the upper floors," Rhys said in a matter-of-fact manner.

"How could anyone ever find anything in all this excess?"

He gave her a reassuring smile. "It's all well organized, and there are a half-dozen sales clerks to attend you." He gestured to a row of attendants, all impeccably clad in black, cream, and the store's signature deep blue. At his nod, Mrs. Fernsby approached. She wore a stylish black dress with a collar and cuffs of cream lace.

"Lady Berwick," Rhys said, "this is my private secretary, Mrs. Fernsby. She's here to assist with anything you require."

Within five minutes, Lady's Berwick's apprehensions had melted into bemused pleasure as Mrs. Fernsby and the sales assistants devoted themselves to gratifying her every wish. While Lady Berwick was shepherded to the glove counter, Pandora and Cassandra roamed among the first-floor displays.

Rhys came to Helen's side. "What's the matter?" he asked quietly.

The bright lighting seemed to pierce into her brain. She tried to smile, but the effort was excruciating. "My head is aching," she confessed.

With a sympathetic murmur, he turned her toward him. His big hand shaped to her forehead and the side of her face as if testing her temperature. "Have you taken medicine for it?"

"No," she whispered.

"Come with me." Rhys drew her arm through his. "We'll find something at the apothecary counter to make you feel better."

Helen doubted that anything would help, now that the migraine had sunk its claws and fangs into her. "Lady Berwick will want me to stay within her sight."

"She won't notice anything. They're going to keep her busy for at least two hours."

Helen was in too much distress to argue as Rhys pulled her away with him. Mercifully, he didn't ask questions or try to make conversation.

They reached the apothecary hall, where the flooring changed to polished black-and-white tile. It was much dimmer here, as most of the lighting had been turned down at closing. Both sides of the hall were lined with cabinets, shelves, and tables, with a countertop peninsula extending from one of the walls. Every shelf was crowded with jars of powders, pills, liniments, and creams, as well as bottles and vials of tinctures, syrups, and tonics. Assorted medicated confectionaries had been arranged on tables; herbal cough drops, cayenne lozenges, maple sugar, and gum Arabic. Ordinarily Helen wouldn't have minded the blend of astringent and earthy scents in the air, but in her current misery, it was nauseating.

Someone was at the peninsula, sorting through drawers and pausing to make notes. As they drew closer, Helen saw that it was a woman not much older than herself, her slim form dressed in a dark burgundy walking suit, her brown hair topped with a sensible hat.

Glancing up, the woman smiled pleasantly. "Good evening, Mr. Winterborne."

"Still working?" he asked.

"No, I'm about to leave for a local orphanage, to visit the infirmary. I'm low on supplies, and Dr. Havelock told me to take them from the store apothecary. Naturally I'll pay for them tomorrow."

"The store will assume the expense," Rhys said without hesitation. "It's a worthy cause. Take whatever you need."

"Thank you, sir."

"Lady Helen," Rhys said, "this is Dr. Garrett Gibson, one of our two staff physicians."

"Good evening," Helen murmured with a strained smile, pressing her fingers against her right temple as a searing knot throbbed inside her skull.

"An honor," the other woman said automatically, but she regarded Helen with concern. "My lady, you appear to be in discomfort. Is there something I can do?"

"She needs a headache powder," Rhys said.

Dr. Gibson looked at Helen across the counter, her vivid green eyes assessing. "Is the pain all through your head, or is it focused in one area?"

"My temples." Helen paused, taking inventory of the various searing pains in her head, as if burning coals had been randomly inserted. "Also behind my right eye."

"A migraine, then," Dr. Gibson said. "How long ago did it start?"

"Only a few minutes ago, but it's rushing at me like a locomotive."

"I'd recommend a neuralgic powder—it's far more

effective for migraines, as it includes caffeine citrate. Let me fetch a box—I know exactly where they are."

"I'm sorry to be a bother," Helen said weakly, bracing against the counter.

Rhys settled a reassuring hand low on her back.

"Migraines are torture," Dr. Gibson said, striding to a nearby cabinet and rummaging through boxes and tins. "My father is afflicted with them. He's as tough as hippopotamus hide, but he takes to his bed as soon as they begin." Pulling out a green-painted tin with a nod of satisfaction, she brought it to the counter. "You may feel a trifle lightheaded after taking one, but I daresay that's better than splitting pain."

Helen liked her manner immensely, capable and friendly, not at all dispassionate as one might expect of a doctor.

While Dr. Gibson pried off the lid of the tin, Rhys took hold of a sliding wood section of the counter, pushed it back, and reached down to extract a wire stand holding four chilled soda water bottles. "A counter refrigerator," he said, noticing Helen's interest. "Like the ones in grocers' shops."

"I've never been in a grocer's shop," Helen admitted, watching as Rhys took one of the bottles from the stand. The bottles were all egg-shaped with perfectly round bases that couldn't stay upright on their own.

Dr. Gibson took a paper packet from the tin of neuralgic powders, and unfolded it to form a vee-shaped channel. "The taste is dreadful," she said, handing it to Helen. "I suggest pouring it as far back on your tongue as possible."

Rhys untwisted the tiny wire cage that affixed the cork to the bottle top, and handed the vessel to Helen. He grinned as she gave it an uncertain glance. "You've never drunk directly from a bottle before, have you?" His gaze was caressing as he stroked the edge of her jaw with a single knuckle. "Just don't tip it up too fast."

Helen held the paper up to her mouth, tilted her head back, and let the bitter powder slide to her throat. Cautiously she brought the bottle to her lips, poured a splash into her mouth, and swallowed the cold, effervescent liquid. The tart lime-flavored soda helped to mask the bitter medicine.

"Have a little more, *cariad*." Rhys used his thumb to wipe at a tiny stray drop at the corner of her mouth. "This time, seal your lips around the edge."

She took another swallow or two, chasing away the taste of the powder, and gave the bottle back to him. Leaving it uncorked, he set it back on the stand.

Dr. Gibson spoke quietly, her sympathetic gaze

on Helen. "It will begin to take effect in five minutes or so."

Helen closed her eyes and lifted her fingers to her temples again, trying to ease the sensation of needles being driven into her skull. She was aware of Rhys's large form beside her, his presence somehow comforting and distressing at the same time. She thought of what she needed to talk to him about, and how he would react, and her shoulders slumped.

"Some people find that an ice bag or a mustard plaster helps," she heard Dr. Gibson say quietly. "Or a massage of the neck muscles."

Helen twitched with agitation as she felt Rhys's hands settle on her exposed nape. "Oh not here—"

"Shhh." His fingertips found places of excruciating soreness and began to knead gently. "Rest your forearms on the counter."

"If someone should see—"

"They won't. Relax."

Although the circumstances were hardly what Helen would have considered relaxing, she obeyed weakly.

Rhys used his thumbs on the back of Helen's neck, while his fingers pressed into the knotted tightness at the base of her skull. She lowered her head, as her muscles were coaxed and inexorably coerced into releasing their tension. His strong hands worked down her neck to her shoulders with sensitive variations of pressure, finding every tight place. She found herself taking deeper breaths, surrendering to the pleasure of his touch.

As Rhys continued to knead and probe, he spoke over her head to Dr. Gibson. "This orphan asylum you're going to—have you been there before?"

"Yes, I try to go weekly. I visit a workhouse as well. Neither place can afford a doctor's services, and the infirmaries are always full."

"Where are they located?

"The workhouse is in Clerkenwell. The orphan asylum is a bit farther out, at Bishopsgate."

"Those places aren't safe for you to go unescorted."

"I'm quite familiar with London, sir. I don't take chances with my safety, and I carry a walking stick for self-defense."

"What good is a walking stick?" Rhys asked skeptically.

"In my hands," Dr. Gibson assured him, "it's a dangerous weapon."

"Is it weighted?"

"No, I can deliver three times as many blows with a lighter cane than with a heavier stick. At my fencing-master's suggestion, I've carved notches at strategic points along the shaft to improve grip strength. He has taught me some effective techniques to fell an opponent with a cane."

"You fence?" Helen asked, her head still down.

"I do, my lady. Fencing is an excellent sport for ladies—it develops strength, posture, and proper breathing."

Helen liked the woman more and more. "I think you're fascinating."

Dr. Gibson responded with a surprised little laugh. "How nice you are. I'm afraid you've disappointed my expectations: I thought you would be snobbish, and instead you're perfectly lovely."

"Aye, she is," Rhys said softly, his thumbs making circles on Helen's neck.

To Helen's amazement, the burning coals in her head were fading to blessed coolness: She could feel the searing agony retreating by the second. After another minute or two, she flattened her palms on the counter and pushed herself up, blinking.

"The pain is almost gone," she said in wondering relief.

Carefully Rhys turned her to face him, his gaze traveling over her. He stroked back a blond tendril that dangled over her right eye. "Your color is better."

"It's extraordinary," Helen said. "I felt so ghastly just a few minutes ago, and now . . ." A euphoric feeling had spread from head to toe, not only chasing away her former worries but also making it impossible for her to recapture them. How odd it was to know exactly what she should be anxious and unhappy about, but somehow not be able to feel anxious and unhappy. It was the effect of the medicine, of course. It wouldn't last. For now, however, she was grateful for a reprieve.

She swayed slightly as she turned back to the other woman, and Rhys instantly slid a supportive arm around her. "Thank you, Dr. Gibson," she said fervently. "I thought I was done for."

"I assure you, it was no trouble," Dr. Gibson said, her green eyes crinkling. She pushed the tin of neuralgic powders across the counter. "Take another of these in twelve hours if necessary. Never more than twice a day."

Rhys picked up the tin and scrutinized it before tucking it into his coat pocket.

"From now on," Helen told Dr. Gibson, "I will send for you whenever I need a doctor"—she paused and gestured to the curved-handle walking stick hooked over the edge of the counter—"or a bodyguard."

The other woman laughed. "Please don't hesitate. At the risk of being presumptuous, you're welcome to send for me if you need a friend, for any reason."

"I will," Helen exclaimed cheerfully. "Yes, you are

my friend. Let's meet at a teashop—I've always wanted to do that. Without my sisters, I mean. Goodness, my mouth is dry." Although she wasn't aware of moving, she found her arms around Rhys's neck, her body listing heavily against his. Warm flushes kept rising through her like sunlight. "May I have some more lime water?" she asked him. "I like the way it sparkles in my mouth. Like fairies dancing on my tongue."

"Aye, sweetheart." His voice was reassuring and pleasant, even as he sent Dr. Gibson a narrow-eyed glance. "What else was in that powder?"

"She'll be much steadier in a few minutes," the other woman assured him. "There's usually an initial sensation of giddiness as the medication enters the bloodstream."

"I can see that." Keeping one arm around Helen, Rhys took the open bottle from the stand and gave it to Helen. "Easy now, *cariad*."

"I like drinking out of bottles." Helen took a long, satisfying draught of lime water. "I'm good at it now. Watch this." She drank again to show him, and his hand closed around the bottle, gently taking it from her.

"Not so fast," he murmured, his eyes lit with tender amusement, "or all those bubbles will bring on the hiccups."

"Don't worry about that," Helen told him, gesturing extravagantly to the woman across the counter. "Dr. Gibson can cure *anything*."

"Regrettably," the doctor said with a smile, picking up her walking stick by its curved handle, "the cure for hiccups has so far eluded me."

After Rhys had replaced the bottle in the stand, Helen slid her arms around his waist, which she knew distantly was a rather shocking thing to do, but it seemed the only way to keep herself upright. "Have you ever noticed," she asked him earnestly, "that hiccups rhymes with snickups?"

Carefully Rhys eased her head to his chest. "Dr. Gibson," he said, "as you leave, please find one of the sales assistants and discreetly tell her to run up to the dressmaker and reschedule Lady Helen's appointment for another day."

"She'll really be quite fine in another few minutes—" the doctor began.

"I don't want her to begin planning her wedding dress like this. God knows what she would end up with."

"A rainbow dress," Helen said dreamily against his coat. "And unicorn shoes."

Rhys gave the doctor a speaking glance.

"Right," Dr. Gibson said briskly. "Good evening to the both of you."

Helen tilted her head back to look up at Rhys. "I was joking about the unicorn shoes."

Rhys was holding her with both arms now, the corners of his mouth deepening. Oh, he was wonderfully large and sturdy. And so very handsome. "Were you?" he asked gently. "Because I'll catch a unicorn for you. There's sure to be enough of him for a matching valise."

"No, don't make him into luggage, let him go free."

"All right, *cariad.*"

She reached up to trace the firm, tempting curve of his lips with her fingertip. "I'm back to myself now," she told him. "I'm not going to be silly anymore."

As Rhys glanced down at her quizzically, she tried to look solemn, but she couldn't help breaking into giggles. "I'm s-serious," she insisted.

He didn't argue, only began to kiss her nose and cheeks and throat.

Helen squirmed, more giggles slipping out. "That tickles." Her fingers slid into his beautiful hair, the locks thick and vibrant, like heavy black satin. His lips lingered at a tender place beneath her jaw until the nerves thrummed with excitement. Clumsily she guided his head, maneuvering his mouth to hers, and he obliged her with lazy, sensuous patience. She relaxed, moving easily with him as he turned to set his back against the counter, his arms wrapped safely around her.

His head moved over hers, one of his hands coming up to support the back of her neck, massaging even though there was no more pain or tension, and she arched against him, purring in her enjoyment. It was heavenly to be clasped in the embrace of her magnificent lover . . . who didn't know that he would soon stop loving her.

That last thought made everything seem just a little less magical.

Sensing the change in her, Rhys lifted his mouth.

Helen kept her eyes closed. Her lips felt swollen, craving more friction and silky pressure. "Do other men kiss the way you do?" she whispered.

Rhys made a sound of amusement, his peppermint-laced breath wafting against her nostrils. "I don't know, my treasure. And you'll never find out." He took a quick taste of her, a flirting tug. "Open your eyes."

Helen looked at him while he appraised her condition.

"How do you feel now?" he asked, cautiously letting her stand on her own.

"Steadier," she said, turning in a small circle to test her balance. She was no longer giddy. The migraine was leashed and held firmly at bay. "And quite energetic. Dr. Gibson was right: I *am* well enough to go to the dressmaker."

"We'll see. If you're still feeling up to it in a half-hour, I'll take you to her. In the meantime, I want to show you something. Do you think you could manage stairs?"

"I could run up a thousand of them."

"Four flights will be sufficient."

A small inner voice warned Helen that being alone with him wasn't a good idea—she would make a mistake and say something she shouldn't. But she took his arm anyway, accompanying him to a wide staircase of travertine marble.

"I didn't think of asking the elevator operator to stay late," Rhys said apologetically as they ascended the steps. "I know the basics of how to operate it, but I wouldn't want to try it for the first time with you in the car."

"I don't ever want to ride an elevator," Helen said. "If the cable snaps—" she broke off and shuddered. Although the store's elevator was of modern hydraulic design, reputedly safer than steam-powered models, the idea of being hoisted up and down in a tiny closed room was terrifying.

"There's no danger. It has three extra safety cables, as well as an automatic mechanism under the car that grips the side rails in case all the cables broke."

"I would still rather climb stairs."

Rhys smiled and kept her hand in his. As they finished the first flight and began on the second, he asked casually, "What have you done for the past few days?"

Trying to sound offhand, Helen said, "We went to the British Museum on Friday. And Lady Berwick has been receiving social visits from her friends."

"How was the museum?"

"Tolerable."

"Only tolerable?"

"We visited the zoological galleries, and I don't enjoy those nearly as much as the art galleries. All those poor animals and their stiff limbs and glass eyes . . ." She told him about Pandora and the giraffes, and how Lady Berwick had darted forward to have a quick feel when she'd thought no one was looking.

Rhys laughed quietly, seeming to relish the story. "Did anything else happen while you were there?"

He sounded relaxed, but Helen's nerves twitched in unease. "Nothing I can think of." She hated lying to him. She felt guilty and unsettled, and nervous at being alone with him, the man she loved. And that made her want to cry.

Rhys stopped with her at the third-floor landing. "Would you like to sit somewhere for a moment, *cariad*?"

The question was gentle and concerned, but for an

instant, as she glanced up at him, there was a look in his eyes she'd never seen before. A cat-and-mouse look. It was gone so quickly that she thought she might have imagined it.

Instead, she forced a smile. "No, I'm quite well."

His gaze searched her face for a few extra seconds. As he led her away from the staircase, Helen asked, "Didn't you say there would be four flights?"

"Aye, the rest of the stairs are in this direction."

Mystified, Helen accompanied him past towering racks of French, Persian, and Indian carpets, and tables piled with samples of oilcloth, matting, and hardwood. The air was tinctured with the odors of cedar and benzene, used to ward away moths.

Rhys guided her to an unassuming four-panel door that had been tucked in a setback near a corner.

"Where does this lead?" Helen asked, watching as Rhys took a key from his pocket.

"To the stairwell that connects to our house."

Perturbed, Helen asked, "Why are we going there?"

With an unfathomable expression, Rhys opened the door and returned the key to his pocket. "Don't worry. It won't take long."

Apprehensively Helen crossed the threshold and entered the enclosed stairwell she remembered from before. Instead of going into the house, however, Rhys guided her up the steps to another landing with a door. "This opens to one of the roof terraces of our house," he said. "It's a Mansard style—the top is flat, with railing all around it."

Did he intend to show her a view of London? Expose her to the elements from the perilous height of the roof? "It will be cold outside," she said anxiously.

Rhys bent to kiss her forehead. "Trust me." Keeping her hand in his, he opened the door and brought her past the threshold.

Chapter 26

Helen was bewildered to find herself surrounded by air as warm as the breath of summer. Slowly she walked into a large gallery, constructed of thousands of flashing, glittering glass panes in a network of wrought-iron ribs.

It was a glasshouse, she realized in bewilderment. On a *rooftop*. The ethereal construction, as pretty as a wedding cake, had been built on a sturdy brickwork base, with iron pillars and girders welded to vertical struts and diagonal tiers.

"This is for my orchids," she said faintly.

Rhys came up behind her, his hands settling at her waist. He nuzzled gently at her ear. "I told you I'd find a place for them."

A glass palace in the sky. It was magical, an inspired

stroke of romantic imagination, and he had built it for her. Dazzled, she took in the view of London at sunset, a red glow westering across the leaden sky. The clouds were torn in places, gold light spilling through the fire-colored fleece. Four stories below, the city spread out before them, ancient streets, dark shapes, and stone pinnacles arranged around the sinuous curve of the river. Distant points of brightness came to life as street lamps were lit.

Rhys began to explain that the floor was heated with hot water pipes, and there would be an earthenware sink with a faucet, and something about how the iron girders had been tested by a hydraulic press. Helen nodded as if she were listening, a crooked smile coming to her lips. Only a man would bring up practical details at a time like this. She leaned back against him, wanting to stay in this moment forever, pin it to the firmament with a handful of brilliant-needled stars.

When he began to describe the prefabricated panels that had enabled the structure to be built so quickly, Helen turned in his arms and interrupted him with her mouth. He went still with surprise, but in the next half-second he responded with wholehearted enthusiasm. Filled with love and gratitude and desperation, Helen kissed him a little too wildly. Her heart broke as she realized she would never be able to fill this beautiful place with her orchids. Although she had thought she'd managed to blink back a blur of tears, she felt an errant drop slip from the corner of her eye, sliding down and flavoring their kiss with salt.

Rhys looked down at her, his face shadowed. His hand shaped to her cheek, his thumb smudging away the faint wet trail.

"It's only that I'm so happy," Helen whispered.

Undeceived, Rhys gave her a skeptical glance and cradled her against his chest. His voice was low and soft against her ear. "Heart of my heart . . . I can't help if you won't tell me what it is."

Helen froze.

Now was the time to tell him. But it would ruin this moment, it would end everything. She wasn't ready to say good-bye yet. She would never be ready, but if she could steal just a little more time with him, a few more days, she would live off that for the rest of her life.

"It's nothing," she said hastily, and tried to distract him with more kisses.

She could feel the reluctance in his response. He wanted to make her tell him what was wrong. Reaching around his neck, she tugged him down and kissed him until their tongues slid together and the intoxicating fresh taste of him filled her senses. All his awareness homed in on her, and he pulled her up against him until she was on her toes. His head angled over hers as he searched the inner silk of her mouth more deeply. Sliding her hands into his coat, Helen followed the slope of his solid, hard torso as it tapered to his lean waist.

Rhys lifted his head with a quiet curse, his lungs working hard, a shiver running through him as she kissed his neck. "Helen, you're playing with fire."

Yes. She could feel the latent power of him, ready to be unleashed. "Take me to your bedroom," she said recklessly, knowing it was one of the worst ideas she'd ever had. She didn't care. It was worth anything, any scandal or sacrifice, to be with him one more time. "Just for a few minutes. It's not far."

Rhys shook his head without even pausing to consider it. "That bloody headache powder," he said darkly. "It's loosened your virtue."

The quaint phrase, coming from him, forced Helen to bury her face against his chest to muffle a laugh. "You took care of my virtue long before now."

Rhys didn't seem to share her amusement. "You haven't been yourself tonight, *cariad*. What upset you badly enough to cause a migraine?"

That sobered her quickly. "Nothing."

Rhys grasped her chin and compelled her to look at him. "Tell me."

Seeing the heated exasperation in his gaze, Helen tried to think of something that would satisfy him. "I miss you," she said, which was true. "I didn't expect it would be so difficult to stay here in London, knowing you're so near, and still never having you."

"You can have me whenever you want."

One corner of her mouth hitched upward. "I want you now." Her hand stole to the front of his trousers.

"Damn it, Helen, you'll drive me mad." But he sucked in a sharp breath as she gripped the huge straining shape of him. His face changed, his dark eyes shot with glints of hellfire. She loved how easily he responded to her nearness, this very physical man, she loved the soul and substance of him.

One last brick-colored wash of light passed over them and melted into shadow, while the winter moon mantled itself with clouds in a distant corner of the sky. It was only the two of them, now, in this high, dark place, while the city stirred far below, its distant noises unable to reach them.

Helen settled her hands on either side of his face, delighting in the masculine texture of his shaven cheeks. How vital he was, how earthy and real. He stood motionless, captured by her light touch, while his body stirred with insatiate hunger, and she sensed how close to the edge of control he was. Desire filled her in showers of sparks, at the tips of her fingers and toes, and the insides of her knees and elbows . . . everywhere. She couldn't keep from touching him, any more than she could stop herself from telling him something she had no right to say.

"I love you."

Shaken to his core, Rhys stared down at Helen. The moonstone eyes were luminous and haunted, and so beautiful that he wanted to sink to his knees before her.

"*Dw i'n dy garu di*," he whispered when he had the breath, a phrase he'd never said to anyone, and he kissed her roughly.

The world sank down to the two of them in this glittering sphere, where there was only darkness, flesh, and feeling. He found himself nudging her backward, crowding her into the corner against a flat-fronted iron support post. She clung to him, writhing as if she were trying to climb up his body. He needed to feel her skin, the natural shape of her, and as always, there were too damned many clothes in the way.

Inflamed, he gripped the front of her skirt and hauled it up in handfuls, and reached into the long seam-split of her drawers. His knee worked between her legs, and she spread them willingly, gasping as he caressed the insides of her thighs where the skin was thin and hot. Helen leaned against the post, moaning into his kisses. The patch of fluff at her groin was warm and dry, but as he shaped his hand to her, cupping gently, he felt humid, intimate heat against his fingers. How delicate she was, how soft. It didn't seem possible that she could take all of him in this sweet, small place.

Gently he pinched each of the plump outer lips, kneading tenderly and splaying them open. She went wet against his fingertips as he circled her entrance and the silky petals around it. Her hips writhed, following the tender stroking. He let one teasing fingertip rest on the little pearl of her clitoris, feeling her fluttering response like the wings of a tiny wintering bird. Her head tilted back, and she gripped the front of his braces with knotted fists.

The whiteness of her exposed throat gleamed in the warm darkness, and he bent to it hungrily, using his tongue on her skin, caressing with his parted lips. Blindly he fumbled with the buttons of his trousers to free his stiff length. Reaching down, he grasped one of Helen's knees and guided her leg around his waist. They both gasped as the head of his shaft pushed against the smoldering wet heat of her. Hunting for the right angle, he bent his knees and drove up to the hilt in a sure, strong thrust. Helen let out a cry, and he hesitated, ter-

rified that he had hurt her. But he felt her body working on his with deep quivers that drew a ragged sound
of lust from him. Letting her weight settle more fully
onto his shaft, he reached down with his thumb and
forefinger to spread her sex open. She whimpered as
he pressed against her and rocked upward, lifting her
slightly with each thrust.

All he could hear were the rasps of their breathing, and the ceaseless rustling of clothes, and the oc-
casional intimate wet sound as he lunged steadily into
her. Deep inside she closed on him sweetly, demanding
more, and he gripped her hips and made her ride him
harder, driving relentlessly, using his body to pleasure
her. They struggled together amid the rising sensation,
pulling closer, closer, until there was no more friction,
only the clamping, writhing, throbbing connection that
held them fast to each other. Helen moaned, her arms
tightening around his neck, and then she fell silent and
began to shudder helplessly. The feel of her ecstasy
delivered him, the release so complete that it was like
losing consciousness, like dying and being reborn.

Crushing his mouth against the side of her head,
Rhys groaned quietly and held her, willing the shaking in his limbs to ease. Helen relaxed against him, her
leg sliding away from his hips. But as he reluctantly

made to withdraw, she gripped his backside with her hands to keep him close, and it felt so good that his flesh twitched and thickened inside her. His lips moved slowly over her face while they stood together with their bodies still joined, heat pulsing within heat.

Her head dropped to his shoulder. "I didn't know it could be done that way," she whispered.

Rhys smiled, and bent to catch at her earlobe with his teeth, and licked the edge of her ear. The delicate salt of her sweat teased him, aroused him like some exotic drug. He would never have enough of her. "You mustn't encourage me, *cariad*," he said huskily. "Someone has to tell me to behave like a gentleman. That's your job, aye?"

Her palm slid gently over his right buttock. "I'll never tell you that."

Rhys continued to hold her. He knew she was keeping secrets, frightened of some nameless thing she wouldn't confess. But he wouldn't force the issue. Yet.

Soon, however, they would have a reckoning.

Reluctantly he loosened his arms and reached down to her hip, holding her steady as he withdrew from her. She gasped as his invasion eased from her body, and he soothed her with a quiet murmur. Taking a handkerchief from his coat pocket, he tucked the soft folded cloth snugly between the lips of her sex, and straightened her drawers. Although he couldn't see Helen blush in the darkness, he could feel the heat radiating from her.

"There are still things that need to be said between us," he warned softly, buttoning his trousers. After pressing a lingering kiss to her temple, he added, "Although I do like your way of distracting me."

Helen had been in a daze for the rest of the evening, unable to discern how much of it was an aftereffect of the neuralgic powder, and how much was from her interlude with Rhys.

Upon leaving the rooftop glasshouse, Rhys had taken her to a bathroom where she'd done her best to tidy herself and neaten her hair. Afterward, he had escorted her to the dressmaker's studio on the second floor and introduced her to Mrs. Allenby, a tall, slight woman with a pleasant smile. She sympathized upon learning about Helen's migraine, and assured her that they had enough time left in the appointment to take her measurements. Helen could return another day when she felt better, and they could begin to plan her trousseau in earnest.

At the conclusion of the appointment, Helen

emerged from the studio to find Rhys waiting to escort her to the first floor. Recalling their torrid encounter of just an hour earlier, Helen felt herself turn a deep crimson.

He grinned at her. "Try not to look quite so guilty, *cariad*. I've spent the past quarter of an hour explaining our disappearance to Lady Berwick."

"What did you tell her?"

"I gave her every excuse I could come up with. Some of it was even true."

"Does she believe any of it?" Helen asked, mortified.

"She's pretending to."

To Helen's relief, Lady Berwick seemed contented and good-humored during the carriage ride back to Ravenel House. She had purchased no fewer than a dozen pairs of gloves, as well as assorted sundries from other departments in the store. Ruefully, the countess admitted that she intended to return soon for another shopping excursion, even if it meant going to Winterborne's during regular hours and mingling with the common herd. Pandora and Cassandra regaled Helen with accounts of everything the sales assistants had told them would be *à la mode* for the coming year. Fancy scarf-pins were becoming all the rage, as well as gold and silver braided trim on dresses and hats, and ladies' hair would be dressed *à la Récamier*, an arrangement of small curls like a poodle dog's.

"Poor Helen," Pandora said, "we're going home with a mountain of boxes and bags, and the only thing you're bringing back is a tin of headache powders."

"I don't need anything else," Helen replied, looking down at the green tin in her lap.

"And while we were having a lovely time shopping," Cassandra said regretfully, "Helen was taking off her clothes."

Helen shot her a startled glance, the color draining from her face.

"At the dressmaker's," Cassandra explained. "You did say they took measurements, didn't you?"

"Oh yes."

"Well, it couldn't have been very entertaining for you," Cassandra said.

"No, indeed." Helen glued her gaze back to the tin of powders, acutely conscious of Lady Berwick's silence.

The carriage arrived at Ravenel House, and the footman carried a towering stack of ivory boxes into the house with the dexterity of a carnival juggler. While the twins went up to their rooms, Lady Berwick informed the butler that she wanted tea brought to the parlor.

"Would you like some as well?" she asked Helen.

"No, thank you, I believe I'll retire early to bed." Helen hesitated, gathering her nerves. "May I speak with your ladyship?"

"Of course. Come into the parlor with me." They entered the room, which was cold despite the fire on the grate. Lady Berwick sat on the chaise and shivered. "Give the fire a stir, if you will."

Helen went to the hearth, picked up a poker, and prodded the coals until she had built up a cheerful blaze. Holding her hands near the flooding heat, she said sheepishly, "About my disappearance with Mr. Winterborne—"

"There is no need to explain. I approve."

Helen gave her a stupefied glance. "You—you do?"

"I told you in this very parlor that you must do whatever is necessary to marry Mr. Winterborne. In other circumstances, I would object strenuously, of course. But if allowing him liberties will bind him closer to you and make the marriage more of a certainty, I am willing to look the other way. A wise chaperone accepts that one must occasionally lose the battle to win the war."

Nonplussed, Helen said, "You are remarkably . . ." *ruthless.* ". . . practical, my lady."

"We must use the means we have at our disposal." Lady Berwick looked resigned. "It's often said that a woman's weapon is her tongue . . . but it's far from our only one."

Chapter 27

In the morning, a penny-post letter came for Helen while Lady Berwick was breakfasting in her room and the twins were still abed.

As the butler brought the envelope to her on a silver tray, Helen saw in a glance that it was from Ada Tapley. Her hand trembled as she picked it up. "I would prefer that you not mention this letter to anyone."

The butler gave her an impassive glance. "Yes, my lady."

Waiting until he had left the morning room, Helen opened the gummed envelope and took out the letter. Her gaze sped over the crookedly penned lines.

Milady,
You wrote to ask about the babe they gave me to

raise. *I named her Charity to remind her she might be set out on the street except for the pity of others, and she must try to be deserving. She was always a good girl what gave me no trouble, but the payments for her upkeep weren't enough. I asked every year for an increase, and they never gave so much as a farthing extra. Five months ago I had no choice but to send her to the Stepney Orphans Asylum at St. George-in-the-East.*

I wrote to the solicitor to say I would fetch her back if he would make it worth my while, but no reply never came. I pray someday there'll be a hard judgment on the heartless old screw for letting the poor child end in such a place. Since she never had no family name, they call her Charity Wednesday, on account that's the day I sent her there. If there is anything you can do for the girl, bless you for it. She's a sore burden on my conscience.

Yours Truly,
Ada Tapley

Helen was grateful that she hadn't yet eaten breakfast. She wouldn't have been able to keep it down after reading the letter. Springing from her chair, she walked back and forth with one hand pressed to her mouth.

Her little half sister was completely alone, and had

been for months, in an institution where she might have been starved and abused, or become ill.

Although Helen had never believed herself to be capable of violence, she wanted to kill Albion Vance in the most painful way possible. She wished it were possible to kill a man multiple times—she would *enjoy* making him suffer.

At the moment, however, she had to think only of Charity. The child had to be removed from the orphan's asylum immediately. A home must be found for her, a place where she would be treated with kindness.

First, Helen had to find out if the little girl had even survived this long.

She tried to push away the panic and fury long enough to think clearly. She had to go to the Stepney orphanage, find Charity, and bring her to Ravenel House. What were the rules for removing a child from such an institution? Was it possible to do it without having to give her real name?

She needed help.

But who could she go to? Not Rhys, and certainly not Lady Berwick, who would tell her to forget the child's existence. Kathleen and Devon were too far away. West had told her to send for him if she needed him, but even though she would trust him implicitly with her own life, Helen wasn't sure how he would react to this. It had not escaped her that West had a streak of ruthless pragmatism, not unlike Lady Berwick.

She thought of Dr. Gibson, who had told her, *"You're welcome to send for me if you need a friend, for any reason."* Had she meant it? Could she be counted on?

It was a risk. Dr. Gibson was employed by Rhys, and she might go to him directly. Or she might refuse to become involved, fearing his disapproval. But then Helen remembered the woman's incisive green eyes and brisk, independent manner, and thought, *she fears nothing.* Moreover, Dr. Gibson was familiar with London, and had been inside an orphanage before, and must know something about how they were run.

Although Helen was reluctant to test a friendship before it had even started, Garrett Gibson was her best chance to save Charity. And for some reason, based on nothing but instinct, she felt sure that Dr. Gibson would help her.

"Why do you wish to see a doctor?" Lady Berwick asked, looking up from the writing desk in her room. "Another headache?"

"No ma'am," Helen said, standing at the threshold. "It's a female complaint."

The countess's lips pursed like the closure of a drawstring reticule. For a woman who discussed the breeding and reproduction of horses with ease, she was surprisingly uncomfortable when talking about the same processes in the human species. Unless it was in the small, exclusive circle of her society friends. "Have you tried the hot water bottle?"

Helen considered how to put it delicately. "I suspect that I may be 'in a situation.'"

Lady Berwick's face went blank. With great care, she set her writing pen back in its holder. "If this concern is a result of your rendezvous with Mr. Winterborne the other night, it is far too soon to tell if there is fruit on the vine."

Lowering her gaze to the patterned carpet, Helen said carefully, "I understand. However . . . Mr. Winterborne and I had another, much earlier rendezvous."

"Do you mean to say that you and he . . ."

"Upon our engagement," Helen admitted.

The countess regarded her with resigned exasperation. "*Welshmen*," she exclaimed. "Any one of them could talk his way past a chastity belt. Come into the room, child. This isn't a subject to be shouted from the threshold." After Helen had complied, she asked, "Your regular monthly illness has ceased?"

"I believe so."

After considering the situation, Lady Berwick began to look somewhat pleased. "If you are in the family way, your marriage to Winterborne is practically a *fait accompli.* I will send for Dr. Hall, who attends my daughter Bettina."

"Your ladyship is very kind, but I have already sent a note to request an appointment with Dr. Gibson, at her earliest convenience."

The countess frowned. "Who is he?"

"Dr. Gibson is a woman. I met her on Monday evening at Winterborne's."

"No, no, that won't do. Females are not meant to be doctors—they lack scientific understanding and coolness of nerve. One cannot trust a woman with a matter as important as childbirth."

"Ma'am," Helen said, "my sense of modesty would be less offended by a lady doctor's examination than one performed by a man."

Huffing indignantly, Lady Berwick lifted a beseeching gaze to the heavens. Returning her gaze to Helen, she said dourly, "Dr. Gibson may attend you here."

"I'm afraid I must go to her private office, in her residence at King's Cross."

The countess's brows shot upward. "She will not examine you in the privacy of your own home?"

"She keeps all the latest scientific and medical equipment at her office," Helen said, recalling Rhys's description of it when he'd told her about Dr. Gibson treating his dislocated shoulder. "Including a special table. And a lamp with a concentrated light reflector."

"That is very strange indeed," the countess said darkly. "A male doctor would have the decency to close his eyes during the examination."

"Dr. Gibson is modern."

"It would seem so." Lady Berwick, who harbored deep suspicion of anything modern, frowned. "Very well."

"Thank you, ma'am." Filled with unutterable relief, Helen fled the room before the countess could change her mind.

An appointment was secured for the next afternoon at four. In her growing agitation, Helen had hardly been able to sleep that night. By the time she finally crossed the front threshold of Dr. Gibson's house, she was exhausted and fraught with nerves.

"I'm here on false pretenses," she blurted out as Dr. Gibson welcomed her into the narrow, three-level Georgian terrace.

"Are you?" Dr. Gibson asked, seeming unperturbed. "Well, you're welcome to visit no matter what the reason."

A plump, round-faced housemaid appeared in the small entrance. "Shall I take your coat, milady?"

"No, I can't stay long."

Dr. Gibson regarded Helen with a quizzical smile, her green eyes alert. "Shall we talk for a few minutes in the parlor?"

"Yes." Helen followed her into a tidy, pleasant room, simply furnished with a settee and two chairs upholstered in blue and white, and two small tables. The only picture on the wall was a painting of geese parading by a country cottage with a rose trellis, a soothing image because it reminded Helen of Hampshire. A mantel clock gave four delicate chimes.

Dr. Gibson took a chair beside Helen's. In the parchment-colored light from the front window, she appeared disconcertingly young despite her presence of manner. She was as clean and well-scrubbed as a schoolgirl, her maple-brown hair pinned in a neatly controlled chignon. Her slim form was clad in a severe unadorned dress of forest green that verged upon black.

"If you're not here as a patient, my lady," Dr. Gibson said, "what can I do for you?"

"I need help with a private matter. I thought you would be the best person to approach, as the situation is . . . complicated." Helen paused. "I would prefer this to be kept confidential."

"You have my word."

"I want to find out about a child's welfare. My chaperone, Lady Berwick, has a nephew who sired a child out of wedlock and abandoned his responsibility for her. The little girl is four years old. It seems that five months ago, she was sent to the Stepney orphan asylum in the parish of St. George-in-the East."

Dr. Gibson frowned. "I know of that area. It's a perfect bear pit. Certain parts are unsafe even during the day."

Helen wove her gloved fingers together into a little snarl. "Nevertheless, I have to find out if Charity is there."

"That's her name?"

"Charity Wednesday."

Dr. Gibson's mouth quirked. "There's an institutional name if I've ever heard one." Her gaze turned questioning. "Shall I go there on your behalf? I won't mention your name, of course. If Charity is there, I'll find out her condition and report it back to you. I'm sure I could make time to go tomorrow or the next day."

"Thank you, that is very generous of you, but . . . I must go today." Helen paused. "Even if you cannot."

"Lady Helen," Dr. Gibson said quietly, "it's no place for a gently bred woman. It exists at a level of human misery that would prove very distressing to someone who has led a sheltered life."

Helen understood that the words were kindly meant, but they stung just the same. She was not delicate or weak-minded—she had already decided that she would muster whatever strength was necessary to do what had to be done. "I'll manage," she said. "If a four-year-old child has survived in such a place, I daresay I can endure one visit."

"Could you not approach Mr. Winterborne? A man with his resources—"

"No, I don't want him to know about this."

Struck by Helen's vehemence, Dr. Gibson regarded her with a speculative gaze. "Why must you be the one to handle this situation? Why would you take such a risk for a child who has only a slight connection to you?"

Helen was silent, afraid to reveal too much.

The other woman waited patiently. "If I am to help you, Lady Helen," she said after a moment, "you must trust me."

"My connection to the child is . . . more than slight."

"I see." The doctor paused before asking gently, "Is the child in fact yours? I wouldn't judge you in the least for it, many women make mistakes."

Helen flushed deeply. She forced herself to look directly at Dr. Gibson. "Charity is my half sister. Her father, Mr. Vance, had an affair with my mother long ago. Seducing and abandoning women is something of a sport to him."

"Ah," Dr. Gibson said softly. "So it is with many men. I see the vicious consequences of such sport, if we're to call it that, whenever I visit the women and children who are suffering in workhouses. To my mind, castration would be the ideal solution." She gave Helen a measuring glance. Appearing to make a decision, she stood abruptly. "Let's be off, then."

Helen blinked. "You'll go with me? Now?"

"I certainly can't let you do it alone. It would behoove us to leave at once. Daylight will start to wane at a quarter past six. We'll have to send your driver and footman home and hire a hansom. It would be foolhardy to take a fine carriage to the place we're going, and I doubt your footman would allow you to set one foot outside it, once he has a glimpse of the area."

Helen followed her from the room to the hallway.

"Eliza," Dr. Gibson called out. The plump housemaid reappeared. "I'm going out for the rest of the afternoon." The maid helped her into her coat. "Look after my father," Dr. Gibson continued, "and don't let him have sweets." Glancing at Helen, she said in a quick aside, "They play havoc with his digestion."

"I never do, Dr. Gibson," the housemaid protested.

"We keep hiding 'em, but he sneaks past us and finds 'em anyway."

Dr. Gibson frowned, putting on her hat and tugging on a pair of gloves. "I expect you to pay closer attention. For goodness' sake, he's as subtle as a war elephant when he comes down the stairs."

"He's light-footed when he's after sweets," the maid said defensively.

Turning to the hall tree, Dr. Gibson pulled out her walking stick by its curved handle, and caught it smartly in midair. "We may have need of this," she said with the satisfaction of a well-armed woman on a mission. "Onward, my lady."

Chapter 28

After the footman and driver were sent back to Ravenel house with the message that the appointment would take longer than expected, Helen and Dr. Gibson went on foot to Pancras Road. As they walked briskly, Dr. Gibson cautioned Helen about how to conduct herself in the East End, especially near the docklands area. "Stay aware of the environment. Take note of people in doorways, between buildings, or beside parked carriages. If anyone approaches you with a question, ignore them, even if it's a woman or child. Always walk with purpose. Don't ever look indecisive or lost, especially if you are, and never smile for any reason. If two people are walking toward you, don't go between them."

They reached a wide street, and stopped near a corner. "One can always find a hansom on the main thoroughfares," Dr. Gibson continued. "Here's one now." She thrust her hand into the air. "They're always running express, so take care not to be mown down as they approach the curbstone. Once he stops, we'll have to seat ourselves and be quick about it. Hansom horses tend to start and jerk, so mind you don't fall from the footboard while climbing in."

Helen nodded tensely, her heart thumping as the two-wheeled vehicle came to a violent halt in front of them. Dr. Gibson ascended first after the folding door opened, ducking beneath the trailing reins.

Grimly determined, Helen climbed up after her, gripping the oval splashguard over the wheel for leverage. The narrow footboard was slippery with mud. To make matters worse, the weight and bulk of her bustle threatened to drag her backward. Somehow she managed to keep her balance, and lunged awkwardly into the cab.

"Well done," Dr. Gibson said. She stopped Helen from reaching for the door. "The driver will close it with a lever." She called out their destination to the driver through a trapdoor in the roof, after using her cane to poke at a newspaper that had fallen across the opening. The door swung shut, the vehicle jerked forward, and they proceeded along the street with rapidly increasing velocity.

Whereas ordinary people rode in hansoms all the time, young women of Helen's rank never did. The ride itself was terrifying but exhilarating. She could hardly believe it was happening. The hansom cab hurtled along at a breakneck pace, threading the mass of carriages, carts, omnibuses, and animals that crowded the thoroughfare, lurching and jolting, missing lamp-posts and parked vehicles and slow-footed pedestrians by inches.

"When it's time to hop out," Dr. Gibson said to Helen, "I'll pay the driver through the hole in the roof, and he'll open the door with the lever. Take care not to let the overhanging reins knock off your hat as you jump to the ground."

The hansom jolted to a rough stop. Dr. Gibson handed up the payment and nudged Helen's side with her elbow as the door opened. Galvanized into action, Helen clambered out and stepped on the footboard. She had to wrench her hips to pull her bustle free of the carriage. With more luck than skill, she leapt to the street without falling on her face or losing her hat. The bustle gave an extra bounce as she landed, causing her to totter forward. Immediately afterward, Dr. Gibson descended to the ground with athletic grace.

"You make it look so easy," Helen said.

"Practice," Dr. Gibson replied, adjusting the angle of her hat. "Also, no bustle. Now, remember the rules." They began to walk.

Their surroundings were vastly different from any part of London Helen had seen before. Even the sky looked different, the color and texture of old kitchen rags. There were only a handful of shops, all of them with blackened windows and dilapidated signs. Rows of common lodging-houses, intended to provide shelter for the destitute, appeared unfit for habitation. People crowded the street, arguing, cursing, drinking, fighting. Others sat on steps or curbstones, or occupied doorways with ghostlike lassitude, their faces sunken-eyed and unnaturally pale.

As polluted as the main road was, layered with filth and wheel-flattened objects, it didn't compare with the alleys that branched from it, where the ground glimmered with dark streams and standing pools of putrid liquid. Catching a glimpse of a dead animal carcass, and a doorless privy, Helen stiffened against a shudder that ran down her spine. People lived in this place. Ate, drank, work, slept here. How did they survive? She stayed close to Dr. Gibson, who appeared coolly unaffected by the squalor around them.

A remarkable stench hung everywhere, impossible to avoid. Every few yards the floating miasma, dark, organic, and rotting, reshaped into a new, even more revolting version of itself. As they passed a particularly foul alley, a pervasive reek seemed to go directly from her nose to her stomach. Her insides roiled.

"Breathe through your mouth," Dr. Gibson said, quickening her stride. "It will pass."

Thankfully the nausea retreated, although Helen's head swam faintly as if she'd been poisoned, and her mouth tasted like pencil lead. They turned a corner and confronted a large brick building with tall iron gates and spiked fencing all around.

"That's the orphanage," Dr. Gibson said.

"It looks like a prison."

"I've seen worse. At least the grounds are reasonably clean."

They walked down the street to a set of tall iron gates that had been left ajar, and passed through to the entrance. Dr. Gibson reached up to tug firmly at a bell pull. They heard it ring from somewhere inside.

After a full minute had passed, Dr. Gibson began to reach for the pull again, when the door opened.

A broad, heavy rectangle of a woman faced them. She looked incredibly weary, as if she hadn't slept in years, the skin of her face drooping in swags.

"Are you the matron?" Dr. Gibson asked.

"I am. Who might you be?"

"I am Dr. Gibson. My companion is Miss Smith."

"Mrs. Leech," the matron mumbled.

"We would like to ask a few questions of you, if we may."

The matron's face didn't change, but it was clear the idea held little appeal. "What would I get out of it?"

"I'm willing to donate my medical services to the children in the infirmary."

"We don't need a doctor. The Sisters of Mercy come three times a week to minister and do nursing." The door began to close.

"For your time," Helen said, discreetly extending a coin to her.

The matron's hand closed over it, her eyelids flicking briefly as she realized it was a half-crown. Standing back, she opened the door wider and let them inside.

They entered an L-shaped main room flanked by offices on one side and a nursery on the other. A squalling infant could be heard from the nursery. A woman walked back and forth past the doorway with the infant, trying to soothe it.

Straight ahead, through a pair of open double doors, Helen could see rows of children seated at long tables. A multitude of busy spoons scraped against bowls.

"They'll eat for ten more minutes," Mrs. Leech said, consulting a pocket watch. "That's all the time

I have." A few curious children had hopped off their benches and had wandered to the doorway to stare at the visitors. The matron glared at them. "Go back to the table, if you know what's good for you!" The children scuttled back into the dining hall. Turning back to Dr. Gibson, Mrs. Leech shook her head wearily. "Some of them insist their mothers will come back for them. Every bloody time there's a visitor, they make a fuss."

"How many children do you have at the orphanage?" Dr. Gibson asked.

"One hundred twenty boys, ninety-seven girls, and eighteen infants."

Helen noticed that one girl had stayed half-hidden behind the door. Slowly the child looked around the jamb. Her hair, a very light shade of blonde, had been chopped into short, uneven locks that stuck out in all directions. It had matted down in some places, giving her the appearance of a half-molted chick. She stared fixedly at Helen.

"Have any of the mothers come back in the past?" Dr. Gibson asked.

"Some used to." Mrs. Leech looked surly. "Troublesome bitches treated this place like free lodging. Brought their children here, left them to live off charity, and came back to fetch them whenever they pleased. The in-'n-outs, we called them. So the Board of Governors made admission and discharge procedures as complicated as could be, to stop the in-'n-outs. But it's made more work for me and my staff, and we already—" She stopped with a wrathful glare as she noticed the little girl, who had taken a few uncertain steps toward Helen. "*What did I tell you?*" the matron exploded. "Go back to the table!"

The child hadn't taken her eyes—wide, frightened, awed—from Helen. "Mamma?" Her voice was small, a mere quaver in the large room.

She darted forward, her spindly legs a determined blur. Ducking beneath the matron's arm, she threw herself at Helen, clutching her skirts. "Mamma," she repeated over and over, in little prayerful breaths.

Frail and small though the child was, the impact had nearly knocked Helen off-balance. She was distressed to see the child yanking frantically at her chopped-off hair, as if trying to find a lock that was long enough to look at. Helen reached down to stop the desperate pulling. Their fingers brushed, and the tiny hand fastened to hers in a grip that hurt.

"Charity!" Mrs. Leech snapped. "Take your grubby paws off the lady." She drew back to cuff the child's head, but without even thinking, Helen blocked the swipe with her own arm.

"Her name is Charity?" Dr. Gibson asked quickly. "Charity Wednesday?"

"Yes," the matron said, glaring at the little ragamuffin.

Dr. Gibson shook her head in amazement, turning to Helen. "I wonder what caused the child to—" She stopped, looking down at the girl. "She must have noticed the color of your hair—it's so distinctive that—" Her gaze flickered back and forth between the two of them. "God's feathered choir," she muttered.

Helen couldn't speak. She had already realized how closely Charity resembled her: the dark brows and lashes, the light grayish eyes, the white-blond hair. She had glimpsed herself too in the lost look of a child who had no place in the world.

The little girl rested her head against Helen's waist. Her grimy face turned upward and her eyes closed, as if she were basking in the feel of sunlight. Exhausted relief had spread over her features. *You're here. You've come for me. I belong to someone.*

As a child, Helen might have dreamed of a similar moment—she couldn't remember. All she knew was that it had never happened.

She could hear the matron demanding to know what was going on and what they wanted with Charity, while Dr. Gibson countered with questions of her own. Continuous squalling came from the nursery. The children in the dining hall had become restless. More of them had returned to the doorway, staring and chattering.

Helen reached down to pick up the child. The small body was light and unsubstantial. Charity wrapped her arms and legs around her, clinging like a monkey. The child desperately needed a bath. Several of them. And the orphanage uniform—a blue serge dress and gray pinafore—would have to be burned. Helen longed to take her somewhere clean and quiet, and wash the filth from her, and feed her something warm and nourishing. For a despairing moment, she wondered what it would take to discharge the child from the orphanage, and what on earth she would say to Lady Berwick when she arrived at Ravenel House with her half-sister in tow.

One thing was certain—she wasn't going to abandon Charity in this place.

"I'm your older sister, darling," she murmured. "I'm Helen. I didn't know you were here, or I would have come for you before. I'm taking you home with me."

"Now?" the child quavered.

"Yes, now."

As she stood there with the little girl in her arms, Helen realized that the course of her life had just been permanently altered, like a train that had crossed a switch-point and moved onto a new track. She would never again be a woman without a child. A confusion of emotion twisted inside her . . . fear, that no one, not even Kathleen, would agree with what she was doing . . . and grief, because she had lost Rhys, and every step she took was leading her farther away from him . . . and a faint, lonely note of joy. There would be compensations in the future. There would be solace.

But there would never again be a man like Rhys Winterborne.

Helen's attention was caught by the other two women as they began to argue in earnest.

"Mrs. Leech," Helen said sharply.

They both fell silent and looked at her.

Helen continued in a tone of command, which she had borrowed from Lady Berwick. "We will wait in one of your office rooms, while you attend to the children in the dining hall. Be quick about it, if you please, as our time is running short. You and I have business to discuss."

"Yes, miss," the matron replied, looking thoroughly harassed.

"You may refer to me as 'my lady,'" Helen said coolly, and took private satisfaction in the woman's glance of surprise.

"Yes, milady," came the subdued reply.

After Mrs. Leech had shown them to a shabbily furnished office, Helen sat with Charity in her lap.

Dr. Gibson wandered around the small room, shamelessly glancing through a stack of papers on the desk and opening a few drawers. "If you want to have her discharged tonight," she said, "I'm sorry to tell you that it probably won't be possible."

Charity's head lifted from Helen's shoulder, breathing heavily. "Don't leave me here."

"Shhh." Helen smoothed a few wild tufts of hair. "You're coming with me. I promise." Out of the periphery of her vision, she saw Dr. Gibson shake her head.

"I wouldn't promise," Dr. Gibson said quietly.

"If I have to break the law and simply walk out of here with her," Helen said, "I'll do it." Rearranging Charity more comfortably in her lap, she continued to smooth her hair. "Why did they cut it so short, do you think?" she asked.

"Usually their head are shaved upon admission, to ward against vermin infestation."

"If they're *that* concerned about vermin," Helen said, "they could give her a wash now and then."

Charity glanced up at her anxiously. "I don't like water."

"Why not, darling?"

The little chin quivered. "When we're bad, the nuns . . . push our heads in the fire p-pail." She gave Helen a glance of childish grief, and laid her cheek back on her shoulder.

Helen was actually glad of the fury that flooded her: It gave her thoughts extra clarity, and infused her with strength. She began to rock the child slightly, as if she were an infant.

Dr. Gibson had seated herself on the edge of the desk, which was possible only because she was wearing the new style of dress, flat and straight in the front, with skirts gathered at the back in lieu of a bustle. Helen envied her mobility.

"What will they require for the discharge?" Helen asked.

Dr. Gibson replied with a frown. "According to the matron, you'll have to fill out administrative papers to apply for what they call 'reclamation.' They'll let you take the child only if you can prove a familial relationship. That means you'll be required to produce a legal statement from Mr. Vance confirming your parentage, as well as hers. Then you would have to go before the asylum's Board of Governors. Once you've explained your relationship in detail, they'll decide whether or not to authorize the discharge."

Helen was outraged. "Why have they made it so difficult for people to adopt these children?"

"In my opinion, the Board of Governors would rather keep the children so they can exploit them, hire them out, and garnish their wages. At the age of six, most of the residents here are taught a trade and put to work."

Disgusted, Helen pondered the problem. As she glanced down at the undernourished little body in her arms, an idea occurred to her. "What if her presence poses a danger? What if you diagnose her with a disease that might spread through the entire orphanage unless she's removed from the premises immediately?"

Dr. Gibson considered it. "Capital idea," she said. "I'm annoyed that I didn't think of it first. A case of scarlet fever should do the trick. I'm sure Mrs. Leech will go along with the plan, as long as you offer her a fiver." She hesitated, her mind sorting through possibilities. "There may be a question of legal guardianship in the future, if the Board of Governors ever took it upon themselves to reclaim her. However, they would never dare go up against a man as formidable as Mr. Winterborne."

"I don't believe Mr. Winterborne will have any part of this," Helen said quietly. "Not after I talk to him tomorrow."

"Oh." Dr. Gibson was quiet for a moment. "I'm sorry to hear that, my lady. For many reasons."

The sun had just set by the time they left the orphan asylum. Aware that their safety was more at risk with each passing minute, now that it was growing dark, the two women walked with ground-eating strides. Helen carried Charity, who clung to her with her legs wrapped around her waist.

They had turned the first corner and began toward the second, when a pair of men began to follow them from behind.

"Two fine ladies must 'ave a bit o' brass wi' yers, to spare," one of them said.

"Go on your way," Dr. Gibson said shortly, her pace unfaltering.

Both men chortled in a way that made the back of Helen's neck crawl unpleasantly. "'Appens our way lies wi' your way," the other one said.

"Dockyard vermin," Dr. Gibson muttered to Helen. "Ignore them. We'll soon reach the main thoroughfare, and then they won't bother us."

However, the men had no intention of letting them walk any farther. "If yer won't give us some brass," the one behind Helen said, "I'll take this little jam tart instead." A rough hand grabbed her shoulder and spun her around. Helen staggered slightly from the weight of the child, slight though Charity was.

The man kept his meaty hand on Helen's shoulder. He was stout and round-faced, his thick skin textured like an orange peel. Hair of an indeterminate color straggled out from beneath a shiny oilskin cap.

He stared at Helen, his beady eyes widening in fascination. "The face of an angel," he breathed, and licked his small, narrow lips. There were black gaps between his teeth, like the sharps and flats of a piano keyboard. "I'd like a leg over yer, I would." Helen tried to pull back from him, and his hand tightened. "Yer not going nowheres, my fine bit o' fluff—*bugger!*" He let out a scream as a hickory cane whistled through the air and struck the joint of his wrist with a sickening crack.

Helen backed away quickly as the length of hickory whistled again, walloping the side of the man's head. A sharp jab with the tip of the cane sank into his stomach, and he bent over with a groan. Deftly flipping the cane, Dr. Gibson smashed the curved handle between her opponent's legs and yanked it back as if it were a hook. The man dropped to the ground, curling up as tightly as an overcooked shrimp. The entire procedure had taken no more than five or six seconds.

Without pausing, Dr. Gibson turned to confront the

other man, who had lunged forward. Before he reached her, however, someone had seized him from behind and spun him around.

The stranger displayed extraordinary agility, dodging to the side with fluid ease as the thug swung at him. He moved in with an effortlessly fast and brutal combination: a jab, right cross, left uppercut, and a full force blow with his right. The ruffian collapsed to the street beside his companion.

Helen whispered to the petrified child, who was whimpering against her neck. "It's all right. It's over."

Dr. Gibson viewed the stranger warily, lowering the tip of her cane to the ground.

He returned her gaze implacably, adjusting the brim of his hat. "Are you unharmed, ladies?"

"Quite," Dr. Gibson said crisply. "We thank you for your assistance, although I had the situation under control."

Helen had the impression that the other woman was annoyed at having been deprived of the chance to demolish the second ruffian as thoroughly as she had the first.

"Obviously you could have managed on your own," the stranger said as he approached. He was a well-dressed young man, slightly taller than average, and extraordinarily fit. "But when I saw two women being harassed, I thought it only civilized to lend a hand."

He had an unusual accent, in that it was difficult to place. Most accents were so specific that one could easily discern what area they were from, sometimes even pinpoint the county. As he drew closer, Helen saw that he was very good-looking, with blue eyes and dark brown hair, and strong features.

"What are you doing in this area?" Dr. Gibson asked suspiciously.

"I'm on my way to meet a friend at a tavern."

"What is the name of it?"

"The Grapes," came his easy reply. His gaze moved to Helen and the child in her arms. "It's not safe here," he said gently, "and night is falling fast. May I hail a hansom for you?"

Dr. Gibson replied before Helen was able. "Thank you, but we don't need assistance."

"I'll stay at a distance," he conceded, "but I'm going to keep an eye on you until you're safely in a cab."

"Suit yourself," Dr. Gibson said crisply. "My lady, shall we go?"

Helen hesitated and spoke to the stranger. "Will you tell us your name, sir, so that we may know to whom we owe our gratitude?"

He met her gaze, and his face softened slightly.

"Forgive me, my lady, but I would rather not."

She smiled at him. "I understand."

He lifted his hat off his forehead in a respectful gesture, the outer corners of his eyes crinkling as they walked away. Helen beamed, remembering West's warning about strangers and heroes in disguise. Wait until she told him about *this*.

"No smiling," Dr. Gibson reminded Helen.

"But he helped us," she protested.

"It's not help when one doesn't need it."

When they had nearly reached the main road, Dr. Gibson threw a quick glance over her shoulder. "He's following us at a distance," she said, annoyed.

"Like a guardian angel," Helen said.

Dr. Gibson snorted. "Did you see the way he felled that thug? His fists were as quick as thought. Like a professional fighter. One has to question how such a man appeared out of nowhere at just the right moment."

"I think he did far less damage to his opponent than you did to yours," Helen said admiringly. "The way you took that ruffian down with your cane—I've never seen anything like it."

"My aim was a bit off," Dr. Gibson said. "I didn't connect squarely with the ulnar nerve in his wrist. I shall have to consult with my fencing-master about my technique."

"It was still very impressive," Helen assured her. "I pity anyone who makes the mistake of underestimating you, Dr. Gibson."

"My lady, the sentiment is returned in full."

Chapter 29

Although Helen had, in the recent past, discovered that she rather enjoyed shocking people, she had now come to the conclusion that it was highly overrated. She felt nostalgic for all those quiet, peaceful days at Eversby Priory when nothing had ever happened. Too much was happening now.

It seemed that Ravenel House was collectively paralyzed when Helen returned with a bedraggled orphan of mysterious origins, in questionable health and decidedly unsanitary condition. Setting Charity on her feet, Helen held her hand, and the child huddled against her. Servants stopped in their tracks. The housekeeper, Mrs. Abbott, came to the entrance hall and froze in astonishment. Pandora and Cassandra descended the stairs, chattering, but as they saw Helen standing in the entrance hall with a ragged child, they both fell abruptly silent.

The most unnerving reaction came from Lady Berwick, who emerged from the parlor and stood at the threshold. As her gaze went from Helen to the child beside her, she comprehended the situation without exhibiting the slightest break in self-control. She seemed like a military general watching his troops retreating from a losing battle and calculating how to regroup his forces.

Predictably, in the horrid, silent tableau, Pandora was the first to speak. "This is like being in a play when no one remembers their lines."

Helen sent her a quick smile.

Without a single word or flicker of expression, Lady Berwick turned and went back into the parlor.

The pencil lead taste was back in Helen's mouth. She had no idea what the countess was going to say to her, but she knew it would be dreadful. She took Charity with her to the bottom of the stairs, while her sisters came down to meet them.

After one glance at the pair, who seemed to tower over her, Charity retreated behind Helen's skirts.

"What can we do?" Cassandra asked.

Helen had never loved her sisters more than she did at that moment, for offering help before demanding explanations. "This is Charity," she said quietly. "I fetched her today from an orphanage, and she needs to be cleaned and fed."

"We'll take care of that." Pandora reached a hand down for the child. "Come with us, Charity, we'll have lots of fun! I know games and songs and—"

"Pandora," Helen interrupted, as the child shrank from the boisterous young woman. "Softly." She lowered her voice as she continued. "You don't know where she's come from. Be gentle." She glanced at Cassandra. "She's afraid of baths. Do your best to clean her with damp cloths."

Cassandra nodded, looking dubious.

Mrs. Abbott came to Helen's side. "My lady, I'll bring up trays of soup and bread for you and the little one."

"Only for her. I'm not hungry."

"You must," the housekeeper insisted. "You look ready to faint." Before Helen could reply, she turned and hurried toward the kitchen.

Helen glanced at the parlor. A chill of dread tightened the skin all over her body. She turned her attention to Charity. "Darling," she murmured, "these are my sisters, Pandora and Cassandra. I want you to go with them, and let them take care of you while I talk to someone."

The little girl was instantly alarmed. "Don't leave me!"

"No, never. I'll come to you in a few minutes. Please, Charity." To her dismay, the child only clutched her more tightly, refusing to budge.

Cassandra was the one to solve the problem. Sinking down to her haunches, she smiled into Charity's face. "Won't you come with us?" she entreated softly. "We're very nice. I'll take you to a pretty room upstairs. There's a cozy fire in the hearth, and a box that plays music. Six different melodies. Come let me show you."

Cautiously the child emerged from the folds of Helen's skirts and reached out to be carried.

After a disconcerted blink, Cassandra gathered her up and stood.

Pandora wore a resigned grin. "I've always said you were the nicer one."

Helen waited until her sisters had reached the top of the stairs. She went to the parlor, thinking that no matter what Lady Berwick said, or how upset she was, it was nothing compared to what she had seen today. It haunted her, the knowledge of what some people were forced to suffer. She would never again be able to look at her privileged surroundings without some part of

knees. She felt the older woman stiffen. "You took Kathleen in," Helen said, "when she was only a year older than Charity. You loved her when no one else wanted her. She told me you saved her life."

"Not at the expense of my own." The countess took a wavering breath, and then Helen felt the light pressure of a hand on her head. "Why won't you listen to me?"

"I have to listen to my heart," Helen said quietly.

That elicited a bitter scrape of laughter. "The downfall of every woman since Eve has begun with those exact words." The hand slid from her head. Another uneven breath. "You will allow me some privacy now."

"I'm so sorry to have upset you," Helen whispered, and pressed a quick kiss to her cool, wrinkled fingers. Slowly she rose to her feet, and saw that the countess had averted her face sharply. A tear glittered high on the time-weathered plane of her cheek.

"*Go*," Lady Berwick said curtly, and Helen slipped from the room.

As Helen ascended the stairs, she became aware of an ache in her lower back, and a weariness that had sunk into her with backward barbs. She gripped the railing at intervals to pull herself upward. Her skirts felt as if they'd been lined with lead. With every churn of her tired legs against the fabric, unpleasant scents wafted up from the hems.

Near the top of the staircase, she heard a buoyant sprinkling of musical notes floating delicately through the air. The familiar sounds came from a rosewood music box that Rhys had once given her. It was so large that it occupied its own special table, with a special drawer containing needled brass cylinders. Following the music, Helen went to the family parlor and looked inside.

Noticing her presence, Pandora came to the door with a finger held to her lips. Her blue eyes were alive with amusement.

Together they stood at the threshold, and watched as Cassandra swayed and turned graceful circles in time to the music. Charity was next to her, dressed in a white chemise with pinned-up straps, the garment ridiculously large for her. Although she faced away from Helen, it was clear that she was excited from the way she bounced on her bare feet. She was so delicate, her bones protruding, that it seemed as if she might float away like dandelion fluff. But she looked much cleaner, and her hair was damp and combed so that most of it lay against her head.

Trying to imitate Cassandra, the child moved in awkward little hops and turned in wobbly circles, like a baby fairy. She kept glancing up at Cassandra, seeking reassurance, as if she were adapting to the idea of playing with an adult.

The sight restored Helen's spirits like nothing else could have.

Pandora took her arm and drew her from the room. "Come with me, Helen—there's a supper tray in your room. You can eat while they play. And I *beg* you, have a bath. I don't know what that smell is, but it was on Charity too, and it's like every bad thing I've ever smelled all mixed together."

"How did the washing go?"

"Not well, Helen," Pandora said darkly. "She is *geologically* dirty. It scrapes off in layers. We could have used chisels. She wouldn't let us wash her hair properly, but we found if we gave her a little cloth to hold over her eyes, she would tip her head back enough to let us pour a teacup of water over it. Twice, and that was all she would allow. Children can be so strong-willed."

"Can they?" Helen asked dryly.

"She ate an entire bowl of soup and some bread with butter. We had no problem cleaning her teeth—she likes the taste of tooth powder. Her gums are red and puffy, but her teeth are like little pearls. None of them are rotting or have cavities, as far as I can tell. I cut her fingernails and toenails, but the dirt goes below the quick on some of them, and I couldn't reach it. She's wearing one of my chemises for a nightgown—I pinned up the straps. Mrs. Abbott is washing her clothes. She wanted to burn all of them, but I told her not to because we have nothing else for Charity to wear."

"We'll buy clothes for her tomorrow," Helen said absently.

"Helen, may I ask you something?"

"Yes, dear."

"Who is she, where did she come from, why is she here, and what are you going to do with her?"

Helen groaned and sighed. "There's so much to explain."

"You can start while you're having soup."

"No, I want to wait for Cassandra. There's too much for me to tell it twice."

After Helen had eaten, bathed, and changed into a nightgown and robe, she sat in her bed with Charity snuggled beside her. They watched as the twins enacted the story of the three bears. Cassandra played the part of Goldilocks, naturally, while Pandora played all of the bears. Fascinated by the story and the twins' antics, Charity watched with huge eyes as the biggest bear chased Goldilocks from the room.

By the time the drama had concluded, the little girl

was breathing fast with excitement. "Again, again," she cried.

"I'll tell it this time," Helen said. While the twins lounged on the bed, taking up every available inch of space, she drew the story out as long as possible. She kept her voice lulling and gentle, watching as Charity's eyes became heavy-lidded.

". . . and then Goldilocks lay on the bed of the little, small, wee bear . . . and it was a nice, soft, clean bed, with linen sheets and a blanket made from the wool of a fluffy white sheep. Goldilocks rested her head on a pillow stuffed with down, and thought it was just like floating on a cloud. She knew that she was going to have lovely dreams while she slept in that warm little bed, and in the morning there would be nice things to eat and a cup of chocolate for her tummy . . ." Helen stopped when she saw the long lashes flutter down, and the child's mouth slackened.

"Your version is far too long-winded, Helen," Pandora said. "How is anyone supposed to stay awake when you drone on and on like that?"

Helen exchanged a grin with her. Carefully she inched away from the sleeping child and pulled the covers up to her shoulders. "She doesn't laugh," she whispered, looking down at the small, solemn face.

"She'll learn." Cassandra came to stand at the bedside. Reaching down, she followed the shape of one miniature dark brow with a soft fingertip . . . and she glanced at Helen, looking troubled.

"Let's go to my room," Pandora said. "I have a feeling this next bedtime story is going to be really interesting."

Helen began with the discovery of the half-finished letter behind her mother's notebooks, and ended with the visit to the orphanage. Any conventional young ladies of high moral standards, upon hearing such a narration, would have been shocked and distraught. Her sisters, however, had been raised outside of society for too long to view it with proper fear and reverence, or to give a fig for its approval. Helen was vastly comforted by the fact that although they were surprised and concerned for her, they took the situation in stride.

"You're still our sister," Pandora said. "It doesn't matter to me whether you were sired by our old terrible father, or your new terrible father."

"I didn't need the extra one," Helen said glumly.

"Helen," Cassandra asked, "are you certain that Mr. Winterborne won't want to marry you when he finds out?"

"No, and I wouldn't want that for him. He's worked hard all his life to rise above his circumstances. He loves beautiful, fine things, and he deserves a wife who will elevate him, not lower him."

"You could never lower him," Pandora said in outrage.

Helen smiled sadly. "I'll be connected with ugliness and scandal. When people see me with Charity, they'll assume she's my bastard child, and I must have had her out of wedlock, and they would whisper about how Mr. Winterborne's wife is a strumpet. And they would pretend to be sorry for him, but they would take malicious delight in shaming him behind his back."

"Whispers can't hurt you," Pandora said.

Cassandra gave her twin a chiding glance. "Whispers can gut and fillet you like a haddock."

Pandora scowled but conceded the point.

"The fact is," Helen continued, "I'll ruin Winterborne's image."

"The man or the store?" Cassandra asked.

"Both. His store is about elegance and perfection, and I would be a chink in the armor. More than a chink: Charity and I would be a large, gaping hole in the armor."

"When will you talk to him?"

"Tomorrow, I think." Helen put a hand over her

midriff as she felt a little stab at the thought of facing him. "Afterward I'll take Charity to Eversby Priory, and we'll stay there until Kathleen and Devon return from Ireland."

"We're coming with you," Cassandra said.

"No, you'll be better off in London. There's more to do here, and Lady Berwick is good for you. She wants very much to make a success of you. I've disappointed her terribly, and she'll need you to lift her spirits and keep her company."

"Will you live with Charity at Eversby Priory?" Cassandra asked.

"No," Helen said quietly. "It will be better for all of us if Charity and I live far away, where no one knows us. Among other things, it will lessen the chance that my disgrace might harm your marriage prospects."

"Oh don't concern yourself about that," Cassandra said earnestly. "Pandora's not going to marry at all. And I certainly wouldn't want a man who would scorn me just because my sister was a strumpet."

"I like that word," Pandora mused. "Strumpet. It sounds like a saucy musical instrument."

"It would liven up an orchestra," Cassandra said. "Wouldn't you like to hear the Vivaldi Double Strumpet Concerto in C?"

"No," Helen said, smiling reluctantly at her sisters'

irreverence. "Stop it, both of you—I'm trying to be morose and tragic, and you're making it difficult."

"You're not going to live far away." Pandora put her arms around her. "You and Charity are going to live with me. I'll start earning money soon, lots of it, and I'll buy a big house for us."

Helen reached out to hug her close. "I think you'll be a great success," she murmured, and smiled as she felt Cassandra's arms go around the both of them.

"I'm going to live with you too," Cassandra said.

"Of course," Pandora said firmly. "Who needs a husband?"

Chapter 30

Helen awakened as Agatha, the lady's maid who attended her and the twins, entered her bedroom with a breakfast tray.

"Good morning, my lady."

"Good morning," Helen said sleepily, stretching and turning on her side. She was briefly surprised to be confronted with the face of a sleeping child.

So it hadn't been a dream.

Charity was so deep in slumber that the slight rattle of teacups on the approaching tray didn't cause her to stir. Helen stared at her with a touch of wonder. Despite the child's pitiful spareness, her cheeks were babyishly rounded. The lids covering her large eyes were paper-thin, with delicate blue veins, thinner than human hairs, etched on the surface. Her skin was pore-less, translucent over her pulses. It frightened Helen to realize how vulnerable this small person was, a fragile construction of delicately joined bones, flesh, veins.

Sitting up carefully, Helen let Agatha settle the tray on her lap. There was a steaming cup of tea, and a silver pot of chocolate next to an empty cup.

"Did the little one sleep well, my lady?"

"Yes. I don't think she stirred all night. Agatha . . . I didn't ask for tea in bed this morning, did I?" She usually took her tea and breakfast downstairs in the morning room.

"No, my lady. The countess bade me to bring it to you, and chocolate for the girl."

"How kind of her." At first Helen thought it was a peace offering, after the uncomfortable scene last night.

She was soon to learn otherwise.

Discovering the sealed rectangle partially tucked beneath the saucer, she picked it up and opened it.

Helen,

Upon reflection, I realized the obvious solution to the muddle you are in. The child, and all respon-sibility for her, belong to my nephew. It is finally time for him to solve one of the problems he has created. I have already sent word this morning that he is to retrieve his daughter forthwith, and do with her as he sees fit.

The matter is now out of your hands, as it should be.

I expect Mr. Vance to arrive within the hour. Have the child dressed and ready. Let us try not to make a scene when it comes time for her departure.

This is for the best. If you do not realize it now, you will soon.

Helen set the note down, breathing shallowly. The room seemed to revolve slowly around her. Vance would come, because he wanted Helen to marry Mr. Winterborne, and Charity was an obstacle to his plans. And if he took Charity away with him, the child would die. He wouldn't kill her, but he would leave her in a situation in which she couldn't survive. Which was more or less what he had already done.

You will take her over my dead body. Picking up the tea, Helen tried to swallow some, finding it difficult to guide the shaking rim to her lips. A splash of hot liquid fell on her bodice.

"Is something amiss, my lady?"

"Not amiss," Helen replied, setting down the cup,

"but Lady Berwick has requested that I have Charity dressed and ready for the day, in very short order. We need the clothes that were washed for her last night. Would you ask Mrs. Abbott to bring them to my room right away? I need to speak to her."

"Yes, my lady."

"Take the tray, please, and set it aside."

After Agatha had left, Helen slid out of bed and ran to the wardrobe. She pulled out a velvet tapestry bag, took it to the dresser, and began to toss articles into it: a hairbrush, handkerchiefs, gloves, stockings, and a jar of salve. She threw in the tin of neuralgic powders— although she wouldn't take one while traveling, she might very well need it by the time she reached her destination.

"Helen?" Charity sat up and regarded her with big, bright eyes. A hank of hair had sprung up near the top of her head like a bird's plumage.

Helen smiled in spite of her suffocating panic, and went to her. "Good morning, my little chick." She hugged her, while small trusting arms clasped her waist.

"You smell pretty."

Helen released her with a fond stroke on her hair, went to the breakfast tray, and poured chocolate into the empty cup. Testing it with the tip of her pinkie finger, she found that it was warm but not too hot. "Do you like chocolate, Charity?"

The question was greeted with perplexed silence.

"Try it and see." Helen gave her the cup carefully, curving the tiny fingers around the heated china.

The girl sampled it, smacked her lips, and looked at Helen with a wondering smile. She continued to drink it in birdlike sips, trying to make it last.

"I'll be right back, darling," Helen murmured. "I have to wake up my sleepyhead sisters." Calmly she walked to the door. Once she was in the hallway, she ran like a madwoman to Cassandra's room. Her sister was deep in slumber.

"Cassandra," she whispered, patting and shaking her shoulder. "Please wake up. Help, I need help."

"Too early," Cassandra mumbled.

"Mr. Vance is coming within the hour. He's going to take Charity away. Please, you must help me, I need to leave Ravenel House quickly."

Cassandra sat bolt upright, giving her a befuddled glance. "What?"

"Get Pandora, and come to my room. Try to be quiet."

In five minutes, the twins were in Helen's bedroom. She handed them the note, and they read it in turn.

Pandora looked wrathful. "'The matter is now out of your hands,'" she read aloud, a flush climbing her cheeks. "I hate her."

"No, you mustn't hate her," Helen said softly. "She's doing the wrong thing for the right reason."

"I don't care about the reason, the result is still revolting."

Someone tapped quietly on the door. "Lady Helen?" came the housekeeper's voice.

"Yes, come in."

The housekeeper entered with a stack of neatly folded clothes. "All washed and mended," she said. "There's not much left of the stockings, but I patched them as well as I could."

"Thank you, Mrs. Abbott. Charity will enjoy wearing nice clean clothes." Helen gestured to the child on the bed, reminding them all that she could hear every word. She gave the note to the housekeeper and waited until she had read it before murmuring apologetically, "I wish I could explain the situation more fully to you, but—"

"You're a Ravenel, my lady," came Mrs. Abbott's staunch reply. "That's all I need to understand. What are you planning?"

"I'm going to Waterloo Station, to take the next train to Hampshire."

"I'll tell the driver to ready the carriage."

"No, that would take too long, and they'll notice, and we'd never be allowed to leave. I have to go to the main road by way of the servants' door and take a hansom cab to the station."

Mrs. Abbott looked alarmed. "My lady, a hansom—"

"Don't worry about that. The problem is that when Mr. Vance realizes I'm not here, he'll follow me to the station. It's fairly obvious that Eversby Priory is the only place I could take Charity."

"We'll stall for you," Pandora said. "We'll lock your bedroom door and pretend to be helping with Charity."

"I'll speak to one of the footmen," the housekeeper said quietly. "Mr. Vance's carriage will be missing a perch-bolt when he tries to leave."

Impulsively Helen snatched up her hand and kissed it.

Mrs. Abbott seemed slightly unnerved by the gesture. "There, there, my lady. I'll send Agatha back up to help you dress."

"We'll take care of the rest," Cassandra said.

The next few minutes were a strange, mad scramble of feverish activity and quiet murmurs. Helen had already donned her chemise and drawers by the time Agatha came to the room, and was struggling with her corset. In her haste, she couldn't match the front hooks up correctly.

Agatha came to her, reached for the top of the busk, and began to hook it deftly. "My mum always says, 'fast is slow and slow is fast.'"

"I'll try to remember that," Helen said ruefully.

After finishing the corset, the maid went to the wardrobe.

"No, don't," Helen said, realizing what she was looking for. "I'm not going to wear a bustle."

"My lady?" the maid asked, looking shocked.

"Just pin up the loose parts of my traveling skirts in back," Helen insisted. "I can't walk in tiny steps today, I have to *move*."

Agatha hurried back to her with a black traveling skirt and a white blouse.

On the other side of the room, Cassandra dressed Charity with remarkable speed, telling her with a smile that she was going on an outing with Helen. "Pandora, she has no bonnet or coat. Will you fetch her a shawl or something?"

Pandora dashed off to her room and returned with a shawl and a small, low-crowned felt hat trimmed with cord. Since there was no significant difference between girls' and women's hat styles, it would work well enough.

After helping Helen to don her black traveling jacket, Agatha asked, "Shall I run to the pantry and fetch something for you to take, my lady?"

Cassandra answered from the window, where she had gone after hearing a noise from outside. "No time," she said tersely. "Mr. Vance's carriage has arrived."

Agatha gathered Helen's loose locks, twisted them with a few violent jerks, pulled a few pins from her own hair, and anchored a simple knot high on Helen's head. Pandora snatched a hat from the wardrobe and tossed it to the maid, who caught it with one hand and fastened it just above the knot of hair.

"Do you have money?" Cassandra asked.

"Yes." Helen strode to the tapestry bag, took out some gloves, and closed the top. "Charity," she asked, shaping her mouth into a smile, "are you ready to go on an outing?"

The child nodded. With the hat covering the ragged mop of her hair, and the shawl concealing most of the orphanage uniform, she looked tidy and presentable.

Cassandra glanced over Helen. "You seem so calm."

"My heart's about to burst," Helen said. "Quickly, let's say good-bye."

Cassandra kissed her cheek. "I love you," she whispered, and crouched down to hug Charity.

Pandora followed suit, kissing Helen and bending to

take Charity's face in her hands. Apparently assuming that Pandora wanted to inspect her teeth, as she had the previous night, Charity opened her mouth to display her lower incisors.

Pandora grinned. Nudging the small mouth closed with a gentle finger, she kissed the child's nose. Standing, she gave Helen a businesslike nod. "We'll buy you as much time as we can."

Picking up the tapestry bag, and taking Charity's hand, Helen followed Agatha from the room. Immediately after she crossed the threshold, the door closed, and the key turned decisively in the lock.

Chapter 31

Along the way to Waterloo Station, in a hansom cab that jounced, tilted, and swayed with suicidal fervor, Helen discovered that it was easier to be brave in the presence of a child than when she was alone. She was so determined to keep Charity from worrying that she found herself making ridiculous comments, such as "Isn't this exciting?" when they nearly crashed into an omnibus, or "How exhilarating!" when the wheels hit a hole in the road and the vehicle was briefly airborne. Charity remained silent, staring at the chaotic world rushing past them. She had a remarkable willingness to endure discomfort or uncertainty without complaining. Whenever Helen had been praised during her childhood, it had usually been for the same quality. She wasn't certain that had been a good thing.

The hansom stopped on Waterloo Road beside one of

the massive train sheds. Helen handed up the payment to the driver and grappled with her tapestry bag as she descended from the vehicle. She reached for Charity, who half-jumped, half-fell into her arms. Catching her neatly, Helen lowered her feet to the pavement. She felt a flicker of triumph. *I couldn't have done that with a bustle.* Gripping the tapestry bag on one side and holding Charity's hand on the other, Helen followed the flow of the crowd as it poured into the station.

The approach to the booking office was a narrow, convoluted path, leading through a collection of temporary structures. The station was in the process of yet another expansion, with the result that the waiting rooms and service areas were crudely constructed and unpainted. Keeping a firm grasp on Charity, Helen waited her turn in line, watching as parcel clerks, booking clerks, and porters rushed back and forth from the row of ticket counters. She reached the front of the line, where a clerk informed her that the train to Alton Station would depart in an hour and a half.

Helen bought two first-class tickets. She was relieved that they hadn't missed the train, but she wished they didn't have to wait for so long. Hopefully the twins and the servants could manage to detain Vance long enough to keep him from reaching the station before her train departed. She took Charity to a cluster of stalls that sold newspapers, books, penny journals and periodicals, boxed sandwiches, snacks, and tea. After buying a cup of milk and a bun for Charity, Helen browsed over the bookstalls and purchased a compendium of illustrated children's stories.

They went to the first-class waiting area, furnished only with backless wooden benches. Some travelers complained about the lack of upholstered seating and the rough, unpainted walls, while others sat stoically. Helen found an empty bench in the corner, and settled there with Charity, keeping her tapestry bag at their feet. While the little girl ate the bun and drank her milk, Helen opened the book and paged through it.

Charity poked excitedly at an illustration of the three bears. "Do that one, Helen. That one."

Helen smiled. "You're not tired of it yet?"

Charity shook her head.

As Helen searched for the beginning of the story, she caught sight of another title: "The Red Shoes." She paused and frowned. "Wait a moment, I have to fix something." With a few deft tugs, she tore the hated story out of the book. Regretfully, a page of "Jack and the Beanstalk" had to be removed with it, but Helen considered it a worthwhile sacrifice.

Hearing the sound of ripping paper, a woman seated nearby glanced in their direction. She frowned in open disapproval at the sight of a book being mutilated in such a fashion. Feeling rebellious, Helen met the woman's disdainful gaze as she crumpled the pages in her gloved hand. After dropping the wads of paper into her tapestry bag, Helen said in satisfaction, "There, that's better." She found "The Three Bears" and read it to Charity in a whisper.

As the minutes wore on, Helen glanced up frequently, fearing she would see Albion Vance walking toward her. What would she do if he found them? Would he try to take Charity by force? In a public conflict between a woman and a well-dressed, respectable-looking man, the man would almost certainly win. No one would lift a finger to help her.

The room was unheated, and icy draughts of air numbed Helen's feet. She wiggled her toes until they prickled uncomfortably. The bench became progressively hard, and Charity lost interest in the book. She leaned against Helen, shivering. Wrapping the shawl more snugly around the child's tiny frame, Helen wished she had brought a lap blanket. People left the waiting area, and others came, and the incessant shouts and train whistles and clamor began to fray Helen's nerves.

Someone approached her directly, and her head jerked up in alarm, her heart hammering. To her relief, it was not Albion Vance but the small, elderly booking clerk who had sold her the ticket. He had a kind face, and a gray mustache with curled waxed tips that gave the impression of a perpetual smile.

"Pardon, ma'am," he said quietly. "You're on the next departure for Alton Station?"

Helen gave him a slight nod, briefly surprised at being called "ma'am" instead of "miss," until she recalled that she had given her name as Mrs. Smith.

"There's been a delay for at least an hour."

Helen regarded him with dismay. "May I ask why?"

"It's being kept waiting outside the station, as we have an insufficient number of platforms. A special train has caused delays for our scheduled departures."

Another hour of waiting. Another hour for Albion Vance to find her. "Thank you for informing me."

He spoke even more softly. "Ma'am, in light of circumstances, seeing as you're the only one in here with a child . . . would you like to go to a more comfortable waiting area? We don't always offer it, of course, but the little one seems cold . . ."

"This other waiting area is nearby?" Helen asked warily.

His smile nudged the points of his mustache higher. "The offices in back of the ticket counter. They're warmer and quieter than here. You could rest in a soft chair while you wait."

The offer was irresistible. Not only would they be more comfortable, but they would be tucked safely out of sight. "I wouldn't want to miss my departure," she said uncertainly.

"I'll watch the clock for you."

"Thank you." Helen straightened Charity's shawl and hat. "We're going to wait in another room where it's warmer," she whispered. Picking up the tapestry bag, Helen ignored a multitude of small aches through-out her body. They followed the booking clerk out past the ticket counters, and went through a door that opened to a row of private office rooms. Heading to the last one in the row, the clerk opened it for Helen.

It was a nice room, neatly kept, with maps on the walls, a desk piled with schedules, books, and pam-phlets, and a shuttered window that revealed a partial view of one of the main platforms. A small chair was positioned behind the desk, and a large comfortable-looking wingback occupied the corner.

"Will this be acceptable, my lady"?

"Yes. Thank you." She smiled at him, even as her nerves crawled with a sudden feeling of apprehension.

The clerk left the office room, and Helen busied herself with making Charity comfortable. She set her in the large upholstered chair, wedging the tapestry bag at one side for her to rest on, and covering her with the shawl. Charity snuggled down in the chair immediately.

Going to the window, Helen stared at the busy platform.

A thought occurred to her. Had the booking clerk just called her "my lady"?

He had. She was so accustomed to the term, it had temporarily escaped her notice. But there was no way for him to know that she had a courtesy title. She hadn't given him her real name.

Her stomach turned to ice.

Striding to the door, Helen opened it. The threshold was blocked by a man in a dark suit and a low-brimmed hat. She recognized the hat first, and then the blue eyes.

He was the young man who had come to help her and Dr. Gibson, when they had been harassed after leaving the Stepney Orphanage.

Staring at him in shock, Helen asked unsteadily, "Why are you here?"

He gave her a faint smile that seemed to be intended as reassurance. "Keeping an eye on you, my lady."

She took a shaking breath. "I'm going to take my child and leave now."

"I'm afraid that's not possible."

"Why not?"

"You'll have to wait a bit longer."

The door closed in her face.

Helen clenched her fists, furious with him, and the situation, and most of all herself. *I shouldn't have trusted a stranger.* How stupid she'd been. Tears stung her eyes, and she struggled to keep from losing her self-control. After taking a few deep breaths, she glanced at Charity, who was drifting off to sleep, having absorbed enough new experiences for the time being.

Wandering to the window, Helen widened the shutters and stared at platform eight. A train had pulled in, bearing the same number as the train listed on her ticket. It hadn't been delayed after all.

Fear and determination raced through her. She went to the chair, picked up Charity, and grabbed the handle of the tapestry bag. Huffing with effort, she carried the sleepy child to the door, and kicked it with her foot.

The door opened, and the young man gave her a questioning glance. "Is there something you need, my lady?"

"Yes, I need to leave. My train is at the platform."

"You'll have to wait for a few more minutes."

"I can't wait. Who are you? Why are you doing this?"

The door closed again, and to Helen's furious astonishment, a key turned in the lock. She closed her eyes, despairing. "I'm sorry," she whispered against Charity's head. "I'm sorry." She carried her back to the chair, made her comfortable again, and paced around the office.

In another few minutes, she heard masculine voices outside the door. A brief, low-pitched conversation.

The door unlocked, and Helen moved protectively in front of Charity as someone came in. Her heart began to thud with sickening force as she looked up at him.

"Rhys?" she whispered in bewilderment.

He entered the office, surveying her with hard obsidian eyes. His head tilted slightly as he looked past her to the sleeping child in the chair.

Helen realized that Rhys had never really been angry with her before now. Not like this.

Unnerved by his silence, she spoke unsteadily. "I'm supposed to be on the train leaving for Hampshire."

"You can take the next one. Right now, you're going to tell me what the bloody hell is going on." His eyes narrowed. "Let's start with an explanation of what you're doing with Albion Vance's daughter."

Chapter 32

It was humiliating to have been outmaneuvered and cornered like this. It was also infuriating.

Helen glanced at Charity, who was sleeping peacefully in the chair. "I don't want to wake her. Is there another place we might talk?"

Without a word, Rhys took her with him past the threshold. She hated the way he guided her with his hand clasped on the back of her neck, as if she were a helpless kitten being carried by the scruff. The fact that he was doing it in front of his . . . henchman, or whatever the young man was, made it even worse. He shepherded her into a little office on the other side of the hallway, pausing to speak tersely to the man in the hallway. "Ransom. Don't let anyone near the child."

"Yes, sir."

This room was smaller, only big enough for a desk, a chair, and a bookcase. Rhys seemed to take up most of the available space. He looked calculating and utterly self-assured, and Helen had an inkling of what his business adversaries must face when they sat across a table from him.

She retreated to the foot of wall space between the desk and the door, still feeling the sensation of his hand on the back of her neck. "That man in the hallway . . . he works for you?"

"Now and then."

"You hired him to follow me."

"At first I hired him to follow Vance. I'd received word about some underhanded business he was involved in, and I had no intention of being duped by the bastard. To my surprise, I received a report that not only had Vance visited Ravenel House, but you and he met again the next day for a private chat at the museum." A chilling pause. "I found it interesting that you didn't see fit to mention it to me."

"Why didn't *you* say something?" Helen countered.

"I wanted you to tell me. I gave you every chance that night at the store."

She felt herself turning very red, as she remembered that night. Seeing her flush, Rhys looked mocking, but mercifully made no comment.

"But I didn't," Helen said. "So you told Mr. Ransom to follow me."

"It seemed a good idea," he agreed with knife-edged sarcasm. "Especially when you and Dr. Gibson decided to traipse through the East End docklands at night."

"Did she tell you that Charity is Mr. Vance's child?"

"No, Ransom bribed the orphanage matron. When I cornered Dr. Gibson to ask about it, she told me to go to hell."

"Please don't blame her—she only went because I told her I'd go by myself if she didn't help me."

For some reason, that broke through Rhys's veneer of control. "*Christ*, Helen." He turned away, seeming to hunt for something in the tiny office to destroy. "Tell me you wouldn't have gone alone. Tell me, or I swear I'll—"

"I wouldn't have," she said quickly. "And I didn't. I took Dr. Gibson with me for safety."

Rhys swung back to her with a lethal glare. His color had risen. "You say that as if she could provide anything close to adequate protection! The thought of you two skipping along Butcher Row through that crowd of whores and thieves—"

"No one was skipping," Helen said indignantly. "I only went there because I had no choice. I had to make certain that Charity was safe, and . . . she wasn't. The orphanage was unspeakable, and she was there because no one wanted her, but I do. I do, and I'm going to keep her and take care of her."

His temper finally exploded. "Damn it, *why?* She's not yours!"

"*She's my sister,*" Helen blurted out, and a wracking sob escaped her.

Rhys turned ashen beneath his bronze complexion. Staring at her as if she were a stranger, he sat slowly on the edge of the desk.

"Vance and my mother—" Helen was forced to stop, coughing on a few more sobs.

There was nothing but silence in the tiny room.

It took a full minute before Helen could control her emotions enough to speak again. "I'm sorry. It was wrong of me to deceive you, but I didn't know how to tell you after I found out. I'm so sorry."

Rhys sounded sluggish and disoriented. "When did you find out?"

Helen told him the entire story—God, she was so tired of explaining it. She was hopeless and unflinching, like a condemned soul at her last confession. It was agony to cut every bond between them, one by one, word by word. But there was also relief in it. After this, there would be nothing left to fear.

Rhys kept his head lowered as he listened, his hands clamped on the desk with splintering pressure.

"I wanted just a little more time with you," Helen finished, "before I ended the engagement. It was selfish of me. I should have told you right away. It's only that—losing you felt like dying, and I couldn't—" She stopped, appalled by how melodramatic that sounded, like a manipulation, even though it was the truth. In a moment, she managed to continue more calmly. "You'll survive without me. She won't. Obviously we can't marry now. I think it would be for the best if I left England for good."

She wished Rhys would say something. She wished he would look at her. She especially wished he wouldn't breathe like that, with tautly controlled energy that made it seem as if something terrible were about to happen.

"You have it all decided, do you?" he finally asked, his head still bent.

"Yes. I'm going to take Charity to France. I can look after her there. You can go on with your life here, and I won't be here to . . . to bother anyone."

He muttered two quiet words.

"What?" she asked in bewilderment, inching forward to hear him.

"I said, *try it.*" Rhys pushed from the desk and reached her with stunning quickness, caging her body with his and slamming the sides of his fists against the wall. The room vibrated. He glared into her shocked face. "Try to leave me, and see what happens. Go to France, go anywhere, and see how long it takes for me to reach you. Not five fucking minutes." He took a few vehement breaths, his gaze locked on hers. "I love you. I don't give a damn if your father is the devil himself. I'd let you stab a knife in my heart if it pleased you, and I'd lie there loving you until my last breath."

Helen wanted to crumple in agony. His face blurred before her. "You—you don't want to end up living with two of Albion Vance's daughters." At least, that was what she thought she had said. She was crying too hard to be sure.

"I know what I want." He pulled her against him, his head lowering over hers.

Feebly she tried to twist away, and his mouth landed on her jaw, dragging hotly over her skin. Shoving at his chest was like trying to move a brick wall. "Let go," she wept, grieving and exasperated, knowing that he had made the decision without thinking. But the force of his will, the strength of his desire for her, couldn't change facts. She had to make him face them.

He was kissing her neck, his beard scraping her

tender skin until it smarted. But his lips gentled as they grazed the hollow at the base of her throat, where her pulse was beating.

"You s-said any child of his is demon spawn."

His head jerked up, his eyes fierce. "I didn't mean you. Whatever damned evil thing I might say, it never means you."

"Every time you look at me, you'll remember that I'm half his."

"No." His hand came to the side of her face, his thumb wiping her tears. "You're all mine." His voice was deep and shaken. "Every hair on your head. Every part of you was made to be loved by me."

He bent over her again, and she tried to push him back long enough to say something, but she was covered by at least fourteen stone of thoroughly aroused male, and soon she was too distracted to remember what she'd wanted to tell him. Her struggles slowed, her resolve weakening, and he took advantage, devouring and seducing every tender place he could find. Somewhere in the middle of it he turned gentle, searching her with slow fire, until she sagged against him with a moan. She felt him pull at the little combs that anchored her hat, and he tossed it aside. His hands went to either side of her head, angling her mouth upward, and he possessed her hungrily.

"Rhys," she managed to gasp against his lips, twisting in his arms. "Stop. This isn't solving anything. You haven't given one moment's thought to what you're promising."

"I don't need to. I want you."

"That's not enough to make everything all right."

"Of course it is," he said, so arrogant and stubborn that she was at a loss for words. He stared at her parted lips, his eyes darkening in a way that sent hot and cold chills down her spine. His voice turned husky. "Damn you for saying I could survive without you. I'll have to punish you for that, *cariad*. For hours . . ." His mouth crushed over hers, dizzying and blatantly sexual, making promises that sent her blood racing.

After a long time, his head lifted, and he reached into his coat, pulling out a soft white handkerchief. He gave it to her and kept an arm around her, his embrace now protective, supportive, as she wiped her eyes and blew her nose.

"Tell me what you're afraid of," he said quietly.

"The scandal will never go away," Helen said miserably. "People would talk behind our backs, and say malicious things, the most terrible things—"

"I'm used to that."

"I was supposed to help you advance in society. But

that won't happen now. Charity and I are"—a residual sob came out in a hiccup—"liabilities."

"Not in my world, *cariad*. Only in yours. Only in that razor-thin layer I was so determined to be part of." A self-mocking smile tugged at his lips. "For no better reason than pride. To show off, and prove that a Welshman could have whatever he wanted. But that means nothing to me now. You're all that matters."

"And Charity?"

Rhys's expression went carefully blank. "She matters too."

Helen knew he was trying to accustom himself to the idea. But she knew how much she would be asking of him. Too much. "It won't be enough for you merely to tolerate her. I grew up with a cold and unloving father, and—" She broke off, swallowing painfully.

"Look at me." He urged her chin upward. "I can love her, Helen." As she tried to look away, his grip firmed. "How difficult could it be? Half of her is exactly the same as half of you."

"The half from Albion Vance," she said bitterly. "You can't dismiss that casually, and say it doesn't matter."

"*Cariad*, nothing about this is casual to me. But if you want a long, sensitive discussion about my feelings, I can't help you. I'm from North Wales, where we express ourselves by throwing rocks at trees. I've had more feelings in the past half-hour than I have in my entire life, and I'm at my limit."

"That still doesn't—"

"I love whatever it is you're made of. All of it."

He seemed to think that was the last word on the entire matter.

"But—"

"Stop arguing," he said gently, "or I'll find a better use for your mouth."

"Rhys, you can't—"

His lips clamped firmly on hers, making good on his promise. She stiffened at first, withholding her response, but as he kissed her with passionate intensity, she soon found herself clinging to him weakly. The kiss turned deep and languid, and she went boneless, sinking through a soft, dark current of sensation into depths of drowsing pleasure.

Thump. Thump. Thump. She moaned in protest at the jarring sound of a fist on the door.

With a grunt of annoyance, Rhys fumbled for the doorknob. Lifting his mouth from Helen's, he shot a lethal glance at Ransom, who stood there with his gaze pointedly averted.

"This had better be worth it," Rhys said. Helen rested the side of her hot face against his chest. She heard a few indistinguishable words over her head. Rhys's chest moved beneath her cheek with a short sigh. "That's worth it." Reluctantly he eased Helen away, gently encouraging her to stand on her own. She was wilted and dazed, her legs shaking.

"Little love," he murmured, "I want you and Charity to go with Ransom—he'll take you to my carriage. I'll join you there, now in a minute."

"Where are you going?" she asked anxiously.

"I have an errand to take care of."

"Does it have to do with Mr. Vance? Is he here?"

Staring into her worried face, Rhys smiled and kissed her. "All I'm going to do is say a few words to him."

Helen went to the threshold and watched as Rhys walked down the hallway with purposeful strides.

"Is that really all he's going to do?" she asked.

Ransom gave her an oblique glance. "For now. But if I were Mr. Vance . . . after this, I'd try to keep a continent between myself and Winterborne."

After exchanging a few words with the gray-haired booking clerk and handing him a gold sovereign, Rhys went to platform eight, where the last of the passengers had boarded, and porters were loading the final carts of luggage.

Albion Vance's snow-colored hair gleamed from beneath a felt bowler hat. He was gesturing to one of the first-class carriages as he stood with three train officials in uniform: a platform manager, a train guard, and a conductor.

Vance wanted them to search for Helen. He was calm and deliberate, a predator who had no idea that he was being pursued by a larger predator.

Pausing at the end of the platform, Rhys couldn't help wondering . . . had he known the first time he'd met Helen that this man was her father, would it have mattered?

Maybe at first. He wasn't sure. But there was no doubt that eventually he would have succumbed to the irresistible attraction of Helen, the magic she would always hold for him. In his mind, there was no connection between Helen and Vance, regardless of physical resemblance, blood, or heredity. There was only good in Helen. That gentle, valiant spirit, that perfect mixture of strength and kindness, was all her own.

It still terrified him to think that she had gone to an East End slum district last night. Even though he'd heard about it after the fact from Ransom, knowing that she was safe, the story had nearly brought him to his knees. "You're sure she wasn't harmed?" he'd asked Ransom a half-dozen times, and the assurances still hadn't been enough to satisfy him.

In the past eighteen hours, Rhys had come to understand far more about poor Ioan Crewe and the choice he'd made after Peggy's death. He would have to make Helen understand that in risking her own life, she had risked his as well. It would break him to lose her. He wouldn't survive it.

But at the moment, what Helen needed most was to be protected from the man standing in front of him. As he stared at Albion Vance, Rhys felt whatever there was of the decent, humane part of his nature being swallowed up by the side he always tried to keep hidden. It was from an earlier, rougher time in his life, when violence had been habitual and necessary. There were things he preferred people not to know he was capable of . . . and what he was willing to do to Albion Vance definitely fell in that category.

Slowly Rhys approached the group of men. The platform manager was the first to notice him, giving a look askance at the big-framed, scowling stranger who wore no overcoat, hat, or gloves. Following the platform manager's gaze, the others turned as well.

As Vance recognized him, a quick succession of emotions crossed his face—surprise, anger, frustration, defeat.

"She's not on the train," Rhys said flatly. "I have her."

Sighing, Vance turned to the railway employees. "It seems there's no need to trouble yourselves. Go about your business."

Since there was no other way to leave the platform, Vance was compelled to walk beside Rhys.

The importunate clanging of a bell rent the air, and the down-train sounded two short, shrieking whistles.

"I should have told Helen the brat had died," Vance said after a moment. "I hadn't expected her to take such an interest in the creature. But that's how women are, their emotions eclipse all judgment."

Rhys didn't reply. Hearing Helen's name on his lips provoked a nearly irresistible urge to seize him, break joints and bones with his bare hands, and hurl him onto the tracks below.

"What will you do about her?" Vance asked.

"The orphan?"

"No. About Helen."

Rhys's fists clenched. *Stop saying her name.* "I'm going to marry her."

"Even now? Oh, my. What a fine litter of mongrels you'll breed." Vance sounded amused. "And my grand-children will inherit your fortune."

As they reached the foundation of an overhead footbridge, Rhys gripped the front of Vance's coat with one hand and shoved him against the support posts.

Vance's eyes widened and his face reddened. He gripped Rhys's wrist, gasping.

Leaning closer, Rhys spoke quietly. "When I was a boy, my father sent me in the afternoons to work for the butcher, who'd hurt his hand and needed help dressing the small stock. Most men have a natural distaste for such work. It turns the stomach at first. But soon I learned to saw along the center of a hog's backbone, cleave through a sheep's ribs, or break the jawbone of a calf's head to remove its tongue, and think nothing of it." He paused deliberately. "If you ever try to communicate with my wife again, I'll carve you like a saddle of lamb. It will take ten minutes, and you'll beg for killing before I'm done." Easing his grip, he released him with a slight shove.

Vance straightened his coat and gave him a hostile, contemptuous glance. "Do you think I fear you?"

"You should. In fact, you should leave England. For good."

"I'm the heir to an earldom, you lowbred swine. You're mad if you think you could bully me into living in exile."

"Good. I'd prefer you to stay."

"Yes," Vance said sarcastically, "so you can have

the pleasure of carving me like a mutton loin, I understand."

"Do you?" Rhys fixed a murderous gaze on him. "You've spent years proclaiming to the world how you loathe the Welsh. How uncivilized my kind is, how brutal. How savage. You don't know the half of it. I've never been able to forget the sound of Peggy Crewe's screams as she lay dying in childbed. Like someone was using a fishing line to hook out her organs one at a time. One day soon I'll try that on you, Vance. And we'll find out if you can scream even louder."

As he heard the vicious sincerity in Rhys's voice, Vance's smirk vanished. He finally wore the look of real fear: the focused eyes, the tiny spasm of tight facial muscles.

"Leave England," Rhys advised softly. "Or your life will be very short."

Chapter 33

After exchanging a few words with Ransom, who had waited outside the carriage, Rhys entered the vehicle and thumped the ceiling to signal the driver. He lowered into the seat next to Helen, who had leaned back in the corner with the child in her lap. She was in uncharacteristic disarray, her hair tousled, and she looked dazed and tense.

"Did your errand go well?" she asked uncertainly.

"Aye." He stroked Helen's soft cheek, staring into her eyes. "Relax now," he murmured. "You're safe with me. He won't bother you again."

As his gaze held hers, her brow smoothed out, and she let out a long sigh. Her anxiety seemed to ease into quiet certainty. "Where are you taking us?" she asked as the carriage pulled away from the station and proceeded along Waterloo Road.

"Where would you like to go?"

"Anywhere," she said without hesitation, "so long as it's with you."

Pleased by her answer, Rhys rewarded her with a kiss, and felt the little girl squirm between them.

Drawing back, he took his first good look at the child he'd promised to raise as his own. She bore a close resemblance to Helen, with those innocent round eyes and silvery-gold hair. To his amusement, she turned and hugged Helen possessively while sending him a sideways glance. The maneuver dislodged her hat. It slid from her head, revealing a thatch of short locks that looked as if they'd been hacked off with spring pruning shears.

"We'll go home to Cork Street for the rest of the day," Rhys said, returning his attention to Helen. "I'll make arrangements for us to leave tonight by special train to North Wales."

"We're eloping?"

"Aye, it's a full-time job to watch over you. I can either marry you and keep you safe with me, or hire at least a dozen men to follow you everywhere." Resting his arm along the back of the carriage, he toyed with a lock of hair that had slid free to dangle at her ear. "You can write a note to Lady Berwick and the twins, to let them know what's happened." A rueful smile played at his lips. "While you're at it, write to Trenear and Ravenel—and try to word things in a way that won't bring them down on me like the wrath of God."

"They'll understand," Helen said softly, and nuzzled her cheek against his hand.

Rhys would have kissed her again, but the child was turning around in Helen's lap, staring at him with open curiosity.

"Who is that?"

"He is . . . soon to be my husband."

Conscious of the little girl's attentive gaze, Rhys reached into his coat and took out a tin of peppermint creams. He popped one into his mouth, and extended the open tin to her. "Would you like a sweet, *bychan*?"

Cautiously she reached out and took one. As she nibbled at the peppermint cream, surprised pleasure spread over her face.

Noticing the traces of dirt beneath her fingernails, and the shadows of grime at the inside edge of her ear and the crease of her neck, Rhys asked Helen, "Why has no one given her a proper bath?"

Helen replied quietly, her eyes filled with concern. "A punishment at the orphanage has left her a bit . . . reluctant."

Wondering what they had done to make a small child afraid of bathing, Rhys frowned. "*Wfft.*"

A few seconds later, he heard an answering "*Wfft.*"

He looked down at the little girl, who had imitated him perfectly. His lips twitched. "Have you tried bubbles?" he asked Helen.

"Bubbles?"

"Aye, a bath topped with foam soap to play with."

Charity spoke to him for the first time. "I don't like baths."

Rhys gave her a quizzical glance. "Not even a nice warm bath?"

"No."

"Would you rather smell like flowers, or a sheep?"

"Sheep," came the prompt reply.

Rhys struggled with a grin. Resorting to bribery, he asked, "Do you want a toy pipe, to blow big bubbles that float in the air?"

Nibbling at the last morsel of peppermint cream, Charity nodded.

"Good. You can have one if you sit in the tub with water and foam soap."

She ate the rest of the sweet before saying, "No water."

"A little water, *bychan*," he coaxed. "You can't have bubbles without it." He demonstrated a space of approximately two inches, with one hand suspended above the other. "Only this much."

The child gave him a considering glance. Slowly her tiny hands came to the outside of his and pushed them closer together.

Rhys laughed. "A born negotiator, you are."

During the exchange, Helen watched them with an arrested expression.

To his surprise, Charity levered off Helen's lap and began to climb over him cautiously. He remained still and relaxed. "You're not a pickpocket, are you?" he asked in a tone of mild concern as she reached into his coat. Perceiving that he wasn't going to stop her, she began to fish inside his coat pockets. Finding the tin of peppermint creams, she pulled it out. "Only one more for now," he cautioned. "Too many sweets will bring on a toothache." She took one white morsel, closed the tin, and gave it back to him, every movement delicate and precise.

He studied her, this small person who would bring about such large changes in his life. Charity. The name didn't exactly roll off a Welshman's tongue. Moreover, virtue names—Charity, Patience, and so forth—were given so often in workhouses and orphanages nowadays that they had begun to acquire the connotations of an institution. A girl from a comfortable family might escape the stigma, but for an actual orphan, it would be a lifelong reminder of her origins.

No daughter of a Winterborne would have a name meant to humble her.

"Charity isn't a name we usually give to girls in Wales," he said. "I'd like to call you something that sounds a bit similar."

She looked at him expectantly.

"Carys," he said. "It means 'little loved one.' Do you like it?"

She nodded, and caught him thoroughly off guard by sitting in his lap. She weighed no more than a cat. Bemused and disconcerted by her ready acceptance of him, Rhys adjusted her on his legs. "Carys Winterborne. It's a fine name, aye?" He glanced at Helen, and saw that her eyes were glistening. "We can call her anything you—"

"It's beautiful," she said, smiling through her tears. "Beautiful." She reached out to caress his face, and nestled into his side.

For the rest of the way home, they both leaned against him . . . and it felt right.

Chapter 34

"Fernsby, I'm eloping."

After settling Helen and Carys at his house, Rhys wasted no time in going to his office and summoning his private secretary for an emergency meeting.

The statement was received with impressive sang-froid: Mrs. Fernsby displayed no reaction other than adjusting her spectacles. "Where and when, sir?"

"North Wales. Tonight."

It wasn't soon enough. Now that an actual wedding ceremony with Helen was within his grasp, he was in a fever to make it happen. He felt damnably giddy, poised at the brink of doing something foolish.

The feeling reminded him of an afternoon, late the previous summer, when he had been drinking with

Tom Severin and some of their cohorts in a public house. They had watched some bees that had flown in through a window and settled on an abandoned pewter quartern with a few drops of rum left in it. The bees had guzzled the rum and had become noticeably inebriated, trying to fly away in dizzy, aimless loops, while one bee had simply reclined with its heels up at the bottom of the mug. Rhys and the others had found it uproarious, especially since they had been drinking steadily and were full up to the knocker themselves.

Now Rhys had far more sympathy for the bees, knowing exactly how they had felt. This was what love did to a man, turned him into nothing more than a half-crocked bee, flying upside down and in circles.

"If you intend to marry by special license," Mrs. Fernsby said, "there might be a problem."

He gave her a questioning glance.

"As far as I know," Mrs. Fernsby continued, "the Archbishop only grants special licenses to peers or peeresses in their own right, members of Parliament, privy councilors, and judges. I'm not certain whether Lady Helen has the right or not, since hers is only a courtesy title. I'll try and find out."

"Tell the Archbishop to make an exception if necessary. Remind him that he owes me a favor."

"What favor?"

"He'll know," Rhys said. Filled with vigor, he paced around his desk. "We'll take my private train carriage to Caernarvon. Arrange for a suite at the Royal Hotel for at least a week."

"Will you want Quincy to travel with you?"

"Aye, and find a lady's maid to come with us."

Now Fernsby was beginning to look perturbed. "Mr. Winterborne, one can't simply 'find' a lady's maid. There's a process—putting notices in the paper—conducting interviews—reading recommendations—"

"Fernsby, of the hundreds of women I employ, can you not find *one* who can arrange a lady's hair and button the back of a dress?"

"I believe there's slightly more to the job than that, sir," she said dryly. "But I will find someone."

"While you're at it, hire a nursemaid as well."

Mrs. Fernsby stopped writing. "A nursemaid as well," she said dazedly.

"Aye, we'll be bringing a four-year-old girl with us. Also, she'll need clothes and toys. Put one of the sales clerks in charge of that."

"I see."

"And Lady Helen will need some new things to wear. Have Mrs. Allenby take care of it. Tell her I want to see Lady Helen in *anything* other than black." Tapping his fingers on the desk, he mused, "I suppose it might be too much to ask for a wedding dress . . ."

"Mr. Winterborne," Mrs. Fernsby exclaimed, "do you *actually* expect all this to be accomplished by tonight?"

"Fernsby, you have the greater part of a day, as long as you don't lollygag over lunch." As she began to protest, Rhys said, "I'll handle the arrangements for the special train."

"What about all the rest of it?" she called after him, as he strode from his office. "What about flowers? A cake? What about—"

"Don't bother me with details," he said over his shoulder. "Just make it all happen."

"So now we're friends again," Tom Severin said in satisfaction, stretching out his legs and resting them on the large bronze desk in his fifth-floor office.

"Only because I want something," Rhys said. "Not because I have any liking for you."

"My friends don't have to like me," Severin assured him. "In fact, I prefer it if they don't."

Rhys sternly held back a grin. "The friendship is contingent upon whether or not you can actually provide the favor," he reminded him.

Severin held up a hand in a brief staying gesture. "A moment." He raised his voice. "Barnaby! The information I requested?"

"Here it is, sir." Severin's personal secretary, a stocky fellow with rumpled clothing and hair that sprang in a wild mass of uncombed curls, hurried into the office with a sheaf of papers. He set them carefully on the desk. "Four private stations I've found so far, sir. Awaiting confirmation on the fifth."

As the secretary hastened away, Severin picked up the pages and sorted through them. "What about this one?" he asked, handing a paper to Rhys. "A small bespoke station with a dedicated line connecting to the Great Western route. We can run a special train from there to Caernarvon. The station building is a two-story structure with a drawing room for entertaining prior to departure. No crowd, no tickets, no waiting. My general manager will personally see to it that your private carriages are coupled with our best rolling stock, including a new locomotive and extra passenger carriages with compartments for servants."

Rhys smiled, glancing briefly over the page before giving it back to him. "There's no way in hell that any other man in England could provide all this on such short notice."

"Two other men in England could," Severin said

modestly. "But they wouldn't give it to you as a wedding present, as I'm doing."

"Thank you, Tom."

"Barnaby," Severin called, and the secretary rushed back in. Severin handed the page to him. "This station. Everything has to be ready by tonight. Make certain Winterborne's private carriage is stocked with ice and fresh water after it's delivered."

"Yes, sir." Barnaby nodded wildly and ran out.

Severin sent Rhys an inquiring glance. "Do you want to walk to a food shop for lunch? Or at least have a whiskey here?"

Rhys shook his head regretfully. "I have too much to do. Let's meet after I return from Wales." It occurred to him that he would be a married man then. Helen, in his bed every night, and sharing breakfast with him every morning . . . for a moment he was lost in a daydream, imagining ordinary life with her, the multitude of small pleasures he would never take for granted.

"Of course." Severin's blue-green eyes were friendly and inquisitive. The angle of the light on his face caught his right eye, illuminating the extra green. "This takes a bit of getting used to," he said. "All this smiling and good spirits. You've never been one of those light-hearted fellows."

"I'm not lighthearted, I'm . . . wholehearted."

Severin smiled reflectively as they stood to shake hands. "It must be nice," he mused, "to be any kind of hearted."

Rhys returned to Winterborne's, finding that most of his executive staff was rushing about at a berserk pace that rivaled Barnaby's. Sales clerks and dressmakers' assistants carried stacks of white boxes and armloads of garments to his private office, where his social secretary, Miss Edevane, was making detailed packing lists. Things were being accomplished, he observed with satisfaction. He decided to find Fernsby and ask about her progress.

As he approached her desk, he found himself following behind Dr. Havelock. The older man carried a tray bearing silver-covered dishes, a glass of iced lemonade, and a tiny vase containing a perfect half-open rosebud.

"Havelock?"

The lionesque head turned as the older man glanced over his shoulder. "Winterborne," he said gruffly.

"Who is that for?" Rhys asked.

"Not you." Havelock proceeded to Fernsby's desk and placed the tray on it. "I heard about the frenzy you've created up here, obligating your entire office staff and three other departments to work themselves to the bone. All the fuses lit at once, as usual. Why must an elopement happen with such all-fired haste?"

"Elopements aren't usually known for being slow," Rhys pointed out.

"Are there parents in pursuit? A rival lover determined to prevent the wedding? No—only an impatient bridegroom who won't cool his heels long enough to allow his hardworking secretary enough time for lunch!"

Just then, Mrs. Fernsby came to her desk. Her gaze fell on Rhys first. "Sir, we found a temporary lady's maid: one of Mrs. Allenby's assistants in the dressmaking department. Mrs. Allenby is altering at least two finished dresses from an order placed by a customer with similar measurements to Lady Helen—the customer agreed as long as we replace them with free dresses of more costly design. As for the nursemaid, Miss Edevane has a younger sister who would be delighted to accompany you and Lady Helen to take care of the . . ." Her voice trailed away as she noticed the other man standing nearby. "Dr. Havelock. Has something gone awry?"

"No, Mrs. Fernsby," Havelock said, "but something might well go awry if you forego proper nutrition, especially at the bruising pace Winterborne has set." He guided her to the desk and urged her to sit.

"You brought lunch for me?" Mrs. Fernsby asked in bewilderment, picking up the linen napkin on the tray and placing it on her lap.

"Indeed." Havelock glanced at her covertly, assessing her reaction. A flash of triumph entered his eyes as he saw how pleased she was, and he quickly covered it with another burst of indignation. "If it were left to Winterborne, you would soon be carried to my door in a state of nervous exhaustion and malnourishment. And I already have enough patients to attend to." He removed the silver covers, and turned the rosebud so that it was shown to its best advantage.

"I am rather hungry," Mrs. Fernsby said delicately, as if she could hardly summon the strength to lift a fork. "Will you keep me company, Dr. Havelock?"

"I suppose I must," came his enthusiastic response, "to make certain Winterborne allows you fifteen minutes of peace."

Rhys tried to sound grudging. "Very well, Fernsby. You can have food. But only because Havelock insists on it." Before turning away, he exchanged a quick glance with Mrs. Fernsby, and her eyes twinkled at him.

Chapter 35

Rhys's private train carriage consisted of two long sections with a flexible covered walkway in between. It was magnificently furnished with luxurious chairs upholstered in bronze silk plush, and floors covered with cut-velvet carpeting. There was a parlor with wide observation windows, and a dining room with a mahogany extension table. Rhys and Helen would sleep in the large bedroom en suite in the first section, while Charity—no, Carys, Helen reminded herself—would occupy one of two smaller bedrooms in the second section, along with her nursemaid.

At first Helen had worried that Carys might be uneasy at sleeping apart from her on the train. However, the little girl had immediately taken to Anna Edevane, the younger sister of Rhys's social secretary. Anna was pretty and vivacious, and she'd had experience helping to raise her four younger brothers and sisters. As soon as they boarded, Anna took Carys to their room, where a collection of new toys and books had been left for her. Dumbfounded by the playthings, including a porcelain doll in a lilac silk dress and a Noah's ark, Carys didn't seem to know what to do with them. Sitting on the floor, she touched the carved and painted animals gently, as if she thought they might break.

Now that Carys had been thoroughly bathed—Rhys's suggestion of foam soap had worked brilliantly—she was clean and sweet smelling. She wore a rose-colored dress with a little skirt made of box plaits, each one headed by a little ribbon rosette.

"It's eleven o'clock," Helen told Anna. "Carys must go to bed soon—it's been a long day, and she had only a short nap."

"I don't want to," Carys protested.

"I'll read her a bedtime story," Anna said. "I heard she has a favorite one . . . I think it was . . . 'Little Red Riding Hood'?"

"'The Three Bears,'" Carys said from the floor.

Anna pretended not to hear. "Maybe it was 'Rumplestiltskin' . . ."

Carys stood and hung onto her skirts. "The Three Bears."

"Three pigs, did you say?" Anna swept the child up in her arms, and fell with her onto the bed.

Carys lay there giggling. "Bears, bears, *bears!*"

The sound of her laughter, Helen thought, was more beautiful than any music.

The rest of the Winterborne retinue, including the lady's maid, Quincy, a footman, and a cookmaid, were all lodged farther back on the private train, in handsome carriages provided by Mr. Severin.

"I'm so glad you renewed your friendship with Mr. Severin," Helen exclaimed as she wandered around their private compartments, pausing to admire a gilded wall lamp. She quoted a popular poem, "*Forgiveness! No virtue surer brings its own reward.*"

"Aye," Rhys had replied dryly, "like a free locomotive."

"That wasn't the only reason you forgave him."

He pulled her against him, kissing her neck. "*Cariad*, are you trying to convince yourself that I'm a man of hidden honor and secret virtues? I'll be changing your mind about that soon."

Helen wriggled in protest as his hand stole to the back of her skirts. She was wearing a ready-made traveling dress, which fit nicely after a few minor alterations made by one of Mrs. Allenby's assistants. It was a simple design of light blue silk and cashmere, with a smart little waist-jacket. There was no bustle, and the skirts had been drawn back snugly to reveal the shape of her body. The skirts descended in a pretty fall of folds and pleats, with a large decorative bow placed high on her posterior. To her vexation, Rhys wouldn't leave the bow alone. He was positively mesmerized by it. Every time she turned her back to him, she could feel him playing with it.

"Rhys, don't!"

"I can't help it. It calls to me."

"You've seen bows on dresses before."

"But not *there*. And not on you." Reluctantly Rhys let go of her and pulled out his pocket watch. "The train should have departed by now. We're five minutes late."

"What are you in a rush for?" she asked.

"Bed," came his succinct reply.

Helen smiled. She stood on her toes and pressed a quick kiss to his cheek. "We have a lifetime of nights together."

"Aye, and we've already missed too many of them."

Helen turned and bent to pick up her small valise, which had been set on the floor. At the same time, she heard the sound of fabric ripping.

Before Helen had straightened and twisted to look at

the back of her skirts, she already knew what had happened. The bow hung limply, at least half of its stitches torn.

Meeting her indignant glance, Rhys looked as sheepish as a schoolboy caught with a stolen apple. "I didn't know you were going to bend over."

"What am I going to say to the lady's maid when she sees this?"

He considered that for a moment. "Alas?" he suggested.

Helen's lips quivered with unwilling amusement.

A whistle signaled their impending departure with two short bursts, and soon they were underway. The locomotive proceeded at a slower pace than the express trains Helen had ridden to and from Hampshire, and the ride was smoother, with subtle vibrations and sways instead of jolts. As the train moved away from lights and buildings and roads, out into the night, the passengers began to retire after a day that had been unusually long and exhausting for all of them.

Rhys went to another compartment while the lady's maid came to help Helen prepare for bed.

"The bow in my dress came loose," Helen said as the maid collected her clothes. "It caught on something." She didn't feel the need to explain that the "something" had been a set of inquisitive masculine fingers.

"I'll stitch it back tomorrow, my lady."

As Helen stood behind the folding doors of the bedroom compartment, the lady's maid handed her a new nightgown to wear. Looking at the thin, silky length of fabric in her hands, Helen asked, "Is this all there is of it?"

"Yes, my lady," came the girl's voice. "Mrs. Allenby selected it for you. Do you like it?"

"Oh it's . . . lovely." Helen held it up in the light of the tiny lamp of the bedroom compartment, realizing that the white silk was semi-transparent. The garment was cut low and open-necked at the front, offering such negligible coverage that it didn't begin to serve the purpose of a nightgown. Blushing, Helen slipped the gown over her head, her breath catching at the coolness of the silk falling over her body.

"Do you need help, my lady?"

"No, thank you," Helen said hastily. She was virtually half-naked in the scandalous garment. "I'll retire now. Good night."

Climbing into the bed, she slid beneath the weight of the soft linen sheets and quilted blankets, sighing in comfort. She was weary in every limb, and the faint oscillation of the train was soothing. Relaxing, she lay with her eyes half-closed.

The folding door was drawn back, and a dark, lean

shape moved across her vision. She rolled to her back, one arm curled loosely above her head.

Rhys stood over her, slowly stripping off his shirt, the soft light catching hard curves of muscle all along his torso. Gently he pulled the covers back, his gaze smoldering as he took in the sight of her. He reached down to caress her, his spread fingertip trailing over the fragile silk. "My beautiful love," he said huskily.

The lamp was turned off, and the gown was drawn away from her slowly. There were movements in the darkness, gentle touches on her body . . . the liquid heat of his mouth, the tip of his tongue stroking in places that made her tremble. He played with the curls between her legs, teasing and stroking with his fingers and tongue, breathing against them until she forgot all modesty and spread her legs wider. His gentle laugh fell against her, and he answered the wanton invitation with a swirling lick.

Helen crooned and moaned and sank her hands into his silky hair. His hands played over her, fingertips following sensitive paths along her skin. Catching the bud of a nipple between his thumb and forefinger, he pinched it in a rhythm that matched the electrifying tugging of his mouth between her thighs.

When he could wait no longer, he levered his body over hers and entered her, his heavy shaft spreading her deliciously, pushing deep. The sway of the train rocked them exquisitely, the subtle hint of motion teasing her senses. Her inner muscles began to close on him help-lessly, and he followed that secret rhythm, sensitive to her every need. Blindly she searched for his mouth, and he gave it to her. He was so deep inside her, his body caressing her within and without, flooding her with pleasure. Her hips jerked up in that ultimate moment, almost lifting his weight. Shivering, she ran a gentle hand down his flexing back. "Now," she whispered. "Come inside me now."

Groaning, he obeyed with one strong thrust, pour-ing his heat into her, holding her as if he would never let her go.

The Royal Hotel was a stately three-story Georgian structure in Caernarvon. Rhys had wanted to bring Helen to the North Wales coastal town partly be-cause it was close to his birthplace of Llanberis, but mostly because he thought she would enjoy its roman-tic appeal. Myths and fairy tales came naturally to this place, with its picturesque ruins and deep green vales, and abundant cascades, pools, and lakes. One could always see the jagged peaks of Snowdon, a moun-tain of which it was said that a man who'd climbed it would come down either a madman or a poet.

Thanks to Mrs. Fernsby's skillful planning, the trip had gone perfectly so far. Upon Rhys and Helen's arrival, they were shown to a spacious suite at the Royal Hotel, with a connecting suite for Carys and her nursemaid. The servants had also been shown to elegant rooms, and seemed very pleased.

The pastor of a local church had consented to perform the wedding ceremony at the remains of an ancient chapel on a hill, just a short walk from the hotel. Massive arrangements of white and pink flowers had been carted to the chapel ruins, which were accessible by a footpath and small bridge. From the top of the hill, one had a view of Caernarvon's castle, the town, the mountain, and the dark blue shimmer of the Irish Sea.

On the morning after their arrival, the sky was clear and cloudless, a rare occurrence for that time of year. As it was planned, the wedding party would gather at the stone terrace at the back of the hotel, walk to the chapel, and return for a lavish breakfast.

Dressed in a morning suit with a cutaway coat and light-colored tie, Rhys waited alone in the ground-floor conservatory of the hotel. He and Helen would meet there before joining the others. Resisting the urge to pull out his pocket watch, he waited with forced patience, thinking he would have paid ten thousand pounds to have the next hour already done with, so that Helen would already be his wife.

A silky rustling sound came from behind him.

He turned, and saw Helen standing there in a white dress made of thin, glimmering layers of silk trimmed with lace. The dress clung to her slender form, the skirts pulled back to outline her hips and cascading gently behind her. She pulled back a filmy white veil sewn with lace and seed pearls, and smiled at him. She was unearthly in her beauty, as light and delicate as a wash of rainbow through morning mist. He held a hand over his hammering heart, as if to keep it from leaping out of his chest.

"I didn't know they'd found you a wedding dress," he managed to say.

"Somehow Mrs. Allenby worked a miracle. I'll have to ask her how she did it when we return."

"You're so beautiful, I . . ." His voice drifted away as he stared at her. "Are you really mine?"

She smiled and came to him. "In every sense but the legal."

"We'll fix that soon," he muttered, reaching for her.

Helen shook her head and touched a forefinger lightly to his lips. "Not until after our vows," she said, her eyes sparkling. "I want my next kiss to be with my husband."

"God help me," he said feelingly, "no man has ever wanted to have a wedding done with as much as I do."

Helen's smile turned rueful. "Have you seen the crowd outside the hotel?"

Rhys shook his head, frowning slightly.

"I'm afraid we'll have more company than we anticipated. When the guests at the hotel and some of the townspeople found out that Rhys Winterborne himself has come here to be married, they all invited themselves to walk to the chapel with us. I was told that in North Wales, it's a tradition for all the neighbors to attend the wedding."

He groaned. "There'll be no getting rid of them. I'm sorry. Do you mind, *cariad*?"

"Of course not. I'll rather enjoy the sight of all those people staring at you with awe."

"They won't be staring at me," he assured her. Reaching into his pocket, he retrieved a smooth white stone and showed it to her on his palm. Helen smiled.

"The oathing stone?"

"Carys found it yesterday while we were out walking."

"It's perfect. Where will we throw it, after we're wed?"

"I'll let you decide," Rhys said, replacing the stone in his pocket. "The Irish Sea is in that direction . . ." He pointed. "The Menai Strait is that way . . . or I can take you to a fair number of good Welsh lakes. I know of one that's said to be the final location of Excalibur."

Helen's eyes brightened at the idea. But in the next moment, a thought occurred to her, and she looked disconcerted.

"I realized this morning that there's no one to give me away."

Rhys lowered his face until their foreheads were touching, and he was lost in the moonstone glow of her eyes. "Heart of my heart, you need no man to give you away. Just come to me of your own free will. Love me for who I am . . . just as I love you for who you are . . . and our bond will last until the stars lose their shining."

"I can do that," Helen whispered.

Drawing back slowly, Rhys smiled down at her. "Come, then, *cariad*. We've a wedding to take care of. A man can only wait so long for a kiss from his wife."

Epilogue

Eight months later

". . . and Pandora said that if her game turns out to be a success, she won't participate in any of the events of the Season," Helen said, deftly hand-pollinating vanilla blossoms. "She told Lady Berwick that she has no intention of being herded from ball to ball like a disoriented sheep."

Rhys smiled and watched her lazily, his back braced against a brick column. He was a handsome sight, his presence incongruously masculine amid the rows and rows of orchids. "How did Lady Berwick react?"

"She was outraged, of course. But before they could start another row, Cousin Devon pointed out that Pandora has only just now filed a patent application, and the Season will probably have begun before we find out if it's been accepted. Therefore, Pandora may as well go to a few balls and dinners, if for no other reason than to keep Cassandra company."

"Trenear is right. There's far more to publishing a board game than applying for a patent and taking the design to the printer. If Pandora is serious about her venture, it will take at least a year before we can stock it on the display tables."

"Oh, Pandora is quite serious," Helen said wryly.

She had just returned with Carys from a morning visit to Ravenel House. They had gone to see Kathleen's newborn son, William, who was healthy and thriving. Carys had been fascinated by the two-week-old infant and had cooed over him for several minutes, until Pandora had coaxed her away to help test her board game prototype. The little girl had loved the game, titled Shopping Spree, in which players moved their tokens around a circuit of departments, collecting merchandise cards along the way. At Pandora's insistence, the game taught no moral values or lessons: it was intended only to be amusing.

"Do you know," Helen said thoughtfully, "I have a feeling that Pandora's game is going to sell very well. Lady Berwick and Carys had a splendid time playing it this morning. They both seem to love the process of collecting all those beautifully detailed little merchandise cards—the umbrella, the shoe, and so forth."

"Human nature is acquisitive," Rhys replied in a matter-of-fact manner. "Aye, the game will sell."

"How well?" Helen used a toothpick to transfer pollen into the blossom's stigma.

Rhys laughed gently. "I'm not an oracle, *cariad*."

"Yes, you are. You know these things." Finishing the last vanilla flower, Helen set aside the toothpick and turned to give him an expectant glance.

"She'll make a fortune," he said. "It's an undeveloped market, the product can be mass-produced with lithographic printing, and as you just pointed out, the game has broad appeal."

Helen smiled, but she was inwardly perturbed. She wanted her younger sister's hard work and talent to be rewarded. However, she was concerned that in her quest to become self-sufficient and independent, Pandora seemed determined to keep from giving any man the chance to love her. Why was she so hardened against the idea of sharing her life with someone else?

"I hope it will make her happy," she said.

Rhys unfolded his arms and approached her slowly. Warm September light, the color of ripe lemons, poured through the glasshouse panes and slid over his dark hair. "Speaking from experience," he said, taking her waist in his hands, "the success will make Pandora very happy at first. But eventually she'll become lonely, and realize there's more to life than financial gain."

Smiling, Helen reached her arms around his neck. "Were you lonely, before you met me?"

Her husband stared down at her, his gaze a simmering dark caress. "Aye, as any man would be, trying to live each day with half his soul missing." Lowering his head, he brushed his mouth over hers in repeated strokes, settling deeper each time until the kiss had turned deep and yearning. "Let's go to bed," he murmured when their lips parted.

Her eyes widened as she felt his hand at her breast. "It's time for lunch."

"You're my lunch." Rhys bent to kiss her again, and she twisted in his arms with a breathless laugh.

"I can't . . . no, really . . . I'm going to see Garrett Gibson for tea."

"You had tea with her the other day," he said, kissing her neck. "I need you more."

"It's not actually for tea. That is, we might have tea, but that's not the purpose of the visit. You see . . ."

Helen paused and blushed as she continued uncertainly. "I have . . . symptoms."

His head jerked up with startling suddenness. Frowning, he asked, "Are you not well, *cariad*?"

Touched by his instant concern, Helen stroked his nape soothingly. "I'm quite well."

His intent gaze raked over her. "Then why—" He broke off as a thought occurred to him, and his mouth opened and closed repeatedly, as if he'd forgotten how to speak.

Helen rather enjoyed his dumbfounded reaction. "We won't know for certain until Dr. Gibson confirms it," she said, lacing her fingers into his vibrant black hair. "But I think by next spring, we'll have another addition to the Winterborne family."

Rhys pulled her close, hunching over her to bury his face against the soft curve of her neck and shoulder. He sounded shaken. "Helen. Helen, my treasure . . . what can I do for you? What do you need? Should you be standing on this hard floor? You're wearing a corset—won't it squash the baby?"

"Not this early," she said, tenderly amused and a bit surprised as she felt a tremor run through him. "There's no need to be anxious. I'll manage this new project brilliantly, I promise. The baby and I will both be strong and healthy."

Rhys drew back until his face was over hers, his breath rushing against her lips with peppermint coolness. "I'll need your word on that," he said huskily. "Because you're my entire world, *cariad*. My heart only beats as an echo of yours."

"Don't doubt it for a moment, my dearest love." Standing on her toes, Helen touched her lips to his. "After all . . . I am a Winterborne."

Author's Note

While researching fashion (always one of the most fun parts of writing historical romance) I learned that there were two periods of bustle-dom in the late 1800s. The first version of the bustle, lasting from 1870–1875, consisted of a massive bag stuffed with straw or horsehair. I imagine it felt like wearing a sofa cushion tied around one's backside. For a few years after that, bustles disappeared and a woman's fashion silhouette was as slim and straight as possible, with very narrow skirts. This is referred to as the "natural form" period, which I would dispute in light of the fact that you still needed a corset to achieve it. However, it was probably preferable to the return of the bustle from 1883–1889, in a new and exaggerated shape. Although the bigger bustle was designed to be lighter and collapsible to allow the poor wearer to sit in a chair, it still doesn't sound all that comfortable!

The torpedo shape of soda water bottles (patented by William Hamilton in 1809) ensured they would be stored on their sides, keeping the cork stoppers from drying out. Also, unlike champagne bottles that were usually made of better quality glass, the cheap glass used for soda water bottles was more likely to shatter from the pressure of carbonated liquids. The torpedo structure was stronger than a flat-bottomed one.

I gave Dr. Gibson the first name of Garrett in homage to Dr. Elizabeth Garrett Anderson, the first woman to qualify as a physician and surgeon in England. She joined the British Medical Association in 1873, and was the only female member for 19 years, after the Association voted to exclude any other women from entering their all male institution. Eventually Dr. Anderson was elected as the mayor of Aldeburgh, making her the first female mayor in England.

Here's a mini glossary of Welsh words and phrases used in the book:

Bychan: little one
Cariad: sweetheart, beloved one
Annwyl: dear
Iesu Mawr: great Jesus

Hwyl fawr am nawr: good-bye for now

Diolch i Dduw: Thank God

Dw i'n dy garu di: I love you

    Owain Glyndŵr: a Welsh ruler, a figure of Welsh nationalism, and the last native Welshman to hold the title Prince of Wales. He lived from 1349–1416

    Eistedfodd: a festival of Welsh literature, music, dancing, and acting

Winterborne's
Peppermint Creams

After reading about the beloved Victorian-era sweets, peppermint creams, I couldn't find any available for purchase. Alas! However, my daughter and I tried different recipes and modified one slightly until we came up with the easiest and best version. Most recipes called for real egg whites, but we got better (and safer) results by using meringue powder, which you can find in the grocery store baking section. If you're not a fan of peppermint, you can substitute any flavor you prefer. Vanilla works beautifully!

Ingredients:

    1 cup powdered sugar
    1 tablespoon meringue powder

1 pinch salt

1 tsp. peppermint extract (or more if you like a lot of flavor)

1 tablespoon milk

Directions:

1. Mix the dry ingredients together, then add the peppermint extract and the milk. Stir and mash with a spoon until the mixture has the consistency of Play Doh. You may need to add a tiny bit of milk if the mixture is too dry, but add just a few drops at a time.

2. Roll the dough into tiny marble-sized balls, and roll each one in some extra powdered sugar. Put them on waxed paper to dry and set for at least 15 minutes. At this point we like to re-roll them in powdered sugar to give them a nice "floury" appearance, but it's not necessary.

3. Make certain to test your Winterborne-fresh breath by kissing someone you love!